"Sacre bleu! _____ *d in a husky voice.* _____ *you not to try your flirtation with me. I am not interested."*

Lowering her lashes to hide the hurt, she dug her now ragged, fifty-dollar sculptured nails into her palms and forced back the urge to claw his face. A layer of protective mud now covered her skin from forehead to toes, at James's insistence after she had been bitten mercilessly by mosquitos the size of mothballs. She pinched her arm, hard, hoping against hope that this time she would awaken from this horrific joke that God, or Damballa, or whoever had played on her.

"Now what? Is this some magic trick where you pinch yourself black and blue, then turn into a beautiful princess?"

Selene blinked against the tears that smarted her eyes. "I may not look like a raving beauty right now, but I'll tell you one thing. I am in desperate need of a Prince Charming to save me from this nightmare. Because you, my friend, are more like a . . . a frog."

He made a low grunting sound of disgust that sounded an awful lot like a frog.

"Heck, at this point," she went on, "a modern-day Rhett would look mighty good." She leaned her head back and studied his glowering face. "You can't even be my Rhett, can you?"

James chuckled softly as he set her on the ground. "I've been called a rat by a few of my enemies, but I've never had a woman ask me to be her rat."

Romances by Sandra Hill

KISS OF SURRENDER
KISS OF PRIDE

THE RELUCTANT VIKING
THE OUTLAW VIKING
THE TARNISHED LADY
THE BEWITCHED VIKING
THE BLUE VIKING
THE VIKING'S CAPTIVE (formerly My Fair Viking)
A TALE OF TWO VIKINGS
VIKING IN LOVE
THE VIKING TAKES A KNIGHT
THE NORSE KING'S DAUGHTER

THE LAST VIKING
TRULY, MADLY VIKING
THE VERY VIRILE VIKING
WET AND WILD
HOT AND HEAVY

FRANKLY, MY DEAR
SWEETER SAVAGE LOVE
DESPERADO
LOVE ME TENDER

SANDRA HILL

FRANKLY, MY DEAR...

AVON

An Imprint of HarperCollinsPublishers

This is a work of fiction. Names, characters, places, and incidents are products of the author's imagination or are used fictitiously and are not to be construed as real. Any resemblance to actual events, locales, organizations, or persons, living or dead, is entirely coincidental.

AVON BOOKS
An Imprint of HarperCollins*Publishers*
10 East 53rd Street
New York, New York 10022-5299

Copyright © 1996, 2013 by Sandra Hill
ISBN 978-0-06-201903-5
www.avonromance.com

First Avon Books mass market printing: February 2013

Avon Trademark Reg. U.S. Pat. Off. and in Other Countries, Marca Registrada, Hecho en U.S.A.
HarperCollins® is a registered trademark of HarperCollins Publishers.

Printed in the U.S.A.

10 9 8 7 6 5 4 3 2 1

Scarlett O'Hara was not beautiful but men seldom realized it when caught by her charm.

—Margaret Mitchell,
Gone With the Wind

FRANKLY, MY DEAR...

Chapter One

NEW ORLEANS, 2012

The South shall rise again, baby . . .

"Hot damn!" Selene stopped dead in the tracks of her designer shoes, slapped an expertly manicured hand over her heart, and gasped, staring straight ahead.

"Umph!" Her agent, Georgia Jones, slammed into her back. With a curse, the statuesque black woman picked up her Hermes handbag from the pavement where it had dropped, checking for scuff marks, and adjusted her white silk Donna Karan suit. "What? What is it?"

"Look, Georgia! Over there. Ooooh!" Selene sighed ecstatically.

Then, like a running back looking for a hole in the line, Selene wended her way doggedly through the Vieux Carre crowd, barely conscious of the cacophony of street vendors, steamboat whistles, soulful jazz music in the distance, and the chatter of the many dialects of the Crescent City. The delicious smells of steaming coffee and fresh baked goods mixed with those of newly cut flowers, in contrast to the pungent products offered by the vegetable and fruit vendors, fishmongers, and butchers.

Finally, Selene stood before a popular beignet stand. Closing her eyes in delight, she arched her neck and inhaled deeply.

"Lord, give me strength. The woman is having an orgasm. Smack dab in the middle of the French Quarter market. Over a sugar pastry, no less." Georgia rolled her eyes heavenward. "Geez! I should've known."

Selene lifted her chin haughtily and turned a deaf ear to her agent's sardonic humor as she ogled the scrumptious baked goods. Licking her lips in anticipation, she opened her purse, preparing to pull out some money.

With a determined snarl, Georgia clasped Selene's wrist in an iron grip and pulled her out of the market and up toward the levee. "What am I gonna do with you? Other women get turned on by drop-dead-gorgeous men," she muttered. "You swoon over a donut."

"Not a donut. It's a New Orleans specialty, a baan-yah," Selene said with careful pronunciation of the French word.

"Baan-yah?" Georgia repeated after her, then added quickly, "I don't care if it's a bloomin' daffodil. It's got two zillion calories, and you have to fit into a size five ballgown for today's shoot. Besides, all that sugar is bound to bring out a zit. Come on, honey. You, of all people, know better."

"You're right," Selene agreed dolefully and dropped down onto a bench at the top of the flat-topped levee overlooking the wide Mississippi. "But I'm so darned hungry. In fact, I'm always famished these days."

"It's all in your mind," Georgia said, not unkindly, and squeezed her hand warmly. "You oughta talk to your shrink about it," she added, laughing softly.

"Dr. Walters would probably say I wouldn't know an orgasm if it hit me in the face, that there's some deep psychological reason why I have this fascination with food."

"Typical shrink! In fact, she'd probably give the disorder

some fancy name like oral dysfunction obsessive mania. Maybe write a book about it. Get on the Today show." Georgia cocked her head thoughtfully. "Hmmm . . . do you think Dr. Walters has an agent?"

"Oh, Georgia!" Selene playfully elbow-nudged her cynical friend, whose opinionated, sometimes vulgar mouth hid a heart the size of Texas. "I don't know what I would've done without Dr. Walters these past six months. Or you, for that matter."

"Hah! Too late to suck up now, sweetie," Georgia said with an affronted sniff, though obviously pleased at Selene's affection. "Do you still miss the bum . . . Devon, I mean?" Georgia smiled guilelessly when Selene glared disapprovingly at her choice of words to characterize her former lover.

"Sometimes," Selene conceded with a sigh. "But not because I still love him. I probably never did. I miss the security, though."

"Security! You are losin' it, girl. Devon made you *insecure*. You did every blessed thing for the man, and it was never enough."

Selene gave a resigned nod. "The last straw was his lack of sympathy for Tessa. I mean, dammit, my best friend died from anorexia, and his version of sympathy was, 'Tessa was a dumb broad.'" Tears welled in Selene's eyes and she blinked to keep them from overflowing. "Still, Devon and I lived together for three years. It's hard to stop caring completely."

"Humph! Seems to me that the woman voted The Most Beautiful Face in America by *We* magazine ought to have dozens of men lined up to help her forget a creep like that."

Selene looked around dramatically. "I don't see any."

"You want me to help you find a man?"

"No way!"

Georgia fanned her face with a widespread hand. "I can't believe I left my nice, air-conditioned Manhattan office for this."

"It is hot, but I love Louisiana. I'm sick of the fast-track life in New York. Life is slower here."

"Of course it's slower. It's too hot to move."

"From the minute we arrived last week," Selene continued, ignoring Georgia's sarcasm, "I've felt a strange sense of belonging, as if fate ordained I be here. I can't really explain it."

Georgia snorted rudely. "Lord! You're here, girl, because I got you a lucrative contract to do this shoot with Phillipe Dubois." She studied Selene for a long moment. "So what's this all about? You always did have this *Gone With the Wind* fixation. You planning a move to the South?"

"No," she said, smiling. "And just because I've seen the movie a few times doesn't mean I'm fixated."

"A few times!" Georgia shook her head woefully.

"We're getting off the subject, Georgia." Selene inhaled deeply for nerve. Georgia had done so much for her. Selene owed her the courtesy of informing her first of a decision that would affect them both. She gave her agent a level look. "This is my last modeling assignment. I start classes at Columbia this fall."

"*What*! Are you nuts? You're twenty-eight years old!"

Selene bristled. "So? I won't be the oldest student at Columbia."

"Humph! I'll bet you're the only one commuting to classes from a half-million-dollar condo, though," she commented cynically, then added, "What kind of classes?"

"Psychology."

"Bull! That Dr. Walters really has worked a number on you, hasn't she?"

"It has nothing to do with Dr. Walters." Selene exhaled wearily. "For a long time I've been fed up with the modeling industry and its perpetuation of unrealistic expectations for the female form. We overemphasize physical appearance. Look what happened to Tessa." Selene's voice cracked with emotion. She was still overcome at the tragedy of her best friend's death six months earlier.

"Selene, be practical. This profession has been very good to you. You've earned six million dollars in the past ten years. And even though you're twenty-eight, I figure you've got at least five more years of making big bucks in high fashion. Then we can try other possibilities—books, videos, the older modeling market."

"Oh, Georgia, you just don't understand. Look at me." She stood up in front of the bench and lifted her arms away from her body. "I'm five-foot-ten and I only weigh a hundred and fifteen pounds. I'm hungry all the time. This diet-for-life regimen is killing me. I should weight at least twenty pounds more."

"Not under the camera, sweetheart."

"I know. And have you seen some of the waifish younger models coming up, following in Kate Moss's footsteps? Criminey! They look like anorexic pre-teens wearing their mothers' clothes. And all these gimmicks you keep having me try!" She slanted Georgia a reproving look.

"Don't start on the collagen injections in your lips again. I like the pouty look on you, and it was right for this assignment."

"How about this *big* hair?" Selene flicked the ends of her long, permed, dark brunette hair that cascaded over her shoulders and down to the middle of her back.

"It's sexy. Besides, the higher the hair, the closer to God."

"Easy for you to say! It takes two hours to dry every day, and if I don't use a diffuser, I frizz up into a god-awful bush."

"No one ever said beauty comes easy," Georgia muttered defensively.

"Then you talked me into getting a full-body tan for those revealing swimsuits last month. I'll probably end up with skin cancer someday. And these dark contact lenses make me feel like I'm wearing sunglasses."

"Well, you didn't follow my advice on the breast reduction surgery."

"And a good thing, too. Breasts are in again, you know."

"Only in *Playboy. Vogue* still wants pancakes. You ready to do a centerfold?" she asked with a snicker.

"Hardly."

Georgia pulled Selene back down to the bench and patted her hand. "Selene, there's a downside to every occupation. You've been paid big bucks for your efforts."

"I have been, I admit that. And I'm thankful, but the bottom line is that I'm getting out. This is my last assignment." Selene felt no remorse over dropping her career, but she did regret having to disappoint Georgia.

"We'll see," Georgia said skeptically. "I'll bet you're bored silly in six months. You'll be back. Don't wait too long, though, babe. You know how the public forgets. And whatever you do, don't balloon up on sugar donuts." She gave Selene a friendly hug and looped her arm in hers. "Come on. We better get back to the hotel before Phillipe has a hissy fit."

They passed through Jackson Square, once called the Place d'Armes, and its surrounding historic buildings known as the Cabildo. When the melodious bells of St. Louis Cathedral pealed out a call to Mass, Selene closed her eyes and fancied the chimes were a divine blessing for her new life.

As they moved on through the quaint streets of the French Quarter with its wonderfully preserved, two- and three-story Creole buildings and intricate, lace-like iron balconies, Selene brooded silently. Finally, she confided, "I have a problem."

"Uh oh! Something besides chucking your whole career for a silly whim?"

Selene smiled at her friend's tart reply. "Yes. Lilith has put a voodoo curse on me. She claims to be a descendant of Marie Laveau, some voodoo queen."

Georgia's mouth dropped open in surprise, and she stopped abruptly before the porte cochere entrance of one of the narrow shotgun houses. Over her shoulder, Selene could see the inner courtyard so prevalent in the Vieux Carre, teeming with lush tropical foliage and cool fountains.

Amazed, Georgia just stared at her, at first. Then she started to laugh . . . and laugh . . . and laugh. "Oh . . . oh . . . I don't believe it . . . a voodoo curse!" She laughed so hard she had to lean against a brick wall, holding her sides. "Lordy, girl, you're gonna make me pee my pants."

Selene ignored her agent's ridicule and went on, "She's carrying around a little doll that looks just like me."

Georgia's saucer-like eyes widened even more. "Why?"

"God knows! But one day she twisted its arm, and I swear I felt the pain myself."

"Get real! This is the twenty-first century. People don't practice voodoo anymore. Girl, I can't believe you let Lilith worm her way under your skin."

"Well, you'd get the willies, too, if someone said you wouldn't be around much longer, and then smiled in a really wicked way."

"Selene, stop it. Right now!" Georgia admonished, shaking a long finger in her face. "It's all in your head. Besides, Lilith is known for her wicked smile." Georgia burst out laughing again.

"It's not funny."

"Yes, it is," Georgia choked out, wiping her eyes with a tissue. "Okay, okay. Tell me all about it. I can see you're taking this curse business seriously."

"Well, the day after Lilith told me about her curse, someone ransacked my hotel room. Nothing was missing except my silver hairbrush."

"The one I gave you for Christmas? The one I bought at bloody damn expensive Tiffany's?" Georgia asked indignantly.

Selene nodded. "Then the makeup technician discovered a snake in my cosmetic case the next day."

"A snake! Holy hell!" Georgia shivered with distaste, her face turning somber. "This *is* serious, Selene. I'm sorry I laughed."

"That's all right. I'd probably laugh, too. In fact, I did . . . *after* I screamed the whole hotel down."

"Did you call the police?"

"No. It was nonpoisonous, and apparently snakes are common in these parts. I couldn't bring myself to complain to the police about something as silly as a voodoo curse. But that's not all. I found a disgusting ball of black wax on my pillow last night. The hotel maid was horrified, called it a voodoo gris-gris. And I just know that the strands of dark hair in it came from my stolen brush."

"And you think Lilith is responsible for all this?"

"Yes. She's been a problem for me ever since she joined the agency two years ago."

"I thought she'd lightened up."

Selene shook her head. "I knew she was upset after *We* did that cover story on me earlier this year, but her jealousy is totally out of control now. When Phillipe asked me to wear the premier gown in his collection for this shoot, she threw a tantrum like you wouldn't believe."

Georgia frowned, deep in thought.

"Also, someone told me that she's seeing Devon."

"Well, that explains it then. He's probably feeding her jealousy."

"Do you think he'd be so vindictive?"

Georgia shrugged. "You know how upset he was when you made him move out."

"Well, I'll be done here in a few days. I just needed to talk to someone . . . a friend. I'm sure I can handle Lilith."

Women did what they had to do, even back then . . .

But Selene wasn't so sure two days later when she awakened feeling exhausted and out-of-sorts. Thank goodness, today was the last day of the shoot.

An hour later, as Selene made her way down the wide staircase of the ballroom where they were shooting, she felt like a character from *Gone With the Wind*. She smiled inwardly at her romantic thoughts. *Gee, maybe Georgia is right. I do keep thinking about that movie.*

She carried her all-important makeup case, having learned long ago to go nowhere without her own cosmetics. Selene felt as utterly feminine as Scarlett as she glided toward the ballroom, wearing the showstopper—a marvelous white, off-the-shoulder gown Phillipe had designed especially for his Women of the Old South collection. Dozens of yards of silk and lace undulated on the wide skirt as she gracefully edged closer to Georgia. Even though Phillipe was showing his ballgowns with hoops, most modern women would probably wear them without.

She gasped with pleasure as she walked into the magnificent Orleans Ballroom, once the site of the famous Quadroon Balls. It was decorated for the occasion with period candelabra and chandeliers. Hundreds of tapers cast a natural, antique lighting for Phillipe's creations. In fact, some of the magazine displays would be done in the old sepia tintype tones.

Dozens of photographers, fashion consultants, and set assistants worked feverishly on last-minute touches while a small orchestra tuned up in the corner, its members dressed appropriately in antebellum attire. Some of the shots called for a romantic waltz scene.

Selene inhaled deeply. The heady scent and vivid colors of thousands of flowers almost overpowered her—gardenias, bougainvillea, azaleas, magnolias. She caressed a luxuriant velvet drapery with a sigh. This was the Old South she'd always dreamed about, a land where all the senses seemed heightened. A perfect setting for Phillipe's whimsical gowns.

Smiling, she headed toward Georgia. Her agent was talking to the world-famous designer near the French doors that opened onto a courtyard.

"*Chérie!*" Phillipe exclaimed, kissing Selene briefly on each cheek in the European fashion. "What do you think?"

He waved his hand with a flourish to indicate the vast ball-room.

"It's magnificent. You'll sell hundreds of gowns from this collection. I just know it."

"*Certainement!*" he agreed unabashedly.

"Honey, you look gorgeous," Georgia said, surveying her gown from all angles.

"Thanks. It's awfully low-cut, though, don't you think?" Selene put both palms on her abdomen, under her breasts, and tried to edge the dress up higher, to no avail. The built-in boning of the bodice pushed her breasts up, and the spidery lace of the décolletage barely covered the tips. "I feel kind of exposed."

"You're the one who said breasts were in," Georgia said with a smile. "You look great, sweetie—for an over-the-hill model, that is."

Selene gave her a playful shove and tried again to shimmy the dress higher.

"*Non, non, non!*" Phillipe cautioned, pulling her hands away from the dress. "The gown is *magnifique.* Perfect." He kissed his fingertips and threw out his hands dramatically. "The white color and delicate lace hint at a virginal quality, while the breasts . . . Voila! . . . the breasts tell another story."

"I just wish I didn't have to be such an open book," Selene muttered, moving closer to the photographers. "Cleavage is one thing. Nudity is quite another."

Phillipe looked pointedly at the Rolex watch on his wrist, then back to her. "Go! Put your face on so we can start." His eyes narrowed suddenly as he scrutinized Selene. "Have you gained weight?"

"No!" Selene and Georgia both burst out together, then laughed at the shared affront.

A short time later, Selene watched as cameras clicked and lights flashed for a set in which Lilith and a number of models, male and female, waltzed around the room in period suits and pastel confections reminiscent of the Old

South. The candlelight enhanced the mocha hue of Lilith's skin. Her coal-black hair was pulled off to one side with a cascade of sweet-scented white roses.

There was nothing sweet about the look of pure hatred she flashed at Selene, though, as she and her partner danced by. "Soon," Lilith mouthed silently in warning as she held Selene's gaze. "Soon."

With a shudder, Selene set her case at the edge of the dance floor, ready for any last minute touch-ups that the makeup consultant might require. Determined to put aside her fears, she turned to Georgia. "You can almost feel the history in this place, can't you?"

"Yeah, and not a very pleasant history, either," Georgia commented in a grim tone. "You know, one of my ancestors went to a Quadroon Ball once—maybe in this very room."

"Really?" Selene raised her eyes questioningly at the curious bit of information Georgia threw out so lightly.

"Fleur was her name. A real beauty, supposedly, and so light-skinned she could have passed for white."

"Georgia, I'm really surprised at you. Why didn't you ever mention this before?"

"It's not something I'm particularly proud of," she said with a shrug. "You do know why they held the Quadroon Balls, don't you?"

"I've heard a little."

"The young—very young—quadroons went to the balls with their mothers, looking for protectors among the wealthy, white, Creole men. *Plaçage*, that's what they called it. The men set the women up as mistresses in cottages over on Rampart Street and had children with them. In return, the women did everything at the men's beck and call—like wives, but more so, with none of the privileges."

Appalled, Selene stared at Georgia.

"And the system was considered honorable for the *placées*. Honorable! Hell, the mothers sold their daughters—pure and simple."

Selene laid a hand on Georgia's in compassion. "How awful for your ancestor. For all those helpless young girls."

Georgia shook her head as if to clear it. "I usually don't get so maudlin, but sometimes I think I have this genetic memory kind of thing. I feel the pain of my downtrodden ancestors. You can see why I don't like to come South."

"What happened to Fleur?"

"Murdered, supposedly. The slimy Creole man who set her up as his *placée* got tired of her eventually and wanted to rid himself of an unnecessary expense. Killed her and the unborn baby she was carrying. Although, oddly, Fleur's name and that of an infant son appear out West about the same time."

"Well, you know how inaccurate some genealogy records are. Did the man—her protector—ever get punished for murdering Fleur . . . or trying to?"

"I doubt it. After all, Fleur was *only a colored*."

Selene put an arm around her friend's shoulder in comfort. "I'm beginning to think this shoot was a mistake for both of us." Selene shivered apprehensively.

She danced her heart away . . .

Hours later, Selene was almost done with her portion of the shoot. She put her left hand on the shoulder of Mark Hiatt, a model she'd worked with many times before, and her right hand in his upraised left one. At the call to "action," the band began to play. They waltzed around the ballroom, the only dancers on the floor. Around and around they danced, dipping and swaying gracefully, as cameras flashed brilliantly and candles flickered in the slight breeze from the open doorway.

Exhausted from her hours under the lights and the back-straining poses, Selene grew dizzy. A tingling sensation at the base of her neck caused her to look over Mark's shoulder. She saw Lilith standing in the shadows of an alcove, holding the voodoo doll in her hands. Smiling evilly, Lilith pulled out a long hat pin. With deliberate care, Lilith pressed the sharp point against the head of the wax figure dressed in a white gown identical to Selene's. Then, with a sly grin, she pushed the pin in completely. At the same time, Mark began to spin her on the dance floor.

A sharp, excruciating pain pierced Selene's skull. Like a spinning top, she felt herself twirling, round and round and round. Pain and dizziness enveloped her. At first she tried to fight it off. But then she surrendered to the agony.

Whirling, whirling, whirling. Selene marveled at her partner's expertise in maneuvering the endless dance step. The photos would be fabulous . . . if she didn't pass out and ruin the shoot. Or worse.

Time flies . . .

Groggily, Selene awakened to a dull ache in her head and the intoxicating scent of flowers. She was sitting on a window seat, leaning back against a bay wall in an alcove just off the ballroom floor. Dazed, she watched the beautifully gowned dancers in front of her smile up at the dark, foreign looking men who moved them through the intricate steps of a quadrille.

Foreign men? Quadrille?

Selene blinked and sat up straighter.

The ballroom setting remained the same. The music was the same. Even the heat and cloying odor of flowers were the same.

But the contingent of male models for Phillipe's shoot had changed. They were all dark-complected men with a foreign look to them, maybe French or Spanish. No, Selene realized immediately. They looked like the portraits in the hotel lobby of famous antebellum Creoles, descendants of the early French and Spanish settlers in Louisiana.

Where had Phillipe come up with these models on such brief notice?

Although quite short, the men made up for their lack of stature with an arrogant hauteur and magnificent clothing— perfectly tailored dark suits with tapered trousers, waist-coats of brocaded satin, silk shirts with ruffled lace, highly polished leather boots, impeccable haircuts, shaves and manicures, even white gloves on some of them.

Geez!

Then Selene noticed something even more alarming. Phillipe's statuesque models weren't towering over these short men. In fact, all of the top-of-the-line female models had disappeared. The beautiful women who wore his delec-table gowns now were light-skinned black women of a very young age, no more than seventeen—every color from café au lait to almost white.

A shiver of apprehension ran through Selene, and she stood abruptly. Feeling a sudden chill from the open win-dows, she looked down.

"Holy cow!" she muttered aloud, noticing that her low-cut gown had slipped even lower. She put her hands to her breasts and pushed the lacy fabric as high as it would go . . . which wasn't far enough.

"Why bother?" a deep voice asked behind her. She turned to see a tall man smoking a thin cheroot. He leaned against an open French door leading out to the balcony. He scrutinized her through narrowed eyes, which showed only a modicum of interest—not the usual reaction her beauty garnered from men.

"What did you say?"

He shrugged in a bored fashion. "Why bother to adjust your bodice, *chérie?* Once you select one of these fine dan-dies for a protector, he will want to examine the merchan-dise before he *buys* it." His voice rang with contempt before he added, more kindly, "*Alors*, as far as I can see, your bosom is your best asset. At your age, you'd best capitalize on what you can."

"Age? Age?" Selene seethed with anger. She was tired of being told she was over the hill, and she certainly wasn't going to put up with a slam from a stand-in model for a photo shoot.

Then the rest of his words sunk in. He'd referred to selling herself. He was probably one of those extremists who considered the modeling industry an immoral form of flesh peddling.

And *bosom?* What an old-fashioned word to use. And offensive! "Why, you arrogant bastard," she snapped finally. Undaunted by the light of anger that ignited in his pale blue eyes, she returned his insult by boldly scrutinizing his body, just as he had hers. From his jet black hair to the bitter lines bracketing his eyes and mouth, down his lean body, all the way to his worn leather boots, her eyes raked him. Then, hands on hips, she curled her lip with disgust as if to say, "Who are you to talk?"

He held her gaze with silent amusement.

Suddenly it occurred to her that this was probably just a new pickup line, and she shook her head ruefully at the poor guy's lack of finesse. "Get lost, buster. If you're looking for a quick lay, you've chosen the wrong place and the wrong woman. I'm not interested. Besides, since you're so free with advice, let me give you a little, darlin'," she offered in an exaggerated Southern drawl. "Drop the brooding look and the biting sarcasm. Dark and dangerous went out with the nineties."

Surprise flashed briefly across his face, quickly masked by the return of his previous demeanor of jaded indifference. Then he flicked his cheroot out the open doorway to the courtyard below.

Looking closer, Selene had to admit that, if it weren't for his somber face, the guy was pretty good-looking. A cross between Eric Bana and Joe Manganiello, he wore the same type suit as the other Creoles, but with more casual, less

perfect attention to detail. With his hands in the pockets of
his slim trousers, the jacket was pulled back over the blue
brocade vest, displaying a well-developed chest and powerful thighs. Probably lifted weights or something. And he
had a nerve remarking on her age. With those lines crin-
kling his eyes and lips, he had to be close to thirty-five.

Suddenly one of the stranger's words struck a discordant
nerve in Selene.

"*Protector?* Did you say something about protectors?"

"*Oui.* Why do you think these wealthy men come to the
Quadroon Balls? For the *glacés*—those ridiculous fruit ices?
Or the excellent music? Hah! And did you think all these
doting mamas were going to allow their precious daughters
to give their favors away?"

"Quad . . . Quadroon Balls?" she choked out, and goose
bumps erupted all over her body. To her chagrin, she saw
the dark stranger staring boldly at a few of them. His darkening eyes and flared nostrils belied his earlier lack of
interest.

A thought occurred to her then, which she immediately
dismissed.

But it wouldn't go away.

"What year is this?" she asked hesitantly, holding her
breath.

At first the man's eyes widened with surprise. Then he
cocked his head and curved his lips into a mirthless smile.
"Eighteen forty-five."

Chapter Two

Virginity isn't all it's cracked up to be . . . or is it? . . .

Selene reeled dizzily for a moment and reached for a nearby column to steady her composure. The fine hairs all over her body raised an alarm of acknowledgment to what she'd already unconsciously surmised. "No, that's impossible! It's two thousand and twelve. It has to be. This must be a dream, or a nightmare."

"Two thousand and twelve! Oh, really!" He looked at her as if she'd just escaped from an asylum. Then understanding seemed to dawn. "Ah, let me guess your game. You don't really have any Negro blood, and you're here at the Quadroon Ball by mistake. You're actually a white woman who's lost and needs someone to help her find her way home. Perhaps you had a blow to the head, or you suffer some illness that makes you forget your name or where you live."

"No, you're wrong. I *am* white, and I know exactly who I am. I'm Sandra Selente, but people call me Selene."

"*Selene!* Hah! You even have a colored name."

"What? You're crazy. There's no such thing as a 'colored

name.' Anyhow, I live in New York City. I was visiting New Orleans for a photo shoot and—"

"Stop this nonsense right now, darlin'. Whether you try to pass matters not to me, but don't ask for my help. And take my advice, my friend, no one will believe your pretty drama. Especially with this hair," he said, leaning forward and rubbing the edges of her frizzed hair between his fingers with slow suggestiveness.

For one tantalizing, dizzying second, the man held her eyes, magnetically, and Selene felt a wonderful aura of heightened sensuality surround them, like a celestial cloud. He was so close, Selene felt his breath against her cheek. She had to fight the inclination to lean into his hand. "It's a permanent wave my hairdresser insisted would go well with this gown," Selene tried to explain in a wavering voice, disconcerted by her attraction to him.

"And those lips! *Mon Dieu!*" he added, grazing the pad of his thumb across their fullness with shocking familiarity.

She unthinkingly put her fingertips to her lips to savor the delicious tingling that lingered even after he removed his hand. "Collagen injections," she muttered in explanation.

"And those dark eyes," he whispered huskily, his eyes locking with hers in an intimate embrace.

"Contact lenses," she said weakly.

He didn't even bother to ask what she meant, his attention already moving to another part of her body. "Not to mention your dark skin," he continued in a low, silky voice as he outrageously skimmed the tops of her breasts with the knuckles of one hand.

Her nipples peaked from his slight caress, and Selene was too stunned even to tell him that her suntan would eventually fade. Panic rippled through her at her uncharacteristic response to this man. Even in the beginning, Devon had never seared her with his touch, or a mere glance, as this handsome gentleman did.

Who was he? What was happening to her?

It was probably one of those erotic dreams some people had, which she'd never experienced herself. Rather wicked, she had to admit. And delightful.

Meanwhile, the man just continued talking. "So, with all those things, *chérie*, there's no way you are going to pass," he concluded huskily. "Not even if you've had some schooling, as your speech indicates."

"Schooling? Well, I've only had one year of college, but—"

"Really? You attended college?" He looked at her with new interest, asking hesitantly, "Hmmm. Are you perchance qualified to teach young children?" Then he waved his hand in the air as if it didn't matter and he regretted asking the question.

"No, I have no teaching credentials. I'm a fashion model."

He looked slightly disappointed, then concluded, "Well, then, *bonne chance!* I wish you much success tonight. May you find a man willing to overlook your age . . . and height . . . and thin body."

Selene stiffened.

"But, in truth, I think you may succeed," he admitted with a grudging nod. "Your breasts are . . . impressive."

Selene made a choking sound of indignation. Even in the twenty-first century, men didn't make such indecent comments to a perfect stranger. But the sharp words with which she was about to lash him died in her mouth as she saw he was about to depart.

"Where are you going? You can't go now," she asserted shrilly, putting a hand on the sleeve of his jacket to stop him.

He looked pointedly at her hand, and she dropped it immediately with embarrassment.

"Can I not? And who is to stop me?"

"Well . . . well . . ." Selene said, licking her lips nervously, unsure why the stranger's presence was suddenly so important to her. "You can't because . . . by the way, what's your name?"

He tilted his head questioningly, then responded impatiently, "James. James Baptiste."

Selene nodded. Nice name. "Well, don't you have to stay for the ball . . . or something?"

"I was downstairs in the gambling rooms. I'm not in the market for a *placée*. In truth, I abhor the whole system of *plaçage*. Not that it's any of your concern." His blue eyes darkened into stormy pools of emotion.

"But . . . but you can't leave me here."

"Really, mademoiselle . . . your impertinence was amusing initially, but now you go too far. You are nothing to me."

"Selene! There you are, chile. I been lookin' for you mos' ever'where. Someone special wants to meet up with you."

Selene and James turned at the same time to see a heavyset black woman barreling toward them with a short Creole man in tow. She came to a halt and wagged a chubby finger in Selene's face. "Girl, you gonna be the death of me. Where you been?"

"Who are you?" Selene asked.

"Raffine. Your patroness," the woman said with exasperation. "What nonsense you spoutin' now? Lordy! Such a trial you been ever since you became my charge!"

"My . . . my patroness?"

"Hush yo'self, Selene," she hissed under her breath. "You gonna make the men folks think you're daft." Then her huge brown eyes riveted on Selene's head. With disbelief, she flicked the tips of Selene's flowing hair with her fingertips. "Where is your tignon, missie?"

"Huh? What's a tignon?"

Raffine put a hand to her turban. "You know the law. *Femmes de couleur libre* mus' wear the tignon. Women of color cain't be showin' their purty hair in public."

Selene scanned the room, and, sure enough, all the black women wore artfully knotted headdresses or scarves, similar to Raffine's turban, except much more elaborate, even decorated with expensive jewels. "That's the dumbest thing I've ever heard."

Clucking with dismay, the black woman went on in an undertone, low enough so the Creole suitor in the background couldn't overhear, "For weeks, I done my best to find a protector for my dead sister's chile, but do you 'preciate my efforts? Nosirree! Over and over, you brung me misery. Now, no more foolishness, missie, or we never gonna find you a man."

"But—"

"Dontcha sass me, girl. Bad enough you're so old, and skinny, and tall," she chastised with a clicking sound of distaste, "but your pert tongue puts the men off. Yesirree, it does."

James snickered behind her in agreement.

"Now, Selene, I wants to interduce you to Henri Gaspar. Y'hear?" With a huge, ingratiating smile, Raffine motioned to the Creole who stood talking to an acquaintance.

Selene looked at the little, preening man, who had to be fifty if he was a day. What right did a man his age have ogling young girls? Humph! Actually, she had to admit, men were the same in her time . . . always looking for youth, even when they were no longer young themselves.

She glared at Henri from her towering position. He was no more than five-foot-five to her five-foot-ten in bare feet, and she was wearing four-inch heels, besides. His eyes—his very appreciative eyes—came just about level with her breasts. He licked his thin lips, framed by a carefully clipped mustache and a goatee, and Selene knew he was thinking about licking something quite different.

James, who'd been about to leave moments before, planted his feet firmly in place and lit up another blasted cheroot, obviously intending to stay for the duration of her humiliation. She shot him a look of disgust, and he had the nerve to wink at her.

"M'sieur Gaspar, I'd be mighty pleased for you to make the 'quaintance of my niece, Mademoiselle Selene, from New York City."

"*Enchanté,*" Henri said with a curt bow to Selene. But

then he immediately turned with distress to Raffine. "*Sacre bleu*, the wench looks a bit . . . old," he whispered worriedly to her patroness. "Are you sure she's still pure—a virgin?"

"Of course!"

His lips pursed skeptically. "How do I know she still has a maidenhead?"

The slimy lech was staring at that part of her lower anatomy as if he could see through her gown. And how dare he demand "purity" of a woman? Odds were that he wasn't a virgin himself.

Raffine slapped a hand to her chest as if offended that Henri would even ask such a question.

"A virgin! A virgin!" Selene shrieked, finally fed up with the whole unbelievable scene. "I haven't had a . . . a *maidenhead* in ten years, not that it's any of your business."

James choked.

Selene darted him a look that she hoped told him how much she would love to whack him on the head.

Raffine gasped and started hyperventilating, as if in the throes of a heart attack. "Oh, Lordy! Now you done it, good and proper. I ain't never gonna find you a protector."

Henri's prissy mouth dropped open. Then he spun on his tiny feet and stalked away, murmuring something about "soiled goods." In moments, she saw more and more people staring her way as word passed of her damaged reputation.

"Tonight . . . you . . . leave . . . my . . . house," Raffine ordered, spacing her words evenly in fury. "Go back to your stepdaddy, or to the devil. I don't care. I don't want nuthin' to do with you no more." With that, Raffine lifted all three of her chins haughtily and stomped away.

For a moment, Selene stood watching the angry woman depart and she questioned her own sanity. This was the craziest dream she'd ever had. But maybe it wasn't a dream, after all. Maybe, with all the stress of Tessa's death, and her breakup with Devon, and then her last modeling assignment in New Orleans, well, maybe she'd gone off the deep end.

Or had she died, and this was the other world? She didn't feel dead. But then, how did one know for sure how death felt? No, she just knew this wasn't heaven. Or even hell.

She fought the idea that Lilith's curse had actually sent her back in time. And, yet, unbelievably, she suspected that was exactly what had happened.

Confused and disoriented, she wondered what she should do next. Her head began to throb with a killer migraine. Noticing her makeup case still sitting on the floor near the window seat, she went over and rummaged until she found a bottle of aspirin. Without any liquid, she popped two of the coated pills onto her tongue and scrunched up her mouth as she forced them down her throat.

Selene turned then to see James still standing in the doorway, smoking his thin cigar. He shook his head in amusement at the show she'd just put on. Eying him speculatively, she made a sudden decision.

"Well, it looks like I'll have to go with you," she announced glumly.

"Never!"

Selene ignored the stab of hurt at his quick rejection. "You asked me earlier about teaching young children. I can do that," she declared more positively than she felt. "How many kids, anyway? And how old?"

"Five years old. And only one—Etienne."

"One child? Piece of cake."

"What?"

"Just an expression, James. Is it your child?"

He nodded, a closed expression on his brooding face.

"Shouldn't your wife be doing the interviewing and hiring?"

"I have no *wife*."

"Oh." Selene felt a curious comfort in that knowledge. Then she thought of something else. "Hey, do you know anywhere we can get a few beignets?"

Selene decided then and there, if she was going to have the dream of a lifetime, she was not going to be on a diet.

That old Black Magic in her soul . . .

James tipped his chair against the wall of the Restaurant
d'Orleans, sipping from a glass of absinthe—his fourth of
the evening, two more than his usual self-imposed limit.
Feeling a slight buzz in his head, he twirled the crystal stem
distractedly as he examined the potent, green liqueur, inhaling deeply of the intoxicating anise aroma.

And he wondered how he could rid himself of the trou-
blesome wench who'd latched onto him at the Quadroon
Ball. In a weak moment, he'd agreed to take her across the
street from the Salle d'Orleans to Gabriel Julian's fine eating establishment. Little did he know that she could consume enough food to fill a starving sailor—seafood gumbo,
crayfish, black beans and rice, beignets . . . oh, Lord, could
she eat beignets!

James berated himself for wasting much-needed money
and time on the stranger. Especially when his plantation
was mortgaged to its crumbling eaves since the bank crash
of '37. Hell, he was lucky to have survived, unlike the more
than 150 planters who were not so fortunate. Even more
depressing, he faced a shortage of workers in his sugar
fields, and that meant he would have to buy more slaves on
this trip, at a time when he wished he could just free
them all.

Most of all, he worried about his five-year-old son, Etienne, who'd become so unruly of late that even his cane-
wielding cook Blossom couldn't control him anymore. And
his *mère* . . . James's poor demented mother, who had managed his household in the past . . . had taken this past year
to locking herself in her room for weeks on end to nurture
her sad fantasies.

With a weary sigh, he pulled his gold watch from a vest
pocket. *Alors!* It was past midnight, and he'd told Maureen
to meet him at his room in the St. Louis Hotel a half hour
from now.

"Ummm," the woman who called herself Selene interrupted his thoughts as she murmured with a deep sigh of contentment. Leaning back in her chair, she patted her stomach. "That was so-o-o good."

"Are you sure you don't want another beignet? You've only had five."

"No, and it's impolite to remark on how much a person eats," she chastised him with a smile that could charm the hair off a swamp hog, "but I'd love another café au lait." Her pink tongue flicked out and she unabashedly licked the sugar off each of her ten slim fingers. Long, slow, lapping, savoring strokes.

James motioned to the waiter for refills but couldn't take his eyes off her tongue and its innocently provocative strokes. Another part of his body took notice, as well, and he felt the fabric of his trousers tighten.

He almost laughed aloud when the wench surreptitiously ran a wet finger over the empty plate and scooped more sugar onto her tongue. She was like a greedy child with its first sweet, uncaring of the stomachache sure to follow.

But Selene was not a child. Despite all her separate features, which should be unattractive to him, James found his gaze continually drawn back to her. Actually, if her face weren't so gaunt, she might be passable in appearance, with her wide eyes and enticingly full, blood-red lips. Looking lower, he groaned inwardly, feeling himself harden. The woman did have magnificent breasts, he would give her that, even though her ribs stood out like barrel staves and her arms looked like sticks.

"What? What are you looking at?"

He jolted to attention, feeling like an untried boy caught in some immodest act. He didn't like the way she made him feel, not one bit, and his eyes narrowed with determination to put her in her proper place. "Do you know that when you eat you look like you're in the throes of *la petite mort?*"

"I know what that means, you brute, and I do not," Selene said, tossing her huge mane of hair over one shoulder.

"*Oui*, you do. You even moan like a woman about to

climax in lovemaking. And the outrageous things you do with your tongue could awaken a corpse. Are you sure you're not a *fille de joie?*"

Her face turned becomingly pink, and she slanted a shy look at him. "I don't moan during lovemaking, nor do I do anything outrageous with my tongue," she blurted out, then immediately slapped a hand over her mouth in regret at her hasty words.

"My condolences to you then," he remarked dryly, trying hard not to smile.

"Really, I don't like the direction of this conversation. I haven't done anything of a sexual nature to lead you on." She threw her shoulders back and shot him a look of sanctimonious disapproval.

If she only knew how her breasts jutted out when she straightened her shoulders, completely obliterating the outraged-spinster image she was trying to portray.

He found that he enjoyed shaking her composure. Perhaps he would amuse himself some more. "Hah! There's nothing more sexual than the sight of your nipples barely restrained by that wispy gown, or that delightful tongue licking everything in sight. Every man in this restaurant is imagining how your flesh would feel and taste in his own mouth." *Well, let's see what your quick retort will be to that, my sanctimonious lady.* James took a long swallow of absinthe and waited.

It took several moments for his words to register. Then her cheeks went from pink to red. In fact, the blush crept down her neck and inched toward the twin mounds in question.

To his chagrin, James felt his own skin grow hot. But not from embarrassment.

He shook his head in disbelief at his reaction to the homely chit. Truly, he'd been too long at Bayou Noir, his remote plantation, if he could be so attracted to an over-tall, bold-mouthed, skinny, sorry excuse for a woman. And a quadroon, at that! He'd always avoided relationships with colored women, with good reason, refusing to take advantage of their lowly status. *Merde*, his own status hadn't been much higher at certain times in his life.

Selene made a discreet coughing noise to alert him to the waiter, who'd finally arrived with their order.

"*Lagniappe*," the waiter said with a smile, placing the extra coffee on the table.

"What's *lagniappe?*" she asked.

"A little something extra a merchant gives a customer in appreciation. No doubt, M'sieur Julian is very appreciative of all the food *we've* consumed."

His subtle criticism passed over her, or else she was just ignoring him. With graceful finesse, her delicate hands wielded the two small pots the waiter set in front of her—one with strong chicory coffee, the other with steaming milk. She poured the two liquids into her cup, then stirred the creamy mixture with a silver spoon.

When she added a heaping spoon of sugar for good measure, James's upper lip curled with distaste.

"I like sugar," she said defensively when she saw his reproving look. "Besides, I don't have to diet now. Especially if I'm in a dream. In fact, I feel as if I've been emancipated. Geez! I can't wait to eat all the forbidden foods that have been denied me these past ten years. Yummm. The possibilities are endless. Lobster with butter. Chocolate chip cookies. Homemade bread. Fettucine Alfredo."

Oh, hell, not the dream business again. If I hear her prattle on about time-travel and voodoo curses one more time, I swear I'll wring her scrawny neck. "Diet! You're thin as a broom."

"Models have to be pencil thin. And I don't appreciate you continually making snide comments about how unattractive you think I am. I'll have you know *We* magazine voted me the most beautiful face in America last year."

He made a snorting sound of disbelief. "Enough of your bold lies! I don't know what your game is, but . . ." His words stopped cold when he saw his father and half brother enter the dining room with a group of laughing men and stop to greet the proprietor. No doubt they came from Madame Felice's establishment down the street.

Too late, he started to turn away, hoping to evade their hated presence. They already approached.

"James, you have not come by to visit for some time. We have missed the pleasure of your company," his father said in a cold, grating tone that belied his warm greeting. "And how is your *mère?*"

Liar! You care nothing for me—your bastard son. Or my mother. You only pretend affection in public places so your friends won't know of your betrayal. How I hate you! I could easily kill you and that weak excuse for a man you honor as your true, and only, son.

These bitter thoughts roiled inside him, but he spoke none of them aloud. Instead, in a voice so calm it surprised even himself, James nodded his head and acknowledged, "Father. Victor."

When he pointedly didn't invite them to sit at the table, his father shifted uncomfortably. A red-faced Victor glared at him, then seemed to notice Selene for the first time. Rather, it was her breasts he noticed, gaping at them with rude insolence.

A rush of anger swept over James at his brother's perusal. He felt strangely protective and possessive toward the wench, whom he'd only met a few hours ago. He signaled Selene with his eyes, and, surprisingly, she immediately understood, putting a napkin coyly to her chest.

"Are manners now lacking in your back-swamp country?" his father chastised him with brittle formality. Then he added with oily condescension, turning to Selene, "You have not introduced us to your companion."

James was not fooled. He'd seen his father's eyes sweep the quadroon's body and dismiss her as of no importance. As easily as he'd dismissed James's own mother at one time. Put aside as carelessly as soiled linen, or an unwanted toy.

"Selene," he said tersely, "this is my father, Jean-Paul

Baptiste, and my half brother, Victor." She inclined her head graciously, but her eyes glittered dangerously. He wondered why, but then decided his father and brother brought out the worst in everyone. With a mental shrug, he continued with his introductions, "And this is . . ." James's words trailed off and he stiffened, seeing his father's thin lips turn up in a smirk as he looked toward Selene.

And Victor! He should have killed him when he'd had the chance. He still suspected his brother of having been involved with Giselle before her death. If he ever found the proof . . .

He'd show them both, dammit. The patronizing bastards! ". . . and this is my fiancée, Selene—Sandra Selente," he finished with a flourish.

Everyone gasped audibly—his father, Victor, especially Selene. He didn't know why he'd made such a ludicrous announcement. He certainly hadn't planned it. But he didn't regret it one bit. The trouble he would have later, extricating himself from the lie, would be worth having seen his hypocritical father sputtering at the prospect of his son marrying a quadroon.

"*Non!* You cannot be serious. Even you would not marry so far beneath yourself, not even to spite me."

"Don't place a wager on it."

"Did you learn nothing from your disastrous marriage to that tradesman's daughter?"

An odd look flashed over Victor's face at his father's reference to James's deceased wife, which he immediately hid with a sneer.

"Ah, what did I expect?" his father continued, throwing up his hands. "You are always a disappointment to me, James."

Outraged, Selene rose to her full height, towering over the short Creole men. Irrelevantly, she noted James's far greater height and figured he must not be pure Creole.

She didn't care that these bozos were related to James. She'd seen the hurt deep in his eyes, the pain he'd tried to hide as soon as he saw his family approaching, not to mention the way his fists clenched and unclenched the entire time they'd stood near the table.

Hey, she knew all about the wounds a parent could inflict on a child. Hadn't her father abandoned her mother and her even before she was born, never to be seen again? Hadn't her mother spent a lifetime, until she'd died of cancer six years ago, hammering away at Selene's inadequacies?

Well, it was past time to put an end to such parental travesties.

"Sir," she said with forced politeness, looking directly at Jean-Paul. "I would appreciate it if you would leave our table. I find there is a stench in the air which is giving me the . . . the vapors." *Vapors? Criminey! Next I'll be swooning.*

"You impudent high yellow putain! How dare you speak to me so! Do you know who I am?" James's father spat out.

"No, and I couldn't care less. I'll tell you something else, mister. I'm not a quadroon, but even if I were, you're not good enough to share the same air as me, let alone a fine man like your son James." *Geez, what am I doing, defending a man I don't even know?* "So get lost before I ask the manager to kick you out. Better yet, you and Victor are such puny little specimens, maybe I'll just pick you up and throw you out myself." She started to advance on them, and the two men backed away a bit, probably more stunned than frightened by her threats.

"Slut!" Jean-Paul spat out before spinning on his heels. He left in a huff then, with Victor mouthing an obscenity over his shoulder and Jean-Paul warning James, "We will discuss this again, of that you can be sure."

She sat back down in her chair, trying to ignore all the curious faces around them. She'd created quite a spectacle. Then she looked at James, whose head was tilted, studying her quizzically.

He smiled at her, the first time she'd seen him really

smile since they'd met, the first time the brooding bitterness left his face, leaving him darkly handsome. Devastatingly attractive. And, holy cow, was that a dimple at the edge of his lips?

Her heart seemed to stop for a split second, then a sweet, tingling feeling rippled through her body, turning her warm and full and wonderfully alive.

She wanted to reach across the table and trace the sharp lines of his finely sculpted mouth. Were the chiseled marble planes cold, or hot as the passion they promised? If she kissed him . . . oh, my, if she kissed him . . . would his firm lips feel hard with demand, or soft with seduction?

He was studying her intently, too, the feathery lines bracketing his eyes and mouth momentarily smoothed out. Finally he said in a whisper-soft voice, "Thank you."

"That's okay. It's the least I could do." She could barely speak over her wildly beating pulse.

"*Au contraire*, it was unnecessary for you to defend me against my father, but it was charming nonetheless. I don't think anyone has ever done so before." He tapped his fingertips pensively on the tabletop as he studied her.

How about Etienne's mother? Didn't she care? "I can't believe you told your father we're engaged," she said nervously, trying to fill the void of silence. "I thought he'd swallow his teeth. And Victor almost had a heart attack."

"You have a most unusual manner of speaking. New York, you say?"

"Yes."

"Well," he said, seeming to come to some decision, "since your prospects with Raffine seem dead, perhaps you should take the next steamboat back to New York. Do you have enough money to buy a fare?"

"Yeah, I think so," Selene said, opening her makeup case, which sat near her feet on the floor. She pulled out her wallet. "Three hundred dollars. Will that be enough?"

"What is this?" James asked, picking up one of the bills.

"What do you mean? It's a twenty-dollar bill."

"It most definitely is not." He shook his head and reached into a pocket of his pants. He shoved several pieces of paper in front of her. They looked like old bank notes she'd seen once in a museum exhibit.

He was examining her money more carefully, then inhaled sharply. "Why is Andrew Jackson on your money? And why do I see the year 2012? Is this a joke someone is playing on me?"

"No, I've been trying to tell you—" Selene stopped abruptly when a bunch of crumbs flew in her face from a nearby table where a young black waiter was ineptly shaking out a tablecloth. "Ouch," she cried when a hard crumb hit her eye. She tried to rub it out with a napkin, to no avail. It was the dumb contact lenses that were causing the problem. Reaching down, she grabbed a small compact from her case, opened it mirror side up on the table, and deftly removed the two dark lenses.

She blinked several times to test, then sighed with relief. "That's better."

"Who in the name of God are you?" James was staring at her in horror. "*Mon Dieu!* Your eyes are green, not black. How can that be?"

"Oh." Now she understood. "These are just contact lenses. The designer of this gown wanted all the models in the photo shoot to have dark eyes. And my eyes are hazel, not green."

"Hazel? Like the nut? Your eyes are hazelnuts?" he choked out, then shook his head in exasperation at the ridiculousness of his own statements. He pointed to the lenses on the table as if they were something repulsive. "Those . . . those things . . . are they or are they not pieces of your eyes?"

"Give me a break. How silly."

"Of course, how silly of me," he remarked dryly, then slapped several of his antique bills on the table. In the blink of an eye, he stood and walked out of the restaurant, leaving her behind.

Selene stared after James's rigid back. Stunned, she tried to comprehend what had just happened. Bottom line, she concluded, "the most beautiful face in America" was being dumped by a man. Worse, she was being dumped in 1845 by an arrogant, brooding, infuriating man she probably wouldn't look at twice in the twenty-first century.

But the thought of drifting alone, without James, in this nightmare or time-travel or voodoo curse or whatever the hell it was threw her into a sudden panic. She wasn't sure why his presence was suddenly so important to her. It just was.

Seizing her makeup case, she hurried after him in her high heels. He was halfway down the street before she finally caught up.

"Wait. I've got a tic in my side."

He said something rude under his breath about where he'd like to put her tic and continued with his long strides.

"Listen," she called after him as she jogged to keep pace, "let's make a deal here. You help me get out of this mess, and I'll—"

"What? Pop out another body part? Spit frogs? Piss smoke?"

Her nostrils flared indignantly. "Don't be so vulgar. I've done nothing to prompt such contempt."

"No?" He grabbed her by the upper arms and shook her, then stopped immediately when he noticed her jiggling breasts. "Bloody hell!" he muttered, turning away. When he looked at her again, he spoke calmly and with forced patience. "Lady, I don't know who you are, but they used to burn people at the stake for stunts like you performed back at the restaurant."

"Oh, really, don't exaggerate. Besides, I'm not a witch."

"What, then? A voodoo priestess? If so, I might just light the flame myself. I've had all the Damballa nonsense I can stand for one lifetime."

She started to speak, but he put up a hand to halt her words.

"Giselle . . . my dead wife . . . fancied herself a voodoo priestess," he said angrily. "If I never hear another drumbeat in my life, it will be too soon. And I don't ever want to see another dead chicken in my bed, or snake eggs in my soup, or eyeballs on my dinner table." For emphasis on his last words, he jabbed her in the chest with a forefinger.

"Huh? Those were not eye parts."

James threw his hands up in the air in disgust and started to walk away again.

"James, please, listen to me. I don't understand what's happening to me, but you seem to be the only one I can turn to for assistance. If you'll just help me get back to my own time, I'm sure there's some way I can repay you."

Reflexively, his eyes shot to her breasts, then darted upward, as if burned, to lock with hers. "No, thank you. I'm not interested."

"I didn't mean *that*."

"Oh? What, then? Will you offer me useless money? Teach me a voodoo spell? Show me how to pop an eyeball?"

"Your sarcasm is unwarranted, James. Just think about it, coming from the future, there must be lots of things I can tell you that would help you to make a fortune, or change history, or improve life for mankind. . . . What's your greatest dream? Maybe . . . just maybe . . . I can help make it come true."

He looked at her warily. "You're serious, aren't you?"

She nodded.

"You're mad."

"I don't think I am." *Am I? A sane person doesn't cartwheel through time.* "Nope, I'm not insane."

"Let's start from the beginning," he offered in a more sympathetic tone, as if he felt sorry for her—poor demented creature that he thought her to be. "Where are you staying?"

"The same place where the ball was being held—the Bourbon Creole Hotel."

"The Creole Hotel," he murmured, then took her by the

hand and led her across the street and back in the direction from which they'd come. Without thought, he twined his fingers with hers, the calloused pads and the hard ridges of his palm at odds with the expected image of a Creole gentleman.

But Selene couldn't dwell on that incongruity. The only thing she could concentrate on was the lightness of his warm palm pressed against hers.

Selene slanted a look at his scowling face through half-shuttered lids, wanting to reach up and smooth the frown that seemed to be perpetually imprinted on his forehead. She sensed a pain deep inside this proud man that she wanted to relieve, and marveled at her presumption in thinking herself capable of such a daunting task.

"Where do you live anyway, James?"

"Bayou Noir. In Terrebonne Parish."

"Tara? Oh, my God, you live at Tara?"

"Terrebonne. Not Terre."

"Tara, Tara-bon. Big difference!" She waved a hand dismissively. "Are you sure your name's not Butler?"

"I'm a planter, not a butler."

"I didn't say . . . never mind. Oh, James, can't you see . . . this is fate that's brought us together?"

In one curt word, he told her what he thought of her theory. It began with the letter "f" but it wasn't *fate*.

Chapter Three

S *tuck on you ...*

A short time later they were back on the street again, the desk clerk of the French Quarter hotel having told a disgruntled James that the register carried no one by the name of Selene or Sandra Selente. Somehow she was not surprised.

"Now what?" she asked.

James raked his fingers wearily through his thick ebony hair. "I guess you'll have to stay in my room at the St. Louis Hotel tonight. Then in the morning you can get on the first steamboat back to New York."

"I'm not sleeping with you," Selene stated emphatically.

"Perhaps you should wait until you're asked before declining an invitation." His eyes raked her with lazy indifference.

Selene felt her face grow warm and stammered, "I'm sorry. I just thought—"

"You can sleep in the dressing room off my suite. I doubt there is a vacant room in all the Vieux Carre tonight. All the planters come to the city in late spring to make arrangements with their agents for the upcoming crops. And they bring their families with them."

"Well, I guess I don't have any other choice."

"How gracious of you to accept my hospitality!"

"That's not what I meant."

"In truth, I don't think you know what you mean, or say, or do. But I give you fair warning, one more body-part trick and your bony backside lands on the street."

Selene made a face at the back of his head as he started to walk on ahead of her, a habit which really annoyed her. But she didn't complain, knowing full well he would be just as happy leaving her behind.

They soon arrived at his hotel, a magnificent structure in the heart of the French Quarter. At this point, exhaustion overwhelmed Selene, and she wanted nothing more than a soft bed for sleeping. More important, she hoped that when she awakened tomorrow she would find the nightmare ended, and she would be back in the twenty-first century.

James started to unlock the door to his second-floor room, but the door flew open before he turned the knob.

"Darling, where have you been? I've been waiting forever." A gorgeous, petite blonde woman, wearing a low-cut red dress that would embarrass a Bourbon Street hooker, stood on tiptoe and threw her arms around James's neck, giving him a welcoming kiss.

James seemed momentarily surprised. "My apologies, Maureen. I was delayed, but—"

"A *ménage à trios,* James?" she asked, noticing Selene for the first time. "I don't recall your tastes being so exotic before."

James grumbled disgustedly. "No, Maureen, I've not become quite *that* depraved yet. This is Selene. She . . . she seems to have lost her way and must catch the first steamboat to New York in the morning." Looking between Selene and the woman, he said, "This is Maureen . . . what is your last name, sweetheart?"

"Rivieux."

"Ah, yes, now I remember . . . Rivieux."

Selene could barely restrain herself from growling with derision. He didn't even know the woman's full name.

"And she's going to stay here tonight?" Maureen asked James with amusement, her hands on her softly curving hips. "That should be interesting."

"She's going to sleep on the pallet in the dressing room." He motioned Selene toward an open doorway and walked over to a sideboard, pouring himself a healthy glass of bourbon. The man drank entirely too much.

James discarded his jacket and turned back to Maureen, dismissing Selene without a second thought. Selene stood frozen, watching Maureen's busy hands sweep his suspenders over his shoulders. Then she started to unbutton his shirt to the tune of soft, cooing suggestions that caused Selene's face to flame.

Revolted, Selene walked into the dressing room, smaller than her walk-in closet at home, and stomped right back out. She tried to avert her eyes from James's bare chest and Maureen's hands, which were already working on his trouser buttons.

"There's no window in there, and it's stifling hot."

James's lips tilted in a mirthless smile. "You know the alternatives." He motioned his head toward the open French doors leading to a balcony overlooking the streets below.

So these were her options, she decided: suffocation, the streets, or sharing a bed, and more, with two other people— not that the offer had been made for the latter, or that she would have accepted. She turned on her heel and slammed the dressing-room door loudly behind her.

Unable to unsnap the back of her tightly fitted gown, Selene had no choice but to remove her hoops and full petticoats, then lie down on the narrow pallet fully clothed. With no light, she couldn't wash or relieve herself, assuming there was a chamber pot available. And, holy cow, this had to be the first time since her tenth birthday that she'd gone to bed without removing her makeup. Her fastidious mother must be rolling in her grave. But no way would she go back into that other room, knowing what she might interrupt.

Within minutes, perspiration pooled in every crevice of her overheated body—her armpits, between her breasts, the vee of her legs. Exhaling loudly, she stood and removed her pantyhose, leaving her body nude up to the waist under the ballgown. Still, the linen sheets soon became soaked, and she began to itch everywhere a seam of the gown touched her skin.

Even worse, she could clearly hear the soft murmurs of a man and a woman through the thin walls, followed by a feminine giggle, then the creak of the rope bed supports as they presumably lay down. To be fair, James probably didn't realize that she could hear them.

Despite her best intentions, Selene couldn't stop herself from picturing a nude James with the beautiful blonde woman.

Was he a good lover? Or selfish as Devon had been?

Did he whisper the soft love words most women yearned to hear? Or was he a silent lover?

Did the prostitute . . . she assumed that's what Maureen was . . . climax for James, or was she so desensitized by her profession that she just faked orgasm? As Selene had learned to do?

Finally, blessed silence reigned, and Selene drifted off to sleep. Later, she was awakened in the quiet night by a husky moan. That was all. Just a moan. But the solitary, intimate sound tantalized her imagination.

Selene slept restlessly the remainder of the night.

She awakened in early morning to a dim light under her door and a full bladder. Unfastening the door to let in a little light, she grabbed one of James's white shirts. With pleasure, she used the fine linen to wipe the sweat off her entire body, then threw the crumpled shirt on the floor.

She opened the door wider and peeked into the bedroom. Only a dim morning light hazed the opulent room through the heavy velvet drapes.

James slept alone, Maureen must have slipped away during the night. Probably to serve another customer, Selene thought meanly.

She saw a screen and figured there must be a chamber pot there. Quickly relieving herself as quietly as she could, she then poured water from a porcelain pitcher into a wide bowl and washed her hands. Despite the long gown, she felt naked and decided to don her pantyhose.

She looked into a small mirror on the wall above the washstand and giggled. She was still wearing her false eyelashes from yesterday's shoot. She removed them carefully and, with the damp end of a linen towel, wiped off the mascara that had seeped under her eyes.

Then, having procrastinated long enough, she made her way toward the bed where James still slept. He lay on his stomach, his lean body exposed from head to waist and thigh to toes, a thin sheet barely covering his buttocks.

"James," she said softly, trying hard not to stare at the wide shoulders and muscled planes of his well-defined back. And, Lord, the man had nice toes—long and slender and somehow vulnerable looking. She put a hand over her mouth to stifle a giggle. *You're losin' it, girl, when you start getting turned on by a man's toes.*

"James, it's time to wake up," she said somewhat louder and almost groaned at the sight of both sinewy arms thrown over his head, as if in abandon. His face was turned toward her, and she could see the dark shadow of his morning beard and his incredibly long lashes, which lay like lacy fans against his tanned skin. In sleep, the bitter lines melted away from his forehead and eyes and mouth. Selene fought the impulse to run her fingertips along his proud jaw, to test the hardness of his muscled biceps, to taste the vulnerable crease behind his knees.

His knees! Criminey! First his toes, now his knees. Get a hold on yourself, girl.

"James, get up!" she said loudly.

His body jerked, but he didn't raise his head. Instead, his

arm shot out with lightning speed and pulled her down to the bed. Then he flipped her onto her back on the other side of him, burying his face in her neck as he adjusted his body atop hers.

"Maureen, what're you doing out of bed? It's early yet, *chérie*," he mumbled, still half asleep.

Maureen! He thinks I'm Maureen. Selene tried to buck him off, and only succeeded in having the brute chuckle and shift his body so he lay more fully atop her.

It was then Selene realized that her bodice had slipped, exposing her breasts, and her blasted gown had twisted up to her waist, exposing about three feet of bare leg. She moaned.

"You like that, do you, sweetheart?" he growled, misinterpreting her sound as he moved his crisp chest hairs back and forth across her now erect nipples. He did it one more time for good measure, and she felt her breasts engorge and ache.

Selene inhaled sharply with disbelief, scrunching her eyes closed tightly. She'd never in all her life felt anything so wonderful.

She immediately amended that thought when his lips covered her left breast. The tip of his tongue created a circle of fire around her nipple before he flicked it several times, then began to suckle in earnest.

Selene bit her bottom lip to stifle her cry of intense pleasure. And parts of her she'd never known were frozen began to melt.

She looked down and saw that his eyes were still closed, even as he moved to the other breast and ministered to it with equal, exquisite care.

Involuntarily, her legs parted more to accommodate him where his nakedness pressed against her. Sensuously she rubbed a stocking-clad calf against the coarse hair of his bare leg. One of his hands reached down and skimmed the edge of her leg, starting at the ankle, moving enticingly up the outside over the calf, past the knee and up the thigh.

And two zillion long-dead nerve endings jump-started to attention.

"Ummm, Maureen, how wicked of you to wear silk stockings to bed," he murmured appreciatively.

Selene stiffened at the reminder that James thought he was with another woman.

At that moment, his hand moved higher, hesitated, then seemed to explore jerkily.

Selene realized almost instantly what the problem was. She wore waist-high pantyhose—something that hadn't been invented yet.

His shoulders pulled back and his eyes flew open to glare at her. "You're not Maureen."

"No kidding, Dick Tracy."

"What the hell are you doing in my bed?" he demanded angrily. He blinked his sleepy eyes several times in stunned surprise. "Seduction will get you nowhere, wench. Get that idea from your head."

"Seduction!" she shrieked and tried to buck him off.

A big mistake.

A very strategic, and highly sensitized, part of her body, pushed against his arousal.

"Oh," she said weakly.

"Oh, indeed," he agreed with a whoosh of breath and quickly put both his hands under her buttocks, holding her in place. "Do . . . not . . . dare . . . move," he ordered through gritted teeth.

He pressed his forehead against hers until he slowly brought his ragged breathing back to normal. And Selene couldn't stop the tears that burned under her closed eyelids, then slid down her flushed cheeks.

"Why are you crying?" James asked with puzzlement, raising his head to peer at her. "I'm the one in pain."

"It's everything," she said on a sob. "I'm lost in this stupid time warp, and I . . . and I don't know how to get back. And I'm hungry . . . all the time. And"—she sniffled loudly, knowing her mascara was probably running again—"and, dammit, it's the first time in five years I've been turned on by a man, and he thinks I'm someone else, and he's almost two hundred bloody years old."

James's lips . . . James's wonderfully firm lips, that had been teasing her breasts just moments ago . . . twitched with laughter. And that infernal, endearing dimple threatened to disarm her. She felt his hardness grow against her.

"I 'turn you on,' do I?"

"Argh! This is impossible!" Selene exclaimed and tried to twist away from under him. Her exertions only caused a section of the boning in her bodice, which was pushed down to her waist, to pop a seam and jab James in the abdomen.

"Damn! You just cut me with one of your ribs," he said in wonder, touching the thin line of blood that formed along the five-inch cut. But his eyes weren't on the wound, they were glued to her exposed breasts as she climbed awkwardly off the bed.

"Sacre bleu!"

"If that's a swear word, I'll second it," she said, pulling up her bodice and straightening the skirt of her gown.

"I don't think I've ever encountered anyone like you." He shook his head in amazement and walked shamelessly in all his nudity toward the screen. She put her hands over her ears when she heard him relieving himself in the chamber pot. *Tsk, tsk, tsk!* Men, whether nineteenth or twenty-first century, had absolutely no modesty about such things, Selene decided.

After that she heard him splashing water in the bowl. Then a loud whacking sound and a harsh swear word. Followed by a long, ominous silence.

She waited apprehensively.

James finally emerged with dark eyes flashing angrily. Bare-chested, he wore only dark pants, no shoes or shirt. His lean, sinewy body exuded masculinity. And sex.

"What the hell are these?" he asked, holding a pair of false eyelashes up in the air, one in each hand. They looked like grotesque spiders. *Flat* spiders.

Selene giggled. "My false eyelashes."

"False . . . false," he choked out. "I killed your eyelashes?"

"Apparently."

He dropped them to the floor with distaste and moved toward her, his eyes glittering with dangerous intent. "You think it's amusing, do you? Spiders are dangerous business in the South. One bite of their poison and a person could die. I think I could very easily kill you, too."

Selene backed away. "Now, James, it *is* funny when you think about it. Don't you have a sense of humor?"

"No." He moved one step nearer, peering closely. "What's that black substance running down your face? Are your eyeballs melting now?"

She put a fingertip to her cheeks and laughed. "No, it's just mascara."

"That explains it, of course."

"It's used to darken the eyelashes."

"Don't tell me. You have orange eyelashes."

"This conversation is getting really silly."

"Everything that's happened since I met you has been silly." He threw his hands up in the air hopelessly.

"Well, you'll be rid of me soon enough. Where's this steamboat office you mentioned?"

"Don't you think you ought to change your dress first?" he asked as his eyes swept her low décolletage and crumpled gown.

"I don't have any other clothes." Suddenly Selene had a ridiculous notion. Looking at the moss green velvet drapes with gold tassels lining the tall windows, she giggled. "Hmmm. Maybe I could make these drapes into a dress à la *Gone With the Wind*."

"What? Don't you dare touch those drapes. The hotel would charge me a fortune." He looked at her as if she were truly crazy. "Do you often make gowns out of hotel drapes? Can't you conjure something out of that magic box you carry around like a—"

A loud knocking on the door interrupted his words.

"James, open the door. Quickly. The city guard will be here soon."

"The police?" Selene mouthed silently. What kind of disreputable character had she attached herself to? He could be Jesse James, or something. No, that was another time period. Wasn't it? "Who is it?" she asked James.

"My overseer, Fergus Cameron."

James opened the door and a large, burly, red-haired man slipped inside. Taking one look at Selene, he cast a reproving look at James and snorted with disbelief. "So Corporal Atwood was right. Well, you've really landed in it this time."

"Why is Atwood coming here, Fergus?" James asked with forced patience.

"For her," he said, pointing accusingly at Selene.

"Me?" Selene squeaked out.

Fergus ignored Selene and addressed James. "Seems your brother Victor went to the authorities. Claims you're harboring an escaped slave. Name of Selene." He inclined his head in her direction. "Can I assume she's Selene?"

James nodded, and Selene gasped.

"Did you really tell Victor and your father that you planned to marry her?"

James shrugged. "I wasn't serious." Then he turned to Selene. "Are you sure you don't have your manumission papers with you?"

Selene counted to ten silently. "Why won't you believe that I'm not black?"

Both men scanned her body disbelievingly.

Selene sighed deeply, struggling for patience. "Listen, you two blockheads. I am not a racist, and I would have no objection to being black, *in my own time,* but read my lips. I . . . am . . . not . . . black!"

"That's what they all say," Fergus commented to James. "Every light-skinned Nigra from here to Mississippi is trying to pass these days."

She turned her back on Fergus and informed James through gritted teeth, "I can prove that I'm white, but I'll be damned if I'm going to expose myself to you creeps."

James lifted an eyebrow cynically. "Lady, I've seen your breasts . . . and a great deal more of your flesh. Your skin is dusky . . . everywhere."

Selene's face flamed. She couldn't believe he would make such a remark in front of another man.

"I told you before that I got an all-over body tan so I could model swimsuits."

"What's an all-over body tan?" Fergus asked James.

James rolled his eyes as if to say, "Who knows?"

"I lay out in the sun in the nude."

Both men turned as one and stared at her as if she'd just sprouted three noses.

"Why?" James asked.

"Because *Sports Illustrated* magazine wanted models with suntans," she answered tiredly, sensing the hopelessness of explaining herself properly.

"She claims to lie bare-assed in the sun?" Fergus asked James with a grin.

"So she says."

"For what reason?"

"Will you two stop talking about me as if I'm not here?"

James walked over to a large mahogany armoire that could bring a fortune some day at Christie's. He began to throw some of his jackets and shirts onto the Persian carpet on the floor. "You'd better hide in here," he told her. "I'll see if I can forestall the guard until Fergus can get some forged documents."

"Argh! Will you listen to me? I can prove I'm white."

He glared at her, hands on hips. "How?"

Selene darted a glance at Fergus, who was leaning against the wall, clearly amused. "Make him step outside."

James hesitated, then told Fergus, "Wait in the hall, and knock if you see the guard coming."

He turned back to Selene, folding his arms across his chest. "Well?"

"I don't suppose you'd just accept my word."

He tapped his foot impatiently.

Selene turned her back on him, leaned down to raise her skirts, then removed her panty hose. She turned around and carefully raised the hem of the ballgown, starting at her right ankle, being sure to expose only the outer side of her leg up to her hip bone.

"See," she said, "I was wearing a teensy bikini bottom. The skin is white right here where the strap went up to the hips."

James squinted at her exposed skin, as if he couldn't see clearly. Then, before she had a chance to protest, he put both hands on her waist, lifted her off the floor, and walked the short distance to the bed. With a whoosh of skirts, he threw her onto her back on the soft mattress and, quick as a wink, tossed her skirts up to her waist.

"You bastard!" Selene shrieked and tried to get up, but he held his left palm on her chest, holding her down firmly.

With the forefinger of his right hand, he traced the band of her pale skin from hip bone to pubic bone and back to the other hip bone. He shook his head back and forth in wonder. "You really are white."

"No kidding. Let me up now."

His eyes locked with hers in challenge. "Perhaps I should examine *all* of your body. Just to make sure."

Selene felt her face flame with humiliation at his perusal of her most intimate body parts. And it didn't help matters to see the sensual parting of his sculpted lips or the erotic hazing of his blue eyes.

"Please . . . don't."

He held her eyes for a few tortuous moments longer, his palm lying hotly against her stomach, like a brand. Then he moved away from her abruptly, leaving her to adjust her clothing.

Opening the door for Fergus, he announced flatly, "She's lily white."

Astonished, Fergus stared at her as she stood by the bed adjusting her gown.

"I'll go to the guard headquarters at the Calaboso and explain that she lived in the Caribee for years where even the white women sometimes live like the natives," James said.

Unconvinced, Fergus raised a bushy red eyebrow.

"If Atwood insists on proof, I'll have his wife examine her," James continued. "I think she lives with him in separate quarters at the jail."

"Well, you'd better hide her in the meantime. If Victor comes by and finds her alone, he won't care if she's white, black, or purple."

"Where's your wife?" James asked.

"Still in bed. Female complaints."

"Is there anyplace in your room you could hide Selene?"

Fergus nodded. "Probably. But . . . are you sure you want to go to all this trouble for the wench? After all, she's just a stranger. Can't you let her fend for herself with Victor?"

James practically snarled, "Do you think I'd let that slimy brother of mine get the best of me? In anything?"

"Does this mean I'll miss my boat?" Selene asked.

"*Oui.*" He didn't look happy at the prospect.

"Can I get another?"

"I certainly hope so. I don't plan on being stuck with you any longer than necessary."

As she followed Fergus through the door, Selene looked back over her shoulder at James, who was watching her intently. She thought of something else.

"James?" she inquired in a coaxing voice.

His face turned immediately distrustful. "What?" he snapped.

"When you come back, could you bring some beignets?"

He said a very, very foul word.

She almost landed in the slammer . . .

"Well, are you satisfied?" Selene asked the police officer later that day, raising her chin defiantly. Corporal George Atwood reminded Selene of a Klansman she'd seen in a movie.

She and James had arrived at the Calaboso, a combination police headquarters and prison on St. Peter Street, two hours ago. They'd been interrogated by Corporal Atwood since then.

James stepped into the corporal's office from another room where he'd been filling out some papers related to the complaint against Selene. He was not a happy camper, having been forced to attest in black and white that Selene was his fiancée and that he would be removing her from the city when he left in two days for his plantation.

"Let's get out of here," he told Selene, ignoring the corporal.

He and Atwood had already exchanged heated words when the corporal had wanted to examine her himself. "Why are you protectin' her, Baptiste?" the rude man had shouted, his ruddy skin turning bright red with anger. "She's nuthin' but a worthless darky, even if she is light-skinned. You kin be sure she'll have to show her flesh—all of it—on the auction block, not that anyone would want to buy such a skinny wench, 'ceptin mebbe for those tits of hers. Bet you been enjoyin' them, Baptiste."

Selene's skin had crawled when his beady eyes lit on that part of her body.

James had very calmly but firmly told Corporal Atwood, "Either you call your wife or I will—in which case, I wonder how she will feel about your insistence on examining a nude woman."

The policeman had reluctantly sent for his wife, but Selene shivered now with shock at how close she'd come to a public stripping, and she began to understand firsthand the defenselessness and utter humiliation of slavery. What if she were trapped in this time flashback? How would she be able to exist in a society that not only subjugated women, but ·sanctioned slavery, as well?

"You'd best watch your step, missie," the corporal called after her now. "I'm watchin' you, an' I agree with Victor. There's somethin' mighty suspicious about your appearance in Naw'leans. Mebbe you're one of them abolitionists. Mebbe you really are a high yaller helpin' niggers escape North."

"Now, that's a good idea," Selene said, putting her forefinger to her chin and tilting her head as if actually considering the possibility. "Where might one go to sign up for that underground railroad thing?"

The corporal's face turned purple with rage, and Selene figured that they'd better leave before he had an apoplectic seizure or came up with some trumped-up charge to hold them both. She tugged on James's coat sleeve, pulling him from the room.

James headed out the door. She hurried to catch up and almost reeled at the wave of humid heat that hit her when she stepped outside. And it wasn't even noon yet.

She executed a few quick skipping steps before arriving at James's side. He continued to walk, ignoring her, as he stared forward with glowering concentration. Criminey! The man took life way too seriously. He was always brooding or angry. Didn't he ever smile or laugh?

And her situation really was humorous, Selene thought, now that she'd escaped the danger of arrest. Imagine being lost in the nineteenth century and mistaken for a quadroon! Even worse, a woman whose whole life—in fact, her whole identity—rested on her beauty was suddenly considered unattractive. Georgia would call it an absolute hoot.

James stopped dead in his tracks and shoved her angrily against the wall of a mercantile. With his palm pressed against her shoulder, he demanded in a cold voice, "Do I amuse you?"

"Huh?"

"You were looking at me and smiling."

"Oh. I was? Actually, I was laughing at myself. Lighten up, James. Get a sense of humor."

"A . . . a sense of humor," he sputtered, dropping his hand from her shoulder. "Do you realize what could have happened back there, you witless wench? If Atwood hadn't believed you, he could have put you on the auction block. There's nothing funny about slavery, I assure you."

"I'm sorry. I've just never been in a situation like this before—"

"And you think I have? *Mon Dieu!* You are senseless."

"I think I take the danger so lightly because you're at my side," she admitted, putting a hand on his coat sleeve hesitantly. "Somehow I don't think you would let anyone hurt me."

"Don't depend on it," he said coldly.

He started to walk in the direction of their hotel once again, but he didn't look quite so angry now.

"James, could we—"

"No! We are not going to eat again."

"That's not what I was going to say."

"Oh?" He slanted her a disbelieving look. "Lady, you'd best understand one thing—the bank crash of '37 brought me and most of the South to its knees. Last summer, a vicious storm destroyed half my cane fields. My land, my home, everything I own is mortgaged to my eyeballs. And mine are not removable, my dear. A man could go bankrupt trying to fill that bottomless pit you call a stomach."

Selene forgot to be insulted for a moment as she gazed at his sparkling eyes, realizing for the first time that their blue color was flecked with gray. Forcing aside her odd attraction to James, she explained, "I merely wanted to ask if I was going to have to hide in Reba's armoire when we get back to the hotel. I mean, your overseer's wife was really nice, but that wardrobe thing was hotter than a sauna. I probably lost a pound."

She saw his lips twitch and knew he was stifling a smile.

Geez! Why did the guy insist on being so somber all the time? If he'd flash that dimple once in a while he'd have the world by its tail. Or at least, all of its women.

"No, there's no need to hide anymore. Unless Victor comes up with some other complaint, or you do something to rile the populace of New Orleans."

"Like what?"

"Like shed your toenails which, incidentally, looked like they were bleeding this morning. Why would you paint them red, for God's sake? Or maybe you'll spin your head on your scrawny neck like a wheel. Or turn your hair purple. What color is your hair really, by the way?"

The anger had disappeared from James's face, and he was almost smiling at her. Almost. Maybe the man had a sense of humor, after all.

"What makes you think this isn't my natural hair color?" she asked, lifting her chin in challenge.

"Because it's darker than your *other* hair," he said flatly, and Selene thought she saw a near-twinkle in his eye, especially when her face heated with embarrassment at his frank observation. As if satisfied that he'd accomplished his goal, he put his hand under her elbow and steered her in the direction of the hotel.

Your point, Rhett, Selene thought. *But remember, Scarlett got the last word.*

Chapter Four

Beauty is in the eye of the be-hold-her . . .

As they walked silently, Selene absorbed the wonderful sounds of the old city. Everywhere she looked, black women carried large baskets or wooden bowls on their heads, singing out their wares for sale in rhythmic chants:

"Nice *calas*, very hot. Come buy my *calas*."

"Pralines, pralines. Sweet and crisp."

"*Bel pom, patat*, madam!"

"Strawberries, fresh and fine."

"*Confiture, coco.*"

The normally closed shutters of the Creole homes would burst open suddenly, and the Vieux Carre housewives would lean out, inviting the vendors into their courtyards.

And bells. All around her bells pealed, and not just those of St. Louis Cathedral. The jingle of a small bell on the horse-drawn milk wagon encouraged housewives and merchants to come out with pitchers and draw their daily requirements from the spigots in the large milk cans. Still another distinctive bell on the Roman Candy wagon with its windows on all sides caused squeals from the children who raced for a taste of the chewy confections made on little burners right in the wagon bed. The water carts, the snowball man, the kerosene wagon—all had their own bells, which the French Quarter residents apparently recognized.

Selene's head pivoted back and forth as she took in all the sights of old New Orleans. She heard James chuckle beside her, probably amused by her touristy fascination.

His amusement quickly disappeared, though, when he noticed something in a shop window, and he pulled her to a halt beside him.

"What?"

"You need another gown," he said studying the window display of the dressmaker's shop.

"I thought you didn't have money for frivolous things."

"I don't, but if we don't soon find a way of keeping your breasts under cover, you won't consider it such a frivolous matter. It doesn't take much to cause a riot in the Vieux Carre."

Selene looked down and, sure enough, her gown had slipped again, the lacy edges of the bodice barely concealing her nipples. She jerked it up with a tsk-ing sound of chagrin, feeling her face turn even hotter with humiliation. "You could have told me," she complained.

"I just did."

"Hah! How long was I walking around letting it all hang out?"

"Long enough."

"And you didn't think I should know?"

He shrugged. "A man deserves a little compensation for his trouble," he said, sweeping her bosom with an appreciative appraisal. "And you have caused me more than a little inconvenience." His damn lips were twitching with amusement again, the beguiling dimple fighting to emerge, as he motioned her toward the shop door with a jerk of his head.

Selene started to tell him what she thought of his sexist tripe, but was interrupted by an exclamation from a blonde woman exiting the shop. "James, *mon ami!*" The woman came forward to kiss him on both cheeks in greeting. Her maid stood quietly in the background.

"Lizette," he acknowledged, holding her at arm's length and gazing at her fondly. "You have grown far lovelier since last we met, *chérie*."

The young woman wore a lemon-colored silk dress trimmed with an embroidery of roses and topaz buttons down the front, complemented by a topaz parure of earrings and necklace. She even wore a lemon-colored bonnet and matching shoes, and carried a fringed parasol with a lemon background and blue cabbage roses. Any more yellow and the sweet young thing would look like a canary.

Selene thought she would gag.

Sniffling, the woman dabbed at her eyes dramatically. "I never had an opportunity to offer my condolences last year after Giselle's death. Such a sad ending for your unfortunate wife! And she left that poor motherless child . . . Etienne, is it not?"

James nodded, his jaw rigid with some strong emotion.

"Ah, well, *c'est la vie.* But that is no excuse for your neglect." Lizette tapped James reprovingly on the arm with a closed fan—yellow, of course—that dangled from her wrist. She pursed her lips flirtatiously. "How long has it been since you visited me, *cher?*"

Selene felt an unaccustomed lurch of jealousy in the region of her heart as James still held the woman . . . Lizette . . . then pulled her to his side with an arm around her shoulder. The woman's blonde head came barely to his neck.

Used to being the center of attention at every gathering, something she'd always thought she hated, Selene found herself feeling unwanted and in the way, almost invisible.

With uncharacteristic meanness, Selene wanted to tell the little Southern belle that if she'd use a little blush on her cheeks it would call attention away from her weak chin, and a few hot rollers would put some body in her lank hair.

Hah! Who was she kidding? Selene didn't think she'd
ever seen a woman with such a pert little nose and such a
disgustingly perfect rosebud mouth in all her life. Lizette
was beautiful, even in yellow, and she and James made a
fantastic couple. *Damn.*

Just then, Lizette noticed Selene, still standing in the
background like a tree. "And this is . . . ?" she asked, peering up at James over the top of her fan with accusing coquettishness. If she fluttered her eyelashes at James one
more time, Selene thought she might gag.

James removed his arm from Lizette's shoulder and
drew her over to Selene, who felt like a gangly, overdressed,
unkempt giant next to the fair damsel with her petite frame
and pristine clothing and hairstyle. Insecurity about her appearance had never been one of Selene's problems, and she
didn't like it. At all.

The dolt didn't even notice her discomfort; his attention
was still on the beautiful woman at his side. "This is Sandra
Selente, or Selene—Etienne's new governess and my mother's new nurse and housekeeper."

Nurse! I can barely put on a Band-Aid.

"And this is my cousin, Madame Lizette Baptiste,"
James told Selene.

Selene honed in on the word *madame*. That meant she
was married, didn't it? And *cousin?* She started to smile.

"*Au contraire*, James. We are not cousins," Lizette immediately corrected. She explained to Selene, "I am widow
to James's second cousin René. He died of the fever two
years ago." After dabbing at her eyes with a snow white
lace handkerchief, Lizette tapped James playfully on the
arm once again with her fan. "We are not blood kin, as you
well know."

Lizette's meaning was not lost on Selene. The jerk
squeezed Lizette's hand in acknowledgment.

Selene wondered where she might buy one of those
fans—a *big* one. She'd like to tap James a few times, too.

Lizette turned back to James. "The opera house is open for a special performance tonight. Will you be there?"

James's face colored and he shifted uncomfortably. "I had not thought to purchase tickets."

"Ah, then you will escort me, *mon cher.* I have plenty of room in my box," Lizette declared imperiously. "You will pick me up at nine. You do still know the way to my home?"

"Oui, certainement!"

"And will you be bringing your governess?" Lizette added, looking Selene over in a thoroughly appraising manner and obviously finding her not much competition for James's favor—something the fair widow obviously wanted for herself.

"Non," he commented quickly, muttering something under his breath about no food being served.

James kissed both of Lizette's cheeks before she departed. Then he turned back to Selene and commented dryly, "Why are you still standing there? I have important business transactions to take care of today. Do you think I enjoy wasting all this time on you?"

Selene decided she was definitely going to buy a fan.

Blonde jokes have timeless appeal . . .

A short time later, Selene walked back to the hotel with James, wearing a full-length, green cambric day dress sprigged with cream-colored flowers and trimmed at the scooped neck and cap sleeves with ruffled ecru lace. She felt like a cutesy, overly tall, overdressed Barbie doll. In deference to the temperature, she scandalously insisted on wearing only one crinoline—one too many, in her opinion. Apparently, most ladies wore five or six. They must be masochists, Selene decided, or else slaves to the dictates of a fashion-conscious society, just like modern women.

"This dress is hotter than hell," she complained.

"Watch your mouth. At least it covers your body, even if it is too tight," he remarked, his insolent eyes honing in on her bodice, which hugged her upper body from scooped neck to pointed waist in what the dressmaker had called the popular Redingote style.

"James, slow down." Even in her new low-heeled shoes, she had trouble keeping up with his long strides on the wide Creole sidewalks, called banquettes. "The smell of that open sewer running down the street is turning my stomach queasy."

"Maybe your stomach hurts from eating too much."

Selene mouthed her opinion to the back of the lout's head.

"Likewise," he retorted flatly, never even turning.

Geez, did the guy have eyes in back of his head, or was she just so transparent? Probably the latter, she decided.

But enough was enough. Her side hurt. All the beignets she'd eaten the night before, topped off with the huge breakfast of fresh sweet rolls, butter, and coffee she'd consumed late that morning, rose bilously to her throat. And a killer headache began to pound under the merciless Louisiana sun. She had to be the only woman south of the Mason-Dixon line not wearing a bonnet.

Finally, she halted with exasperation, put her hands on her hips and glared at James as he blithely continued on without her. She knew he resented her latching onto him, but he didn't have to be so darn obvious. She wished she had some other choice; he should know that. Lord, she'd like to pick up one of those clods of horse manure on the street and hit him on the back of his stubborn head.

Seeing a nearby stone bench in a small park, she sat down with a whoosh of relief, too fatigued to care if he left her behind. If flesh could melt, Selene figured she would soon be a puddle. She really could use one of those fans the Southern belles favored. Or about two million BTU's of air-conditioning.

It took James a few moments to realize she wasn't beside

him. He stomped back. Towering over her, he demanded, "What now?"

"I'm tired, and hot, and I don't feel well. And we have to talk . . . about this governess and housekeeper and nurse-maid business, among other things. Would you *please* get me a cup of lemonade, over there?" she asked, pointing to a street vendor who was chipping ice off a big block to put in the beverages.

James's jaw tightened and she knew he considered balking at the delay. Instead, he muttered something about her being more trouble than a polecat in heat and went off reluctantly to purchase two metal cups of cold lemonade. He came back and handed her one of the frosted cups, then sat down next to her. Too close, she thought, as their eyes met and held for a long moment. A new and inexplicable warmth surged through Selene, despite the cool cup that trembled in her hands.

Selene's mind spun with bewilderment as she tried to weigh the sequence of events that had led to her present dilemma. A strange wall separated her from her past. Her future loomed shadowy and uncertain. She had only this crazy, ever-changing present, and a man who was becoming too important to her. Amazed that she reacted so strongly to a brooding, cynical, rude man like James, she fought desperately to control her swirling emotions.

James continued to gaze into her eyes, as if unable to look away, and Selene sensed his confusion, as well, over this illogical bond that was growing between them. Finally breaking eye contact, James stretched his long legs out lazily and sipped his lemonade.

Selene watched, fascinated, as his beautiful fingers, slender and work-worn, circled the cup and traced the edge distractedly. She imagined those same fingers . . . *oh, Lord, I am in big trouble.* Forcing her eyes upward, she was struck by the starry highlights in his ebony hair. He had had no time to shave that morning, and his face carried a bristly overnight shadow that was not unattractive.

Yes, Selene really could use a cold shower.

Slowly relaxing, James's lean body eased into a casual slouch as he surveyed his surroundings and the bustling people going about their business—white-robed nuns in their cowls and wimples hurrying toward the nearby Ursuline Convent on Chartres Street, more tradespeople hawking their wares from pushcarts, ladies and their maids ambling toward the French Market for their daily provisions.

And, to her chagrin, she saw James's eyes halt appreciatively in appraisal of one platinum-blonde beauty whose hips swayed seductively as she passed on the other side of the street. She glanced with interest toward James, and he tipped his head, acknowledging the bimbo's unspoken invitation.

"You like blondes, do you, James?" Selene asked in a voice thick with sarcasm.

"Hmmm?" He turned to her, tilting his head questioningly. She saw then that the edges of his jacket were frayed and the elbows shiny with age.

She felt an odd tug of sympathy at the proud manner in which he carried his obvious poverty. She fought for a way to halt her weakening resistance. "Blondes. Your companion last night—Maureen—was blonde, and you liked her a whole heck of a lot by the sounds of your moans."

"You heard?" he asked, a surprising blush rising up his neck.

"Half the hotel heard," she exaggerated, then continued, "Back to the question of blondes. First there was Maureen. Then, Lizette is blonde, too, and you obviously like her looks. And that blonde woman across the street—don't try to deny she turns you on, too."

"Turns me on?" he choked out. "Moans! *Mon Dieu!* You are coarse, for a lady. If you are that."

"Oh, I'm too vulgar for you, am I?" His criticism cut Selene deeply. Stiffening with pride, she snapped, "Hah! You're probably critical of me just because I'm a brunette, not a blonde. You know what they say about blondes, don't you?"

"What?"

"Dumber than doornails. Is that what you like? A woman who lies down like a door mat for a man?"

"What I like or don't like is none of your affair. And don't you think you're overreacting a bit?"

"Yeah, well, I'm sick up to here," she said, slicing her neck with a forefinger, "of men who are more interested in a woman's boobs than her brains."

His mouth dropped open with surprise. "Surely, *surely,* that word does not mean what I think it does." When her face colored with embarrassment, he shook his head in disbelief.

Selene was tired of James's lack of humor. He never smiled. He never laughed. He took himself entirely too seriously. Well, she'd show him. "Do you know how to get a blonde to laugh on Sunday?"

His eyebrows shot up in surprise, but he wouldn't answer, no doubt sensing he would be the butt of her strange question.

"You tell her the joke on Friday."

He didn't crack a smile, just scowled at her.

"Okay, what did the blonde say when she found out she was pregnant?"

He set his empty cup on the bench next to hers, and a little black boy immediately scooted over and took them away. James stared at her as if she were truly hopeless and refused to answer.

"The blonde said, 'Are you sure it's mine?' "

She saw in his marvelously luminous blue eyes the moment he began to understand her jokes.

"Are you implying that blonde women have lesser intelligence?"

"Yeah."

He glared at her, stone-cold somber. "And that I am lacking in mental discernment for appreciating their beauty?"

"You got it, buster."

He sat there like a blasted statue, glowering at her. Oh well, she might as well jab him some more. "Two blondes were walking through the woods and came to a set of tracks. One said they were moose tracks. The other said they were deer tracks. They were still arguing when the train hit them."

James made a clicking sound of disgust with his tongue. "You have a warped sense of humor."

"You have none at all," she accused, then decided to go for the kill. "Why did the blonde climb the glass wall?"

"To see what was on the other side?" he retorted, surprising her with his quick rejoinder. He tilted his head in a So there! attitude. "See, I do have a sense of humor, but it finds nothing to appreciate in your weak excuses for wit. Perhaps you try so hard with these sorry attempts at amusement to make up for your lack of beauty."

Once again, Selene felt a stab of hurt at his criticism. "You know, I'm really fed up with you looking down your nose at me. You might think I'm unattractive, but I want you to know that in my time I'm considered *very* beautiful."

"So you've told me before."

Selene blushed. She hadn't meant to blow her own horn, but he goaded her so. "James, I would have to be considered a beautiful woman in order to be a model, and I'm one of the most sought-after models. Do you know how much I was being paid for this one-week shoot in New Orleans?"

He stubbornly refused to ask, but Selene saw the spark of interest in the tilt of his head.

"One hundred thousand dollars."

He gasped, then quickly controlled his composure. "You lie."

"I do not lie. It's hard work. I've struggled to establish a reputation. And I *am* beautiful."

He still looked skeptical.

"Listen, do you even know what a model does?" She could tell by the blank expression on his face that he did not. "Okay, just sit there and I'll show you. Pretend you're the photographer, and I'm modeling, oh, let's say a new hair product. But it could be anything—clothing, makeup, even . . ." She was about to say cars, but quickly amended, ". . . carriages."

She walked a few feet away to a white birch tree and mentally psyched herself for her poses.

"First we'll go for innocence," she said, leaning against the tree trunk and setting her face into a demure expression, peeking up at him shyly through half-lowered lashes.

A tiny crack in James's implacability showed in his softening expression of curiosity.

"Then there is the playful look." Quick as a wink, she grabbed onto a low branch and swung herself up. With her legs swinging freely, she laughed mischievously and smiled widely, then held the pose.

"Come down from there. At once," James hissed, scandalized by her unladylike behavior. He stepped forward, prepared to come after her. "This is a public park."

She dropped down and added quickly, "Then there is sexy."

He halted immediately. And waited watchfully.

Selene pressed her shoulder blades to the tree trunk, arched her back so that her breasts jutted forward, tossed her huge mane of hair, licked her lips, and then gazed at him invitingly through sultry, half-lidded eyes.

"Well, I'll be damned!" he whispered hoarsely. The interest in James's smoldering eyes and tense body was unmistakable.

Before he had a chance to pounce on her, Selene plunged on, "Of course, sometimes I do runway modeling, as well." She walked some distance down the sidewalk from him, ignoring the passersby who watched her curiously. "Imagine music playing, very loud and upbeat." Selene pulled out all the stops then, strutting her stuff for James, using every bit of expertise she'd gained over the years. With long, fluid strides and swinging arms, hips swaying seductively, she sashayed back and forth in front of him with a springy bounce to her steps, flashing haughty glances, then blatantly sensual body language of invitation.

At first his wonderfully firm lips remained rigid with displeasure. Then she noticed a slight twitching at the edges. Throwing his hands out in resignation, he broke into a full-fledged grin. "You win," he said with a laugh, pulling her down to the bench beside him.

Selene smiled back at him, unsure whether he meant that he now believed she had been a model, or that she was, in fact, beautiful. She was afraid to ask.

"We've got to get back to the hotel," James said and shifted on his seat, about to stand.

Selene realized they still hadn't discussed the jobs he'd mentioned for her. "James, you told Lizette that I was going to be your governess and help your mother. Did you mean that?"

He raked his fingers through his thick hair and shook his head slightly, as if he must be crazy. "*Oui*, it appears I have no choice. My brother is a vengeful man. He probably has us watched even now. The minute you are alone, even boarding a steamboat for New York, he would capture you."

"For what purpose?"

"He needs no purpose. Perhaps he would rape you and keep you as his mistress for a while, but somehow I doubt that. He has his own *placée* on Rampart Street. Besides, you are not quite to his usual tastes," he commented, sweeping her with a cursory glance.

"There you go again, denigrating my appearance."

"That's not what I meant. Victor prefers young women, *very* young. Tiny . . . fragile in appearance. And most definitely colored. He likes the master-slave relationship. It fits well with the sadistic pleasure he gets from humiliation and pain."

"That's not a very pretty picture you paint of your brother."

"He's *not* a nice man, make no mistake about that. You would not like being in his clutches."

Selene sighed wearily. "I'm sorry about all this, James. I know you don't want to be responsible for me."

"What's one more person, one more burdensome responsibility?" he remarked enigmatically and stood, then pulled her up beside him.

As they walked along the banquette, the sun beat down on them in unrelenting waves and Selene could feel perspiration beading at her armpits and between her breasts. She squinted up at him, noticing that the grim lines of bitterness had returned to etch his eyes and mouth.

"What about this fiancée business?" she persisted. "How are you going to explain that relationship away?"

He shrugged. "You can break our betrothal once we get to Bayou Noir."

"For what reason?"

"*Alors!* You ask a lot of questions. How should I know? Perhaps you could say I forced my beastly attentions on you."

"Would you?" she asked stiffly.

"What?" he asked with exasperation. "Force myself on you? Or be beastly?"

"Oh, never mind," she said huffily.

"Just don't do anything to draw attention to yourself."

"I won't," she promised, "but . . ." Selene's words trailed off as she noticed a small cottage with a number of people coming and going—mostly women, whose eyes lowered furtively before entering. Some even wore black veils over their faces. Selene felt an ethereal sensation pass over her, like an invisible vapor. She shivered apprehensively and pulled James to a stop. "What is this place?"

"Marie Laveau's home," he snarled, "though I would describe it more as Satan's lair."

Selene's eyes widened in surprise at his vehemence, but before she had a chance to study him closer, she felt something warm and furry rub against her ankle. With a soft shriek, she jumped and moved closer to James, almost knocking him over. It was only a large tabby cat. Actually, as she looked around with disbelief, she counted dozens of cats, at least fifty of them, of all sizes and colors, roaming the front yard, over the porch, even on the roof of the pastel blue bungalow.

Shuddering with revulsion, Selene suddenly remembered Lilith claiming to be a descendant of this woman. "Marie Laveau . . . wasn't she a voodoo something or other?"

" 'Something or other' describes her very well." James clamped his jaw, and his eyes flashed angrily. "She fashions herself the Mamoloi, the high priestess of Damballa."

"And what do you think?"

"I think she's a shrewd, evil woman who manipulates people for her own gain." His lips tightened into a thin line of barely controlled fury, and he looked at the house with such loathing, Selene suspected he would tear it to the ground with his hands if he could.

"Can I go in and talk to her?"

"What?"

"Don't panic," Selene said quickly. "I told you before I'm not involved in voodoo. I don't believe in it any more than you do, but . . . well, there was this curse put on me. Maybe this woman can help remove it . . . if it's really there . . . and I could—"

"—go back to your own time," James finished for her on a groan. "Why don't you just admit who you are and stop this time-travel foolishness?"

"Listen, it's my last chance. I've got to give it a shot, at least try to return to my own time. I suspect that once I go to your plantation, I won't be able to go home from there."

A look of dismay flashed across his face, which James immediately covered with disdain. Was he upset that she might leave him, or at the idea that she might not ever be able to leave? He soon set her straight . . . the brute.

"Well, I must admit, the prospect of being rid of you does appeal, but I refuse to step inside that cesspit of intrigue."

Selene wasn't too happy about his wanting her gone. No woman relished rejection . . . in any form. But she wished to leave him just as badly. Didn't she? "Why don't you wait for me in that restaurant over there? Give me fifteen minutes. C'mon, James, maybe this is your chance to get me out of your life."

"What makes you think you're in my life?" he reminded her rudely, then seemed to consider the significance of her words. "So if you don't come out in fifteen minutes, am I to assume that Marie put you on a broom and you've flown off to the twenty-first century?" He stood with his legs spread slightly and his hands on his hips, an unreadable expression on his face.

"Something like that," she muttered and turned to walk away. She'd gone only a few steps when she stopped and did an about-face. He still stood in the same place, watching her with what almost seemed like longing. The silent sadness of his face pulled at Selene, and she walked back.

"Did you forget something?" he asked softly, his husky voice belying his testy words.

She licked her lips nervously and felt an electric current of desire shoot through her when his eyes, his glittering blue eyes, followed the action of her tongue. Shuffling uneasily from foot to foot, she tried to come up with the right words.

"I just wanted to say . . . well, thank you."

He arched a brow, but said nothing.

"I mean, if for some reason I don't return . . . not that I really think Marie Laveau can help me . . . but if I do go back to my own time, I wanted you to know how much I appreciate your help. I would have been lost without you." Her last words came out on a heartfelt whisper, and she reached up, putting her hands on his shoulders, to kiss his lips lightly.

It was meant to be a kiss of thanks, and good-bye.

But a low hissing sound came from James's parted lips at her feathery kiss and he put both his hands on her elbows, pulling her closer. Then, with his right arm wrapped around her waist and his left hand at the nape of her neck, he pulled her flush with his body. "Not much of a farewell, to my way of thinking, or a proper display of gratitude," he murmured against her lips, and took control of the kiss.

Selene's knees turned to butter at the first touch of his warm lips on hers, and she moved her hands up around his shoulders, holding on for dear life. Expertly, he molded her lips to fit his, nipping at her bottom lip until she parted for him. Then his tongue seared her with its molten heat, and Selene's world tilted on its axis. Shock waves of passion ricocheted through her body, and Selene knew her life would never be the same again.

Almost as quickly as the kiss began, it was over. James pulled away from her slightly. Tracing the moistness on her bottom lip with the pad of his thumb, he gazed at her with unquestionable desire, and a puzzled frown.

Finally he stepped back completely, his arms at his sides. He no longer touched her, though his eyes still embraced her with soulful yearning.

"That was a proper good-bye." Only then did he turn and walk away toward the restaurant.

Selene just stood there, watching his departing back. And, for the first time since she'd left the twenty-first century, she wondered if she really wanted to return.

Chapter Five

If one door shuts, does that mean? . . .

When Selene entered the low-ceilinged shop, her senses were assailed by the myriad smells of dried herbs hanging about. Some of them she recognized, like lavender, verbena, coriander, and sweet basil. Others, exotic and repellent, spoke of secrets and danger and illicit thrills.

Dust motes danced in the streams of sunlight that filtered through the small windows, casting narrow, shifting patterns on the counter and cluttered shelves. Two ladies whispered, heads together, on the other side of the room as they examined amulets and little packets of potpourri.

"Ah, finally you have arrived," a petite black woman said in a sultry, low voice, coming up behind Selene. "I have been expecting you for weeks."

Selene almost jumped out of her skin. "Me?"

"*Certainement!* You are Selene. Lilith, my granddaughter many times removed, first began casting her spells weeks ago. You must be strong to have withstood them for so long."

Selene studied the woman closely. She had to be about

fifty, but her skin was almost ageless. Supremely beautiful, she carried her small body in a majestic manner. Although she was shorter and her skin much darker than Lilith's, the resemblance was remarkable.

"What can I do for you, Mam'zelle Selene?"

Selene's brows furrowed in surprise at the woman's knowing her name, and Lilith's. "Ah . . . well . . . I was wondering if you could help me—"

"Non."

"No?"

"I can do nothing to break the spell. 'Tis a powerful gris-gris that Lilith put on you."

"Listen, I don't really believe all this voodoo stuff, but—"

"You'd best believe, missie. How else do you explain your . . . predicament?"

"A dream?" Selene asked hopefully.

"Please, *chérie*, let us be honest with each other. You have traveled from another time. Now, you may credit voo-doo, or *le bon Dieu*, or dreams, or whatever," she said with a shrug, "but the fact remains that you are here."

Selene sighed woefully. "But what can I do?"

"The time is not right. For now."

"And later?"

"Oui, later, *certainement*. The spirits will tell when your time is right. I do know this, only one person will be permitted to go forward through the time door. And you must be wearing the same gown you came in."

Selene made a mental note to get the dress back from the dressmaker as soon as possible and guard it with her life.

"The choice will be yours, Selene—whether to go or stay."

"Why ever would I want to stay here?" she asked incredulously.

Ms. Laveau's full lips turned up slightly in a secretive smile.

"How will I know when the time is right and what I should do?"

"I will tell you."

"How?"

Marie Laveau make a tsk-ing sound of disapproval at Selene's persistent questioning. "I will send you a message with directions."

"Will I have to be standing on the same spot in New Orleans?"

The woman shook her head. "The magic knows no boundaries—of time or place. You may go with Mr. Baptiste to his plantation."

Selene was not terribly surprised that the voodoo woman knew of her plans to leave New Orleans.

"*Oui*, 'tis best to leave the city," she continued. "Much danger awaits you here."

Selene thought immediately of Victor.

Marie Laveau took two jars off the shelf behind her and gently shook out two mounds of seeds onto pieces of parchment—one white pile, one black. Then she folded them over and twisted the ends tightly. Handing them to Selene, she advised, "I will send you a wax doll like the one Lilith used. When you prepare to enter the time door, you must wear the ballgown and hold the doll in your hands, with one seed pressed into the wax for each year you want to travel—black forward, white backward." She looked intently at Selene. "Do you understand?"

Selene nodded hesitantly. "You mean I can go to whatever year I want, either backward or forward in time?"

"*Oui.*"

"But that's remarkable. Have you met other people who've come from another time?"

Marie Laveau smiled enigmatically, but refused to answer.

Selene quickly left the small house, almost tripping over a sleeping cat the size of a ten-pound sack of potatoes. Inexplicably, she harbored no doubts in her mind that Marie Laveau was correct in all she had said. And Selene felt reassured by the black woman's words that she would not have to remain in the city to return to her own time. Now she could go to James's plantation with some degree of certainty that she wouldn't be closing the time door behind her.

Some visits are longer than others . . .

When Selene entered the cool restaurant, she searched the dimness for James and found him sitting alone near the back at a small table. She slipped into a chair opposite him. James eyed her questioningly as he sipped a glass of green liquid—that potent Creole liquor called absinthe. And it wasn't yet noon.

"You drink too much," she remarked without thinking.

"You talk too much."

"Don't you want to know what happened with Ms. Laveau?" She felt oddly hurt that he didn't show some stronger emotion at her return, particularly after their special kiss. Apparently it had affected her a lot more than him.

He gave her an indifferent look. "You're still here. Was she out of brooms?"

"Yeah. Looks like you're stuck with me." Selene smiled tentatively, trying to hide her bruised feelings. She explained all that Marie Laveau had told her, emphasizing the importance of safeguarding her ballgown. "Will you take me with you now?" she asked as she slipped a hand into her dress pocket, guiltily patting the seed packets, which she'd failed to mention.

He studied her for several long moments, his eyes brilliantly intelligent and unfathomable. "I shouldn't."

"I promise to do my best with your son . . . and your mother."

He scrutinized her steadily, unconvinced.

"How long will you want me to work for you? It appears I won't have to return to New Orleans, if what Ms. Laveau says is true." She wrung her hands, knowing she was rambling. "But perhaps you'll want me to stay only for a short time, until this problem with your brother Victor blows over."

Selene forgot momentarily that just a short time ago she'd been wondering whether she even wanted to return to the future.

He looked surprised at her question. "I thought I told you, my plantation is in a remote bayou, four days by boat from New Orleans to Terrebonne Parish, beyond Bayou La Fourche."

Selene frowned. "I thought your home was only about a hundred miles away."

"Oh, it's not so far as the bird flies," he added, sensing her confusion, "but the streams are sometimes nearly impenetrable, and there are no roads, for the most part. Once there, you will have to stay . . . for a time."

"How long?" she asked suspiciously. "When will you come back to New Orleans again?"

"I come once a year."

"A year!"

Dr. Ruth, she was not . . .

"Men are insufferable," Selene commented to Reba Cameron later that afternoon as they walked through the French Market gathering supplies from the list James had given the overseer's wife.

The pale woman's superfine strawberry-blonde hair hung lankly under her bonnet, onto her flat chest and down to her protruding shoulder blades. It had been obvious to Selene almost from the first moment they'd met that the overseer's wife was chronically shy. Self-consciously, she kept her eyes lowered and never looked at a person directly, even when talking.

"Men are wh . . . what?" Reba asked, her wide periwinkle eyes blinking nervously. Reba's lashes were so pale, they appeared almost nonexistent. Her ankle-length gown of blue- and brown-striped cambric hung pathetically loose on her slim frame, despite the three or four crinolines she must be wearing. Selene had to stop herself from gawking at the woman's incredible lack of color sense—not just the dull brown and blues of her high-necked and tight-wristed dress, but the ridiculous apricot-colored gloves and frivolous straw bonnet she wore with a profusion of pink ribbons and white veiling. Gawd! It was enough to give a person color blindness.

Selene thought idly that she could do wonders with this young woman with a little makeup, a layered cut to give her hair thickness, a curling iron, and, of course, a color chart. Geez! What was she thinking? Just a short time ago she'd been bemoaning her society's overemphasis on beauty, and the first thing she noticed about a woman in another time was her lack of it.

"Men," Selene repeated, calling herself back to Reba's question. "I was saying that men are real jerks. James keeps harping away about my being too skinny, or too tall, or sharp-tongued, or whatever fault he's thinking about at the moment. And I heard what your husband said to you." In a deep voice, she mimicked, " 'Must you always be stuttering about, lassie? And for God's sake, stand straighter, Reba love.' "

"Fergus is trying to help me," Reba asserted with the first show of life Selene had seen in the drab woman. "He knows how timid I am, and he's trying to help me overcome my shortcomings. Sometimes he sounds sharp-tongued, but he's a good man, and . . ." Her words trailed off as she realized how strongly she'd been defending her husband.

Selene almost retorted that women of all times had an obligation to fight gender oppression, even when it came from their spouses. But James had warned Selene about discussing her modern notions with anyone, including Fergus and his wife, Reba. They thought Selene had come to New Orleans from some Caribbean island, and Selene had to continually watch every word she uttered for fear of betraying her knowledge of the future.

"I apologize if I misjudged Fergus. I tend to forget that all men aren't the same. Hey, who am I to criticize? I've been tolerating put-downs from Devon for years."

"Devon?" Reba asked, her curiosity overcoming her innate shyness.

"My ex-lover. We lived together for three years . . . until recently."

Reba merely gawked, tongue-tied with surprise.

"Oh, Devon was a master at undermining my self-confidence." Selene frowned in remembrance. His words still rang in her ears. " 'Selene, aren't you putting on a little too much weight?' " she parroted his cruel, masculine voice, uncaring of the way Reba looked askance at her. " 'Don't you think you should have hired a decorator? Don't just lie there under me like a loaf of bread; do something, for chrissake. No wonder your father left before you were born. No wonder your mother always said you could do nothing right. You're worthless, Selene, worthless.' "

Reba's mouth dropped open in fascination. "Ex-lover?" Her attention focused on that one irrelevant detail. "You were a mistress? Oh, my goodness! I don't think I've ever met a real fallen woman before, except for the slaves, of course. Do you think—" She slapped a hand over her mouth in horror at what she'd been about to ask.

Selene smiled. After cartwheeling through time, being mistaken for a black woman, being verbally assaulted by an arrogant Southern "gentleman," then kissed till her toes melted, she didn't think anything could shock her now. "Go ahead, honey, ask."

Reba wrung her hands nervously, still having trouble looking her directly in the eye. She fought to get the words out. "Well, seeing as how you've had all this, ah, experience, well, I, oh, tarnation, how can I say this . . . well, I was wondering if you could tell me . . . things." Blinking

nervously, Reba's lashless eyes looked everywhere—
everywhere but at Selene.

"Things?"

Reba's already flushed face turned scarlet, but she raised
her chin with determination. These "things" were apparently more important to her than her painful reticence.
"About what a husband and wife do together," she whispered, mortified. "You know, man-woman things."

"Man-woman things?" Selene choked out. Oh, this was
rich. Sandra Selente, the "sexless mannequin of the bedroom," as Devon had once referred to her, being asked for
lovemaking advice.

"Yes, you see, I married Fergus five years ago when I
was only fourteen, and—"

"Fourteen? You got married when you were fourteen?"

Reba looked puzzled at Selene's astonishment. "Yes. My
parents died on the ocean crossing. Fergus was a passenger
on the same ship. He had been a sugar maker in Santo Domingo with Mister James, but he'd gone home to Scotland
for his mother's funeral. And, oh, he was ever so handsome." Reba's face glowed with the obvious love she had
for her husband, and she looked almost pretty then. Yes,
Selene decided inwardly, the girl had possibilities. She
would definitely have to help her with a makeover.

Reba had continued to talk while Selene's mind wandered. ". . . and, even though he never says anything, I just
know I'm not very exciting. I wish I could please him more.
I really do. Can you help me?"

"Reba, I'm the wrong person to ask about sexual tricks.
Take my word for it. But I can help you look prettier. Maybe
if you had more self-confidence, you wouldn't have any inhibitions in bed. That might help." Oh, Lord, Devon would
burst a blood vessel laughing at her playing the role of sex
counselor.

"Me? You could make *me* pretty?" Reba asked in an
awestruck voice.

"Sure. Also, I did read a book recently . . . oh, never mind."

"What?"

Selene clammed up, realizing too late that she really, really, shouldn't be offering advice to this woman from the past.

"What?" Reba insisted. "Please tell me."

"Oh, heck! I read this book called *The Perfect Fit*. The authors claim there is this one sexual position where the male and female bodies are so perfectly aligned that the sexual pleasure can go on for hours and hours before climax."

"Hours and hours!" Reba's face brightened hopefully. "See! I knew you could help me," she gushed. "That's just the kind of information I need. *The Perfect Fit*, you say. And it works?"

"I don't know if it works," Selene said, immediately defensive. Hey, she'd mentioned it to Devon once, and he'd laughed cruelly at her as if she'd been grasping for straws in a hopeless attempt to be more sexual.

Reba grabbed Selene's hand and squeezed it in thanks. "I'm so glad you're coming back to Bayou Noir. I just know we're going to be good friends." When she realized she was holding Selene's hand, she dropped it immediately and looked down with embarrassment.

They entered the St. Louis Hotel, and Selene saw a large number of people in the central rotunda with its marvelous skylights. "What's going on?"

"The auctions. People come from all around for the daily sales. See, Fergus and Mr. Baptiste are over there."

Selene had been to a few auctions in the past . . . at Sotheby's. This was vastly different. Some auctioneers shouted out details about household furnishings from bankrupt estates—Turkish rugs, Italian marble, furniture from Paris, London, Philadelphia, and New York, silks from China, casks of French wine, coffee from Martinique.

Other auctioneers pointed to cotton bales and barrels of
sugarcane syrup. But Selene sensed that most of the people
weren't there to bid on fine art, or antiques, or plantation
products.

A slave auction drew the liveliest bidding.

And James was one of the bidders.

Damn him!

One shock after another . . .

James needed a drink. Badly.

He motioned for Fergus to sign the papers for the young
buck he'd just purchased, bringing his total up to twelve
Negro slaves, all males under age twenty, to work his sugar
fields. One of them, younger than the rest, sobbed quietly
with humiliation. James forced himself to look away, raking his fingers through his hair with frustration. He understood too well the boy's shame in being purchased—like a
horse, but less prized. As soon as he completed his transactions here, James intended to lock himself in his hotel room
with a bottle of bourbon. Hell, maybe two bottles.

He watched as an obese merchant next to him ogled a
coal-black Mandingo girl, no more than twelve. He wouldn't
intervene. In truth, her fate was no worse than most, and
better than some. She could have been sold to the Fancy
Trade, not an easy life for beautiful Negro women, sen-
tenced to a lifetime of prostitution. Fancy Girls, they were
called, but there was nothing fancy about their sordid life.

Even worse, there were evil men like Jake Colbert, his
father's overseer, who stood across from him, fingering
his huge drooping mustache and a knotted whip—both
his trademarks. The vicious Colbert bought only prime
young males to work the Baptiste cotton fields. Within a
year, they'd be worn down to skin and bones, working fifteen to twenty hours a day, scarred for life.

Hell and damnation! How he hated slavery! Almost as

much as he hated owning slaves himself. Five years of working side by side with the natives on a Santo Domingo sugar plantation as an indentured servant had taught him good and well what servitude felt like. But he'd had an opportunity to buy his freedom in the end, unlike these helpless slaves.

Well, that wasn't quite true, at least for *his* slaves. James, much to the ire of his fellow planters, offered his slaves an incentive to freedom. If they worked to his satisfaction for five years, he freed them on the condition that they gave him five additional years of indenture. Thus far, his slaves had worked harder than those on any of the surrounding plantations.

But still, slavery was slavery, no matter how he sugar-coated it, and it left a bitter taste in his mouth. Selene had asked him about his dreams, his fondest wish. Escape . . . that was what he yearned for—escape from the burdens of running a struggling sugar plantation, escape from the responsibilities of a family that was splintering apart, escape from the loneliness of his self-imposed exile. Most of all, escape from the system of slavery he abhorred and yet benefitted from.

Sometimes he thought he was as much a prisoner as his slaves.

James noticed Selene enter the hotel with Reba. Fergus approached the two women, taking an overflowing basket from his wife's hands. James thanked God for his good fortune in Fergus Cameron, who'd hired on as his overseer five years ago. He was an honest, hardworking man. A friend. And an experienced sugar maker—an invaluable asset which James unhesitatingly rewarded with a percentage of the cane profits each year.

Selene moved away from Reba and Fergus and continued onward, stomping toward him in a most unfeminine manner, a storm brewing in her hazelnut eyes. Slipping his hands into the pockets of his trousers, he waited, wondering what he'd done to raise her ire this time. It didn't take much.

He gazed at her indulgently, rather amused by the strange woman who'd come into his life only yesterday. It seemed like a lifetime ago.

A group of men accidentally jostled Selene as they passed, but, other than perfunctory apologies, she garnered no attention from them, being too tall and thin for most tastes. Hell, her bony body had more angles than a Louisiana bayou.

Amazingly, he was beginning to see an attractiveness in Selene that he hadn't perceived at their first meeting. Oh, he wouldn't call her beautiful, despite all her claims of being a beauty in her time. *Time!* That was another thing James couldn't accept. No, the mad wench was probably just a little unsettled in her mind. High-strung women often were.

But to give her credit, these men in the rotunda who ignored her hadn't seen her "strut her stuff," as she'd so vividly called that outrageous demonstration in the park. He grinned at the recollection. He'd like to see her repeat the performance wearing a lot less clothing.

And the lady did kiss rather nicely, James thought, honing in on the thick, sensual lips that invited a man's touch. He felt a quickening at the juncture of his thighs at the memory of her soft lips under his. He ran the fingertips of his right hand across his lips, as if he could still feel her touch.

Selene's face flushed prettily as she followed the movement of his fingers. For a brief second, their eyes held and he knew Selene was remembering the kiss, too.

Hmmm. Maybe he would forget the bourbon and just take Selene back to his hotel room. If he drew the drapes, he might be able to ignore her jutting ribs and bony arms. As he recalled, her legs were long and nicely shaped. And her breasts, of course. Ah, yes, her breasts could balance out a thousand imperfections on the beauty scales.

He opened his mouth to suggest just such a proposition, perhaps even offer to purchase some beignets at a *boulangerie* along the way as further enticement. But then he noticed that the flush of sensuality on her tanned face had turned to anger. Her eyes practically threw sparks at him.

Uncaring of the spectators around them, she placed a palm against his chest and backed him up against the rotunda wall. He was too stunned to protest.

"You low-down dog! I have a bone to pick with you."

"What now?"

Selene clenched her fists at her sides, forcing herself to calm down and not smack James, as she'd like to do. Where was that fan she'd just bought in the mercantile?

"You're creating a spectacle of yourself—the very thing you promised not to do," James pointed out matter-of-factly.

She looked around. Sure enough, men and women strolling through the wide central rotunda watched them with open interest.

Selene probably would have exercised more caution if she hadn't seen amusement flickering at the edges of James's lips, that maddening dimple struggling to emerge. He was laughing silently at her. The lunkhead! She raised both hands into claws and advanced on him.

Recognizing her intent, James grabbed her wrists and pulled her into a corridor off the main lobby, and then into a private courtyard for hotel guests. Lush tropical plants created a cool oasis around the softly bubbling fountain with its dolphin centerpiece.

He shoved her down into an ornate wrought-iron settee, then slouched into a matching high-backed chair. He sat so close his knees almost touched hers. Selene whisked her skirts aside in exaggerated distaste and edged away.

He moved his chair even closer, just to annoy her.

She shifted herself over to the other side of the settee.

He and his chair followed.

James raised a brow as if daring her to move again.

She looked to the right, into the fountain. She had no place else to go.

Stretching his long legs out straight, he crossed them at

the ankles and arrogantly rested his shoes on the settee next to her.

"You are so childish."

"And you are so mature? Now tell me, what's all this fury of yours about this time?"

"Slaves . . . that's what. You're buying slaves," she accused, glaring at him.

Exhaling wearily, he folded his long fingers tent-like in front of his mouth, but she could see his lips tighten into an angry line and his blue eyes glitter icily.

"*Oui*, I am."

There was no one else in the courtyard, and silence sounded like a death knell between them. It seemed to go on forever.

"That's all? No explanation? Good heavens," she cried on a sob. "I thought you were better than that."

"Why would you think so? I own fifteen thousand arpents of land, most of it in sugarcane. One hundred slaves . . . yes, *slaves* . . . work my fields. Were you thinking I planted and harvested the cane alone? Or used voodoo magic instead of a plow?"

"No, but—"

"Let me guess, there are no slaves in your land."

"That's right," she snapped, "but never doubt that it's the same land—the United States of America. It's just another time."

"Hah! Pop another eyeball and maybe I'll believe that." He waved a hand dismissively. "It doesn't matter where or *when* you've come from. Just know this, sweetheart, if you dare to preach abolitionist words in public, you will not only find yourself in prison, but hanging from a lynchman's rope, as well."

"That might very well be, but in my time—"

"And no more prattling this time-travel nonsense. I've had your fantasies up to here," he said, slashing his neck.

A huge lump formed in Selene's throat at his coldness. "I

thought you were different, James," she said, barely above a whisper. "I sensed somehow that you and I were—"

"What?" he snapped. When her face heated with embarrassment, he hooted with derision, "*Sacre bleu!* Just like a woman! One bloody kiss and she's baking the wedding cake."

"Oh, you egomaniac! I never said I wanted to marry you."

"Pray you never do. Never, *never* will I make that fatal mistake again."

Furious, she stood and kicked him in the shin.

"Ouch! You crazy witch," he yelled and lurched for her. His iron fingers grasped her waist and she tripped, causing them both to fall to the stone patio.

"Geez! You're nuts. Do you know that?" she shrieked, turning her face and body under him.

"Nuts? I'm not sure what that means, but you are insane. Why did you kick me?"

"You're changing the subject. We were talking about slavery, James. Explain to me how you can condone such a barbaric practice."

His jaw tightened with suppressed tension. "I owe you no explanations whatsoever."

Selene felt tears welling in her eyes. For some reason, James's being a slave owner was a betrayal of sorts to her. It wasn't that she harbored romantic notions about him. She really didn't. But he represented her safe haven in this roller-coaster ride through time, and she couldn't bear to think that her security hinged even indirectly on the misery of slaves.

"Save your blubbering for something you can change," he said tautly. "Slavery and the South go hand in hand."

"That won't always be so. In fact, there will be a black president of the United States," she said softly, wiping her eyes with the back of her hand. "After the Civil War, all the slaves will be emancipated."

"The *what* war? No, forget I asked. Spare me your predictions of the future."

His hard body still lay half on, half off her, pinning her to the ground. "Get off me, you big hulk. I can't breathe, and I'll probably be covered with bruises."

"I'm the one who'll have injuries. Your hipbone almost emasculated me."

"Well, wouldn't that be the South's great loss!"

"Your sarcasm is highly unflattering."

"Big deal!"

With a snarl of disgust, James moved lithely to his feet and motioned her to follow.

She stood petulantly, wanting to argue further with him over the issue of slavery, but his stubborn chin rose defiantly. And besides, what choice did she have? She would have to go with him for now, but later . . . later she would try to convince him to release his slaves.

She made a big production of dusting off her gown and asked, "Where are we going now?"

"*We* are not going anywhere. I'm going back to my hotel room where I hope to consume a bottle of bourbon. It's been a hell of a day."

"You really do drink too much."

"You really do talk too much."

Selene stuck out her tongue at him and immediately felt silly for doing such a childish thing. But she refused to apologize to the maddening dolt. "Don't think I'm going to swelter in that little closet while you drink yourself into oblivion."

"You have a nasty habit of making demands when you are in no position whatsoever to do so. And I would suggest you keep that tongue in your mouth, or I'll find a better use for it."

It took Selene a moment to realize what he meant. Her hormones jump-started into a low hum with just those simple words. And he knew it, Selene could tell, by the way his blasted dimple kept trying to emerge.

"Actually, I hate to disappoint you, but I was able to find a room for you at the hotel. A planter's wife became ill suddenly and had to leave the city." He gazed at her speculatively as he held out an arm to escort her from the patio. "Unless, of course, you'd like to share a bottle . . . and a bed."

Her heartbeat quickened at his offhand offer. Was he serious? Or just goading her again? His closely guarded expression hid his true feelings. She hadn't thought she interested him in that way, except for that glorious kiss this morning. But when he tucked her arm through his, his large, callused hand enfolded hers, and Selene could feel the rapid pulse of his wrist against hers. Yes, he was definitely . . . interested.

Selene decided to steer the conversation away from this dangerous territory. "If I thought booze would help my situation by sending me back home, I'd drink a barrel. As it is, I'd probably fall asleep after one glass."

"Glass? Who said anything about glasses? This is drinking-from-the-bottle time, *chérie*."

Selene wondered what had prompted this sudden need for the forgetfulness of alcohol. And she couldn't stop thinking about the other part of his offer—the enticing part—where he'd mentioned sharing a bed. "I thought I was too tall, and skinny, and mouthy, and, well, unattractive for your tastes."

His eyes crinkled a bit with mischief as he immediately understood her reference, and Selene berated herself for inadvertently offering him another opportunity to bait her.

"*Oui*, but your breasts make up for a world of defects, and your legs in those odd silk stockings aren't so bad, either."

Selene should have been outraged, but, instead, she felt a thrum of pleasure course through her at his backhanded compliments. Her delight soon turned to chagrin when he added, "And we could always put a gag in your mouth and a feed bag over your head if I'm not able to rise to the occasion."

She tried to pull her hand from his grasp, but James refused to let go. Chuckling, he bowed to her with exaggerated gallantry and proceeded to lead her back to the rotunda where Fergus and Reba awaited them anxiously.

Selene bit her bottom lip furiously to prevent a hasty retort to his needling. Finally, when she calmed down enough, she asked with forced politeness, "What about your date?"

"Date?"

"With Lizette. The opera."

He groaned. "I forgot." Then he looked at her, rubbing his fingertips thoughtfully over his full lips. A dark shadow of whiskers covered his face, and fatigue underlined his eyes. "I don't suppose you'd like to attend the opera with Lizette, taking my place?"

"Me? Hardly. And I don't think Lizette would consider me a good substitute. I doubt I'm what she has in mind for the evening's entertainment."

"What's that supposed to mean?"

"It means that your little Southern belle has got her eyes on you, babe. Criminey, Lizette made it perfectly clear back there in the dress shop that she'd like to take you home and have you for an afternoon delight. Hey, I wouldn't be surprised if she's already monogramming the sheets."

"Afternoon delight!" His eyes widened slightly. "You're wrong. Lizette doesn't think of me in that way."

"Oh, Lord! Men are so blind when it comes to single-minded women. Their favorite organ isn't their brains, that's for sure, and when a blonde woman is involved, well, their common sense just flies out the window."

"Please spare me. Not another blonde joke."

"Actually, James, did you hear about the blonde and the brunette who jumped off a cliff? No? Well, guess which one hit the ground first?"

"The brunette, of course," he answered sarcastically.

"Well, you're right, because the blonde had to stop and ask directions."

The edges of James's lips turned up slightly as he shook his head from side to side. "You really do have a bizarre sense of humor, Selene."

"Do you think so? Boy, you should have met . . ." Selene's words trailed off with a gasp as she saw a younger, more beautiful version of her agent Georgia standing in the rotunda. Clutching at James's arm, she cried frantically, "Oh, my God, there's Fleur. And she's with Victor."

"Fleur? Victor's *placée? Mon Dieu!* How do you know her?"

But Selene had already taken off across the exchange floor. Fortunately, Victor left the beautiful quadroon's side for a moment and stopped a short distance away to speak to a man with a large handlebar mustache, who was carrying a lethal whip in one hand. Selene had to warn Georgia's ancestor of the danger. She knew, without a doubt, that Victor was the man her agent had told her about, the one who'd murdered, or tried to murder, his pregnant *placée*, Georgia's ancestor.

Anxiety caused a rush of adrenalin to soar through Selene. The young girl, no more than sixteen, looked just like Georgia, yet she was innocently pretty in her off-the-shoulder pink organza gown, which highlighted her silky mocha skin and tiny waist. *Tiny waist.* Either Fleur was not yet pregnant or not very far along. Maybe it wasn't too late.

James grabbed her upper arm in a pincer grip and pulled her to a halt. "Where do you think you're going?"

She motioned toward Victor's mistress with a jerk of her head. "I've got to save Fleur. She's in grave danger."

"That girl has been in danger from the moment she first agreed to be Victor's *placée*, and you, my troublemaking wench, are not about to become her savior."

"Yes, I am."

"I beg to differ. You go anywhere near Victor, or his property, and I wipe my hands of you."

"Property?" Selene bristled.

"Yes, property," James hissed, practically nose to nose with her. "Get it through your thick head, once and for all. Slaves and *placées* are a fact of life here, like it or not. Nothing you say or do can change that."

"But—"

"There are no buts," he snapped, his fingers digging

painfully into her upper arms. "And you're doing just what I warned you about—creating a scene."

Selene looked around quickly. He was right. People were watching their angry interchange with curiosity. Luckily, Victor hadn't yet noticed them.

"Listen, just give me five minutes to talk to Fleur. That's all I ask. Can't you distract Victor for a few moments? Please," she begged tearfully. "He's going to kill her, you know, along with their unborn child. Georgia told me so."

James flinched at her revelation, and his eyes involuntarily went to the young girl who waited patiently for her master, eyes lowered demurely. Turning back to Selene, he studied her intently, then finally loosened his grip on her arms. "Five minutes," he agreed stonily, then spun on his heel and stormed over toward his brother. Within seconds, she heard their angry exchange of words and all eyes in the rotunda turned to the two brothers.

Selene rushed over to Fleur and pulled her toward a shadowy alcove before the girl had a chance to protest.

"Fleur, listen carefully. I'm not going to hurt you," she told the frightened girl quickly. "I've been sent by a relative of yours—"

"A relative? Who?" Fleur inquired, curiosity overcoming her alarm.

"It doesn't matter," Selene said, waving a hand dismissively. "I need to know something. Are you pregnant?"

The girl gasped and put a tiny hand to her flat stomach. "How did you know? I haven't told anyone yet, not even Victor."

"Oh, God, whatever you do, don't tell him."

"Don't tell the child's father? Whyever not?"

"Because he's going to try to kill you."

Fleur cried out softly and tears of terror pooled in her dark eyes, but the girl didn't protest the allegation as impossible.

Fleur's soft outcry caused Victor's head to jerk toward

them. His eyes darted suspiciously between James and her, and Selene knew she'd only have a few more moments.

"Listen to me carefully, Fleur. I'm a friend. I'll do anything I can to help you. Do you understand?"

The girl nodded hesitantly, her brown eyes wide with fear.

"My name is Sandra Selente . . . Selene. I'm staying at the St. Louis Hotel with Victor's brother, James. We'll be there four more days. Then we're going to his plantation at Bayou Noir. Please come to me for help. Anytime. Anywhere."

Squeezing the young girl's hands in hers, she held her gaze for a long time until Fleur finally nodded in understanding. Then Selene stepped away and addressed James's vicious half brother with exaggerated exuberance, "Why, Victor, how wonderful to meet up with you again!"

Victor snarled something obscene and grabbed Fleur's arm, yanking her brutally toward him. Fleur cried out softly in pain, but did not try to pull away.

"What the hell are you doin' with mah woman?" he growled in a deep Southern drawl.

"Why, I was jus' introducin' myself to yoah lovely *wife,* Fleur," she mimicked through gritted teeth, gleeful at the purple color that infused Victor's face at her referring to the quadroon as his spouse. "Y'all mus' come and see us sometime at Bayou Noir," she continued in a honeyed accent.

It was James who swore then and grabbed her arm. Pulling her out of the rotunda, he muttered something about "stupid women, stupid schemes, and stupider men who listened to stupid women."

Chapter Six

*S*ome men really are bad to the bone . . .

Victor shoved Fleur through the door of their Rampart Street cottage and slammed the door behind them. Finally he would be able to vent the rage he'd had to restrain since the exchange with his half brother.

"What did James's fiancée want with you?"

"Noth . . . nothing."

"Liar," he gritted out, advancing on her.

"She mistook me for someone else . . . a relative of a friend. I swear."

"Tell me everything. *Everything.*"

"At first she did not believe me when I said I did not know her friend. It is as I say, Victor. When have I ever lied to you?"

"I don't know, my little *putain*," he said coldly, narrowing his eyes suspiciously. "But I have ways to find out, don't I?"

Whimpering, Fleur backed away and cowered in the corner like a frightened kitten. His lip curled with disgust. The spiritless wench who had been his *placée* these past two years, since her fourteenth birthday, held little appeal for him these days. Thank the Lord she'd borne him no children; it would be that much easier to rid himself of her.

What he wanted was a woman who would fight back when he twisted her arm, who would shriek with outrage at his verbal abuse, who would be a joy to tame.

Like James's new slut, he thought suddenly. Or his old one.

And that made him even more angry. That bitch Selene had mocked his small stature the first time he'd met her, threatening him with bodily harm, and today she'd mimicked his accent. No woman did that to Victor Baptiste.

She would pay. Oh, *oui,* she would pay, along with his bastard brother. And soon.

But for now, the timid Fleur would have to suffice. Charging toward his mistress, Victor raised an arm and backhanded her across the cheek. Fleur put the back of her hand up to her bleeding mouth to stifle her cries. She knew better than to scream. Only one time had she screeched out in protest at his touch, and she had been unable to walk for a week.

"Go into the bedchamber and make yourself ready for me," he ordered.

Fleur merely nodded, backing away from him warily.

"And prepare the ropes," he added.

"Oh, *non, s'il vous plaît,* Victor. I will please you today, I promise."

Victor liked it when she begged for his mercy. Ignoring her pleas, he pointed toward the back of the house. "How is *she* today?"

"Agitated. She has had no . . . medicine since yesterday."

"Good. It is time to wean her from the laudanum. The document is still unfound, and now this new woman has entered James's life. It is unacceptable that he marry again and beget more heirs. I can wait no longer." He jerked his head once more toward the back of the house. "*She* has work to do for me, work that requires a clear head."

"Against James?"

His eyes shot up with outrage that his *placée* would dare to ask about his plans.

She immediately realized her mistake. "*Pardonnez-moi*, I did not mean—"

His nostrils flared angrily. "And the whip, *chérie* . . . don't forget the whip."

She almost swooned against the door frame, so fierce was her fright, and Victor felt an immediate surge of arousal. It would be a long night of pleasure, he promised himself, and headed toward the back of the cottage to a small hidden room.

At first Victor recoiled at the condition of the body on the pallet. Then he untied the restraints and removed the gag from the wretched woman, softly murmuring, "'Twas for your own good, darling."

"Oh, thank *le bon Dieu*, you have finally come. Where is my medicine?" she gasped out.

"Ah, the medicine," he teased, taking a small vial out of his pocket and holding it out of reach. "I don't think you deserve it anymore, *chérie*. I have given you a year and still you have not accomplished our goal."

"But I tried, Victor. Truly I did, *mon couer*. Even with my talent for voodoo, James is just too sly for me."

He threw the brown bottle to the floor and crushed it under his shoe. The eyes of the once beautiful woman rolled madly in her head, and she screamed, coming at him with long-clawed fingers. "I loved you. Damn you, I loved you. Is this my reward?"

With one deft movement of his foot, he tripped her, flipping her back onto the bed, then straddled her weakened body. Over and over, he struck her face and neck and breasts until she was covered with blood and darkening bruises. When her shrieks had died down to mewling sobs, he sat back on his haunches, across her stomach.

"I give you warning, bitch. Ready yourself to return to Bayou Noir and finish the job you started. I give you six weeks—till St. John's Eve—to get your body restored to its former beauty."

"I would be beautiful for you again, Victor," she said

softly, gazing up at him with adoration through her swollen eyelids.

His anger flowed out of him then. Truly, this woman was the only one to love him unconditionally, despite his . . . flaws. His touch turned suddenly tender as he traced a forefinger along her jawline. "Ah, *chérie*, you know how much I love you. Why do you force me to treat you so?"

She smiled then, a macabre, bloody smile and opened her arms to him. She was ready for him when he slammed his body into her sheath. It was always so with them.

The road to Tara was full of potholes . . .

Four days later, Selene and Reba stood on the riverbank, watching three huge flatboats, each about fifty feet long, being loaded with all of their supplies.

Fleur had never shown up at their hotel after the meeting in the rotunda, and James had forbidden Selene to go to the cottage the young girl shared with Victor on Rampart Street. Selene obeyed him, grudgingly, but she had sent the girl a note, without James's knowledge, repeating her offer of assistance. Selene could only hope that Fleur would remember the invitation to come to Bayou Noir if she needed help.

Putting her concerns aside, Selene pulled the damp cloth of her white spencer, a sort of antebellum blouse, away from her neck and tried to blow inside the steamy confines of her garment, to no avail. Her breath was as hot as the humid air surrounding them. When they reclaimed her gown from the dressmaker, James had purchased four spencers for her, along with two dark skirts and three new gowns. They would probably all rot from perspiration before the week was out, she thought ruefully.

"How do you people stand this heat?" Selene asked Reba.

"You get used to it."

"I never will. Already the makeup I applied this morning has melted away. And when my deodorant runs out, I'll probably smell as ripe as everyone else here." That should be something to look forward to, Selene mused. With a mother who had started her on antiperspirants when she was nine years old, Selene didn't think she'd smelled her own sweat in her entire life.

"You think I smell?" Reba asked, raising her chin in affront.

"Not you, honey, but just about everyone else. People start out fresh in the morning here, but by noon they can't help having a case of prime body odor with all this sweating. Will it be cooler once we move inland?"

"Sometimes it's cooler in the shade," Reba said, not very enthusiastically.

"How will we sleep on those glorified rafts?"

"The men will camp on the bayou banks. We'll sleep under the canopies on the flatboats," she said, pointing to the primitive, open-sided shelters erected in the center of each wide raft. "We can pull mosquito netting down around us at nighttime."

"Why couldn't we just continue on the steam packet, like we did from New Orleans?"

Reba looked askance at her. "Do you have any idea where we're going? Steamboats could never navigate the narrow passageways."

"Oh."

"Even the flatboats can only go so far when the streams are low."

James had told her his plantation was on a remote bayou in "Tara-bon" Parish. Obviously it was more remote than she'd first imagined. And the way Reba looked away guiltily every time she asked a question about the plantation made Selene decidedly uncomfortable.

Hmmm. She'd been picturing a *Gone With the Wind* style mansion nestling on a green lawn along a glorious river. Okay, she admitted to herself with a grimace, she'd probably even been hoping that James would turn into Rhett Butler. Every woman's fantasy.

Hah! Fat chance!

She looked down the riverbank where James and Fergus, both shirtless, were working along with the slaves, loading the heavy supplies onto the boats. She had to give James his due—he worked as hard as his slaves, whom he'd released from their chains as soon as they'd arrived at the river. Sweat glistened on his wide shoulders and muscled arms. Lean and sinewy, he looked like a man who worked hard for a living, not an indolent planter.

Nope, he definitely was no Clark Gable. Then again, she decided, scrutinizing his tapering waist and lean hips, he might be better. Especially if he would flash that dimple once in a while. Selene had to be realistic, though. James wouldn't consider her much of a Scarlett O'Hara. He always made smart remarks about how bony she felt in his arms. Or that she was too old to be attractive.

On the other hand, she'd noticed a look of appreciation in his eyes sometimes when she'd caught him off guard. What if he really did find her attractive? What if he stormed all her defenses and swept her off her feet, like good old Rhett, carrying her away to his bedchamber where he would have his way with her? Selene giggled. *Have his way with me? I'm losing my mind.*

Still, for one brief, tantalizing second, Selene's thoughts wandered and she tried to imagine the brooding planter in the role of the romantic Rhett Butler. They would be standing at the base of a wide, curving staircase, arguing . . .

"You've been teasing me from the day we first met, Selene. Your time of reckoning has finally arrived."

James's wonderfully expressive eyes flickered with sensual sparks of blue ice as he swept her up in his arms and proceeded to carry her up the stairs.

*She fought against his steely arms, as well as her wild
attraction to a man she should not love. To no avail.*

*She tried not to think of the massive four-poster bed that
awaited their bodies at the end of the hall. Against her will,
she wondered if she would finally experience all the sexual
delights her body craved.*

*As if he had read her thoughts, James's hot lips nuzzled
the curve of her neck. He whispered hoarsely, "Tonight . . .
tonight, my love, I will discover all of your body, all your
secrets. You will beg me for mercy and scream when I give
it, finally."*

*Selene moaned. The tips of her breasts hardened into
aching pebbles, and blood rushed madly to all the erotic
points that he would soon investigate.*

"Why are you standing there looking like a moon-eyed
calf?"

"Huh?" Selene emerged slowly and embarrassingly from
her reverie.

"Are you going to stand there all day like a broom handle?"

Selene jolted to awareness. Reba had left her side and
stood next to Fergus near the boat, talking animatedly. To
Selene's embarrassment, James was standing in front of her,
hands on hips, legs widespread. Still under the spell of her
romantic fantasy, she felt an insane inclination to use the
hem of her wide skirt to wipe the perspiration that ran down
his face, dripping off his chin, making rivulets through the
crisp black hair on his chest, all the way down to a delicious
vee near the low-slung waistband of his trousers.

He made a clucking sound of disgust as his eyes followed
the path of her gaze. He knew exactly what she'd been
thinking, Selene realized with dismay. Then his eyes latched
onto the pointed nipples which showed through her blouse.

"That must have been some daydream," he remarked
dryly.

She put the fingertips of both hands to her warm cheeks, hoping he would attribute the flush she felt to the hot sun.

No such luck.

"Your timing is way off, sweetheart, if you have in mind what I think you do."

"I do not . . ." she protested weakly. "Have in mind what you think I do, I mean." She realized with chagrin that her stammering betrayed her guilt even more.

"You don't lie very well, but since we're on the subject, I think we should make one thing clear. I'm not looking for a mistress."

Selene inhaled sharply with outrage. "Why, you overbearing chauvinist!"

He ignored her words and continued, "I might have considered bedding you back in New Orleans, as unwise as that would have been. But I have too many problems at Bayou Noir to handle the entanglements of a mistress. So, *please,* no games of seduction."

The nerve of the guy, thinking she would try to seduce him. As if she knew how! "You are an arrogant bastard."

"*Merci.* I try."

"I have absolutely no interest in you . . . that way."

He slanted a look of disbelief her way.

"And I'll thank *you* not to try any games of seduction on *me,*" Selene countered. "Because I'm going home the first chance I get. I hate this time. I hate this heat. And most of all I hate you." Swiping at the tears rimming her eyes, she turned her back on him and started to stomp away.

"*Je m'en fous.*" When she didn't react, he repeated in English, "Frankly, Selene, I don't give a damn."

Selene stopped.

A chill began in her fingertips, traveled up her arms to her brain, making her light-headed, then careened all the way down to her toes.

"What . . . did . . . you . . . say?" she asked incredulously, spinning on her heel to face him.

"Nothing," he snapped and brushed past her on the way
to the boat.

Selene stared after him for a long time before she finally
murmured on a groan, "Welcome to my fantasy, Rhett."

They were gator bait . . .

Hours later, Selene was sitting on a wooden crate under the
shady keelboat shelter watching the mysterious bayou
landscape pass by. Like a piece of intricate lace, the Louisiana bayous wove throughout the state. In some places,
they joined together as wide as rivers. In others, like this
one, the waterway was so narrow that the giant, Spanish-
moss-bearded oak trees on either side almost met, like
fingers raised in prayer, forming a canopy not unlike a cathedral.

A whispery, ethereal silence pervaded her senses, broken by the occasional swish of the sluggish current and the
myriad, sometimes mellifluous calls of the birds from the
dense trees.

Suddenly Selene heard a loud noise. Looking to the side,
she saw an alligator the size of a Buick, no more than six
feet from her, casually ramming the side of the raft. She
looked about, only to see a dozen of the beast's brothers
and sisters floating about the bayou stream, some showing
off a dazzling display of teeth that could snap an iron bar
with no effort at all. And enough leathery skin to furnish
Louis Vuitton with handbags and luggage for the next year,
Selene thought with morbid irrelevance.

Frantically her eyes darted about the boat. Apparently
she was the only one who'd noticed the danger. Everyone,
including James, Fergus, and the slaves, was working effi-
ciently, propelling the boat with long poles, and rearrang-
ing the supplies. Reba was resting indolently on a pile of
fabric bolts under the shelter, her eyes closed, her hand ab-
sently fanning her face.

Selene did the natural thing, of course. She screamed her terrified head off.

Hundreds of birds rose from their nests in trees and undergrowth, raising a ruckus that would wake the dead. Even a huge turtle, weighing at least two hundred pounds, stopped its slow amble along the bank and peered toward her curiously. The gator yawned widely, showing off a vast assortment of yellow, industrial-sized teeth, and then just stared at her with its big eyes, waiting.

James lurched and almost fell off the boat near the front edge where he had apparently been teaching a slave how to steer with the long poles. He hurried to her side.

"What? What happened?"

Selene put one palm to her chest, feeling as if her heart might explode from fright. With the other hand, she pointed at the alligator, which hissed and then made a low rumbling noise, like a belch. She shivered, imagining what it might have had for lunch. Then the animal resumed its casual gnawing on the side of the wood boat.

James looked at the alligator, then back at her. Grabbing her by the forearms, he pulled her back roughly and asked with concern, "Did it bite you? Where?"

"No, it didn't bite me. But it would have. It wanted to," she stammered out.

"What are you talking about?" he snarled impatiently, dropping his hands from her arms. "Are you hurt or aren't you?"

"No, not exactly. But look all around us, the alligators."

"This is a swamp! What did you expect? Swans?"

"They want to eat us."

He put his hands on his hips. "So?"

"What are you going to do about it?"

"I'll tell you what I'm going to do if you scream like that again. I'm going to throw you in the water. And you'd better hope that bones float, sweetheart, because I'm not jumping in to save your scrawny hide."

She said a very vulgar word, one she had never spoken aloud.

"Likewise," he retorted angrily and stomped away.

Sometimes a lady has to be her own Knight in Shining Armor...

It took a long time for Selene's adrenaline to settle down. Actually, she felt a little silly now. She should have been prepared for the dangers of the Louisiana swamplands.

She sat back against a wooden crate and let the primitive beauty of the age-old bayou with its teeming wildlife soothe her nerves. Loons cried piercingly, ducks took wing, egrets rose in wispy white spirals. A thousand frogs rasped out their throaty mating calls, and muskrats made small splashes as they dove into the murky water.

Selene saw the bayou as a microcosm of the world's ever-regenerating soul and felt privileged to be a silent observer of its wonder. But she knew too well that it was a deceptive calm, and she shivered briefly at its vaporous shadows and the overpowering musk of centuries of decaying vegetation.

"Are you all right now?" Reba asked with concern.

"Yeah. I suppose I made a fool of myself."

"Well, if you've never seen an alligator, I guess your reaction was understandable." She looked dubious, though.

"But James overreacted a bit, too, don't you think?"

"Actually, no. When you screamed like that, someone could have jolted with surprise and fallen overboard, especially one of the new slaves who aren't yet steady on a flatboat."

"Oh, I didn't realize I'd put anyone in danger." Selene promised herself to be braver in the future, not to scream at the least little thing. Not that an alligator was a little thing, no matter what these Southerners thought.

Her brave front lasted about twenty minutes.

Reba slept lightly at her side, and Selene had been half dozing herself, staring at a long grayish black stick that stretched across the deck. With eyes barely open, she wondered if one of the slaves had forgotten to pick up a pole used to propel the boat. But she realized almost immediately that it couldn't be a pole, at least not one used for that purpose. It was too thick and would weigh too much.

Then the damn pole moved.

Her body broke into a cold sweat, and blood roared in her ears. Selene felt her mouth open wide, almost in slow motion, preparing to scream. But then she remembered that she'd promised James not to scream again. *Oh, Lord, oh, Lord, what should I do?*

She clamped a hand over her mouth to stifle her silent cries. Frantically, her eyes darted from side to side. When the snake inched forward on its yellow underbelly, Selene grabbed Reba's arm. Shaking Reba awake, Selene pulled her sleep-disoriented body upright. With a soft shriek, she jumped up onto a bale of wooden barrel slats, and Reba followed without question, gasping.

The serpent's coal-black tongue darted out and trembled in the air, testing. Then it opened its mouth wide, exposing the pure white, cottony interior. *Cottony! Oh, great! It must be a cottonmouth . . . one of those poisonous water moccasins.*

With no one nearby to help them, Selene reached for the first thing in sight—a huge burlap bag full of apples. She threw the first one and missed the monster snake's spade-shaped head by a country mile. But the second one landed smack between the reptile's elliptical eyes. "Did you see that?" she excitedly asked Reba, who was gaping open-mouthed at the snake, horrified into silence.

Of course, the apple didn't kill the snake, but it did make the reptile pause. Selene threw a half dozen more. Only one more hit, but her efforts weren't in vain. The snake seemed to stare at her with its lidless eyes, then slithered away, heading toward the edge of the boat.

"What the hell are you doing?" James barked as he rushed toward her and Reba.

Selene and Reba both pointed, too frightened to speak. They all watched as the enormous snake began to slide into the murky waters.

"Sonofabitch! A water moccasin!" Even James's eyes widened with concern, although Selene could see now that the snake was not as big as she'd originally thought.

She watched, fascinated, as the snake dipped soundlessly several inches below the water's surface and headed toward its new prey—a young soft-shelled turtle. In a matter of a few seconds, the snake emerged, caught the unsuspecting turtle in its mouth, and carried it to the shore. The helpless turtle struggled frantically, trying to bite the snake, to no avail. With a skill as old as its species, the snake used its strong mouth and body muscles to swallow the turtle whole, squeezing it with internal spasms toward its stomach where the body parts would be digested over a period of time.

I want to go home, Selene thought. *Back to nice, safe Manhattan where the only danger is from muggers, or terrorist bombers.* She whimpered involuntarily in shock. *Oh, Lord, I'm becoming hysterical.*

Fergus walked up and lifted his wife down, crooning softly to her in comfort. Selene stood shaking, an apple still clutched in one hand. Tears streamed down her face.

"Come down, Selene," James urged, not unkindly.

"I . . . I ca . . . can't," Selene stuttered, shaking uncontrollably as a delayed reaction to the danger settled in.

James felt a bit shaky himself. *A cottonmouth! Bon Dieu! Why hadn't the halfwit screamed?* Then he remembered. He'd warned her not to raise her voice again or he'd throw her into the swamp.

Sacre bleu! The fool woman had tried to kill a water moccasin with an apple. *An apple!* He should be laughing, but he wasn't, knowing full well how close she'd come to death just moments ago. Was she full-blown insane? No, he admitted right away, she was just a damn brave lady who was trying to survive the hand that life had dealt her. Like him.

He reached up and put his hands on her waist, pulling her forward into his arms, gently. Then, sitting on a wooden crate, he forced her into his lap and the cradle of his arms.

The woman was too tall, too skinny, too bony. But, damn, she fit just right against his body.

James closed his eyes to savor the feeling of rightness, to inhale the sweet floral scent of her wild hair that felt like silk against his lips. Protectively, he brushed wisps of damp hair off her forehead and cheeks and rubbed her back soothingly. Sweet heat emanated from her body, having nothing to do with the sun, and warmed his soul. Her heart thumped madly against his in perfect counterpoint.

And James realized in that moment that, frankly, he did give a damn.

She dreamed of Rhett, but got a rat, instead . . .

Two days later, Selene took one look at the ramshackle Cajun house where they'd stopped and turned on James. "That's where we're stopping? That's my big reward for behaving?"

He nodded. "*Oui.* The Gastoneaus have kindly offered us an opportunity to bathe and eat. And if I hear one more complaint from you, *chérie*, I swear you will be riding an alligator the rest of the way to Bayou Noir." Selene made a face at him as he grabbed her hand, leading her toward the edge of the boat.

The unpainted plank structure sat high off the ground on lopsided stilts along the bayou shore. Filthy children of all ages, wearing little more than rags, peeked shyly from every corner of the long front porch, from behind bushes, even from above in centuries-old cypress tree branches.

After two days and nights of living on the flatboat as it

wended its way through the bayou's maze of interlocking waterways, Selene would give a fortune for a bath, a bed, and a gallon of calamine lotion. She'd never admit it to James, but she couldn't have been more pleased to get off the rocking boat if the glorified shack had been the Plaza Hotel.

Even though she meticulously applied her makeup every morning, as always, she knew without seeing a mirror that she looked like hell. Her eyes burned grittily from lack of sleep. Who would be crazy enough to close their eyes with the danger of snakes and alligators lurking about? Dirt, grease, and probably a few dead bugs matted her tangled mass of hair.

A layer of protective mud covered her skin from forehead to toes, at James's insistence after she had been bitten mercilessly by mosquitoes the size of mothballs. Someday James would pay for the pleasure he took in slathering that goop on her.

"Up you go, sweetheart," he said with exaggerated cheerfulness, undoubtedly knowing his good mood would irritate her. To her chagrin, James had done a complete about-face from the tenderness with which he'd held her after the snake incident. He either ignored her or criticized her for every little thing. His flip-flopping moods were driving her mad.

Lifting her easily into his arms, James waded the short distance from the boat toward the river bank. Remembering the sweetness of his other soothing embrace, she wrapped her arms around his neck and laid her head against his chest, uncaring of his sweat-soaked shirt, wanting to feel safe and cherished, even if only for a moment. She shifted slightly for comfort, and her innocent action caused a not-so-innocent response as her breasts brushed against his chest, and peaked.

James inhaled sharply and tripped, almost dropping Selene in the murky water. "*Sacre bleu!* Stop squirming," he ordered in a husky voice. "I told you not to try your flirtation with me. I am not interested."

Lowering her lashes to hide the hurt, she dug her now ragged, fifty-dollar sculptured nails into her palms and forced back the urge to claw his face. When would she learn? Every time she softened toward the jerk, he brought her quickly back to harsh reality with one of his caustic remarks. Just like Devon, he made her feel less than a woman, deficient, undeserving of love.

She pinched her arm, hard, hoping against hope that this time she would awaken from this horrific joke that God, or Damballa, or whoever had played on her.

"Now what? Is this some magic trick where you pinch yourself black and blue, then turn into a beautiful princess?"

"Argh! I *am* beautiful."

"You're demented, that's what you are," he said. "Wait till you see a mirror."

Selene blinked against the tears that smarted her eyes. "I may not look like a raving beauty right now, but I'll tell you one thing. I am in desperate need of a Prince Charming to save me from this nightmare. Because you, my friend, are more like a . . . a frog."

He made a low grunting sound of disgust that sounded an awful lot like a frog, then muttered something about women and foolish fairy tales.

"Heck, at this point," she went on, "a modern-day Rhett would look mighty good." She leaned her head back and studied his glowering face. "You can't even be my Rhett, can you?"

James chuckled softly as he set her on the ground, but, she noted idly, even his laughter rarely warmed his sad eyes. It was probably a sign of her codependent personality—a need to be needed—that she was drawn to men with dark sides, like James, Selene mused.

"I've been called a rat by a few of my enemies, but I've never had a woman ask me to be her rat."

Selene furrowed her brow in confusion. Then she couldn't hold back the smile that twitched the edges of her lips. "Not *rat*, you fool. Rhett. Rhett Butler was the quintessential Southern gentleman."

"Well, darlin'," he drawled. "I've never had a woman ask me to be a gentleman, either." He winked meaningfully.

"Actually, Rhett wasn't much of a gentleman, now that I think about it. He was a bit of a frog at times, too. Just like you," she said forlornly.

"Poor Selene," James said suddenly. "You've had a rough couple of days, haven't you, *chérie?*" He brushed some strands of hair off her muddy face with gentleness, surprising her after his cutting observations of a few moments before.

Oh, great! Another mood swing to shake my balance. Heck, I'm already teeter-tottering between lust and loathing here, between the urge to kill and the urge to jump his bones. Selene groaned inwardly. Even the slight graze of his knuckles across her cheek heightened her awareness of him as a man. Despite her weariness, despite his brutish nature, Selene yearned inexplicably for James to touch her again.

Days-old whiskers shadowed his face. Perspiration plastered his thin white shirt to his lean body. Rolled-up sleeves exposed the corded muscles of his forearms. The silky, ebony hairs on his chest peeked out from the gap created by three undone buttons.

James was a male chauvinist to the nth degree. Disgustingly arrogant. Blatantly, handsomely virile. He was cynical, even cruel at times. And definitely crude and vulgar. Everything Selene hated in a man.

And she was beginning to fall in love with him a little, she feared, sighing dejectedly. *This must be how Scarlett felt: drawn to Rhett even as she was repelled by him.*

"You're looking at me like I'm a beignet, Selene," James chided her with a mocking laugh.

She came immediately to her senses. "Oh, you are such an egotist! I'm just tired," she lied.

James gave her a patronizing pat on the behind and pushed her toward the house. "Well, that's a good thing . . . because I wouldn't touch you with a barge pole. You smell like swamp mud, and you look like a warthog."

That was the last straw for Selene. She had been slingshotted back 167 years in time, attacked by alligators and monster snakes . . . well, almost attacked . . . devoured by kamikaze mosquitoes, and belittled and berated by the world's most insufferable man. Enough!

Selene turned abruptly and made a flying leap for James's startled body. He fell backward in the wet earth near the riverbank, and she landed on top of him. Then Selene rubbed her muddy face back and forth against his. With relish, she ran her dirty arms over his white shirt, over and over, until it was as filthy as her dress. Sitting up, she straddled his stunned body and exclaimed, "There! Now *you* smell like swamp mud, and *you* look like a warthog, too."

The effect of her raging tirade was lost, however, when James burst out laughing, and continued to laugh and laugh until tears streamed down his face, making muddy rivulets down to his chin. Startled, Selene watched with fascination the first spontaneous laughter she'd seen James exhibit. The unrestrained emotion transformed his somber face, turning him youthful and impossibly handsome.

He was still laughing when she stood up haughtily and stomped up the bank to the house, ignoring the astonished faces of Reba, James's men, and their hosts, Pierre and Amelie Gastoneau, not to mention all the children.

Chapter Seven

Life on the bayou was no joke . . .

Several hours later, James sat beside an open cookfire, sipping a cup of strong Acadian coffee. He felt like a new man, having bathed in a clear stream behind the Gastoneau house, shaved, and donned clean clothing. He ran a callused hand over the rough cloth of his dark work trousers and the worn fabric of his blue homespun shirt. He would not miss the finer trappings he was forced to wear when in New Orleans. His father would say his English peasant blood from way back showed through.

James was a man of the soil, not society, and had ever been so. That was what had annoyed his wife, Giselle, so much. From the start, she had hated his remote plantation. She had hated his refusal to move back to the French Quarter she loved. She had hated his dirty fingernails and honest sweat when working alongside his slaves in the sugar fields. She came to hate his "vulgar" touch. She had even hated the child he bred on her, poor Etienne.

But James blamed himself. He should not have taken the innocent Giselle from her home and family. He should have understood that her increasing complaints about the wildness and utter desolation of his home bespoke a greater inner turmoil. He should have seen the signs of her mental strain and rescued her before she ran away into the dangerous swamps. Yes, he blamed himself for many things, including his wife's death.

He would never, never remarry. And he most certainly would never allow himself to be sucked again into that deceptive abyss some dared to call love. James had failed miserably at marriage, and he'd come to accept that some men were just not suited to the wedded state.

Besides, he had more problems and responsibilities than any one man should have to carry. His time and his energy had to be focused exclusively on the land and making his plantation succeed. A wife . . . even a mistress . . . would be a complication he could not handle in his overburdened life. Look how his plantation had floundered on the chasm of ruin during his argument-filled marriage, and during the months after Giselle's death when he had wallowed in self-recrimination.

That was why he had to keep himself removed, emotionally, from Selene.

Truly, the woman was a puzzle to him. Certainly she did not come from the future. Could she be running from a husband or lover . . . or even a crime? Was she mad? Or suffering some physical ailment that caused her to hallucinate?

Despite all his misgivings, he barely stifled a smile as he watched her make her way carefully down the steep outside steps of the Gastoneau house, talking all the time to Reba. Lord, the woman could talk, and talk, and talk. He couldn't believe she had actually knocked him down and covered him with, her mud, not that he didn't deserve her furious reaction after teasing her so. He bit his bottom lip to hide his amusement, then tilted his head in amazement as he realized how much he had smiled in recent days . . . more than in the last few years, for a certainty . . . ever since Selene had dropped like a boulder into his life.

He studied her closely as she approached the cookfire, trying to comprehend his unexplainable attraction to her. She had washed all the mud from her body, and her hair had been brushed and clubbed back at the neck with a ribbon.

A clean dress of pale gold trimmed with cream lace hung loosely from her too-tall, too-thin form. Even though she had slathered on her usual coating of "makeup" from her magic box, mosquito bites still dotted her sunburned face and arms. Her beet-red nose was starting to peel.

So why did her mere presence make his heart soar . . . and another part of his body, as well? James groaned low in his throat at the hardening evidence between his thighs that belied his useless denial of her attraction. He probably should have spent another week in New Orleans, slaking his lustful appetite on Maureen's lush body.

"What are you growling about now, James?" Selene commented acidly as she sank down on the wooden bench next to him. Reba went over to talk to Fergus, who leaned against a tree smoking a cheroot.

Unfortunately, Selene looked down at his lap before he had a chance to rest his arms across his thighs. Her greenish eyes widened and her face turned even redder. "I thought you said I looked like a warthog," she said with unwelcome frankness. He could tell she immediately regretted her hasty words.

With relish, he lifted his shoulders in a hopeless gesture. "Some men get aroused by warthogs, I guess."

"Yeah, right. You just can't admit that I'm beautiful, can you?"

He slanted her a disbelieving look. "Selene, you are *not* beautiful. I don't mean to be cruel in telling you so, but surely you are opening yourself for hurt if you expect to snare a man with your unremarkable appearance." His eyes shifted lower, to her full breasts outlined by the close fit of her gown. Although . . .

"What makes you think I'm out to snare a man?"

"All women are."

"Not this one."

"Hah!"

The arrogance of the man! Gritting her teeth and counting to ten for self-control, Selene thought about bopping him one over the head. She wasn't sure if James was serious or not in his assessments of women, and her in particular, but she couldn't let him continue to put her down.

"Listen carefully, James. Maybe you'll learn something. I've been living on my own since I was sixteen. I earn more than most men I know. I own a $500,000 apartment in New York, and I have $200,000 in the bank. Why would I need a man?"

His mouth dropped open at her angry retort.

"Why do you tell so many falsehoods, *chérie?* First, your tales of the future. Now, your claims of a great fortune. Truly, lying ill becomes you."

"It's the truth, and I can prove it."

He lifted one brow scoffingly.

"I found a magazine yesterday at the bottom of my makeup case. A 2012 magazine with me on the cover."

To humor her, James sent Rufus, one of his new slaves, back to the flatboat to get her "magic" case. Selene had to admit that he treated his slaves very well. From the time of the auction back in New Orleans, she'd witnessed James's personal attention to the men who would be working for him. He made sure they were well fed and clothed. He spoke to them with consideration, asking about their needs and talents. He even told them that if they worked hard for him for a period of five years, without trouble, he would change their bonds of slavery to a limited indenture.

Her introspection was broken suddenly when James asked, "Why are you so preoccupied with your appearance? Do you really think beauty is so important?"

"Me?" Selene jerked her head back as if he had slapped her. "That's not true. At least, I hope I'm not that superficial. Don't get me wrong, beauty is very important in my society, but I think that's wrong. And I want to do something to correct it."

"Really? How? By wearing false eyelashes and face paint? By darkening your skin and sticking colored glass in your eyes?"

She closed her eyes wearily against his criticism, which was not entirely unwarranted. Then she looked at him directly. "You're right. I do place too much value on beauty, but I'm working on it. You have to understand that, from the time I was a child, my mother indoctrinated me with the idea that a woman's only asset is her appearance. And everyone I work with has pretty much the same attitude. I want to change, though. And the shoot in New Orleans was to be my last modeling assignment. I am . . . was going back to school—"

"School! School! At your age?" He regarded her skeptically.

"I'm not *that* old." Selene thought she might bop him one, after all.

Rufus returned before Selene had a chance to follow through on her violent inclinations. She rooted around in her box and pulled out a copy of *We* magazine. "See," she said, pointing with a flourish to the front cover, which proclaimed, "The Most Beautiful Face in the World."

A woman with dark brown, luxuriant hair and pouty red lips was staring out dreamily from the front page. A gorgeous woman, surely even James would admit that. And the date on the cover read January 5, 2012.

He looked at her, back to the cover, then back to her again. "You must have forged the date."

"Why would I do that?"

"I don't know. Perhaps you work for Victor. Perhaps he wants you to spy for him . . . worm your way into my affections—"

"Is that possible?" she scoffed. "That I, a homely twit like me, could break through that chunk of ice you call a heart?"

"Your sarcasm is uncomely, Selene," he remarked, slanting her a deprecating look. "And no, a homely twit like you could not melt my icy heart," he returned with equal cynicism.

Before she could answer, he began flipping idly through the pages of the magazine. He rubbed the glossy paper between two fingers, fascinated with the texture. The colored photos and the quality of the printing repeatedly drew soft exclamations from him of "Unbelievable!"

Then he halted at some page that caught his interest. "*Bon Dieu!* I can't believe what I'm reading." He read several more lines before looking up at her through sinfully long lashes and grinned. "Do you know this Dr. Ruth person?"

"Wha-at?" Selene squeaked out and tried to grab her magazine.

He held it out of reach and read a few more lines. "Hmmm," he said, turning back to her with amazement. "Have you read this interview with Dr. Ruth Westheimer about female sexuality?"

Oh, my God! Her face grew hot and not from sunburn. And she could see that James was enjoying her discomfort immensely.

"And this oral sex that the majority of all women enjoy . . . what might that be?" he asked, blinking innocently at her. He read more. "*Alors!* Can these figures be true? Do ladies, other than *putains,* really do all these scandalous things the author claims?"

Mortified, Selene stood and bent over him with an outstretched hand. "Give me my magazine, you lout," she demanded, afraid he would read more, not sure what else the article included. "And don't you dare read any more."

He did read on, of course, wanting to see what it was she didn't want him to read. He chuckled when he arrived at the crucial part of the article. "And multiple orgasms? Women of your 'time' demand this of their men, do they? And mastur—"

She slapped a hand over his mouth, halting his words. "Stop it. Right now."

He ran the tip of his tongue over her fingertips, which were still pressed against his lips. She pulled them away as if burned.

"I just wanted you to see the cover. I didn't mean for you to read the magazine."

"I'm sure you didn't, *chérie*." Then he frowned and studied her face for a few moments. "On the other hand, maybe you did. Maybe you were just planning a seduction."

"Seduction? Me?" For the first time, she noticed his sensually parted lips and the haze of passion in his pale eyes. Without thinking, she looked down at his lap and watched, fascinated, as he grew under her steady gaze. She quickly averted her eyes. "Seduction?" she repeated. "Don't flatter yourself, you dumb schmuck!"

"What did you call me?" he exclaimed in a stunned voice. "I am shocked that even you would use such a coarse word."

"Huh? What coarse word?" When realization dawned, she made a very unfeminine snorting sound of disgust and sank back down to the bench. "I said *schmuck*. Not that other word."

At first, James just gaped at her in amazement. Then he wrapped an arm around her shoulder, squeezing her close to his warm body. "Oh, Selene, you are a jewel, after all. You continually surprise me. And any woman who can keep a man on his toes like that doesn't need beauty."

Selene was about to jab him in the ribs for his indirect insult when he leaned down and lightly kissed the top of her head. Just that slight caress left her speechless. Could he hear her thundering heart?

She probably would have done something really foolish, like cuddle closer, but he dropped his arm and began to peruse the magazine some more.

"What is that?"

"A car."

He waited impatiently for an explanation.

"It's a horseless carriage."

He made a clucking sound of disbelief. "And I suppose that thing up there flies through the skies," he said derisively, pointing to the top of an advertisement for American Airlines.

"Actually, it does. It's an airplane. I rode on one when I came to New Orleans. It took only three hours."

He gasped sharply and stared at her in horror. "No, it's impossible," he muttered, his eyes drawn involuntarily back to the magazine. Turning the pages slowly, he was surely amazed at the unusual clothing and the mixture of black and white models in the photo shoots.

"What's a tampon?"

Selene inhaled sharply and started to choke.

He slapped her heartily on the back and repeated his question, "What's a tampon?"

Oh, Lord. "A feminine product."

"For what purpose?" he persisted.

With face flaming, Selene thought about evading the question, but he was gazing at her with such honest curiosity that she shrugged with resignation. "A woman's monthly flow."

His brow furrowed with confusion as he cocked his head in several different directions, studying the advertisement. When he finally understood, he laughed softly. "How remarkable!"

Flicking through more pages, he stopped again. "What's this?" he asked, pointing at another advertisement.

She exhaled loudly. "Birth control pills."

"Huh?"

"Women take one pill every day to prevent conception."

He raised his eyebrows dubiously.

She smiled at his incredulous expression.

"And they work?"

She nodded.

He seemed to ponder the concept for a long time, then

commented, "Those wonder pills must have a liberating effect on women's sexual activity . . . and men, as well, of course."

"You could say that."

Suddenly he slapped the magazine shut and gazed at her with horror. "*Sacre bleu!* You truly do come from the future, don't you?"

"That's what I've been trying to tell you. I'm here by means of time-travel."

"Time-travel! Time-travel! How? How could it be possible?"

"I don't know," she confessed forlornly. "One minute I was dancing in the ballroom, and the year was 2012. The next moment, I was standing in the same ballroom, but the year was 1845. Maybe it was Lilith's voodoo doll. Maybe it's reincarnation. Maybe I'm dead and this is the afterlife. Who knows?" She threw out her hands in puzzlement.

"Well, you can't tell anyone about this. And for a certainty, you must not show the magazine to anyone else." He rolled up the publication and tucked it in his back pocket. "Can you imagine what Victor would do with this information? They don't burn witches anymore, but there are laws against the open practice of voodoo. And, believe me, the black arts would be the only explanation any logical-thinking person could come up with for your outrageous claims."

"But you believe me, don't you?"

"*Oui,*" he admitted reluctantly, "but then I haven't had a logical thought since you entered my life."

"What are you going to do . . . now that you know?" she asked nervously.

Whatever answer he was about to give was forestalled by the arrival of Mrs. Gastoneau, who insisted on being called Amelie.

"The dinner, she is ready, *chers,*" she told them in a rich Acadian dialect, a local combination of French, Indian, and English. "You will like the Cajun food, yes. It is good-good."

Reba and Fergus came to sit beside them on the bench,

along with Pierre Gastoneau, a bearded, long-haired man of indeterminate years, wearing a ragged palmetto hat.

"Everyone, quiet!" Pierre yelled at the squealing children. They silenced immediately.

Without apology, Pierre spat tobacco juice from a huge plug in his cheek onto the dirt at his feet. The crude backwoodsman stared at her with open curiosity, and then grinned at James. "That one, she is your mistress, yes?"

"No, I'm not," Selene denied.

Unconvinced, Pierre winked with manly camaraderie at James.

"How's the trapping been this year?" James asked Pierre, changing the subject.

"Good, good, my friend," Pierre said in a thick Cajun accent, waving his hands dramatically as he spoke. "*Le bon Dieu* shines his blessing on the bayou this year. Yes, he does." He pointed to the hundreds of dried skins that were stretched on racks and every conceivable surface around the house—muskrats, beavers, even alligators.

Pierre turned toward Fergus, who engaged him in a heated discussion on deflated prices being offered in the city for bayou products. Throughout the conversation, James glanced continually toward Selene. And she could see that he was trying to understand all that she had told him about coming from the future.

Amelie Gastoneau spoke little as she handed them wooden platters with crude metal utensils. The woman was probably plumb tuckered out; thirteen of the children scooting about the clearing were hers, and she wasn't even thirty-five years old.

"Poor man's opera," James whispered to her when he saw her observing the large number of children.

"What?"

"I saw you counting all the children. Haven't you ever heard the expression 'Sex is the poor man's opera'?"

"My, my! Quite the philosopher, aren't you? And what is sex to the rich man?"

"I wouldn't know, not being rich. Probably his dessert."
A companionable silence thickened between them. "Speaking of food . . ." he finally said, motioning her to hold out
her plate toward Jolie, the oldest of the Gastoneau children,
a thirteen-year-old girl who moved with the body language
of an oversexed porno star as she carried a cauldron and
ladle toward them. Her fully developed breasts strained
against the feedsack-style fabric of her dress, the nipples
standing out through the thin cloth like two beacons flashing her availability.

Reba and Selene exchanged disgusted looks when the
girl's come-hither eyes lingered on James and Fergus as she
served their food. Selene wondered uneasily if the Gastoneaus offered up their daughter, along with the food, for a
few coins.

"No, thank you," Selene said, declining the gumbo that
Jolie offered her. It had a slimy texture due to the okra that
was its main ingredient.

"That one, she is skinny-skinny," Jolie remarked to
James, as if Selene weren't even there.

"Bless the Lord, there is some food she won't eat. The
South's food supply is no longer in danger of extinction."
Even as he teased her, Selene could see that he was still
deeply troubled, having difficulty accepting the reality of
her time-travel.

Selene lifted her chin with a forced sniff, pretending
wounded pride as she accepted a piece of fire-blackened
catfish, some swamp chicken, and a helping of greens, accompanied by a thick slice of homemade bread slathered
with fresh butter. At first she concentrated on her food, being ravenously hungry . . . as usual. When her stomach was
finally full, she sipped a cup of the thick chicory coffee and
watched the maneuverings of the girl, especially in front of
James.

"Will the m'sieurs be staying for the *fais-do-do* tomorrow night?" the young girl asked. "The gentlemens will be
coming from miles aroun' for the joliment, I tell you."

"*Non*," James answered with a knowing smile. "I must return at once to my home."

Jolie pouted prettily. "Don't you like to dance with the pretty girls, m'sieur?" Before he had a chance to answer, she continued, "Me, I love to dance. I love to stay up late-late."

Yeah, and I'll bet there are some other things she loves to do, Selene thought.

Jolie turned to Fergus. "And you, m'sieur? Do you like to . . . dance?"

Before Fergus could answer, Reba jabbed him so hard in the ribs that he choked on his food.

Undaunted, Jolie leaned forward to pour James some more coffee and offer a second helping of dinner, while the gaping neckline of her dress exposed her bare skin practically down to her navel. She held his appreciative eyes for a telling moment before she straightened and tossed back her greasy blonde hair, in classic California-girl fashion.

Blonde hair! Lord, what was it about men and blondes?

Selene leaned over and took Reba's fan from her hands. Then she flicked it open in front of her face. "Hey, James," she said, trying to get his attention, which wasn't easy since the little tart was bent over the cooking pot, providing a tantalizing view of her rear end. "James!" she snapped, and he finally turned to her with an infuriating grin.

Selene still held the fan in front of her face. Then, moving her head from side to side, keeping the fan immobile, she asked in a purring voice, "Do you know what this is, James darlin'?"

He looked at her as if she'd grown a horn between her eyeballs. "No. What is it?"

"A blonde fanning herself."

It took several moments for the joke to register. When it did, his eyes immediately shifted to the blonde Lolita who was still casting her sultry eyes his way, flinging her hair over her shoulder.

"Why does Selene tell you these blonde-woman riddles all the time?" Fergus asked.

"Because she thinks I have a preference for blonde women."

Fergus nodded. "You do."

James shot him a condemning glare, and Fergus laughed.

"What did the blonde say when asked to spell Mississippi?" Selene continued.

James sipped his coffee, pretending not to hear her.

"Which one—the river or the state?"

Fergus guffawed and Reba giggled, but James ignored her, refusing even to look her way. Geez, the man was entirely too stoic. He hardly ever laughed or grinned.

"Why is beauty more important than brains for a blonde?"

"Selene, don't push me," he warned in a soft voice, staring straight ahead.

"'Cause plenty of men are stupid but not many of them are blind."

"I'll tell you what's stupid, *chérie*," he said, standing abruptly. "It's you and your—"

"What does a blonde say when you blow in her ear?"

He sat back down. That question clearly caught his interest. His eyes held hers while he waited impatiently.

She ran a forefinger around the edge of her chipped cup and pretended to forget she had stopped in the middle of a joke.

"Well?" James prodded finally.

"What?" she asked with unnaturally wide eyes.

"Don't you flutter your spider lashes at me. Finish the damn joke and be done with it. What does a blonde say when you blow in her ear?" he prompted.

"Thanks for the refill."

They all stared at her, puzzled. Mr. Gastoneau hadn't seemed to get any of her jokes. "Me, I don't understand," he kept saying, asking Fergus to explain.

"You know . . . blondes have only air in their heads, not brains," she started to explain.

"I understood your joke, Selene," James said, moving closer. Before she grasped his intent, he leaned close to her exposed ear and whispered, "What do you say when *I* blow in *your* ear?" Then he expelled his hot breath softly into her ear.

Sweet, sweet ripples of pleasure spiraled out from her sensitive ear to her breasts and the vee between her legs. She parted her lips on an involuntary sigh. "I say . . . I say, 'Could you do it again?' " she admitted candidly.

Gotcha! . . .

James couldn't possibly have heard what he thought he had. Had Selene really said she would like him to . . . ?

He jolted away from her and her enticing temptations. Her subdued admission painted all kinds of impossible pictures in his mind. His tongue laving the tiny ear lobe. His tongue tracing the shell-like whorls of her outer ear. His tongue plunging into its inner depths in imitation of other even more pleasurable activities.

His long fingers flexed nervously around his coffee cup, and he pressed his parted lips together into a firm line. The woman was driving him mad with need. He was almost tempted to take up the offer of Gastoneau's nubile daughter, but he was not quite that perverted yet. Or that desperate.

The future! 2012! He was having a hell of a time accepting Selene's stories, but how could he not? The facts were there in black and white . . . and color . . . in the blasted magazine she'd carried with her. Still, *time-travel!* Maybe he was the one finally driven insane by all the pressures of his never-ending problems. Maybe the maladies of Giselle and his mother had rubbed off on him.

Finally, when he got his emotions under control, he looked back at Selene, who grinned from ear to lovely ear, gloating that she'd disconcerted him with her ridiculous blonde riddles. Well, he would show her. With seeming consideration, he asked, "Tell me, Selene, how did you enjoy your dinner?"

His question clearly surprised her. *Good!*

"It was delicious, especially the chicken. I've always liked chicken."

"Ah, yes, the chicken . . . the swamp chicken," he said smoothly, allowing mirth to tinge his voice. "You do know what swamp chicken is, don't you?"

"Wha-at?"

"Rattlesnake," he said flatly and cast her a "Voilà!" look.

Her red face turned greenish and she clamped a hand over her mouth. Then she jumped up and ran toward the privy. Oddly, he didn't feel quite so much the winner of their verbal sparring as he followed after her to see if she was all right.

Merde, maybe he really ought to turn his boat around and take Selene back to New Orleans as she'd suggested . . . before he did a whole lot more than blow in her ear.

Chapter Eight

he boy was a chip off the old block-head...

The next afternoon, when Selene got her first look at
Bayou Noir and James's sugar plantation in Terrebonne
Parish, she realized why they called it Bayou Black. Bayou
Bleak was more like it.

The flatboats had docked at the bottom of an incline,
which at one time would have been a carefully clipped alley
of lawn, almost a city block long, leading up to the plantation house. The centuries-old oak trees, about thirty feet
apart, had been trained to form an arch over the alley, but
now their gnarled branches stretched out in distorted
shapes, dripping moss.

The lush tropical flowers and bushes of the swamps—
vivid reds and pinks and oranges—encroached steadily,
crowding out anything as civilized as mere grass. And everywhere the odor of pungent flowers, stagnant water, and
decaying vegetation hung in a thick miasma.

At the top of the sloped yard stood a once-stately, raised
plantation house. Massive wood columns at least fifty feet
high stretched from the ground to the top of roofed galleries

or porches that encircled all sides of the mansion's second and third stories. A wide staircase rose majestically to the center of the second floor, which was obviously the main living quarters.

The floor of the broad second-floor gallery formed a roof for the open veranda that encircled the house on the ground floor, where servants could be seen entering and exiting its wide expanse. Selene knew there would be no basement since a spade stuck in the soil almost anywhere in the Louisiana lowlands brought forth water. It was the reason also why cemeteries had to be built above ground.

Looking higher, Selene saw that most of the tall windows were open in deference to the heat, even on the dormered fourth floor. Much of the mansion's whitewash had long since faded away, leaving bare, cold wood in those places where ivy and wild wisteria had not snaked out their vines. In some places, shutters hung from single hinges, a sad commentary on the beautiful structure's neglect.

"To think that I was expecting Tara," Selene muttered as she stepped off the flatboat onto a rickety dock.

"Tara?" James asked, coming up beside her. He took her elbow and led her forward. "Don't tell me you're still blathering about that *Gone With the Wind* nonsense."

She raised her chin haughtily. "No wonder you were cruising the Quadroon Ball looking for a governess. No sane person would come willingly to this godforsaken place . . . this . . . this Last Chance Plantation."

His head jerked back. For one brief second, unspoken hurt glittered in his beautiful eyes at her insult. Then they became remote again. "You're right. God has forsaken Bayou Noir. And He certainly forsook me long ago."

Selene inhaled sharply at the hopelessness in James's cold words. She immediately regretted her hasty condemnation.

"And as for Last Chance Plantation, well, you're closer to the mark than you may think," James continued before she had a chance to apologize. "This *is* the last chance for me. If I don't make this land thrive, not only will my future be bleak, but there will be no future at all for the hundred slaves who depend on me."

His eyes narrowed and hardened. "What were you expecting, Selene? No, don't tell me. Your damned fairy-tale Tara and a prince named Rat." With a grunt of disgust, he stepped off the dock to the shore.

"Oh, James!" she said, giggling, probably from hysteria. "You're getting my stories all mixed up."

"Which isn't difficult. You tell so many."

She made a face at the back of his head. Then, failing to watch her step as she followed him, she sank ankle deep in mud.

James turned at her squeal, and a smile crept through his mask of aloofness. Under the impact of his disarming smile, Selene momentarily forgot where she was standing, and her already shaky defenses began to melt. *Just keep that dimple hidden, James, or I won't be responsible for my actions.*

"You're beginning to look good in mud, Selene," he said with a low chuckling sound, jarring her back to reality. "In fact, you could start a trend when you go back to your own . . . country." A brief look of dismay flashed across his face, and Selene knew he was still having trouble accepting that she came from the future. "You and that Dr. Ruth person could write a book on how to have multiple orgasms and turn a man hard while standing in a load of mud looking like a warthog."

James hadn't returned her magazine and was apparently having a grand old time reading more of the articles. His mockery was like a dash of cold water, locking her defenses firmly back in place, where they should be, of course.

"You are a rat."

"So you've said before."

"No. I said Rhett, not Rat."

"I know."

"And I told you to stop reading my magazine."

"I know." He bowed mockingly and, instead of helping

her, walked away. He was still smiling when he addressed a crowd of slaves nearby, giving them orders for unloading the boat.

Clucking with disapproval, Reba came up and put a hand under Selene's elbow, helping her pull her feet out of the mud. One shoe stayed behind.

"I'm going to kill the bum," Selene said as she reached down and gingerly lifted the leather slipper from the disgusting sludge.

"Shhh," Reba warned at her side. "It's your own fault for belittling Mister James about his home."

"Huh?" Selene cast a quick look of surprise at Reba, who had lost some of her shyness in the close proximity they had shared the past few days.

Reba blushed at her temerity. "It's just that he has struggled so hard to make Bayou Noir prosper. So many planters have failed, you see, especially after the bank crash eight years ago. It is very important to Mister James that he succeed."

"I don't see much prosperity here, Reba," Selene said, although she had to admit that the acres and acres of sugarcane, being worked by slaves with hand hoes, looked very well tended. And the slave quarters—those rows of cabins to the left and behind the main house—were neat and better cared for than the mansion itself.

Reba shook her head woefully. "He has let the house go since his wife—that evil demoness, Giselle—died last year, but . . ." She let her words trail off, and her pale face flushed as she realized the impropriety of discussing the private life of her husband's employer. "Just be careful, Selene. I think Mister James has come to care for you, and I would not want to see him unmanned by one of your cutting remarks."

Selene's chin jerked up defensively at Reba's criticism, but, in all honesty, she had become quite the shrew. And most of her barbs were directed at James. "You're wrong to think that James cares about me."

Reba looked skeptical. "Maybe."

"He doesn't even think I'm attractive. He says I look like a warthog."

Reba's mouth formed a soft "O" of surprise. "A warthog? Oh, he never said *that!*"

"Yes, he did. And he said he wouldn't touch me with a barge pole."

Reba put a hand over her mouth to stifle a giggle. "Oh, I daresay he would like to touch you with a pole, but not a wooden one."

When the meaning of Reba's words and her bright red face sank in, Selene teased her, "Reba! A shady remark from a shy little thing like you?"

Reba ducked her head sheepishly. "Well, it's your fault."

"My fault?"

"Yes, I've been watching you and learning to be more . . . what did you call it? Assertive. Fergus says you're a bad influence on me."

"Oh, great! That's just what I need. Another man who—"

Her sentence was broken off by a loud shrieking noise as a little boy no more than five came barreling down the hill. "Papa! Papa! Papa!"

The child's too-short trousers barely reached his bony ankles, and his cotton shirt was buttoned wrong, with several buttons missing. His unkempt hair was probably as black as his father's under all the dirt that covered his grubby body from head to bare toes. And the pale blue eyes that sparkled with joyful tears were an exact replica of James's.

He came to a screeching halt, halfway up the incline, in front of James, stared up at him soulfully for a minute, then swung his skinny arm in a wide arc and punched his father in the stomach. "There!"

"Oomph!" James exclaimed on a loud exhale.

The rascal followed with a kick to James's shin, then hobbled about on one bare foot, having hurt himself more than his father. "Damn it all! That hurt."

James narrowed his eyes at the boy's swearing and advanced on him with outstretched arms. He scooped up his son's flailing body, no easy feat since the boy was kicking and clawing wildly.

"You shoulda taken me with you, Papa. You shoulda," he cried. "And you promised to be back two days ago. I been waitin' and waitin'."

James held the boy tightly against his chest with one hand under his buttocks and the other stroking the back of his filthy head. "Shush, Etienne. Shush, now, *mon fils*," he soothed. With a sniffle, the boy quieted and burrowed his head into the crook of his father's neck, sobbing.

Tears welled in Selene's eyes at the poignant scene, and her heart expanded in her chest almost to bursting. When James closed his eyes, still embracing his son, it was hard to tell which one was holding on tighter, the father or the son.

In that moment, Selene knew she was lost. It was one thing to be attracted to the man's physical appearance, or to be touched by the painful vulnerability he sometimes failed to hide, or to see how gently he treated those who worked for him. But to witness the open love he showed for his son caused Selene's world to tilt on its axis, spinning her off into a galaxy of new emotions she'd never experienced before.

She loved the man. She really did. Hopelessly, breathlessly, totally.

For some time, she'd been fighting her attraction for the infuriating planter, but there was no way she could deny her feelings now. Her heart soared. Her blood sang. She wanted to shout with joy, and scream with frustration.

In a flash of clarity, she realized this was the love she'd been searching for all her life. She didn't understand how fate had accomplished what she never could in her failed relationships. She certainly hadn't come looking for love . . . at least, not knowingly. It was just there.

While her future loomed uncertain and perilous before

her, Selene's troubled spirits quieted under the unquestionable knowledge that she loved James.

James set Etienne on his feet and hunkered down in front of him. With both hands holding the child's upper arms, James spoke to him intently in a soft voice. Intermittently the boy would nod his head. The tears had stopped, leaving white tracks down his dirty face.

Finally James rumpled the boy's hair affectionately and stood, noticing Selene for the first time. Reba had gone off to the home she shared with Fergus, a small cottage behind the main house. He motioned for her to come closer.

"Etienne, this is Mademoiselle Selene. She will be your new governess."

"Don't want no governess. You and *Grandmère* can teach me."

"*Non.* We cannot. I am too busy with the sugar, and your grandmother is not . . . well," James asserted firmly. "You need to study your books *every* day, Etienne."

"*Every* day? I'll die," he moaned.

James's lips twitched with a suppressed smile. "You'll live."

The boy glared at Selene, as if she were the cause of all his troubles.

"Do you want to grow up to be an ignorant swamp farmer?" James continued.

"*Oui.*"

"Well, I won't allow it."

The little boy seemed to weigh all his choices, then nodded reluctantly. "You won't send me away to that school in New Orleans then—the College d'Orleans?"

"We'll see," James replied evasively. "Now take Mademoiselle Selene up to the house and show her the schoolroom."

"Me and Jacob's been usin' it to dry muskrat skins."

James's eyebrows shot up in surprise. "In the house? You're drying animal skins inside the house? In the schoolroom?"

"Well, no one was usin' it anyways." He lifted his chin defensively.

"Etienne!"

"Oh, all right. I'll take 'em back to the shed, but the roof's leakin' somethin' fierce. And any damn fool knows wet skins are worthless."

"Etienne, what have I told you about using that word?"

"What word?" he asked innocently, peering up at his father with wide blue eyes.

"Perhaps you need to be reminded with a willow switch across your bottom."

The child grimaced, then hitched his little trousers up and gave his father a level stare, facing off with foolish bravery. "You use bad words sometimes, like—"

"Etienne," James warned.

"—damn, and shit, and *Sacre bleu*, and *mon Dieu*, and—"

"Etienne."

"—and that other word. Begins with F, I think." The miniature version of James tapped his head thoughtfully as if trying to think of the forbidden word.

"If you dare—"

"Now I remember. It was f—"

James clapped one hand over his son's mouth and lifted him by the back of his shirt with the other. To James's surprise, the worn material ripped and Etienne fell, giggling, to the ground.

Selene and James exchanged looks of incredulity at the boy's antics, then both burst out laughing as the imp rolled around in the dirt, hooting with amusement.

After a while, James forced a stern look back onto his face and wagged a finger at the boy. "We will discuss this later. I have to help the men unload the boats now. Take Selene up to the house."

He turned and started walking toward the flatboats where the slaves, under Fergus's direction, were unloading the goods.

"Didja buy me a present?" Etienne called after his father.

"I don't remember," his father answered without looking back.

"It better be a wagon. A red one." When his father still ignored him and continued walking, the scamp narrowed his little eyes with determination and yelled at his father's back, "Hope you bought some tobacco. I could use a good smoke."

James's step faltered and it seemed he might turn around. But he quickly regained his composure and continued on his way, his fists clenched at his sides.

Then Etienne turned to Selene. "You sure are an ugly wench. Where did Papa find you? In an ugly barrel?"

Selene hadn't had much experience with children, but no way was she going to let a three-foot gremlin intimidate her. "I think we'll start your lessons tomorrow with two hours of arithmetic."

"Arithmetic? Arithmetic! I hate doin' numbers. Makes my head fuzzy."

"Then maybe we'll read some poetry."

"Poetry!" Etienne put both hands on his hips and scowled at her, trying to figure out whether she was serious or not. Then he turned defiantly, dropped his pants, and stuck his bare back end out at her.

Selene's mouth dropped open and her eyes almost bugged out. *He mooned me. The little brat just mooned me. And why the heck isn't the kid wearing underpants?* Selene had never laid a hurtful hand on anyone in her life, let alone a small child, but she reached out now with evil intent.

Quickly pulling his pants back up, Etienne scooted out of her reach, running up the hill.

Selene closed her eyes wearily, seeing a long, miserable summer stretching in front of her, despite all her newly discovered feelings for James. Maybe she had died and gone to hell, after all.

Etienne didn't get far. He had run only a few feet toward the house when he ran into a brick wall. Actually it was a short, very heavy black woman leaning on a cane, waiting for him on the ground-floor veranda. The child's eyes widened with fear and he tried to swerve out of her way, but the woman wielded the crook of her cane with expertise, catching Etienne by the ankle and knocking him to the ground.

"Ouch! Blossom, lemme go. I was just showin' my governess to the house, like Papa told me."

Blossom. James's cook.

Grabbing the lying little imp by the ear, the woman pulled Etienne to his feet. "Don't you fib to me, boy. I warned you 'bout misbehavin' today. If your papa don't give you a whuppin' fer all that cussin' I jist heard, then I surely will. Yessirree. And didn't I tell you to take a bath and wash yo'self? Lordy, you gonna be the death of me."

Still holding onto Etienne's ear with her left hand, the woman turned to Selene. Her coal-black skin was smooth as ebony silk, but her short, frizzy hair was peppered with gray. Selene figured she must be at least sixty, especially when she noticed her swollen legs and feet encased in comfortable house slippers, bespeaking long, long hours and possibly years spent on her feet.

Selene stepped closer. "Hello. My name is Sandra Selente, but everyone calls me Selene. Mr. Baptiste brought me here to be Etienne's governess—"

"Oh, Lordy!"

"—and a sort of nurse for his mother—"

"Oh, Lordy!"

"—and, I guess, to just help get his house in order."

"Oh, Lordy!"

"I heard Etienne call you Blossom," Selene continued, ignoring the woman's doleful exclamations. "I think James told me you have been the cook here for years, even before he bought the plantation."

She held out her hand for Blossom to shake, and the

woman looked at her as if she were crazy. Blossom's left hand still held onto Etienne's ear, but her cane slipped from her right hand to the ground. Selene took advantage of the opportunity and vigorously pumped the woman's hand. "I'm so pleased to meet you, Blossom."

The black woman stared at their clasped hands for several long moments, then she smiled widely, exposing a mouthful of pure white teeth. The cook released Etienne, telling him, "You best go hide Bob fast-like and tie up Dreadful afore your papa knows they still be here."

Etienne, surprisingly, did as he was told, without any argument.

"Who is Bob, and what is Dreadful?"

"You don't wanna know," Blossom said, rolling her eyes.

Selene picked up Blossom's cane and handed it to her.

Clearly surprised at her consideration, Blossom motioned for Selene to accompany her. "Come with me, chile. You look like you could use a bath and some of Blossom's good cookin' "

"Do you by any chance know how to make beignets?"

Blossom beamed a prideful smile. "I wuz makin' beignets in my cradle."

"Maybe I won't hate it here as much as I thought."

And then he kissed her! . . .

Hours later, James approached the back of his house, heading toward the kitchen. He had finally got all the equipment and goods unloaded from the flatboats, showed the new slaves to their cabins, ridden out over the fields with Fergus to see how the cane was coming up, and helped install some of the new equipment in the sugar mill.

His muscles ached, his skin itched with sweat and dirt, and his stomach growled hungrily. But it felt gloriously good to be home.

James soaped his hands and arms in a washbasin on a

bench outside the back door, sloshing some of the water over his stubbled face. He heard the low murmur of voices as he entered the large detached kitchen and stopped in the doorway, unseen for the moment. His heart lurched at the warm domestic tableau, one he couldn't recall ever seeing when Giselle was alive.

Selene, her smooth skin shining from a recent bath and her long hair lying in a wet swath down her back, sat at the table talking companionably with Blossom. They were drinking coffee and eating . . . beignets.

He smiled and shook his head with wonder at Selene's enthusiasm for food, especially sweets. He was not repulsed. In fact, the years of food deprivation she often spoke of tugged at his sympathies, and, oddly, he wished he could make up to her for all the things she'd missed in life.

If she spoke the truth, she had never had a normal childhood, having worked modeling clothes from an early age. She'd never experienced paternal love—her father having left before her birth—or maternal love, being raised by a cold mother with an eye for profit.

But then, his father and mother had never been there for him, either. His father had not cared enough, and his mother, in her self-absorption, had spent a lifetime pining for a man who never loved her enough. She'd had no affection left over for a little boy's needs.

He still shuddered when he thought of his childhood in New Orleans, neglected by his mother, ignored by his father. A bastard child who ran wild, like a native, through the French Quarter and the outlying bayous.

But back to Selene. James sensed, from what Fergus had relayed of Reba's conversations with her, that Selene had been made to feel less than a woman in her dealings with men, too. Hell, he knew more than anyone how failure felt, especially after his debacle of a marriage.

Reba claimed Selene had been mistress for years to a man who had never appreciated her worth. An unfamiliar thrum of jealousy swept through him at the image of Selene in the arms of another man. He should not feel possessive toward the strange woman from the future, but he did. And that was dangerous.

He had to concentrate his efforts on making his plantation prosper. He had to spend more time with Etienne, whose behavior was clearly out of hand. He had to help his mother overcome her mental problems. He had to do something about the slaves who depended on him. So many burdens and responsibilities weighed him down.

Love was out of the question. Even lust was a complication his over-encumbered life could not handle.

". . . and then I met James at the Quadroon Ball, where he thought I was one of those light-skinned black women looking for a protector," Selene was telling Blossom, meanwhile licking the sugar off her fingers with maddening sensuality.

"Tsk tsk! Is that man daft? Anyone can tell you ain't got a drop of the blood in you, chile."

James stepped into the room. "So I'm daft, am I, Blossom? Now isn't that a fine welcome home?"

The woman got up clumsily from her bench and rapped him affectionately on the shoulder with her cane. "Dontcha be sassin' me, boy."

He leaned down and kissed the old woman affectionately on the cheek, even as she swatted him away with embarrassment. "I toldja before, boy, it don't look good for a master to be kissin' one of his slaves, even one as old as me." But he could see that she was pleased.

"And I told you, Blossom, that you're no more a slave than I am. I gave you your papers."

He laughed and sat down next to Selene on the bench. Her face turned pink as his thigh brushed hers and she scooted her bottom over, creating a short distance between them. Suddenly he stiffened, remembering Giselle's distaste for his body after a day in the fields. In his foolishness, he had painted Selene as different. He told himself he didn't care.

He turned back to Blossom. "Is there any food left over? I'm sure you've already discovered that Selene's stomach is a bottomless pit."

Blossom's wide mouth pursed with disapproval. "Watch your tongue 'round a lady, boy. And you know well and good that I made all your favorites, like I always do when you come home—turtle soup, seafood gumbo, jambalaya, greens, biscuits, and beignets."

"Beignets?" Selene exclaimed, turning to James accusingly. "You never told me you like beignets, too. Why, you brute, you made me think I was the only one with a gluttonous passion for the pastries."

He couldn't help but grin. Selene rose to the bait so easily.

Blossom's observant gaze swiveled back and forth between the two of them as they exchanged barbs. "I 'spect you're hungry. So you just dig in here," Blossom said, putting a bowl of gumbo and a heaping platter in front of him, accompanied by a cup of hot coffee. She placed a dish of beignets in the center of the table, and James saw Selene eye them hungrily. He chuckled and tapped her fingers lightly with a spoon when she reached tentatively for another one. "Those are mine."

"Selfish!"

"Prudent."

"You should share."

"You're going to get fat."

"I'm starting aerobics tomorrow."

"Arrow-backs?"

"No, aerobics. Exercise."

"Wonderful. You need a few more bones jutting out." He ignored the comical face she made at him and dug into his food. After a short time, he took pity and handed her a beignet. "Here. I don't want you drooling on the table."

"I was not drooling. I never drool. Besides, you should give me two beignets since you're being so churlish."

"You should thank me for my generosity."

"Oh, yeah, I can just imagine how you'd expect to be paid."

"*Chérie*, you can't begin to imagine the payment I would like."

Her mouth . . . her lush, full lips . . . parted in wonder as she pondered the possibilities of his words. Their eyes clung while a delicate thread of intimate promise grew between them. He was unable to drop his eyes before her steady gaze, even though he feared she could hear the loud thunder of his heart, feel the heat of his attraction. He had already noticed the blossoming of her breasts under the thin gown . . . the passionate need in her greenish eyes . . . the sensual parting of her lips.

Mon Dieu! He needed to get a grip on his careening emotions.

Blossom's loud guffaw of delight interrupted the erotic haze that hung over them. "Bless the Lord. He done sent a woman to mend the master's broken heart."

"Me? A broken heart?"

"Yessirree. I can see how you cotton to the lady. Afore you know it, there'll be a whole passel of young-uns runnin' about."

James made a loud grunting noise of disgust and turned back to his food. "Where's my mother?"

"Locked in her room."

"How long this time?"

"Two weeks, ever since you left. Been seein' haints again, and those voodoo drums het her up somethin' awful."

James nodded stoically in acceptance. His mother had managed his household in the past, but of late her "spells" had increased in frequency and intensity. And Blossom was too old and ill-equipped to handle those responsibilities. As a result, the mansion had deteriorated badly. Perhaps Selene could help, but, with her background, he doubted her capabilities in that regard.

Selene laid a hand on his arm in commiseration, as if

reading his mind. "I'll do whatever I can to help. Do you want me to go to her tonight?"

He shook his head, trying not to be affected by her concern. "She's probably asleep by now. Tomorrow will be soon enough." Looking pointedly at her hand still resting on his sleeve, he remarked, "You shouldn't touch me. I'm dirty from working in the fields."

Her eyes blinked with confusion. "From honest toil, James. There's nothing repulsive about a hardworking man."

James closed his eyes for a moment and felt himself sinking.

"By the way, that marble tub is a luxury I never expected here. Even without running water, it's marvelous. There's plenty of lukewarm water left in the cistern, though. Do you want me to go up and draw a bath for you? I wouldn't want Blossom to have to climb those stairs again tonight with her ailing feet."

Stunned, James stared at her as she rambled on. She would draw a bath for him? And her consideration for a mere slave amazed him. *She'd better say something dumb or shrewish soon or I might just kiss her. Or ask her to share a tub with me.*

Selene saw the myriad emotions rippling across James's handsome face. And, yes, despite the day-old shadow of whiskers, despite the lines of weariness that furrowed his forehead, despite his infuriating, biting tongue, he was a devastatingly handsome man. Unconsciously, he licked his dry lips, as if relaying a message.

"Wha . . . at?" she asked. "Why are you looking at me like that?"

Blossom chuckled knowingly, and James shook his head as if to clear it. Then he turned on Blossom with a scowl. "Where's Etienne?"

"Hidin' from you, I 'spect."

He frowned. "Why? No, don't tell me now. I'd rather save some bad news for tomorrow."

"The boy missed you somethin' fierce."

James's Adam's apple moved visibly in his throat, but he said nothing.

"Don't be too hard on him."

"Blossom, what has he done now?"

"Nothin'. Just you remember he's only five years old. The poor, motherless, helpless mite!"

"Hah! Helpless doesn't begin to describe—"

An ungodly squawking noise, followed by shrieks of laughter and loud barking interrupted James's sentence.

His pale eyes widened with disbelief. "You told me Dreadful died," he accused Blossom as his eyelids slitted with suspicion.

Dreadful?

Blossom ducked her head sheepishly. "Well, I thought the dog died. He looked dead. Yessirree, he did."

Oh. Dreadful is the name of a dog.

"That mutt always looks half dead."

The chicken squawked again as if the hounds of hell were on its heels.

"And I ordered you to kill that damn Bob," he said angrily.

Bob? He wanted Blossom to kill a man?

"I ain't killin' no voodoo chicken. Nosirree. And no one else will, either. You wants that rooster dead, you gonna haf to wring its neck yo'self."

Bob is a chicken. Criminey! Who ever heard of naming a chicken at all, let alone Bob? Selene giggled.

James shot her a glare and said a foul word under his breath before stomping toward the doorway. Selene and the cook followed after him with Blossom muttering, "Lordy, the feathers 're gonna fly now."

James moved swiftly into the midst of the amazing scene in the backyard. A huge mangy dog—half sheepdog, half horse—was galloping around in circles, chasing a mutant three-legged rooster. The clumsy dog—appropriately named Dreadful—kept tripping over its own big feet, but it never broke stride in its relentless pursuit of the chicken with the crippled gait. Suddenly fed up, the rooster turned on the dog, and now it was Bob in hot pursuit of the whimpering dog. Etienne rolled in the dirt, laughing hilariously.

James grabbed both his son and the dog by the scruffs of their equally filthy necks and kicked at the rooster pecking at his ankles. "Somebody get this blasted chicken away from me," he shouted, and the new slave, Rufus, came forward, shooing it into the trees. Rufus also managed to grab the dog and hold its squirming body as the friendly beast licked his stunned face with slavish affection.

James was left with only Etienne to handle. The child suddenly seemed to realize he was in big trouble. "I was only tryin' to help, Papa. Blossom told me to tie up Dreadful and hide Bob afore you could see 'em," he whined, placing the blame on the poor cook.

Blossom exhaled loudly with outrage, putting her hands on her hips, and flashed Etienne one of those ominous "Just you wait, boy!" looks.

Selene started to laugh and couldn't stop. Tears welled in her eyes and streamed down her face. Even after Etienne had been dispatched to the house to take a bath and get ready for bed, even after all the curious slaves had left and Blossom had returned to her kitchen, muttering dire threats, Selene held her sides and wiped her eyes with the sleeve of her dress, but she couldn't stop laughing.

"You find me amusing, do you?" James asked, coming closer, putting his hands on his hips.

"Hilarious," she gasped out.

"I don't like being laughed at." An easy, sensual smile playing at the edge of his mouth contradicted his words.

"I couldn't stop if I wanted to."

"I could stop you," he said in a voice thick with double meaning.

Selene hadn't realized that he had moved so close until

he leaned down, his lips descending an infinitesimal notch at a time until they were a hairbreadth from hers. She could feel his body heat radiating toward her, enveloping her.

"How?" she whispered.

"You know," he said against her mouth.

Her breathing suspended.

His sounded ragged and loud in the heavy stillness.

He put one hand on the column of her neck to hold her in place and rubbed the callused pad of his thumb across her bottom lip. Then, tunneling his fingers through her hair, he angled her face. With a soft sigh, she welcomed his impending kiss.

At first he just brushed his lips softly against hers. "I've wanted to do this for days."

"So have I," she confessed on a groan.

He moved his body against hers urgently and deepened the kiss. She made a soft mewling sound low in her throat, and he responded with a deep masculine groan of satisfaction. Molten desire exploded throughout her body, but at the same time a peaceful sense of completeness swept her senses. She felt his heart beat against hers, with the same rhythm.

When she parted her lips for his searing tongue, he made a low hissing sound. Wrapping her arms around his waist, she drew him closer, then jerked with awareness at the evidence of his arousal pressing against her belly.

"You taste like beignets," she murmured when he allowed her to take a breath.

He laughed . . . a low musical sound to her ears. "So do you." He licked the seam of her lips with the tip of his tongue, and currents of sharp electric pleasure darted to all the sweet nerve endings in her body.

Within seconds, James had made her want him in ways she'd never thought imaginable. He'd shattered her carefully erected defenses with the hunger of a mere kiss. *A mere kiss! Hah! There was nothing "mere" about his kiss.*

Caught in the throes of passion, Selene didn't want to remember why involvement with this man from the past was
not a good idea. He was a gift from the gods and she would
not question the priceless bequest.

"I thought you weren't attracted to me," she said, tracing
the line of his strong jaw with a forefinger, lovingly. "You
said you wouldn't touch me with a barge pole."

"I lied." He kissed the warm hollow of her slender neck
and pulled her body more intimately against his.

"Is she yer mistress?"

James halted his kiss with a groan of dismay at the
sound of Etienne's voice, and for a brief second leaned
against her, forehead to forehead, until their breathing
calmed. Then they both turned, still in an embrace, toward
the kitchen where Etienne was leaning against a chair,
watching them with insolent arrogance, munching on a
beignet.

"I thought she was supposed to be my governess. Guess
I won't be needin' to clean out them skins if ye're plannin'
to share a bed with her," he remarked cheekily.

James pulled away from Selene, a regretful expression
on his face. He trailed the edges of his fingertips over her
kiss-swollen lips, gazing at her with unfathomable soulful-
ness. Then he put her away from him with obvious reluc-
tance and moved into the kitchen.

"I guess you forgot that I told you to take a bath and
prepare for bed."

With lightning speed, the scamp turned and ran for the
back stairs. "I wuz just goin', Papa. Tarnation! Can't a
starvin' boy even stop to eat?"

For a long moment, James stared after his son, shaking
his head with dismay. Then he turned back to Selene. His
shoulders slumped in delayed reaction to all the problems
that had hit him since his arrival home. "You must feel like
you've landed in Bedlam," he said, raking his fingers
through his overlong hair.

Still feeling the aftershocks of his devastating kiss, Selene nodded. "But I'm glad I came," she admitted on a soft whisper.

"That's what you say now. But tomorrow is another day."

Tomorrow is another day?

Tingles of synchroneity swept over Selene like goose bumps. "Don't count on it, Rhett," she murmured as he walked away. "Don't count on it."

Chapter Nine

*B*ig *tushes . . . the eternal bane of women . . .*

A short time later, even though it was barely eight o'clock, Selene headed for bed, exhausted from the cumulative effects of her long trip. Not to mention a delayed reaction to her time-travel experience. And the emotional wallop of James's mind-shattering kiss.

She dragged her feet wearily as she followed a slave, Iris, from the kitchen on the lower level through a corridor to the front of the house.

"Are you ailin', mam'zelle? You lookin' mighty peaked."

Selene shook her head, smiling weakly at the beautiful woman who peered down at her. Iris had to be six feet tall. She was big-boned but statuesque, with high cheekbones and full, sensual lips—a cameraman's dream. Her tight curls were clipped close to her finely formed head, calling attention to smooth, obsidian skin and finely sculpted features. The only flaw in her perfectly proportioned body was a huge behind, which couldn't be hidden, even by her full-skirted gown.

Geez! Here I go again. Thinking about a person's phys-

ical attributes. Selene giggled, a thread of hysteria tugging at her wandering, exhausted mind.

"I guess I'm more tired than I thought, Iris. Just point me toward a bed and I'll be fine in the morning." *The morning?* Today had brought a staggering kaleidoscope of new scenery and people and experiences. She could only wonder what tomorrow would bring.

An unbidden thought crept into her consciousness, and the fine hairs on the back of her neck stood out with alarm. Perhaps this brain-numbing paralysis creeping in her bones was the precursor of her return to the future. Once she fell asleep, maybe she would wake up in her nice, air-conditioned bedroom back in New York, surrounded by all the modern trappings she valued so much—electricity, television, running water, telephones.

So why did the prospect no longer appeal? Why did a return to the future loom cold and uninviting before her?

Selene reeled with dismay when the answer came immediately to mind. *James.*

How could she leave . . . without James? How could she ever be happy in her old life without him?

With this new worry to weigh her down, Selene could barely crawl up the wide staircases—first the narrow enclosed one to the second floor, which was really the main living area, and then the wide, open one to the third floor where the main bedrooms were located. She had no idea, at this point, what rooms were on the dormered fourth floor.

A broad central hallway ran through each floor, giving brief glimpses of cloth-draped furniture in many unused rooms.

"Here it is, mam'zelle," Iris said deferentially, holding the door open for her. Selene's bedroom was one of six on the third floor, located at the end of the corridor. It overlooked the backyard, beyond which were the overseer's cottage and the slave quarters, resembling a miniature village in the moonlight. Like the rest of the house, her room suffered from neglect—dust on priceless antique furniture, mildew on exquisite drapes, fly-specks on faded wallpaper and gilt picture frames.

"I changed the bed linens, but you gots to 'scuse the dust," Iris offered apologetically. "Me 'n Verbena will give the room a good cleanin' tomorrow."

Selene had been raised in an antiseptic house where dirt was anathema. Her mother had designated each day of the week for certain household duties, in addition to managing Selene's career. Aside from the daily dusting, vacuuming, scouring, and scrubbing, Selene's mother insisted on certain weekly rituals. Religiously, all the woodwork and walls had to be washed with disinfectant, the mattresses turned, toilets and tile grout scrubbed with an old toothbrush, and windows Windexed till they sparkled like mirrors.

Until Selene's career brought in enough money to hire domestic help, she had been expected to clean alongside her mother. She had carried on the tradition in her own apartment, even after her mother died of cancer five years ago.

Her mother was probably dusting the clouds in heaven. Heck, she probably had the angels organized into cleaning crews. Did the celestial beings cringe with guilt as Selene always had? Did they ever feel inadequate, unable to measure up to her mother's lofty ideals?

Somehow none of these things seemed quite so important to Selene now. Not her indoctrinated fastidiousness, nor her mother's rigid expectations.

She sank down with a whoosh onto the edge of the bed and began to remove her mud-caked shoes. Suddenly Selene realized that she hadn't seen her all-important ballgown since she'd left New Orleans. "Iris, where are my clothes?" she asked with panic.

"Don't you be frettin' yo'self." The slave walked over to a tall rosewood armoire and opened the double doors, exposing Selene's meager wardrobe, including the ballgown and her makeup case.

With Iris's help, Selene stepped out of her gown and

full-length petticoat. Underneath she wore a sleeveless camisole-type undergarment and drawers that extended only to the top of her thighs. Since James had neglected to buy her a nightgown, this would have to do for sleeping. She looked down at her flat stomach, which had always been somewhat concave. Criminey, before she knew it there would be a pot belly there. "I'm going to have to start on a diet tomorrow," she remarked aloud.

"A diet?" Iris looked up from where she was idly dusting a side table with the edge of her long apron.

"I've been eating too much the past week. I'm going to get fat if I'm not careful."

Iris made a clucking sound of disagreement, eying her skeptically. "You gots a fine figure, mam'zelle. Y'hear?"

"James says I'm too skinny."

"Men! They's all the same. Sayin' they wants their womenfolks to be slender, but sniffin' after a hunk of flesh to hang onto when the hunger hits 'em. Why, I onct knew a man who . . ." Her words trailed off as she recognized the inappropriateness of her conversation. "Beggin' your pardon, mam'zelle."

"Don't apologize. And isn't it the truth? About men, I mean. They keep throwing out these mixed messages. Supposedly 'thin is in' for women, but when men are being perfectly honest about their sexual fantasies, their preference is really for more voluptuous women." Selene shrugged and grinned companionably over the universal hopelessness of understanding men.

Iris hesitated, then grinned back at her. "Sexual fantasies?" the slave said and seemed to like the sound of the words. "Well, I sho-nuff gots a good hunk to hold onto." She clapped a hand onto her wide bottom with a self-deprecating grimace. "The menfolks are always commentin' on my . . . well, you know. No matter what I be sayin' or doin'— washin' clothes, servin' food, goin' to services when the travelin' preacher comes by—their eyeballs be glued to the same ol' spot, my backside. Makes a body shamed, it does."

"Iris, you're one of the most beautiful women I've ever seen, and I'm not just saying that. Besides, a couple thousand tush crunches could probably tighten up your behind and . . ." Selene stopped herself, remembering James's warning about talking of the future.

"Tush crunches? What's a tush?"

"Never mind."

Iris looked down at the floor, disappointed and obviously thinking she, a slave, had no right to question a white woman.

Hell! "Tush is another name for the buttocks." She patted her own posterior to demonstrate.

"And a tush crunch?"

Selene winced at the realization that her running mouth had gotten her into trouble once again. "An exercise to reduce the tush," she disclosed with a loud exhale of self-disgust. "And that's all I'm going to say on the subject."

She began to pull the mosquito netting around the bed, yawning widely. When she turned, Selene almost jumped at the sight of Iris standing right behind her with her hands braced belligerently on her hips.

"Are you sayin' there's a way to get rid of this big butt of mine and you're not gonna tell me?"

A short time later, Iris left the room, smiling widely. Selene had promised to demonstrate tush crunches and other aerobic exercises that might help the slave correct her physical problem.

James was going to kill her.

He almost rocked her world! Who was she kidding? He did rock her world . . .

Selene awakened late the following morning, feeling deliciously rested, even though every muscle in her body ached. She stretched hugely, sitting up in the netting-swathed four-poster bed of exquisitely carved rosewood. James had told her that she could wait a day before starting her duties, but still Selene felt guilty for oversleeping.

She tried to rake her fingers through her hair, but they got caught in an ungodly number of snarls. With a moan, Selene remembered that she'd fallen asleep without drying her hair. A big mistake. It would probably take her hours to comb the tangles out of her hair now.

Well, today was the first day of her new life, Selene decided, choosing to be optimistic. She pushed the mosquito netting aside and walked behind a screen where she relieved herself in a chamber pot—not an experience to be cherished. She decided she would take a bath, then look for Etienne to start their lessons. On the way to the armoire, she passed an oval free-standing mirror on serpentine legs, giving it a passing glance. She jolted back in a double take.

Then she shrieked the roof off.

James was in the back of the house talking to Rufus about some chores he wanted done when he heard Selene's first scream, followed by a horrific, mournful wailing.

With lightning speed, he shot into the house and up the back stairs, rushing into her room without knocking. "What? What happened?" he shouted. "Are you hurt?"

"No, I'm not hurt," Selene blubbered out between sobs, intermingled with hiccups. She stood in front of a mirror, crying loudly, wearing only a lacy chemise that showed off the tops of her magnificent breasts and brief drawers that exposed a huge expanse of legs—exceedingly long and nicely formed, he had to admit.

Unable to sleep last night, James had spent hours thinking of this strange woman from the future. With noble intentions, he had vowed to avoid her at all costs. It was one thing to have a short sexual encounter with a woman like Maureen, but he just knew that making love to Selene would involve commitments he could not make at this time, perhaps never. Besides, Selene was living in his home. He couldn't very well leave, or send her away, when the affair ended, as it surely would.

As tantalizing as their kisses had been the night before, he had decided he would not touch her or kiss her again, and certainly he would not make love to her. But, *Sacre bleu*, as she stood before him now in delectable dishabille, his determination faltered. And he acknowledged just how hard it would be to carry out those intentions.

He could picture those slender legs wrapped around his hips. He could taste the nipples that jutted out from their lacy confines, begging for his suckling. He could rub his coarse chest and leg hairs against her smooth skin with sweet abrasiveness. He could . . .

With a mental curse, he cut himself off. Girding himself with resolve, he hit the side of his head with the heel of his hand to clear it of the sensual images. Dangerous images. Images that led down a path of self-destruction for them both. Quicksand.

"Is it a snake again?" he choked out, looking over the bare skin of her arms and legs and feet for fang marks.

She shook her head and let out a small sob, muttering something about buckwheat.

"Buckwheat?" he asked incredulously. "You were attacked by buckwheat?"

"No, you fool. I wasn't attacked by buckwheat. I *look* like Buckwheat. From the Little Rascals," she wailed, flicking out the ends of her monstrously big hair.

He looked more closely at Selene then, noticing her hair for the first time. He didn't know who Buckwheat was, but Selene looked like a cypress tree with dark brown moss exploding haphazardly in all directions from her skull. "What happened, *chérie?*" he asked, trying hard not to smile. "Is this a hairstyle from your time?"

She shot him a look of absolute disgust. "You are an idiot. Only an idiot would think that any woman would choose to look like this."

He shrugged. "You are not *any* woman," he reminded her. "You are a woman who pops eyeballs and wears fake spiders on her eyelids. You diet to look like a skeleton. You—"

"What's your point?" she snapped.

"—you tell a slave that you know how to reduce her ass," he continued.

Her face grew pink at being caught in this latest outrage. "I didn't intend to tell Iris about tush crunches. It just slipped out."

"Oh? Would that be like the words that just slipped out when you informed Reba of the most ideal sexual position in the world—the Perfect Fit?"

Selene's pink face gradually turned beet red. A ghastly contrast to the dark bush on her head.

James should have been repelled. Instead, he was thinking seriously about continuing where they had left off the night before with that bone-melting kiss. Perhaps on the bed. Or on the floor. Against the wall wouldn't be so bad. Or in front of that mirror . . . oh, yes, definitely the mirror. A flame of searing desire shot through his vitals.

He shook his head like a wet dog to bring his roiling senses under control, especially when he realized that Selene had been talking and he hadn't been paying attention.

"—and it's not really my fault if Reba feels so insecure and was asking for my advice." She slanted him a sly, speculative look from under her thick lashes, which really did not need the aid of fake spiders, he decided.

He leaned lazily against a bed post. "Well, darlin', Fergus keeps asking me to describe this 'Perfect Fit,' and I'll be damned if I know what he means. Would you care to explain it to me?"

"No."

"No?"

"I forget what it is."

"Liar."

"Well, it's not the kind of thing you can describe anyway. You have to—"

"—demonstrate?"

"I thought you had to be in the sugar fields today."

"I should be, but, for an orgasm that lasts for hours and hours I might be willing to let Fergus take over. That is what you told Reba, isn't it? Hours and hours?"

"You're teasing me, aren't you?" she asked, narrowing her eyes suspiciously. "You know I'm nothing great in bed, and you think that's funny. Devon told me that men can tell that about women." Tears welled in her eyes as she looked at him accusingly.

"Devon was a fool."

She blinked in confusion.

"Selene, *chérie*, after the kiss we shared last night, how could you doubt that you and I would be anything less than spectacular together? I don't think we would need any special positions, either."

She stepped toward him, the yearning in her vulnerable eyes clearly evident. *Mon Dieu*, if she didn't do something repulsive soon, like pop an eyeball or belch a bird, he would be lost.

He felt a roaring in his ears, probably the wall of his carefully erected good intentions falling brick by brick. Backing up a pace, he put out a halting hand. "No. Don't touch me."

She recoiled, mistaking the curt words he lashed out.

Merde! The look of shame in her eyes would soften a strong man's heart, and he was becoming weaker by the second. "Selene, sweetheart, have mercy. If I touch you . . . if you touch me . . . I won't be able to stop. And that would be a mistake. You know it. I know it."

A single tear slipped down her face, and he groaned inwardly, grasping for some thread of logic in his disintegrating brain. "Selene, I'm drowning in responsibilities. I can't afford to be distracted by romantic notions."

"I know," she said, and another tear slid out of her misty hazelnut eyes.

"We have no future."

"I know," she agreed, but her traitorous eyes willed him

to come closer. "But tell me one thing. If I were blonde, would you be able to resist me so easily?"

He laughed mirthlessly. "Don't for one moment doubt that I want you more than . . . anything. Even a blonde."

She smiled tremulously, and his heart expanded and threatened to burst the walls of his chest. Through the haze of his passion, he fought for strength, some way to save them both from sinking into the magnetic pull of their mutual attraction.

She, too, seemed to be fighting off the heavy lethargy of the thick air that surrounded them. After a long, charged silence, she dropped her eyes before his steady scrutiny and turned back to the mirror. Clearly seeking to change the subject, she made a tsk-ing sound of dismay. "I need my hair diffuser."

"What's a diffuser?" he asked, thankful for her efforts to relieve the tension between them, hoping he would be able to escape the room without making an utter debacle of both their lives.

"A diffuser keeps the hair from getting frizzy. I shouldn't have fallen asleep with wet hair last night, but I was tired and you kissed me, and I didn't want you to stop," she rambled on in a rush of words, and James saw that her emotions were no more in control than his. "Now I'm so mixed up. I'm not even sure I want to go home. But what would I do here in this godforsaken place without my job? Oh, Lord, what am I going to do?" She put her hands to her eyes and began to sob pitifully.

More bricks crumbled from the wall of his good intentions as James gazed helplessly at Selene. She looked so forlorn that James couldn't help himself. Casting caution aside, he stepped right into the quicksand of the most powerful temptation of his life.

He told himself it would only be for a second. He could step away at any time.

Hah! He was fooling no one, least of all himself.

He took her into his arms and soothed her, patting her shoulder, running a palm over the smooth planes of her back and the sharp shoulder bones.

Closing his eyes, he buried his face in her neck and inhaled deeply of her seductive scent. He tried to resist. He truly did. But he was sinking fast. He knew it even before she turned her face up to his, offering her lips.

Like a starving man, he devoured her mouth. Hard and soft. Demanding and coaxing. Giving and taking.

She returned his kiss with a reckless abandon that shocked, and tantalized, him.

"Selene . . . oh, *ma chérie*, I cannot help myself," he moaned against the sweet curve of her neck.

"I know, James. I know," she whimpered.

With fingers tunneled in her hair, framing her scalp, he turned her this way and that, unable to get enough. He nipped her lips. He plunged his tongue deep into her mouth, then growled low in his throat when she drew tentatively on him.

Mounting urgency caught him in its painfully sweet agony. "Tell me to stop, *chérie*. Quick." Pulling her flush against his body, he let her feel his arousal.

She gasped and stared at him wide-eyed, as if he'd asked her to jump off a cliff. Instead of telling him to stop, she boldly parted her legs and gave him closer access. When he touched himself against her in that certain place, soft shudders shook her body, and her legs buckled. They both sank to the floor, on their knees, never breaking their frantic kiss.

"Sweet Lord! I . . . have . . . never . . . wanted . . . like . . . this . . . before," he gritted out. Gasping for breath, he pulled away, staring down at her. With her bruised lips and passion-hazy eyes, not to mention her mussed hair, she looked wild, and wanton, and wonderful.

Lowering his head, he took a pebbled nipple into his mouth through the sheer cloth of her chemise and drew on it with feverish intensity. She began to keen . . . a low, erotic sound as old as Eve . . . and he suckled harder, matching the rhythm of his lower body, which was pressing spasmodically against hers.

His knees grew weak and he pressed her to the floor, settling between her parted thighs with a growl of immense satisfaction. Pleasure, hot and painfully intense, lodged between his legs, and grew, and grew, spiraling out to his fingertips and toes, even his scalp.

I should not do this. He looked down at the wet cloth that revealed in all its transparency her beautiful breast, and he proceeded to minister to its mate.

I should not do this. He wrapped her legs around his waist.

I should not do this. He ground himself against her damp womanhood.

I should not do this. He lifted her hips off the floor at the stiffening of her thighs, which portended the beginning of her pleasure.

"O-o-h," she whispered, her eyelids fluttering.

He could see the first quivers of her orgasm in the startled widening of her eyes, the parting of her lips. Her legs jerked and she tried to pull away.

He wouldn't let her go.

"Come for me, *chérie*," he coaxed rawly. "Let it go. For me."

"I don't know how," she confessed softly.

She didn't know how? With sudden understanding, he told her tenderly, "Relax, darling. Just unstiffen and relax."

When she finally did as he instructed, he watched her face closely and began to buck against her with light, controlled movements. Her eyes glazed over with passion, and she writhed from side to side. "No," she protested. "No, it's too much."

Relentlessly, he held her body against the cradle of his hips and rocked and rocked against her until she arched and screamed as the first wave of her climax hit her. Her womanhood pressed reflexively against his hardness.

A violent shiver overtook him. He couldn't help himself. He couldn't wait.

Pounding against her, he sought his own release. Over and over, he hammered her, unable to think beyond her soft wails of pleasure, his own low moans and coaxing love words, the devastating, nerve-splintering explosion of his senses. He was caught in a spiral of ever-increasing arousal beyond anything he had ever experienced in all his life.

A hoarse, animal sound of surrender erupted from deep in his chest. His senses hurtled through space, disintegrating into a million sparks of progressively larger, more intense peaks of pleasure.

He floated slowly back to sanity. Sated, he lay against her heavily, stunned by the sheer perfection of ecstasy he had just experienced and the even more complete satisfaction he felt in just holding her in his arms. He pulled back slightly, needing to see if she was equally affected.

"I didn't know," she said, gazing up at him in utter astonishment.

"Neither did I, *chérie*," he rasped out. "Neither did I."

With a deep sigh, he nuzzled his lips against her neck.

He should feel regret over his foolish actions. He felt only elation.

He should return to the sugar fields and the many responsibilities that awaited him. He couldn't move.

For a long time he lay atop her, breathing raggedly, his heart pounding loudly. He raised himself on straightened arms, gazing down at Selene, who still looked at him with absolute amazement.

Suddenly, without warning, Blossom stormed in, crying, "What happened? We heard the screamin' all the way down to the kitchen, and . . . oh, Lordy!" Quickly, with her brown eyes practically bulging from their sockets, she took in the scene, then shooed Iris and Reba out the door, along with a number of slaves, not to mention Etienne with Iris's little twin boys, Cain and Abel.

"The mistress fell, and the master is jist tryin' to help her up," Blossom quickly explained.

James thought he heard snickers. Then his son remarked crudely, "My papa is prob'ly pokin' his pizzle in the skinny wench."

A loud whacking sound followed.

"Ouch! Wha'dja swat me fer, Blossom? I wuz jist tellin' Cain and Abel—"

"You be doin' any more tellin' and you gonna have blisters on your backside," Blossom scolded. Soon their voices faded away as they descended the stairs.

"Oh, I'm so embarrassed," Selene said. "How will I ever be able to face anyone?"

James could just imagine the reaction of Fergus and his workers when he finally returned to the fields, but he decided Selene didn't need to know that.

"Once you make yourself presentable, I'm sure no one will remember what they saw," he comforted her. But he didn't believe his own words. *Mon Dieu,* the woman's bruised and swollen lips alone proclaimed their recent activity. And the brushburns on her face and neck from his morning stubble probably wouldn't fade for days.

He tried to push the wild hair off her face with both hands but it kept springing right back up, and out, with a will of its own . . . like its owner. Finally he gave up.

"Well, perhaps you are going to be the talk of the South but more for your hazelnut eyes and buckwheat hair," he teased. "I wonder what other foods you have hidden on your person."

"I'm serious, James."

"So am I. Let's see what other edible body parts you have." He examined her thoughtfully, then grinned mischievously. "Berries?" he offered, looking at the hardened peaks on her chest. "Or honey, perhaps?" he asked, casting his eyes lower.

"Oh, you!" She shoved him playfully, and he rolled off her. Moving out of his arms, she stood and almost fell as her knees threatened to fold with weakness from their recent activity.

He was inordinately pleased.

She walked toward the mirror, and her mouth dropped open in shock. "Oh, my goodness!" Wet circles of fabric clearly displayed her breasts and the vee of her drawers.

He chuckled, folding his arms behind his head, and watched her with smoldering eyes. Suddenly shy, she grabbed a long wrapper and held it in front of her exposed body.

"It's a bit late for that, don't you think, *chérie?*"

She blushed becomingly. "If you're getting such amusement out of my condition, perhaps you should examine yourself." She looked pointedly at the joining of his thighs.

He glanced down and grinned, seeing the wide, damp stain on his trousers.

"Aren't you even embarrassed?"

He should have been. But he wasn't. "Selene, sweetheart, I haven't gained such enjoyment from spilling my seed since I was twelve years old."

Selene put both hands on her hips and glared down at James—the arrogant, infuriating, wonderful man. His pale eyes glittered with the afterglow of passion, caressing her admiringly. She noticed then that her posture called attention to her half-clad body. With a tsk of disgust, she went over to the armoire where she selected a light poplin day dress and pulled it over her head. She turned, about to ask James to help her fasten the back of the gown when she noticed that he no longer lay on the floor watching her. Nor was he smiling.

He had straightened his shirt and trousers, and the usual somber expression had returned to his face. He was staring past her shoulder, almost with horror.

She jumped out of the way quickly, fearing that one of the many bayou pests had crept into her room, maybe even a snake. "Oh, Lord! What? What is it?"

James brushed past her without speaking and opened the double doors of the armoire wider. Lifting her white

ballgown out, he held it toward her accusingly. His blue
eyes pierced the distance between them, and she shivered
with apprehension.

"I forgot. May all the saints curse me for a fool, but I
forgot." He regarded the precious gown with such disdain
that Selene feared he might rip it to shreds.

"You forgot?"

"*Oui.*"

"I don't understand." The icy expression in James's eyes
frightened Selene. A suffocating sensation tightened her
throat. How could he go from hot passion to cold revulsion
so quickly? Selene had put up with so much verbal abuse
from Devon over the years. He would appear to want her,
would seduce her with soft words, then ridicule her with
cruel taunts after she'd surrendered her body to him.

Oh, Lord, please don't let this man be the same. James
had made her feel feminine and desirable for the first time
in such a long time. She didn't think she could bear condemnation from him now.

But what if she'd mistaken his ardor? What if he'd felt
sorry for her? Maybe he'd just been . . . well, horny . . . and
she was convenient. Now he was repelled by her.

She had to know the truth. Swallowing the bitter taste of
despair in her throat, she pleaded hoarsely, "James, please
don't say that you regret our kiss."

"Kiss? You call what just occurred between us a kiss?"
He slanted her a look of utter disbelief and dragged his fingers through his hair distractedly.

"What do you call it?" she asked in a low voice, willing
herself not to cry.

"We were making love, Selene," he told her, spacing his
words slowly and carefully, as if instructing a small child.
"The fact that the act was not consummated doesn't make it
any less lovemaking, and you know it."

She nodded. "Then why are you acting so . . . strange
now?"

"Strange?" He regarded her gravely. "I'll tell you what's

strange. Me. How could I forget who you really are?" He shook the ballgown in her face for emphasis. "Any minute now, you could slip this garment on and slide out of my life. Without a backward glance."

Selene inhaled sharply with sudden understanding. He was right, she realized with horror. At least, about the possibility of her leaving this time period . . . and him . . . without a moment's notice. But he was wrong about the backward glance.

"I'll tell you what else is strange," he continued, dropping the gown to the floor with revulsion and beginning to pace the floor in agitation. "My lack of control. *Mon Dieu!* I have fifteen thousand arpents of standing cane and one hundred slaves out there, and I'm rolling around on the floor like a brainless lad with an equally brainless witch from the future."

"James, I understand. Please let me explain."

"I'm thirty-four damn years old," he continued, ignoring her plea, "and I'm behaving as wildly as my son, who is clearly in much more need of a father than you are a lover."

She gasped.

"I warned you about seducing me. I told you my responsibilities were stretched to the limit. Oh, don't look at me with such outrage, *chérie*. I take equal blame for this seduction, but it must stop. *Now*." He grabbed her by the upper arms, lifting her toward him. "Do you understand?"

Her unfastened dress began to slip off her shoulders, and for a moment Selene thought he was about to pull her into his arms again as his eyes fastened on her bare shoulders and lower. But he made a savage hissing sound and dropped his hands, turning away from her, clearly agitated.

"I'm going mad," he muttered.

"James, listen to me," she said, putting a hand on his arm in sympathy.

He shrugged her away. "Do . . . not . . . touch . . . me."

Selene drew her hand away, but she was not insulted. She understood the bolt of electricity that seemed to shoot between them with just a mere touch. "I wasn't thinking, either, James. And I accept what you're saying now, but surely you don't think I take these . . . feelings . . . between us lightly. That I could leave here and have no regrets."

He looked at her intently, his mouth tight and grim. "Are you saying that you won't leave?"

Selene's shoulders slumped. "I don't know."

"Would you destroy the gown, cutting your bridge back to your own time?"

"*No!*" She clapped a palm over her mouth at her too-quick retort.

James's lips twisted cynically.

"I mean, not yet."

"Ever?"

She winced at his scathing tone. "I don't know. I just don't know."

A dark cloud seemed to settle over them.

"Tell me this, Selene. Are you taking those birth control pills that were advertised in your magazine?" He threw the icy words at her like stones.

She shook her head slowly. "Not anymore." Her very breath seemed to burn in her throat.

"And what were you planning to do if you became pregnant? Would you leave with my child, as well?"

"I hadn't thought . . ."

His nostrils flared with outrage.

Selene couldn't believe that she had failed to examine the consequences of her actions. It was so unlike her.

"So we are in agreement then?"

She nodded.

"We won't be making love."

She nodded again, unable to speak.

His eyes held hers intently, intimately, for several long moments. Then he left, closing the door quietly after him. And one word clanged painfully in the air, unspoken. *Love.* Neither of them had spoken of love.

And that's what might have made the difference.

Chapter Ten

You could say she was Mary Kay to the rescue . . .

After much frustration and two broken combs, Selene washed her hair one more time using a special cream rinse concoction Blossom gave her that smelled faintly of vinegar. The cook assured her it wouldn't leave a lasting odor. Then, with Reba's help, Selene cut three inches off the ends of her hair all around.

"What do you think?" Selene asked, turning her head this way and that before the mirror in her bedroom.

"I don't know," Reba said, glancing dubiously at the large clumps of dark hair scattered on the sheet Selene had spread on the floor.

"I think it's perfect. I should have cut it long ago, despite my agent's advice."

"I vow, Selene, you say the strangest things. Everyone knows men hire agents to factor their goods, like cotton and sugar. Imagine a woman having an agent!"

Selene remembered James's admonition not to speak of the future and decided not to explain. Instead, she stood, shaking the linen towel from her shoulders onto the sheet.

Then she cast a calculating look at her new friend. "Your turn now, Reba?"

Reba turned startled, frightened doe eyes on her.

"Sit down and let me trim your hair a little."

"Oh, no. Oh, blessed Lord, no. Fergus would never allow me to cut my hair."

"Allow?" The scathing tone in Selene's voice could slice concrete.

Red blotches bloomed on Reba's pale cheeks, and she raised her chin defensively.

"I wouldn't be cutting it short, hon," Selene said, trying not to be so judgmental of another time. "Just trimming the edges and, most important, layering it for added thickness. Believe me, Reba, most women aren't born beautiful; they just learn how to improve on the gifts God gave them."

"Hah! What if God didn't give them any gifts?"

"Reba, listen to me. The one thing I know is beauty. You're already a pretty girl. I can make you prettier."

Reba sighed wistfully. "Do you promise not to cut it short?"

"Cross my heart and hope to die," Selene said, making an X mark over her heart.

Reba backed away from her slightly. "Was that a voodoo sign?"

Selene laughed and pushed Reba onto the low stool. "No. What is it here with you people and voodoo?"

"Did you hear the drums last night?" Reba asked with a shiver while Selene adjusted a clean towel on her narrow shoulders and combed her fine hair out of the coil at the nape of her neck.

"What drums?"

"The voodoo drums out in the swamps. I hate them. Truly I do. Fergus says there's nothing to fear in all the mumbo jumbo. But I remember all the bad times when Giselle was alive, and everyone knows about the ghost that appears here sometimes. Giselle's ghost."

"What drums? I didn't hear a thing," Selene said,

clipping expertly, choosing to ignore the ridiculous remark about Giselle's ghost. Reba was entirely too impressionable. "I'm usually a light sleeper, but I guess I was too exhausted last night."

Luckily, their conversation soon veered away from voodoo and ghosts. A short time later, Selene fluffed the ends of Reba's hair, standing behind her before the mirror. "Now doesn't that look better?"

"Oh, Selene, you're a magician." Reba preened before the mirror, beaming.

"Hardly a magician. And, *please,* don't repeat that word in association with me. James gets decidedly uncomfortable anytime people connect magic with me." She helped Reba to her feet, then added, "Also, the next time you wash your hair, you've got to scrunch it dry."

"Scrunch?" Reba put her fingertips to her lips to stifle a girlish giggle.

"Yeah, scrunch." Bending over from the waist, Selene demonstrated, tossing her own still-long hair over her head, repeatedly bunching and unbunching thick clumps of it. "Scrunching makes your hair even thicker and bouncier. Do you think you can do that?"

Reba nodded, memorizing her every move.

Selene tilted her head to the side, studying Reba. "One more thing. Don't move." Going over to the armoire, she took down her makeup case and examined the contents carefully before selecting a small compact of powder, brown mascara and eye pencil, and a tube of Pink Passion lip gloss.

"Oh, no! Never! I might be able to convince Fergus about the haircut, but he would never accept face paint."

"Sit," Selene ordered with mock sternness. "Honey, do you know how many thousands of men have said that they hate makeup, that they like 'the natural look,' just like their own wives or girlfriends have? Hah! Little do they know, it took hundreds of dollars and a carload of Revlon to achieve 'the natural look.'"

"Red-lawn? Oh, Selene, please, no face paint. The haircut is enough."

"If you don't like the makeup, you can wash it off."

With a groan, Reba gave her reluctant permission. A short time later, Selene stood back and let Reba get her first look in the mirror.

The hair layering had made an improvement in Reba's appearance; the makeup brought about a miracle. Using only the tiniest amounts of mascara on her lashes and pencil on her brows, Selene heightened the vivid cornflower blue of Reba's eyes. The powder added a tint of color to her toneless skin, and the gloss gave definition to lips that Selene hadn't noticed were full and rather sensual.

Reba was a knockout.

Stunned, Reba gaped at her reflection. Then she did the natural womanly thing. She started to cry.

"Reba! Sweetie, we can wash it off if you don't like it."

"I . . . love . . . it," Reba blubbered out, throwing her arms around Selene's neck and hugging her thankfully. "Fergus will love it, too, but I'm not going to tell him. No, I'm not. It's just like you said. He'll think I got some sun, or was eating berries. Men see what they want to see. Oh, Selene, I'm so glad you came to Bayou Noir."

It took Selene another ten minutes to repair the damage from Reba's tears. Then Selene handed her the cosmetics she had used, as a gift, and they headed downstairs, arms linked companionably. Halfway down the second set of stairs they met Iris, the tall slave that Selene had met the night before, carrying an armful of clean linens. Iris took in Reba's new appearance with a startled glance, then shot an accusing look at Selene. "When you be startin' on my backside?"

"Maybe tomorrow, Iris. I overslept today," Selene said with a laugh.

"I tol' Hyacinth 'n' Rose Petal 'bout your arrow-back exercises and they wants to do 'em, too. Do you mind, mam'zelle?"

Oh, Lord. James is not going to be happy.

"Hyacinth's bosoms are big as cow udders, and Rose Petal's got feet big as cow pies," Iris went on.

"Oh, my goodness, Iris! There's nothing a person can do to reduce the size of feet," Selene said, trying hard not to laugh. "And breast reduction, well . . ." Selene stopped herself from discussing twentieth-century surgical methods.

"Don't you be worryin' none, mam'zelle. I reckon anyone who can do magic like this," she said, waving a hand toward Reba, "can surely make feet and tits *look* smaller."

"Yeah, right." And there it was again. That word. *Magic.* James was definitely not going to be pleased.

Reba's eyes widened. "Can you make mine bigger?" she asked, blushing, as she looked down at her flat breasts.

"No! Absolutely not!" Selene asserted firmly. Geez, these people treated her like some deity, a goddess who could dole out perfect body parts on a whim. Then, feeling bad at having snapped at poor Reba, she added, "Maybe."

"Wait till I tell Lily," Iris said with a whoop of joy. "She ain't got no tits atall."

Yup! James is not going to be a happy camper.

A woman's work never changes . . .

An hour later, Selene was sitting at the kitchen table with Blossom, sipping her second cup of strong Creole coffee. It was already past noon, and she had consumed a combination breakfast and lunch of corn cakes, hominy, bacon, eggs, greens, homemade bread, and freshly churned butter. Aerobics were number one on her menu for the next day.

She dipped a quill into the inkwell in front of her and began to scratch out words on the paper Iris had brought for her. "Okay, now give me the names of all the slaves and free workers on the plantation, those not engaged by James in the sugar fields or other hard labor." After much deliberation, and consultation with records she'd found in the library, they came up with about thirty names, mostly women, and children over the age of seven.

"Now we can make a schedule of duties to assign to these servants so that at least the inside of the house, the yard, and kitchen gardens can be brought back to order."

"'Bout time," Blossom agreed. "Mam'zelle Baptiste always did this before, but she been . . . well, indisposed, of late. An' my legs jist won't allow me to climb those stairs no more. Nosirree. What this house needs is a new mistress. Yessirree, it does." She eyed Selene speculatively at her last words.

"Not me," Selene said with a laugh. "I'm just here for a brief . . . vacation." *Vacation, huh! Club Med of the Bayou, not!*

Selene inhaled deeply of the delicious scents wafting about the cozy kitchen, so unlike her antiseptic white enamel one back home. Cooking was done in an open hearth and a brick oven but mostly on a unique *potager,* which was a tile counter with built-in "stew holes" over charcoal burners. Selene assumed this was a forerunner of the stovetop ranges to come.

Right now, the traditional jambalaya was simmering on the *potager,* redolent with smoked ham, shrimp, onions, tomatoes, rice, and red peppers.

"By the way, why do you call Mrs. Baptiste Mam'zelle?" Selene asked, calling herself back to the job at hand. Then she remembered that James's father had never married his mother. "And it is Mrs. *Baptiste,* isn't it?"

"All the white ladies are Mam'zelle," Blossom said with a shrug. "And Mam'zelle always called herself Baptiste, as far as I knows. Don't know if she gots a legal right. Don't knows that it matters much here."

Selene nodded. "When can I meet Mrs. Baptiste?"

James had gone out to the *garçonnière*, a separate building to the side of the house sometimes used as a bachelors' quarters, to see his mother the night before. She'd refused to budge from her self-confinement.

Blossom hedged. "Mam'zelle don't want no visitors till she be feelin' better."

Selene turned back to her list. "I just noticed something," she said with a laugh. "Almost all the women slaves have flower names, and the male ones are from the Bible. Look here. We have Blossom, Hyacinth, Verbena, Lily, Iris, Rose Petal, Daisy, Gardenia, Azalia, Violet. And the men . . . Abraham, Jacob, Ezekiel, Cain and Abel . . . holy cow, *Cain and Abel?*"

"Those be Iris' twin boys."

Selene shook her head with amazement at a mother choosing those particular biblical names for her babies, and continued, "Isaiah, Moses, Noah, Matthew, Mark, Luke, John—"

"Yessirree," Blossom agreed with a smile. She had been kneading bread dough the entire time Selene was making her list and chatting with her. "Those be the slaves what come with the plantation when Master James bought it ten years ago. The old master just opened the Bible ever' time a new boy was borned, and the mistress had a sketch book of flowers from France what she used to name the girl babies. Didn't have to do much thinkin' that way."

Selene shook her head ruefully.

"Master James gave most of those slaves their freedom papers las' year, includin' me, but we's stayed on, all of us," Blossom declared proudly.

"Really?"

"Yessum, when he first come here ten years ago, Master James done tol' us if we works hard for him and don't cause no trouble, after five years he would give us a five-year indenture. Was 'bout twenty-seven of us las' year. Should be 'bout ten more after this harvest season, and every year to come."

"And do you get paid? I mean, I know James doesn't have much money."

"A bit," Blossom said, "but the menfolks gets to clear a piece of land for their own sugar crops and sell 'em along with the master's. It's more'n most of us have ever had."

"Well, that's . . . remarkable," Selene said. These policies didn't make James's being a slaveholder right, but he was redeemed somewhat in her eyes. Not that he needed or wanted her admiration. He'd made that clear when they'd parted this morning. Selene put that painful thought aside, not wanting to think about the powerful attraction that had almost resulted in their making love without thought for the consequences.

"And, believe you me, it don't sit too well with the other planters in Terrebonne Parish, or down the bayou, for that matter." Blossom patted the huge ball of dough with a final flourish and set it aside, wiping her floury hands on her long white apron. "Now, let's see what you gots on that chart of yours."

Within the hour, they had set up a daily schedule for inside the house. Taking one room at a time, the mansion would be given a thorough cleaning, from ceiling to floor. Wool carpets and heavy draperies would be taken outside, beaten clean, then wrapped in tobacco leaves until the winter as protection against moths. Clean rush mats would be laid over polished wood floors, and lighter lace curtains hung on the windows.

A thorough housecleaning would probably take at least a week, but Selene vowed the windows would sparkle, the furniture would gleam, and the interior of the house would be as clean as any human being could possibly make it. Then, using her mother's organizational skills, Selene drew up a daily schedule of duties to be performed on a regular basis. She assigned Iris to be the head housekeeper, Blossom the cook, of course, and Verbena the head laundress.

She was just beginning to realize how much work was involved in cooking and doing laundry by hand for more than one hundred people every day. A daunting task, but one she looked forward to with an odd relish.

Selene felt a sense of satisfaction as she laid the papers aside, knowing she would have full days ahead. But first she had a more important responsibility.

All day a nagging image kept flitting through her mind. It seemed to her that, when she and James had been inopportunely interrupted in their lovemaking that morning, one of the spectators at the door had been a small, filthy boy with black hair and pale blue eyes . . . one who hadn't obeyed his father's command to take a bath.

"Blossom, can you tell Iris to fill the tub upstairs and provide a bunch of clean towels and lots of soap?"

The cook nodded. "I thought you already took a bath this mornin'."

"I did. Now I'm going to bathe the brassiest brat on the bayou."

"Not Etienne!" Blossom looked at her incredulously.

"Exactly."

Blossom started laughing, a deep belly laugh, as Selene went off to find her victim.

The little shit was adorable . . .

Selene started her search on the fourth floor of the mansion in Etienne's large dormered bedroom. Upon opening the door, she immediately amended her schedule for organizing the household, deciding she would need more than one week to give the house its first complete cleaning. Etienne's room alone was going to require at least two days.

Abandoning her search for a moment, she began picking up his dirty clothing. She wished she were wearing gloves, unsure just what might crawl out of some of the pockets. Most of the threadbare apparel would have to be thrown out, or passed on to some of the slaves of smaller stature.

On the way back from her third trip to the laundry shed behind the house, carrying a pile of dirty clothing wrapped in an equally dirty sheet, Selene ran into Iris. The slave held a tray of coffee and cakes, along with a carafe of tafia, the locally brewed rum, toward the *garçonnière*. Obviously for Mrs. Baptiste. For the first time, Selene began to suspect that Mrs. Baptiste's melancholia might be related to alcohol.

"Iris, why hasn't Etienne's clothing been washed for such a long time . . . or his room cleaned?"

"'Cause the li'l master won't allow no one into his room."

"Won't allow? Won't allow?" Selene sputtered. "Criminey, the kid's only five years old."

"Hah! You won't be feelin' so brave the first time you find a snake in your bed—"

"He wouldn't dare!" *I'd better start locking my door.*

"—or that Dreadful dog of his sittin' on your face when you wake in the mornin'—"

"He wouldn't dare!" *That mutt is going to be put on a leash.*

"—or all your clothes gone when you step out of the bath . . . and a passin' stranger standing there awatchin', bug-eyed—"

"He wouldn't dare!" *Geez! And I've been leaving my clothes right next to the bathroom door . . . the unlocked bathroom door.*

"—or, worst of all, he gits that voodoo chicken of his to put a curse on you. Onct he made Bob peck me on the leg an' I broke out in the itchiest rash . . . jus' 'cause I tossed out a box of spiders he was savin'."

Spiders! Oh, Lord, give me strength.

"And Noah got boils on his private parts for refusin' to help the li'l master ride a bull."

Enough was enough! Selene made a clucking sound of disgust. "Really, Iris! Did it ever occur to you that Noah got the boils on his genitals because he put *it* into something he shouldn't have?"

Iris made a matching sound of disgust, casting her a scornful glance. "Noah is seven years old."

"Oh. Well, regardless, I was brought here to help control Etienne, and that's just what I'm going to do."

Iris rolled her beautiful brown eyes skeptically. Before

she went off with her carefully balanced tray, she reminded Selene, "Don't be forgettin' about my . . . what you call it? . . . tush. And did I tell you, I gots another two folks what wants to come to your arrow-backs?" Iris made a short bob of a curtsy and went off to perform her duties.

Selene laughed, but Iris's warning took seed about the dirty tricks Etienne would undoubtedly employ. Snakes and spiders were not her cup of tea. Tapping her chin thoughtfully, Selene finally came up with an idea . . . an insurance policy, so to speak, against any forms of retaliation the little wretch might choose to throw her way. She went back to her room to obtain a few modern "good luck charms."

Then, smiling with satisfaction, Selene began to search every room in the four-story mansion, starting at the top where, in addition to Etienne's room, there was a nursery converted to a schoolroom. All the skins the brat had been drying there were removed, but the large room still smelled rank, so Selene opened the windows wider, leaning out to get some fresh air.

Sugarcane fields stretched for miles and miles in the distance, divided into neat rectangular plots of about forty acres each. A road, fifty feet wide, ran through the center of the fields, with deep irrigation ditches on each side. Other, narrower roads, also with the drainage trenches, ran parallel and perpendicular, every twenty-five feet or so, all of them crisscrossing the crops.

The red and green cane . . . ribbon cane, it was called . . . rose only about a foot tall, having been planted only a few months ago. James had told her they wouldn't harvest the cane until October. Actually, the grinding season, *roullaison,* the most grueling and yet merriest of times on a sugar plantation, would last two to three months once it started.

Selene could see the monumental effort it would take to make such a vast enterprise prosper, and she had to admire James's efforts to succeed. Was he out there now, working alongside the slaves and free workers?

All day Selene had pushed aside thoughts of James and

his lovemaking that morning. It had been spontaneous, explosive, and wonderful. Even now, Selene's lips felt full, kiss-swollen. She touched them softly with the tips of her fingers, savoring the memory of his lips on hers. Her breasts still ached with erotic fullness.

What would it be like to really make love with him? If this heavy petting was so incredible, what might the real thing be like? Selene raised her chin with wounded pride, knowing she would never find out. James was right. They had no future. And an affair would just make their parting all the harder.

Well, at least she could help make his job easier by getting his house in order. And his son.

Selene grimaced at that last thought and pushed away from the window. She searched through the empty servants' rooms that occupied the rest of the fourth floor, then the bedrooms and bathroom on the third floor. She noticed that the tub was already full, and clean towels, as well as clothing were laid out. The only thing missing was Etienne.

After leaving the house, she walked down the wide street that ran through the double rows of slave cabins with their fenced-in vegetable plots where chickens and an occasional pig wandered about. Reba had told her that James allowed his workers to sell their excess products to the *caboteurs*, the grocery boats that came by on occasion. Nursing mothers nodded at her from their doorways, along with elderly women knitting socks and a few infirm gentlemen rocking in their front-porch chairs.

After passing through the neglected orchard with its many fruit and nut trees, Selene finally found the missing brat up in a grape arbor. He was throwing grapes, one at a time, up in the air, and the mangy dog, aptly named Dreadful, was catching them in his mouth before they hit the ground.

Grapes! He's feeding a dog grapes. Even a city girl like me knows grapes can't be good for an animal. Can they?

The dog was yipping wildly at the game, and purple

slobber dripped in globs from his huge mouth. *A real Kodak moment.* Curling her nose with distaste, Selene walked casually up to the trellis, not wanting to warn Etienne of her intentions.

"Etienne, I found the strangest bug near the house," she lied silkily, pulling an empty handkerchief from her pocket, pretending to be intrigued by its contents. "The bug has red eyes and big pincers. Do you know what it is?"

He made a loud, raspberry noise with his mouth, ignoring her question.

She gritted her teeth, stifling an angry admonition. "That's all right if you don't know," she said in dulcet tones. "I just thought you knew a lot about bugs, and this one is *so-o-o* big. Oh, well . . ." Turning, she began to walk back toward the house.

A shuffling noise behind her alerted her to Etienne's descent from the arbor. But she kept walking.

"Oh, let me see the thing," he grumbled, obviously intrigued, coming up next to her. Geez, the child smelled as if he'd been wallowing in a manure pile.

"Aha!" she exclaimed, grabbing him by the waist and throwing him over her shoulder. He kicked and flailed and bit at her shoulder, calling her every colorful, foul name he could think of . . . and there were a lot of them . . . but she held on doggedly, rushing toward the house. The barking dog and a bunch of astonished black children who'd been playing nearby followed after her. Several times, Selene's grip slipped, but she managed to keep hold of the squirming whelp until she reached the bathing room. Setting him on the floor, she reached behind her, locked the door, then threw the key out the open window.

"You are going to take a bath," she said, advancing on him.

"Yer an ugly *salope* . . . a bitch . . . and I ain't gonna take a bath."

"Young man, you're getting one swipe of soap across your tongue for that bad word."

"Bitch, bitch, bitch, bitch, bitch, bitch," he shouted.

"That makes seven swipes, I think."

"If you touch me, you . . . you *maigrichon*, I'm gonna tell my papa."

"*Maigrichon?*"

"It means skinny bones."

"Thank you for teaching me so many French words, Etienne."

He snarled like a rabid dog.

Selene chucked him under the chin. "And, by the way, do tell your papa. I think he will thank me for giving you a bath."

"I'll tell him you tried to rape me."

Selene had to laugh at the boy's vivid imagination. "I doubt that you even know what that word means."

She saw the quick look of confusion on his face and knew her guess was right. In that moment of vulnerability, she attacked and wrestled the boy to the floor. Finally she had to straddle his stomach and hold his hands over his head, tearing his clothing off his body until he was naked. She stood and threw all his dirty clothing out the window, then held him to the floor once again.

"Now, Etienne, you can either get in the tub yourself and scrub your own body or I'll do it for you. Which will it be?"

He narrowed his blue eyes, miniature versions of his father's, and answered too quickly, "I'll take a bath myself. You can go away now."

"Nice try, kiddo. No way! I stay right here until you're spit clean and dressed in clean clothes."

He gave her his version of the evil eye, but when she didn't cower, his shoulders slumped with resignation. "Oh, all right. I'll do it, but no soap in the mouth," he bargained.

Selene agreed, but before she allowed him to get up off the floor and climb into the tub, she had to make sure he wouldn't be retaliating afterward. It was time for her insurance policy, her good luck charms.

"Etienne, we have to come to an understanding. There

will be no snakes or spiders or ghosts or voodoo curses or anything else done to me. Do you hear?"

He gazed up at her slyly, saying nothing but clearly already plotting his revenge.

"I know you're not going to do anything nasty to me, Etienne. And the reason is that I know more tricks than you do." With that, she dropped her hold on his hands, still sitting on his body, and popped her contact lenses out of her eyes, holding them out for him to see in her palms.

His devious little eyes grew wide with amazement. "You popped yer eyeballs out! And you changed their color!" he exclaimed.

Then Selene proceeded to pull off, one by one, each of the long fake fingernails she had glued on a short time ago.

"Are you a voodoo priestess, like my mama was?"

"No. No voodoo. I just have a few . . . powers that I have to use sometimes when little boys misbehave."

Etienne studied her eyes and then the long fingernails in her palms. He shuddered, as if considering the implications. "You musta put a curse on Papa. No wonder he was tryin' to put his pizzle in such an ugly wench as you."

Selene made a low snarling sound in her throat, but managed not to throttle the troll. "Well, I could put a curse on you, too, if you should somehow try to get back at me for making you take a bath. How do you think you would like to have your eyeballs pop out? Or your fingernails?"

His bottom lip quivered, but still he went on bravely, fighting tears. "I could tell my papa. He hates voodoo. *Oui*, he does."

"Oh, I think this will be our little secret," she said with a smooth voice, its underlying threat loud and clear. She put the contact lenses in a plastic case in her pocket, then examined her fingernails in a bored fashion, still pinning the child to the floor. "I'm rather good at popping toenails, too," she bragged unabashedly. "Once I even made a man's . . . pizzle fall off."

Selene almost choked on that last outrageous claim. She

should feel ashamed of lying to the child, scaring him so, but she didn't. Extreme measures were called for if she was going to get the spoiled brat to toe the line.

Finally Etienne agreed to her terms, also promising not to tell anyone of her "magic." Selene stood, releasing the scamp. His cute little buns were the last thing she saw as he sunk all the way under the water, then came up with a curse. "The water is bloody damn cold."

Then he looked her in the eye in a calculating fashion and deliberately farted in the water.

I'm going to kill him.

Blinking with wide-eyed innocence, he said with awesome politeness, "*Pardonnez-moi.*"

Selene had won a minor skirmish with the imp. But, obviously, the battle was far from over.

She sat down on a stool and propped her elbows on her knees, chin in hands. "Etienne, your name is an awfully big mouthful for such a little boy," she remarked idly as she watched him bathe. "Don't you have a nickname?"

"*Non,*" he replied, soaping his body with gusto, ducking under the water repeatedly, sloshing water carelessly over the side of the tub. Now that he was in the tub, he was having a grand time with the bath. Too bad she didn't have a Rubber Duckie to give him, she thought with a chuckle. "Besides, there is no nickname for Etienne. Everyone knows that. What did you expect, Et?" he sneered.

Selene smiled at his quick wit. "No, but maybe E.T. Yeah, that would be great. Just like the alien, E.T."

"What's an alien?"

"A being from another planet." Selene bit her tongue, knowing James would not like her speaking of her world, let alone another world. She proceeded carefully. "Where I come from, there's this wonderful . . . story about a creature who comes to earth." She relayed to Etienne in capsule form the story line from the famous movie, pleased at the fascination that gripped the small child. When she finished, he asked if she would tell the story again.

"Later. Right now, I want you to get out of the tub so that I can cut your hair."

"*Non!*" he protested. Then his eyes fixed on hers, probably fearing she would pop some more eyeballs, or maybe a nose or tongue this time. Grumbling, he climbed out of the tub and began to dry his body with the towels. "So that'll be my nickname then. E.T."

"Okay."

A short time later, Selene stood back, admiring the new Etienne. His black hair fell barely to the collar of his shabby but clean shirt, accenting his sparkling clean face. His pale blue eyes were shaded by magnificent ebony lashes, almost feminine in their thickness.

"Oh, Etienne . . . I mean E.T., you are beautiful."

"Beautiful? Beautiful?" he shrieked with outrage. "Where's a mirror? *Mon Dieu!* If you made me beautiful, I'm gonna get back at you, I swear I am. I don't care if you do pop my pizzle. Beautiful! Oh, shit!"

Aliens 'r Us . . .

It was past five o'clock when James sent the slaves and other workers back to their quarters for the day. They'd been laboring since six that morning. Other plantation owners worked their slaves from dawn to dusk, but he felt guilty keeping them out in the grueling sun this long. There was just so much work to be done.

He would like nothing better now than a bath and dinner. Then he would have to check over the repairs on the sugar boilers, see to the mare that Ezekiel had told him was about to foal, try to coax his mother out of her rooms, talk with Rufus about the yard work he'd asked him to start today . . .

Sacre bleu, his responsibilities never ended. But he wasn't unhappy. There was a satisfaction in working hard and seeing some tangible results at the end of the day.

"When will dinner be ready?" he asked Blossom when he entered the kitchen. She smacked his hand away when he picked a freshly peeled crayfish off a plate she was about to dump in a stew kettle on the *potager*. His stomach growled at the wonderful aroma, and he popped the raw shellfish hungrily into his mouth, noting that the kitchen table had not yet been set. That was where he and Etienne had been eating whenever his mother was "indisposed."

"Mam'zelle Selene says you all should be eatin' in the dining room, like civilized folks. I asked Fergus and Reba if they wants to come for dinner, too." She grinned with some secret knowledge at that last bit about Reba and Fergus. He was too tired to inquire further.

"Where's Etienne?"

Blossom chuckled and rolled her eyes in one of those "You don't really want to know" ways she had.

"What's he done now?"

"He ain't done nothin' . . . leastways, nothin' I knows about. He's takin' a bath."

"A bath?" James repeated dumbly.

"Yup. Miz Selene is givin' him a bath. Di'nt you hear the screamin' out there in the fields?"

"No." He filched another piece of crayfish before Blossom could swat him with her cane. Leaning against the wall lazily, he asked, "Who was screaming? Etienne or Selene?"

"Both, I reckon. Oh, Lordy, what a day this has been. You seen Reba yet?"

"No. Why?" he asked suspiciously.

"I reckon you won't believe it. Nosirree, you won't believe your own eyes when you see her."

When Blossom refused to tell him more, turning back to her food preparations, he started up the back stairs, deciding to see for himself what all the fuss was about. Just outside the bathing-chamber door, he heard Etienne exclaim, "Oh, shit!" James gritted his teeth. Something would have to be done about the boy's coarse tongue.

Trying the door, he realized it was locked. "Etienne? Selene? What's going on in there?"

There was a long silence before Etienne replied sweetly, "I just took a bath, Papa. Like you tol' me."

"Why is the door locked?"

Another long silence.

"I threw the key out the window," Selene said finally, with no explanation offered.

He turned around with a grunt of disgust and walked down two flights of stairs, then outside to find the key. He returned and unlocked the door. At his first sight of the room, and of Etienne and Selene, he jerked back with shock.

The bathing room was a shambles. A black scum covered the top of the water in the tub, which was still half full. The other half of the tub water was on the floor . . . and the walls . . . and Selene.

Both Etienne and Selene had had haircuts. Etienne's was drying nicely about his face . . . his recently scrubbed face. But Selene's hair was plastered wetly about her head, looking as if she had been in a dog fight. She probably had . . . but the dog was Etienne. And at this point she looked as much like a dog as that Dreadful animal who'd followed him up the stairs and was whining behind him in the hallway, wanting to enter the room.

Black hair was scattered about the room—on the washstand, on the lamp, floating on top of the tub water.

"I wuz just about to clean up here, Papa. Would you like me to draw some bathwater for you when I'm done?" Etienne asked with sweet consideration.

Selene gaped at James's son as if he'd just popped one of his eyeballs, which was, of course, her trick, not his.

"Well, that would be nice," James replied, beginning to think that Etienne's misbehavior of late had perhaps been exaggerated by Blossom. "And, by the way, you are looking very handsome."

Etienne cast Selene a knowing look. "Handsome, yes. Beautiful, no," he told her haughtily. Then he looked back at him, "But my name is E.T. now, Papa. Not Etienne. It's my nickname."

"Huh?"

"E.T. is a creature from another world, Papa."

James shot Selene a condemning look. Had she been speaking of the future and time-travel with his son, against his orders?

"It's just a story, Papa. Like a fairy tale. And E.T. was this person . . . who was not really a person . . . he was a . . . ?" Etienne looked up at Selene questioningly.

"An alien," Selene said on a soft moan, probably realizing that he would not be happy with her. "E.T. was an alien from another world."

He looked back at Etienne, who was gazing up at him with such enthusiasm that he found it difficult to dash his dreams. "Well, then, I guess your new name will have to be E.T. *for now.*"

His son flashed a dazzling smile of adoration at him, and he reached out his arms for him, swinging him high in the air, then into his embrace. That small move on his part gave the dog an opportunity to squeeze past him into the bathing room, where he made a flying leap for the bathtub. Water flew in a million directions, drenching Etienne, Selene, James, and everything else in the room.

Selene stared at him for a moment, stunned, while dirty water ran in rivulets down her face, dripping from her chin. Then she started to laugh, gasping out, "Oh, Lord, I think I'm the alien here. And I've landed in another world, all right."

James laughed, too, pulling her against his side in a three-way embrace with Etienne. Yes, she was an "alien," that was for sure, and he didn't know how he was ever going to let her return to her "world."

Well, that wouldn't be his concern much longer. Selene would be leaving Bayou Noir within the week.

Selene had troubled his spirits the entire day. In the end, he'd been forced to take drastic measures. If a tooth aches, you tear it out. If the temptation grows, you remove its source.

Just before he'd left the fields, he'd sent a note to a neighboring planter. The plan for banishing Selene was already in motion.

His motives were pure. His conscience was not.

How would he tell the wench she could no longer stay at Bayou Noir?

For one insane moment, as he continued to embrace her and his son, he almost wished he could be her blasted "Rhett."

Chapter Eleven

In the end, Rhett was just a rat, after all . . .

"And the aliens have big heads with bi-i-i-g eyes and little bodies," Etienne related with enthusiastic gestures at the dinner table for Fergus and Reba's benefit. Once, he almost knocked over the huge epergne in the center of the table, a tiered centerpiece with ten separate crystal vases dripping fresh gardenias. James hated the monstrosity. Giselle had loved it.

Turning back to Etienne, he smiled with bemusement while his son repeated Selene's story about a creature who'd come to earth from another world. He'd already told him the tale three times, embellished a bit more in each retelling.

Fergus and Reba listened politely, but they really had eyes only for each other. *Sacre bleu!* They behaved like newly-weds, unable to stop touching each other.

Fergus kept gaping like a lovesick cow at his wife's remarkable change in appearance . . . a "makeover," Selene had called it. *Merde*, he'd like to show her a makeover.

Reba's hair, which had always lain rather limply down

her back, now fluffed out about her face like silky strands
of pale wheat. Her surprisingly lovely eyes looked bigger
and her lips appeared fuller. She was beautiful. Amazing!

He slanted a quick, suspicious look at Selene, who probably had had something to do with this magical transforma-
tion. She avoided his eyes, as well she should. He'd warned
her about any more magic tricks. He bit his bottom lip to
stifle an admonition, though. After all, he would have to put
up with her antics only a short time longer, now that his
plans were set in motion.

"And did you know, Papa, that the earth is a planet?"

"Huh?" James's attention was called back to his son. "A
plant? I don't think so, son."

"Not a plant, Papa." Etienne slapped his knee with a
childish squeal of laughter. "A plan-et. And there are lots of
planets in the sky. And nobody knows for sure if there are
people on these other planets, like E.T., but I think there
are. Don't you, Papa? Don't you?"

James listened indulgently to his son's excited chatter,
but his eyes kept coming back to Selene, who sat quietly
contemplating the bowl of soup Hyacinth had set before
her. Selene probably feared his wrath over her stories of
another world. Etienne, with his running tongue, would
have rumors flying up and down the bayou within days.

"Don't you care for your soup, Selene?" he asked. "Blossom prides herself on her crayfish gumbo."

"What? Oh, no, the soup is delicious." She took several
more sips from her spoon. Dainty sips through slightly
parted lips. And James remembered how those lips had
felt against his, parting for his, under his, above his. A
yearning—so intense he could barely contain it—overcame
him. He wanted more than anything to take her hand and
lead her up the stairs.

If she belonged to him . . . if he were free to take another
woman into his life . . . if he had met her long ago, before
Giselle . . . *If! If! If!*, he chastised himself. *This dreaming
has to stop. Truly, the woman must have placed a spell on*

me. Perhaps she is involved in voodoo, after all. Thank the Lord, she will be gone soon.

"Why are you looking at Selene's mouth?" Etienne asked. "Did she dribble soup on her chin?"

Selene ducked her head with embarrassment and dabbed at her chin with a table linen.

James laughed. Leave it to his son to bring him back to reality with a jolt. "No, E.T., she did not dribble. I was just watching to see that she eats her soup, like a good girl. She must keep up her strength if she is to do a good job teaching you." *Even if it's only for a few days.* He winked at Selene and was pleased at her quick blush. "And you must show your new teacher more respect. She is Mademoiselle Selene to you."

Etienne took several noisy slurps of his soup before narrowing his eyes craftily. "Is it respectful for a teacher to use the word pizzle, Papa?"

All four adults at the table gasped, looking at Etienne with horror.

The scamp blinked back at them with the innocence of a fox caught in the henhouse.

"Exactly what do you mean by that outrageous remark?" James asked, throwing his napkin to the table.

"What outrageous word? Oh. Pizzle." He waved his hand loftily. "I think *Mam'zelle* Selene said somethin' today about voodoo curses and makin' my pizzle fall off."

"Why, you little brat," Selene exclaimed, starting to stand. She looked as if she might leap over the table and throttle his son. Frankly, the prospect appealed to him, too. Still, he placed a restraining hand on her arm.

She calmed herself down with visible effort, digging her nails into her palms. Soon she was sending dagger looks at Etienne, with her elbows propped on the table, her cupped hands holding up her defiant chin. Etienne flushed and shifted uncomfortably, seeming to realize belatedly the extent of Selene's seething anger.

"Would you care to change your mind about what you

just said, E.T.?" Selene asked with exaggerated sweetness. She made her eyes go extra wide with question, and the scamp's eyes looked as if they might just pop out with fright.

"Well, maybe it wasn't Selene . . . Mam'zelle Selene, I mean," Etienne stammered out, gulping. His eyes darted guiltily, looking everywhere but at Selene. "*Oui*, I think it was Cain . . . or maybe it was Abel who said that word. And I told 'em it was a bad word, just like you told me, Papa."

Two small voices gasped with outrage from the corner. Cain and Abel were pulling the cords of the punkah, the maharajah-style fan that hung over the dining-room table to shoo away flies and provide a cool breeze. The twins glared indignantly at Etienne for his obvious lie.

James was developing a horrible headache.

And he still had to check on the mare, repair the extra boiler, and review the yard-work schedule with Rufus. Plus he really should disclose to Selene the plans he'd made for her departure.

"Hmmm. I think we can discuss this matter further away from the dinner table," Selene offered to Etienne in a conciliatory manner. "Perhaps in the morning when we begin your first lessons."

Etienne nodded enthusiastically, no doubt figuring he'd escaped her wrath. But then Selene added, "I wonder what subject we should study first." She tapped her fingertips on the table thoughtfully.

Etienne avoided her scrutiny, his eyes riveted with odd concentration on her short, blunt fingernails. Then his shoulders slumped with resignation. "Numbers. You're gonna make me do numbers, aintja?"

"Exactly."

Etienne made a rude, blowing sound of disgust with his tongue and asked to be excused, rushing off before James could correct him again. Fergus and Reba left, as well, and James didn't have the heart to remind Fergus that he was supposed to meet him in the barn later. Somehow he didn't think he'd be seeing Fergus again tonight.

Selene stood, too, about to help Hyacinth clear the table. "Wait. I need to talk to you a moment."

She swerved suddenly and her newly cut hair swirled about her shoulders in a cascade of brown silk waves. It was still long and very curly, despite her haircut. He couldn't help picturing it spread out on his pillow, framing the clear skin of her face, staring up at him expectantly, surrendering to him, demanding his surrender in return. . . . *Merde! My brain is melting.*

"James, don't."

"What?" So lost had he been in his fantasy that he hadn't realized she'd moved back to the table and was proceeding to sit back down next to him. He felt confused and disoriented. "Don't . . . what?"

"Don't look at me like that. It's hard enough for me to resist you without you . . ." She let her words trail off.

She has trouble resisting me? I am lost. "How was I looking at you, Selene?" he asked softly. Then, shrugging with resignation, he allowed his pent-up passions to spill out, like dammed-up water through a broken levee. "Like I want to run my fingers through your hair to see if it feels as silky as it looks?" He reached out a hand and tugged on one curl near the curve of her neck, rubbing it between his thumb and forefinger.

He felt her pulse jump against the back of his knuckles. His pulse jumped, too, in a not-so-obvious place.

"Or was I looking at your smooth skin, wondering how it would taste . . . all over?"

She made a small whimpering sound deep in her throat, but didn't pull away when his fingertips grazed her jaw, slowly, from ear to ear. He felt like whimpering, too, from the sweet pain of arousal building between his thighs.

"Or was I looking at your mouth like a starving man," he continued recklessly, "wondering if you could give me the succor I crave?" The pad of his thumb skimmed her lower lip, which trembled deliciously.

"Oh, James," she moaned helplessly, and parted her lips, anticipating his kiss.

He leaned closer.

Selene's heart leapt in her breast at the smoldering desire revealed in James's beautiful eyes. Lord, how she loved the man! Could he see it in her face? She laid a hand over his. "Oh, sweetheart, is this what you wanted to talk to me about? Have you thought of a way for us to be together?"

"What?" He pulled his hand out from under hers as if burned and shook his head to clear it. Standing abruptly, he knocked his chair to the floor and began to pace, raking his fingers distractedly through his hair. Casting her a look of horror, he exclaimed, "What have you done to me?"

James's harsh tone was a splash of cold water on her flaming emotions. "Me? What have I done to you?" Selene was not pleased by James's sudden change of mood. How could he look at her with such yearning in one moment and loathing the next? "How about what you're doing to me? Damn, I'm sick of these roller-coaster mood swings of yours."

"You made this rollercoaster, *chérie* . . . whatever the hell a rollercoaster is."

She growled with frustration, searching for the right words to tell him just how she felt. "A few moments ago I was leaving this room. You're the one who asked me to stay. You're the one who said you had something to tell me. Hah! All you want to do is seduce me with your sexy words, and then when you set my blood to boiling, you turn off the heat."

"Zut alors!"

"You're a tease, James . . . a male tease . . . that's what you are."

Speechless at her accusation, he gaped at her in amazement for several seconds, then turned to brace his arms against the frame of a tall window overlooking the side yard. In the distance could be heard the mating call of a loon and the chirping of crickets as the swamp lands bedded down for the night. Still, James said nothing, just stared out, sightlessly, looking frustrated and miserable. *Good!*

Finally he pushed away from the window and walked back to her with resolution. "Selene, listen to me—"

"No, you listen to me. This morning you kissed me till my bones melted, practically made love to me on the floor . . . *on the floor, damn you.*" She inhaled deeply, continuing, "Then you turned around, big as you please, and said you didn't want to have anything to do with me."

"That's not quite how it happened, *chérie*," he said, stepping closer to the table.

She stood warily and backed around the other side, away from him.

He continued talking while he stalked her. "The way I remember the event is that *you* kissed me till *my* bones melted, wrestled me to the floor, made me come in my trousers . . . and, *oui*, I used the word 'come.' Then you *agreed* with me that we have no future together."

"That's what I said, you fool."

"You did?"

"Of course." She crinkled her nose at him. "Maybe you've been inhaling too much of your own sugar lately, because it sure appears as if you've got cotton candy between your ears."

"I don't understand one word of what you said."

"Well, fiddle-dee-dee!" Selene exclaimed and then winced. "I can't believe I just said that. I'm turning into a blooming Scarlett O'Hara."

"Really, Selene! There is a reason why I wanted to talk to you now. I just got distracted." He rubbed a hand wearily across his forehead.

A wave of foreboding rippled across Selene's skin. She had a feeling she wouldn't like what he had to say.

"I've invited the Collins to visit on Sunday." He looked at her expectantly.

Selene failed to understand the relevance of that bit of

information or the significance of his nervously flexing fingers as he spoke. "Who the hell are the Collins?"

He winced at her swear word. "The Collins—Andrew and his wife, Ellen—own a sugar plantation about an hour down the bayou. They're coming because . . . because I sent them a note telling them about you. Andrew and Ellen have two young children who are in need of a governess—"

"You didn't!" she accused, suddenly understanding. She looked at him through misty, wounded eyes. "Please say you didn't."

"—and I think it would be best if you left Bayou Noir and went to work for them." He lowered his eyes guiltily and added weakly, "After all, you will probably be returning to your own time soon."

"When did you send them a message, you bastard? And how could you make such an important decision about my life without consulting me?"

"You don't have to go with the Collins if you don't like them. There are other planters—"

"And what if they don't want me, James? The Collins or the other planters? Geez, I don't believe you!"

"Be reasonable, *chérie*—"

"Reasonable! Just what am I to you? A piece of meat? A commodity like one of your slaves to be put up for bid?"

His head jerked up as if she'd slapped him. She'd like to. Oh, Lord, she'd like to slap the man silly. Shake some sense into his stubborn head.

"You deliberately misunderstand me. I'm only trying to do what's best for you . . . for both of us."

"That's not the point. How dare you go behind my back and try to get rid of me? Do you hate me so much, James?" she asked on a small sob.

"No. I don't hate you at all," he said, groaning. "Surely you know that. Selene, even now I have work waiting for me. Piles of work. Enough work for twenty men—"

"I could help. Really, we could work together."

He ignored her offer. "I can't think about anything but you. You distract me."

"Then you do care for me," she asserted, suddenly hopeful, about to tell him of her newly discovered love.

"Lust, Selene. Pure lust. Make no mistake about that." He raised his stubborn chin, his eyes flashing defiantly. "The drive to mate is a powerful one, and women have been using this weakness to manipulate men since the Garden of Eden."

She inhaled sharply at his insult.

"You make me want things that can never, *never*, be. Two people from two different times—impossible! The only way for me to go on about my business in a rational way is to cut you out of my life."

"You bastard!" She wiped angrily at her eyes.

"You said that before. And your coarseness is becoming redundant." Then he seemed to look at her more closely. "Oh, Selene, don't cry," he said, reaching out a hand to comfort her. "*Mon Dieu!* I have handled this situation badly. All I'm trying to do is make things better for us both. Truly, I never meant to hurt you, *chérie.*"

She slapped his hand away. "Don't . . . touch . . . me," she said evenly. "Don't ever touch me again. I'll be ready to leave here on Sunday, you can be sure of that. In the meantime, I'll do the job you hired me to do. Just stay out of my way. Do you hear me? Stay . . . out . . . of . . . my . . . way."

She spun on her heels and started for the door.

"It's for the best, Selene," he called after her. "You'll see that when you have a chance to think more clearly. We'll talk again when you can see things more rationally. Remember, *chérie*. Remember what that crimson lady said—"

"Huh?" Then understanding dawned. "Not crimson, you dolt, Scarlett," she snapped over her shoulder.

"Ah, well, then, remember what Scarlett said. Tomorrow is another day."

Her step faltered but she didn't turn around. "Screw you, Rhett."

Dead man . . . uh, woman . . . walking . . .

Selene had to keep a tight rein on her unraveling despair. She couldn't break down yet. *He's getting rid of me.* First she had to go to the kitchen and discuss the next day's cleaning schedule with Blossom. *The bum.*

"Blossom, I want to get started early in the morning with the cleaning. About seven. Will you make sure the women are all here?" *My heart is breaking and he tells me, "Tomorrow is another day." The jerk!*

"Yessum," Blossom agreed and went on kneading bread dough, which she would set out in the spring cellar to rise through the night. Hyacinth and Lily were washing dishes in large basins. *I'll show him. He'll see what he's missing.*

"I need to give Etienne his first lessons tomorrow morning, too. Once I get the servants working, I should be able to leave."

"Leave?" Blossom looked up. "What's ailin' you, honey?"

"Nothing," she said, barely able to speak past the lump in her throat. *And I thought I loved him. Thank God I didn't tell him.*

"You look like the end of the world done come, chile. Now tell ol' Blossom what happened." She wiped her hands on her apron and pulled Selene down to the table, pouring her a cup of coffee.

"The Collins are coming on Sunday," she explained and started to choke on the scorching liquid.

"You're about to cry 'cause the Collins are comin' for a visit. Lordy, girl, we'll get the house cleaned up by then. Dontcha het yo'self up over such a triflin' matter."

"And James is sending me away with them." Her voice broke with emotion.

Blossom's mouth dropped open with surprise. Then she clamped it shut with a snap. "The master can't do that. You're his fi-an-cée."

A little hysterical giggle bubbled out of Selene's mouth.

"No, I'm not." *I'm Crimson O'Hara, and he's Rat Butler, and this is Tara-cum-Bedlam.*

"Honey, he told his father you're his fi-an-cée. And the master ain't never lied before."

"It was a trick. To keep his father and Victor from thinking I was a quadroon and taking me away."

Blossom frowned, stunned at that news. "And now he's gonna send you away? No, he's not. I'll have a talk with that boy. Yes, I will."

"No, Blossom, leave it be. This is the way James wants it, and . . . and he's probably right. It's for the best." *Oh, yeah, right. And tomorrow is another day.*

Blossom made a snorting sound of disgust, then looked up with concern when thunder rumbled in the distance. "Best you lock your doors t'night. The ghost always comes when there's a storm."

"The ghost? Great! James doesn't want me, and a ghost is on the prowl." Shaking her head, Selene went off to find Etienne and tuck him in for the night.

Surprisingly, he was in his bedroom, where he should be. He sat examining a jar of about fifty lightning bugs he'd collected in the yard.

Etienne took off his clothes down to his underdrawers and slipped into bed, yawning widely. Then he wriggled around a bit until he got comfortable.

"You gonna yell at me now, or give me a whippin', or"—he gulped loudly—"pop my eyeballs?"

"Not this time, Etienne. But tell me, why did you do such a mean thing to me at the dinner table?"

"'Cause I don't like you takin' over. My papa and me are in charge here. Not you."

"Oh, Etienne—"

"E.T.," he corrected her.

"E.T. then. I don't want to take anything away from you or your father. I just want to help. Your daddy has so much work to do running the plantation, and he's worried about you and his mother and the house. That's all."

Lightning cracked loudly close to the house, and Selene sat down on the bed next to him. "Are you afraid of storms, E.T.? I'll stay with you till you fall asleep if you are."

"Me? Afraid of storms? Hah! But the ghost'll prob'ly come t'night."

The ghost again. "Are you afraid of the ghost?"

He shook his head. "It never hurts me none. Just stands by my bed and looks at me. Then it goes away."

Holy cow!

"But it doesn't like Papa. Once it tried to set a fire in his room."

Selene gasped.

"And 'nother time it put a dead rooster in his bed."

James had once mentioned a dead rooster to Selene, hadn't he? And snake eggs.

"Even snake eggs in the soup Blossom made for him." He giggled at the remembrance. "*Merde!* Blossom was so-o-o mad. She said if she ever catches that ghost, she's gonna wring its neck. Blossom is so dumb. Everyone knows you can't kill a ghost," he said with a hoot of laughter.

Selene stifled a laugh herself. "Do you want me to tell you a story?"

"E.T. again?"

"I could retell that one, or I could tell you a ghost story. Oh, don't look at me with those wide eyes of yours. It's not a scary story. This one is about Casper, the Friendly Ghost."

By the time she'd finished one story about Casper and made up two more adventures for the Friendly Ghost, specially tailored to the bayou setting and a little boy with a big dog, Etienne's eyes were closing.

"I like your stories, Selene . . . Mam'zelle Selene."

She started to smile.

"I hate you, but I like your stories."

Well, one for one, Selene figured. "Does your father usually tuck you in at night, Etienne?"

"I'm not gonna answer you anymore if you don't use my nickname."

"Does your father usually tuck you in at night, *E.T.?*"

"Sometimes. When he's not too busy, or when he remembers."

Selene inhaled sharply at the hurt in the little boy's voice.

"Actually, I think he prob'ly comes up all the time, even after I fall asleep. One time I woke up and he was just sittin' by the bed watchin' over me. I liked that."

Her throat constricted. "Goodnight, E.T."

"G'night, Mam'zelle Selene."

A wave of self-satisfaction at his polite response swept over Selene. She must be making progress with the incorrigible child.

But then he added mischievously, "Hope the ghost don't getcha."

Later in her room, after Selene had removed her clothing and washed herself with a cloth and rose-scented soap in the china bowl, she slipped into a thin nightgown Iris had given her. It belonged to the older Mrs. Baptiste and was too short, but it would have to do.

She could hear the house settling down for the night. All the servants slept in the quarters, even the free ones, except for Blossom, who had a bedchamber off the kitchen on the ground floor.

Slipping into bed, Selene pulled the mosquito netting around her. Now that she had the privacy to break down and cry over James's devastating news, she couldn't do it. The more she thought about it, the angrier she got. It wasn't so much what James had done, but how.

Her heart told her James had dealt her a crushing blow by planning to send her away, but her mind recognized the logic of his actions. He knew she was going to return to her time, possibly any day now. And he had no time in his life for a new relationship, even if he hadn't been burned so badly by his wife, Giselle. Why start a relationship that couldn't go anywhere?

James was right.

But why did it feel so wrong?

Over and over, Selene pondered all that had happened to her since coming back in time, trying to find rational explanations for an irrational occurrence. She didn't think there was a scientific explanation, but she did believe in miracles. Perhaps God, or whatever Being existed up there, had a purpose in sending her back in time. Perhaps He wanted her to help James.

But how could she help James if she were no longer with him?

Or perhaps God felt it was she who needed saving. Maybe He'd seen the collision course her life was on, and He'd sent her here to learn a lesson about redirecting her life. And maybe James wasn't the one He wanted to do the redirecting.

That last thought made Selene feel even more miserable. For some reason, she wanted James to be "the one."

Between the coffee Blossom had given her and the voodoo drums that began softly after Selene had lain down, she couldn't sleep. For what seemed like hours she lay staring at the ceiling, listening to the steady beat-beat of the muted drums, and the rhythmic tapping of rain on the rooftop.

If she hadn't been awake, she wouldn't have seen the figure flit by the gallery outside her open bedroom doors. A figure clad from head to ankle in wispy material, not unlike the gauzy mosquito netting. A ghost?

No, Selene didn't believe in ghosts. She climbed out of bed and grabbed a poker near the cold fireplace, going out the door to the gallery. The ethereal figure had just turned the corner. Selene followed and saw it look both ways before it entered James's bedroom.

Suddenly she remembered Etienne's words about the ghost threatening James. With her exceptional night vision, Selene realized that the shining object in the hand of the "ghost" must be a knife.

Rushing forward with alarm, she entered James's bedroom. *Oh, my God! Please, don't let him be dead.* The "ghost" was raising the dagger above the heart of the sleeping body on the bed. Cackling in a demonic female voice, it shouted, "Die, James! Finally you shall die, *mon amour!*"

"No!" Selene screamed, dropping her poker and pulling on the arm of the "ghost," which was definitely not a ghost by the feel of the flesh under the gauzy veils. "No, I won't let you kill him!"

She struggled with the killer, and the knife grazed her bare arm from elbow to wrist. She cried out with pain but would not release the murderer until the knife clattered to the floor.

"You *salope!*" the woman exclaimed. "You bitch! For that, you will die, too."

"Selene! *Sacre bleu!* What are you doing here?"

Surprised, Selene looked over her shoulder to see James rush in from the hall, where he must have been hiding. Her eyes darted quickly between him and what was obviously rolled-up material under the bed sheets.

Her momentary surprise gave the killer an opportunity to slip out of her grasp and escape through the gallery door. James hesitated for a long moment. "Are you all right?"

When she nodded, he ran after the specter. He came back a short time later, alone, and glared at her as if she were to blame for the escape of his assassin. She probably was.

"What the hell are you doing here?" he asked icily, lighting an oil lamp. Rain dripped from his hair and plastered his shirt and trousers to his body from that short excursion into the storm.

"Saving your life, you ungrateful clod." But Selene couldn't be angry at James. He was alive. Thank God. The "ghost" hadn't killed him as she'd feared when she entered his room.

But she was wounded, she realized, almost in slow motion, as she felt a throbbing in her arm. A warm liquid— blood—was running down her arm to her fingertips and dripping to the carpet, like raindrops.

Finally a delayed reaction set in. A strange lassitude swept over her in waves, and Selene began to shiver violently, then slid to the floor.

James rushed forward, then dropped to his knees beside Selene. "Selene! *Mon Dieu!* You're bleeding."

Quickly he lifted her limp body in his arms and placed her in the center of his bed. Her skin, clearly visible from neck to toes through the transparency of her rain-wet gown, was ice cold. He pulled her soaking garment over her head and threw it to the floor, unaware of her nudity, his focus being on her safety. Taking some warm blankets from a chest at the foot of the bed, he wrapped her tightly, then brought a bowl and water to the bedside table, crooning to her unconscious body the entire time, "Do not worry, *chérie.* You will be fine. I will take care of you."

She awakened when he was almost done cleaning her wound, which, luckily, was not deep.

"You gave me a scare, *chérie,*" he said in a low, husky voice.

"So did you, James," she said softly, her eyes watching his every move as he wrapped a thin strip of linen around her forearm and tied the ends with a neat knot.

He leaned down and kissed her cheek lightly, pulling away almost immediately, fearful he would not be able to stop if he did more.

Her eyes widened with surprise and confusion. "I thought you were dead when I first came into the room. You were setting a trap for the 'ghost,' weren't you?" she stammered out, still shivering with shock.

He nodded. "This has been going on for the past year, though more frequently of late. I have posted guards about the house and grounds, but thus far the intruder has evaded my traps."

"But who is it? Surely, not a ghost."

"Giselle."

Selene gasped. "Your wife? I thought she was dead."

"She is. It's someone pretending to be Giselle."

"Victor . . . it's Victor who's behind this, isn't it?"

He shrugged with uncertainty. "Probably."

"Why does he want you dead? What does he have to gain?"

"Victor doesn't need a motive for killing. He hates me. Always has. But he also fears that my father may leave me something in his will when he dies. As if I want anything from the bastard!"

"But, James," she wailed, "you could have been killed tonight."

"And you, as well." He clenched his jaw tightly. "That was very foolish of you, attacking a dangerous murderer like that." He stood and studied her, trying to understand why she would risk her life for him.

Selene inched herself off the bed and stood shakily.

"Perhaps you should stay here tonight," he offered tentatively.

She tilted her head questioningly. "Have you changed your mind? Have you decided not to send me away?"

He tried not to think. He tried to follow his impulse, which was to gather her in his arms and throw all caution to the wind. Tomorrow. He could worry about the consequences then—how he would feel when she returned to her time, what his life would be like without her, how thoughts of her kept distracting him from his responsibilities.

But, no, he had almost lost the plantation during the bad times with Giselle, before and after her death. He would not risk it again. Too many lives depended on his total commitment. Besides, Selene might not be safe here now. More guards would have to be posted immediately.

Bleakly he shook his head. "You must go."

"I love you, James. Surely you know that."

His heart lurched against his chest walls. *No. Don't say the words. If you don't say them, they don't exist.*

His thoughts must have shown on his face, because her

shoulders slumped with resignation. He knew she'd wanted him to tell her he loved her in return, but he couldn't. He didn't. Oh, blessed Lord, he couldn't.

Selene lifted her chin with wounded pride and was about to turn toward the gallery doors. "I feel sorry for you, James. Everyone . . . *everyone* . . . needs to love and be loved. Love is like breathing to the soul. Without love, you are dead inside."

Still, he couldn't bring himself to speak. If he uttered a word, he feared what thoughts would spill out, what secrets of the heart he might reveal. He turned his back on her, biting his bottom lip.

"You don't even care, do you?" she said on a soft sob.

"I care," he whispered in a low, raw voice. "God forgive me, but I care too much." He turned.

But Selene was already gone.

Chapter Twelve

They were arrows, but not the weapon kind...

The first thing Selene saw the next morning when she entered the kitchen was Blossom grabbing Etienne by the ear. "Look, look at what that dog done to my clean kitchen. Purple dog biz'ness everywhere."

The grapes, Selene thought with a giggle.

Etienne's blue eyes widened with sudden understanding. Amazed and somewhat impressed, he looked down at Dreadful sprawled in the corner like a rug, huge head resting mournfully on its front paws. Dreadful whimpered a dog hello to Etienne, sort of under his breath. Both of them were treading a thin line with Blossom, whose cane stood propped against the wall, within arm's reach.

"You're gonna clean up this mess yo'self, boy. No, no, no. Don'tcha flutter them big lashes at me. I toldja not to bring that beast into the house. What you been feedin' him anyway?"

"It wasn't me, Blossom. I swear."

"Don't lie to me, boy. Din't you come into the house yesterday with a mouthful of purple grapes?"

Etienne began to argue with Blossom, his hands braced on his thin hips. With a chuckle, Selene decided to bypass the kitchen and went to the outside privy—not one of the more pleasant aspects of living in the nineteenth century.

On the way back, she had to dodge Bob, the wildly clucking, three-legged voodoo chicken, which still managed to escape the meat cleaver. Bob had a tendency to peck the ankles of anyone—human or animal—who came within ten feet of his self-proclaimed territory, usually the periphery of the outhouse.

When she returned to the kitchen, Etienne and Dreadful were both gone, along with the dog's mess. Blossom was still muttering under her breath, something about dogs and little boys being the death of her.

"So you saw the ghost last night," Blossom commented idly, handing Selene a cup of strong chicory coffee.

"James told you?" she asked with surprise.

Blossom nodded, looking pointedly at the scratch on Selene's arm. "Don'tcha be worryin' none 'bout the master, though. He kin take care of hisself." She smiled at Selene and patted her shoulder. "Especially with you here to save his stubborn hide," she added. "He tol' me how you rushed in and attacked the ghost."

"Impressed was he, huh?" Selene asked, suddenly hopeful.

Blossom cast her a knowing glance. "More like amazed."

Selene's shoulders slumped.

"But 'amazed' is good, too," she comforted her. "Don'tcha be frettin' over the master sendin' you away. I'm gonna get you a love potion from one of the swamp women. Like a dead duck he'll be, jist right for the pluckin'. The master won't be able to resist you then."

Selene wasn't so sure. And voodoo? Criminey! But the idea of "plucking" James, now that was a thought fraught with possibilities.

After breakfast, Selene and her cleaning crew assembled in the front parlor. Iris had brought with her Hyacinth of the big breasts, Lily of the nonexistent breasts, and Rose Petal with the big feet. Plus a half dozen other chattering girls and women who soon told her of their problems, which they somehow expected her to cure. Everything from zits to buck teeth to excessive facial hair.

Selene would have laughed if she wasn't so miserable. She was lost in the nineteenth century with the only man she'd ever truly loved, and he intended to send her away. If she stopped to really think about all her problems, she'd probably start to cry and never stop. Work . . . that was the key to getting through the next few days, she decided.

First she had the younger boys drag the heavy wool carpets—priceless Aubussons and Tabrizes, not to mention some fine, vintage hooked rugs with unique local designs—out to the clotheslines in the backyard where they beat them with wire whisks. The weighty velvet and damask draperies followed suit, leaving a trail of dust bunnies in their wake.

The boys, joined by Etienne and the twins, treated the chore as a game. They were soon laughing and teasing each other, like youngsters anywhere, anytime.

Two slave girls of about ten clapped their hands with delight to be given the less arduous job of polishing all the silver. Selene set them up on the side loggia, or gallery, off the dining room. Perched on a long bench with lyre carvings on the back and arms, they giggled with delight when she pulled a work table up in front of them. Armed with several basins of water, polishing cloths, homemade silver cream and piles of Sheffield flatware, coffee and tea services, and various dishes and vases, the girls would, no doubt, be kept busy the entire day.

When Selene placed two glasses of lukewarm lemonade in front of them, they gaped at her with adoration as if she'd handed them the moon.

The first and second parlors were separated by sliding wood doors that could be opened to create one large room occupying a whole side of the house. Selene and her work crew pushed all the furniture out of these rooms. Starting from the ceilings with their carved plaster moldings and center medallions, they dusted and scrubbed. Patterns began to show through on faded wallpaper. Woodwork looked brighter. The tall, floor-to-ceiling windows literally sparkled from Blossom's vinegar cleaning solution.

They carried bucket after bucket of water in from the well, and dumped as many dirty buckets off the gallery. Some of the water bounced off the flourishing plant life, which was being trimmed by the new slave, Rufus, an extremely tall, very handsome man with coffee-colored skin.

Selene noticed that Iris made a point of being the one to dump the buckets, using the opportunity to bat her wonderfully full eyelashes at Rufus. And Rufus, eyes twinkling with appreciation, was not complaining. Once, the poor man almost raked the porch rail with his hoe, so transfixed was he by the sight of Iris's huge behind swaying away from him—one buttock going up while the other went down, up and down, the rhythm a sensual invitation. All the while, Iris flashed him a little secret smile.

Maybe Selene could learn a few tricks from her. If she were more sexy, James wouldn't be able to resist her. He would be so mad with desire for her, he'd give in and keep her at his side forever.

Forever? That was the rub, Selene realized immediately. There could be no forever for them.

Still, she should be the one who decided whether to go away or to stay. The more she thought about it, Selene did not like the idea of being cast aside by James, as if she had no worth.

Raising her chin, she determined that she was going to make the insufferable man sorry. Using all the wiles at her disposal, she would make him pant after her, just like Rufus did for Iris. James would beg her to stay. Then she would thumb her nose at him.

She smiled with anticipation, thankful to finally have a plan.

After scrubbing and waxing the wood floors, they took a break for lunch, eating together companionably in the kitchen with Blossom. Reba joined them, her hair having been scrunched up rather nicely. Selene couldn't help but notice the pinkness of her cheeks, caused not by rouge but by the abrasiveness of a man's whiskers. And the crushed rose petal color of her lips could only be the result of her husband's heated kisses. A lot of her husband's heated kisses.

The quiet glow of Reba's bright blue eyes and the womanly, knowing carriage of her slim body told volumes about the kind of night she had spent. Selene couldn't remember ever feeling so well loved by a man.

"Thank you," Reba mouthed silently to Selene.

Perhaps Selene should be taking lessons from Reba, as well. Or perhaps she should start listening to her own advice.

"We gonna do them arrow-backs today?" Iris asked, after having taken a tray to Mrs. Baptiste, along with her usual ration of tafia. Selene wondered if James's mother got herself crocked before noon each day, convinced now that alcohol was her real problem, not depression. Maybe today she would get to meet the mysterious recluse.

"If you'd like," Selene said, picking at the cold chicken and greens on her plate, her massive appetite having finally settled down. "Can you women come up with some pants to wear . . . something that would let you have free body movement during our aerobics?"

"Trousers?" Hyacinth asked, her huge eyes going huger. "You wants us to wear men's trousers?"

"Well, just for the exercise program."

"I s'pose Verbena could find some for us in the laundry," she said dubiously.

"And we need music," Selene said, trying to get into the mood for this exercise thing. "Maybe we could sing. I don't suppose you ladies know any songs with a good beat."

They all gawked at her.

"You know, like 'Give me that old time rock 'n roll,' " she crooned, snapping her fingers in cadence to the song.

"Rocking roll?" Iris asked. "What's that?"

"Never mind. Just repeat the song after me."

They did, several times, until they got at least a few lines down pat.

Wracking her brain for songs that would be suitable for aerobics, Selene launched into, "Jeremiah was a bullfrog." She was snapping her fingers and bopping in her chair the whole time.

Two of the women exchanged looks with each other that clearly questioned her sanity. But Hyacinth's mammoth breasts were bobbing up and down as she got into the swing of the music's rhythm, clapping in counterpoint to Selene's snapping. And Rose Petal's shoebox-size feet marked time on the stone floor to the boogie beat.

She thought about teaching them the Trace Adkins' song "Honky Tonk Badonkadonk," but didn't want to offend Iris since revolved around women's behinds.

"Of course, there's always 'Achy Breaky Heart.'"

Iris smiled widely. "I likes the sound of that one."

When Selene got to the part of the Billy Ray Cyrus song with the "whoo-whoo" refrain like a train whistle, she knew she'd found their hallmark aerobics exercise song.

A short time later, the women practically line danced from the kitchen to the second parlor. Snaking along in their ill-fitting homespun trousers and work shirts with rolled-up sleeves and knotted-at-the-waist tails, they sang in tandem better than any Nashville back-up group.

Soon they all dripped with perspiration, but it was a good feeling. Selene was showing Hyacinth, Lily, and Reba how to hold the palms of their hands pressed together in front of their breasts, elbows up and out. "Now keep holding the pressure as long as you can. See. Press, release, press, release. Do that twenty times and then alternate with the front and back shoulder rolls, like I showed you."

"Are you sure this will make my tits get smaller?" Hyacinth asked crudely.

"And make ours get bigger?" Lily asked, looking at

Reba who stood beside her, murmuring in concentration, "Press, release, press, release . . ."

Selene cringed. She was beginning to think that the only thing that would help Lily-of-the-lilypad-chest was a lifetime supply of Wonder Bras. "No, no, no. I never said it could enlarge or reduce breasts. It will just build up muscles around the breasts, make them firmer, uplifted. Frankly, Hyacinth, if you'd lose a little weight, it might help more. And exercise."

Hyacinth grumbled but agreed to try.

"Now let's get back to the tush crunches."

"Not again," Iris groaned. "Lordy, my behind feels like I been ridin' a horse for two days."

"That's good. That's good," Selene said, dropping down to the rag rug at her feet. She waited until all the other ladies had done the same and lay on their backs, legs spread, knees bent. "Now remember, every time you thrust your pelvis up, you've got to squeeze your tush cheeks together and hold for a few seconds, like you're trying to crush a piece of straw between them."

They all moaned as one.

"Now you start singing, and I'll do the count."

They began singing enthusiastically, and she marked time with them, calling out rhythmically, "Thrust, up, hold . . . harder . . . harder . . . now release. Thrust, up, hold, release. Thrust up, hold, release."

Men like to watch. It's just a fact of life . . .

"Some of these hoes need to be sharpened," Fergus told James as they both stood in the hot sun of the cane fields, wiping perspiration from their foreheads and necks with already sodden handkerchiefs. James pushed his hat back on his head, surveying the workers who lined up before the food and water wagon, then sank down into whatever grassy spots they could find in the shade.

"I'll go," James offered. "I want to see how Rufus is doing with the yard work I set him to do."

"He seems to know a great deal about plants."

James nodded. "Says he helped landscape some plantation in Virginia before the owner died. He's a good worker. I think he'll work out well."

"Do you still hope he'll be able to take over as driver for Amen?"

"I don't know. Amen has been head of all the field workers since I arrived here ten years ago. He's free now, of course, but the man's sixty years old, and Blossom thinks he's suffering from the lung disease."

"Why don't we have Rufus work alongside Amen starting next week and see what Amen thinks? He's always been a good judge of men."

"Oui." Then, untying his horse's reins from a tree and mounting, he gazed down at Fergus, who was still pondering the situation with great seriousness. James decided the man needed some gentle ribbing. "By the way, *mon ami,* you might want to have Blossom look at those bites on your neck. You wouldn't want them to get infected." His lips twitched with suppressed laughter as he spoke.

Not to be ruffled, Fergus touched his neck almost with pride, and puffed his chest out like a randy rooster. "You wouldn't be jealous now, would you, James? You wouldn't be wonderin' how many of those bites I've got on other parts of my body, as well?"

James guffawed, shaking his head at his friend's obvious pleasure in a night well spent.

"Well, I for one intend to thank Selene," Fergus went on. "She's certainly added some zest to my life."

Mine, too. Unfortunately.

"I can't wait to see what she does next."

Me, either. Unfortunately.

"Do you suppose you could ask her about that 'Perfect Fit' thing?"

"Are you demented?"

"Well, it doesn't hurt to ask," Fergus countered defensively.

"Ask her yourself," James snapped, turning his horse. *Sacre bleu! Time-travel, popping eyeballs, aliens from another world, attacking ghosts . . . now the world's most perfect sexual position.*

As he neared the house, he saw Rufus on the second-floor gallery near the parlor window, peering inside in a clandestine fashion. *What the hell?* Sliding from his horse, James tied the reins to a rail and moved quietly up the outside stairs.

Then he heard the train whistle. *Train whistle?* He knocked the side of his head with the heel of his hand to clear it.

"Whoo-whoo, whoo-whoo."

There it was again, but it wasn't a train whistle. It sounded like female voices imitating a train whistle. The whistles alternated with loud caterwauling. Some strange, rhythmic song about . . . huh? . . . achy, breaky hearts.

James tapped Rufus on the shoulder and the slave almost jumped out of his skin. "Oh, Lordy. You skeered me somethin' fierce, Mastah James."

"Whoo-whoo, whoo-whoo," a group of shrill voices sang out again.

In between the train whistles and the achy breaky song strains, he heard Selene's voice calling out, "Thrust, up, hold, release. Thrust, up, hold, release."

"Rufus, what are you doing here peeping in windows?" James demanded sternly. The black man cupped a hand to his ear, barely able to hear him over the screeching voices in the background.

"Watchin' the arrow-backs," Rufus answered, jerking his chin over his shoulders in the direction of the parlor. "Mam'zelle Selene is holdin' an arrow-backs class. Right now they's doin' tush crunches. That be another name for pelvic thrusts," he informed James as if imparting some great wisdom. "Lordy, I tell you, Master James, that Iris can do pelvic thrusts in my bed anytime. Yessirree." He rolled his eyes in emphasis.

James pushed Rufus aside and looked through the window . . . a very clean window, he noted idly . . . and his mouth almost dropped to the gallery floor. Eight women were lying on their backs on Blossom's best rag throw rugs spread about on the bare floor. Selene, Reba, and six servants. Wearing form-fitting men's trousers and thin cotton shirts, they were all singing louder than bullfrogs during the mating season and moving their bodies in a most scandalous way.

"Thrust, up, hold, release. Come on, ladies, we're working for buns of steel here, not cinnamon buns. Thrust, up, hold, release. . . ."

James grinned. "Hurry," he whispered to Rufus, "go get Fergus. Tell him he has to see this. Tell him . . . tell him you've got something better than the Perfect Fit to show him."

Then James turned back to the window. His eyes homed in on Selene, whose thick, dark hair was pulled back off her face with a ribbon into a long queue, accenting the fine bones of her cheeks and jaw, her straight nose, her full, sensual lips.

"Thrust, up, hold, release. . . ."

Oh, merde!

Lying on her back, she had both hands folded behind her neck. Her legs were spread wide, knees bent, and bare feet planted firmly on the floor. To the tempo of the singing, she thrust her hips upward, almost in imitation of the sex act, held that pose, then lowered herself. Over and over, she repeated the enticing exercise.

"Thrust, up, hold, release. . . ."

Oh, merde!

James leaned against the window frame lazily, fearing that his suddenly weak body couldn't withstand much more of this teasing of the senses. Not surprisingly, he felt himself grow hard, and with each rhythmic thrust, he imagined

Selene was moving against him thus. Naked. Pulling him inside her warm folds, then almost out. Up, down. In, out.

"Thrust, up, hold, release. . . ."

Oh, merde!

He wiped his hand across his upper lip, not knowing how much more of this he could stand. Not knowing if he could walk away. Not caring.

He felt as if he'd stepped into the middle of the ocean and was sinking fast. A heavy lassitude pulled at his limbs, but he couldn't fight the delicious lethargy. Reflexively he placed a hand against his arousal, then jerked it back despite the throbbing need.

Forget about the Perfect Fit. He could think of a hundred sexual positions he would like to try with this seductive witch, and all of them would be perfect. He just knew it.

Two can play this game, buster . . .

Like a robot, Selene called out the exercise chants, pleased with the enthusiasm of her "students" thus far. Her eyes swept the room, then came to a halt as she noticed James leaning against the frame of the tall window.

His luminous eyes held hers captive, smoldering, while conflicting emotions swept his tight features—anger and passion. Anger, no doubt, because he did not like the complications she posed to his very controlled life. Passion, which he could not control, despite his best efforts, despite his plans to send her away.

Selene remembered her vow earlier that day to make him sorry for sending her away. She wanted him to regret not loving her. With that in mind, she smiled with ageless, wanton intent.

He stiffened, recognizing the challenge.

Slowing her chant and her body movements to a more sexual rhythm, Selene watched his fists clench and his jaw tighten, but he seemed unable to tear his eyes away from her. She arched her breasts and felt them peak against the taut fabric. She held her pelvic thrusts higher than necessary, tantalizing his senses.

With outrageous insolence, James palmed himself, showing her his arousal. Clearly he was throwing the gauntlet in answer to her challenge.

She gasped and turned away, realizing that teasing could be a two-edged sword. In the taunting of his desire, she had kindled her own, as well. And he knew it.

When she turned back to the window, James was gone. With a groan, Selene stopped her chants and stretched out flat on the floor. "Party's over, ladies. Time to get back to work."

But her thoughts still dwelled on James. *Hold onto your chauvinistic butt, Rhett. Here comes Scarlett. Believe me, this war's not over yet. Not by a twenty-first-century long shot. And don't think for a minute that I'm settling for "Tomorrow is another day."*

She was turning into a bleepin' Martha Stewart . . .

By the end of the afternoon, Selene had spent three concentrated hours with Etienne in the schoolroom, setting out lesson plans and daily schedules. First she reviewed the basics in a number of subjects, like arithmetic, reading, writing, and elementary science, to get a feel for his abilities.

The boy was a genius.

Selene should have guessed that a child with Etienne's talent for mischief was gifted intellectually. Not only was his reading level that of at least a ten-year-old, but he had a quick grasp of the sciences, probably due to his fascination with the bayou biological wonderland that surrounded him.

"Why are you frowning? You look like a bullfrog when you make those wrinkles in your forehead," he said.

"How nice of you to notice!"

He smiled, guilelessly for once, and she ruffled his clean hair. James had apparently given his son strict orders to bathe once a day, wash his face and hands before every meal and before his tutoring sessions. Selene didn't know what threat James held over Etienne's head to get such compliance, but it must have been a powerful one.

She sat watching him solve yet another long addition problem, biting his tongue in concentration as his squat, square pencil skimmed the page. The brat loved challenges of any kind.

"How many minutes did that one take?" he asked, putting his pencil down resoundingly. They both peered up at the banjo clock on the wall.

"Three minutes," Selene said, checking his answer for accuracy. Her grimace told him his answer was correct, again.

"I win. I win. Tomorrow you gotta go into the swamp with me to study . . . what did you call it?"

"Biology." She shuddered at the prospect of entering that haven of snakes and bats and who knew what kind of slimy creatures. But she'd foolishly promised Etienne that some of their classes could be outdoors if he solved three of her more difficult problems within five minutes. Her entire session today had been one bargaining match after another. "Are you sure it's safe, Etienne?"

Standing, he put his hands on hips and glared at her.

"E.T. I forgot."

"You always forget. And, *oui*, you're safe with me," he boasted. "Will you draw a picture of E.T. for me now?"

"Will you read some more of *Oliver Twist* for me?"

"*Merde!* Read, read, read. My head is swimming."

"Etienne . . . E.T.," she amended at his immediate scowl, "didn't you agree to stop swearing?"

"I don't remember. Did I?" he asked, kicking at a ball of paper on the floor. Then, seeing that she wasn't going to give in on the reading deal, he growled, "Oh, all right. I'll read one more page, but then you have to draw a picture of

E.T. for me. I promised Cain and Abel I would show it to them."

Selene glanced through the open doorway where the two black children sat in the hallway waiting patiently for Etienne's lesson to end. Actually, they listened so avidly that they probably soaked in as much information as he did. Selene intended to ask James about including the other children in the lessons.

When he finished reading, stumbling over the harder words, Selene drew a rudimentary pencil sketch of an E.T. style figure and even added a spaceship in the background.

Etienne gaped in awe at the drawing. Then he turned his dazzling eyes on her in appreciation and smiled. Selene could have sworn he almost hugged her in thanks. Her heart expanded with warmth.

After Etienne left, she tidied the room a bit, then returned to the second floor where the servants, under Iris's orders, had already laid clean rush matting. They finished polishing the furniture and returned it to the two parlors and the dining room.

She walked about the rooms, inhaling deeply of the pungent odors of lemony cleaning solutions and strong beeswax polish. Here and there she touched a piece of furniture in admiration—Hepplewhite nesting tables in the corner, a mahogany upholstered sofa that could very well be Duncan Phyfe, a tall case clock with a scroll top and ogee bracket feet, an American empire sideboard, fine Hitchcock chairs.

Most of the furniture was in the simple federal style, using rich reddish brown mahoganies or highly grained native cypress, all stained to resemble the satinwoods so popular in Europe. But the most exquisite pieces, with their delicately molded panels, were made of *palissandre*, or violet ebony, and signed by a New Orleans furniture maker named Seignouret.

Selene vowed to research Seignouret when she returned to the future to see if his work was appreciated in her time.

Then her spirits plummeted at the reminder that she would, in fact, have to leave this period in history, these people . . . James . . . all of whom she was beginning to cherish.

Shaking away those unwelcome thoughts, she listened as the grandfather clock chimed five times. Then she told Iris, "I think we can stop for the day."

Iris nodded. "Are we gonna do arrow-backs again tomorrow?"

Selene smiled. "If you want. We'll have to find another place to work out, though, since we've replaced the furniture in here. Maybe Etienne's schoolroom, or even outside if the weather's nice."

The black woman patted her bottom and winked at Selene. "I feel smaller already, Mam'zelle. Betcha I could catch that Rufus if I had a smaller backside. Betcha he would stay longer 'n the other men I knowed if my body was more . . ." She searched for the word.

". . . perfect?" Selene wept inside at the universal weakness of women who kept trying and trying to please others in order to be happy themselves. "Iris, I think you've already caught Rufus. But can't you see that it's wrong to try to change yourself to please someone else?"

"How else I gonna catch a man, and keep 'im?"

"Men are important. Hey, I like men *a lot.* But having a husband, or a lover, shouldn't be the way women define themselves."

"Huh?"

"Listen, women throughout time have been running in place, thinking that if they were only prettier, or smarter, or sexier, or more docile, or more aggressive, men would love them more. It doesn't work. Believe me. It's taken me five years of group therapy to understand that women need to be stronger, to learn to love themselves first."

"Oh, Selene, everything you're saying is just what I need to learn," Reba interrupted enthusiastically.

Selene realized then that all the women were listening with interest to her conversation with Iris.

"Therapy?" Iris asked, her beautiful eyes wide with curiosity. "What's that? Is it like arrow-backs for the head?"

Selene burst out laughing. "You could say that. Oh, Iris, really, you could very well say that therapy is like exercise for the mind."

"Good! Then we can do therapy right after our arrow-backs everyday," Iris declared excitedly, and all the rest of the women nodded their heads in agreement. "Lordy, I'm gonna be so perfect when you're done with me there won't be no man good enough for me."

They all laughed and began to pick up the cleaning materials.

"*Salut!* May I join in your therapy group, as well?"

Selene turned with a jolt to see a slim, fiftyish woman standing in the doorway. Her black hair, sprinkled with strands of silver, was pulled back into a neat bun at the nape of her neck. Her blue eyes were hazy with deep sadness.

Walking with refined elegance toward Selene in a dress of gray silk moiré edged with snow-white lace and accented by an exquisite cameo brooch at the collar, the lady extended a frail hand in greeting. "You must be Mademoiselle Selene. I am Marie Baptiste, James's mother. May I offer a long overdue welcome to Bayou Noir?"

Selene stood speechless with shock at finally meeting James's reclusive mother.

Mrs. Baptiste smiled faintly, aware of her discomfort. "I'm so sorry if I interrupted a private conversation, my dear. But I could not help myself when I heard you say that women must learn to be stronger. Truly, even at my age, I could stand to learn that lesson."

Selene acknowledged her greeting with a slight nod, then belatedly caught the implications of Mrs. Baptiste's reference to learning something from Selene . . . to joining her amateur therapy group.

James, James, James. You are definitely not going to be happy with me today.

Chapter Thirteen

Amazing, the people who enjoy a good blonde joke! . . .

James did not show up for dinner that evening, sending word via Blossom that he had to go to a neighboring plantation for a part to replace a broken boiler coil. Selene wondered if the damage was related to Victor's misdeeds, as James had suggested to Blossom, or if James was just finding excuses to avoid her.

Mrs. Baptiste did come, along with Etienne, Fergus, and Reba. James's mother added a touch of refinement to the atmosphere of the now sparkling dining room with her soft-spoken, Creole-tinted language, her dainty mannerisms and polite conversation.

Selene listened with fascination to her accounts of her arrival at Bayou Noir ten years ago, when James would have been less than twenty-five years old, and Mrs. Baptiste a healthier and more enthusiastic woman.

"Ah, *chérie*," she said, looking kindly toward Selene, "you would not consider the state of this plantation today quite so sad if you could have seen it then."

Selene started to protest, but Mrs. Baptiste waved a hand

dismissively and continued, "*Alors!* I think there was a whole battalion of mice and as many bats inhabiting the house. And the swamp . . . *mon Dieu*, the swamp! . . . had grown right up to the doorsteps."

"Weren't there people living here then?" Selene asked. "I mean, Blossom mentioned that she and some of the other slaves were here when James arrived."

"*Oui,* but M'sieur Declouet and his wife had been traveling abroad and left the property in the care of an overseer. They never realized until their return how negligent he'd been in his duties." She made a low tsk-ing sound of disgust as her eyes misted with memory.

Their conversation was interrupted by the arrival of the first course, a rich turtle soup carried by Hyacinth in a magnificent china tureen. Next came salty, home-cured ham with parsleyed Irish potatoes, sweet peas, dandelion with hot bacon and vinegar dressing, fresh bread and butter. And, of course, the table was never missing the sassafras-flavored Creole gumbo served over fluffy white rice.

After a sinfully sweet caramel *glacé* dessert, Reba and Fergus excused themselves, still unable to keep their hungry eyes off each other.

Then Etienne proceeded to leave, too, having consumed three of the custards, with the permission of his *grand-mère.* He reminded Selene with a roguish grin that tomorrow they were going to study "bye-olive-gee" in a favorite marsh setting he wanted to show her. Blossom had told her it would be all right as long as they didn't go too far.

"Don't forget to bring that book of animal drawings and their descriptions that I bought in New Orleans for your classes."

"*Sacre bleu!* You're gonna make me read, even outdoors." He rolled his eyes comically as he left.

Selene and Mrs. Baptiste lingered over delicate china cups of strong Creole coffee. Selene wished Mrs. Baptiste would resume her earlier conversation about James.

As if reading her thoughts, Mrs. Baptiste proffered suddenly, "He is a good son, you know. He must seem hard to you, but to me he is just a good son. You are aware, of course, that he is illegitimate. Well, he was never able to accept our . . . situation. It was a mistake, I see now, to live in the city where daily he saw the contrast between our manner of living and his father's family. Always, *always*, he compared his life to that of his half brother, Victor, and saw that he came up short."

Selene swallowed hard over the growing lump in her throat, not sure she wanted to hear anything about James that would make her care more than she already did.

"And, most of all, it pained him to see me brought so low. I was not raised to be a mere mistress, you see. My father was an English trader and my mother a Creole, disowned by her family when she married beneath herself. We were not wealthy, but we lived well, until my parents died in a shipping accident just before my planned wedding to Jean-Paul."

"Wedding?" Selene gasped. "But I thought . . ."

Mrs. Baptiste tilted her head in understanding. "*Oui*, I can see how you would think otherwise, but Jean-Paul did love me. That is why I accepted such a demeaning role in his life." She ran the tip of her forefinger around the rim of her cup, lost in reverie. "But it was selfish of me because I never considered the effect our love would have on my son. James grew up wild and increasingly bitter. I realize now that his forays into the bayous, which I considered mere boyish pranks then, were really a means of escape for him from the degradation of our life . . . a cry for help which I failed to heed."

"Mrs. Baptiste, perhaps you shouldn't be telling me all this."

The lady raised her eyes resolutely. "*Non*, I want to tell you. I beg you will not judge him too harshly."

Selene tried to protest, but Mrs. Baptiste raised a halting hand and continued, "When my parents died just before my wedding, I lost my dowry and was left penniless. Jean-Paul needed to wed a wealthy woman, his own finances having suffered from some unfortunate gambling losses. If I had been wealthy, there never would have been a problem."

"Oh, this is intolerable," Selene said, throwing her napkin to the table with disgust, unable to bite her tongue any longer. "This is just what I was saying this afternoon to Iris. Women . . . women throughout time . . . keep blaming themselves. If only they were better in some way—richer, prettier, slimmer, fatter, whatever—then everything would work out all right. When . . . *when, in the name of God* . . . are women going to learn that changing themselves to please another person . . . a man . . . isn't the answer?"

Mrs. Baptiste's small mouth opened in amazement.

"I'm sorry. I had no right."

"*Non*, do not stop because you fear offending my sensibilities." She scrutinized Selene speculatively. "You are a very interesting woman, *ma chérie*. I look forward to seeing the role you will play in my son's life."

"None, actually. He's sending me away."

"Never! He would not do so."

"Well, he invited the Collins here on Sunday with the intention of having me go away with them."

"Really? How curious! Hmmm. We shall see. In any case, I wanted you to understand the reasons why my son is . . . the way he is."

Selene frowned, unsure what message she was supposed to glean from Mrs. Baptiste's remark.

Seeing Selene's confusion, Mrs. Baptiste went on, "When he was thirteen, James could no longer tolerate the ignominy of our position in the city, dependent on his father's generosity for our every coin. He ran away, signed a document of indenture with a shipping firm, which took him to Santo Domingo and the sugar plantations there. For more than ten years, he worked as little more than a slave until he earned enough to return for me and purchase Bayou Noir."

Selene inhaled sharply with sudden understanding. Now she comprehended James's insistence that he not get involved in an affair with her. Without commitment, theirs would be a less than honorable relationship, just like the one his father had foisted on his mother. And James knew better than most the pain that could emanate from the momentary easing of lust, especially if a child were involved.

"Oh, Mrs. Baptiste, please forgive me if I've seemed condescending of this plantation, or you, even of James. It's not James's work here that upsets me . . . although I do hate slavery. It's James himself. He's always saying or doing something to rile me."

"He riles you, does he?" Mrs. Baptiste smiled softly, knowingly. "That is good. *Oui. Très bien.*"

"No, no, no. I can see what you're thinking, and you're wrong. James has told me on numerous occasions how unattractive he finds me, how unwomanly and shrewish my speech is, how . . . how I'm just a bother to him. And, besides, I'm not blonde."

Mrs. Baptiste laughed, a soft tinkling sound of delight. "Blonde? Oh, my dear, blonde? But, *oui,* I can see how you would think that. Giselle was blonde, and—"

"Giselle was blonde?" Selene interrupted, her heart sinking further.

"You didn't know?"

"No, I've just noticed that James's eyes always home in on blondes, no matter where he is. Haven't you heard about the blonde jokes I keep telling him?"

"Blonde jokes? *Non.*" She slanted Selene a look of mischief then, tapping her hand with her folded fan. "But I demand you tell me one. Now."

Despite her misgivings, Selene asked, "What does a blonde call her pet zebra?"

"What?"

"Spot."

It took a moment for Mrs. Baptiste to understand the

joke. Then she laughed merrily, clapping her hands together in glee. "A riddle. Now I see."

"How does a blonde kill a bird?"

Mrs. Baptiste frowned with concentration. "How?"

"She throws it off a cliff."

Smiling girlishly, Mrs. Baptiste demanded, "Another."

"Well, this one is rather risqué."

"So?"

"What's the difference between a blonde and the Grand Old Duke of York?"

"What?"

"The Grand Old Duke only had ten thousand men."

Mrs. Baptiste giggled behind her hand. "Oh, that was scandalous, but so deliciously wicked. Of course, I understand your point completely. Jean-Paul's wife is blonde, you know," she confided with a grimace. Taking a final sip of her coffee, she pushed the cup and saucer away. "You are amazing, my child. No wonder I have been hearing so much merriment about the plantation since your arrival. *Non,* I do not think my son will be able to let you go so soon."

Before Selene could answer, Mrs. Baptiste, looking suddenly tired, rang a small bell on the table. When Iris came in, she told her she wanted to return to her rooms. Then she patted Selene's hand. "You will come to visit me tomorrow and we will continue our conversation. Perhaps we can have tea after our therapy group . . . that is what you called it, is it not?"

Selene groaned inwardly. The therapy thing again! "Oh, no, Mrs. Baptiste. I don't think it would be wise for me, an unprofessional, to conduct counseling sessions. Absolutely not. Now, the tea, that would be nice, but no way on the group therapy. No way."

Mrs. Baptiste and Iris just smiled, blocking out her protests with their silence. Wincing, Selene accepted the fact that she had somehow maneuvered herself into not only providing aerobics instructions on a nineteenth-century

Southern plantation, but into becoming a psychologist, as well.

What was her world coming to?

And did she really want to know?

When logics and war conflict, passion always wins . . .

Selene took a bath after dinner and brought a book up from the library to read in her bedroom. She hadn't read *Pride and Prejudice* since high school.

Sitting in a wingback chair next to a table, Selene soon realized why people in this century went to bed so early. Even with a many-branched candelabra, the lighting was abysmal.

The grandfather clock chimed nine o'clock before Selene heard James finally come up from the kitchen where he must have grabbed a bite to eat from the tray Blossom had left for him. Soon she heard water splashing into the tub, the sounds of bathing, and then the rustling sounds of clothing being donned again. Once she heard a swear word when James presumably knocked over the stool.

She waited, her book lying in her lap, her heart thudding wildly as his steps took him past her room. Instead of going to his bedchamber in the front, however, she heard him go back downstairs. By the direction of the footsteps, it sounded as if he'd entered the library.

Should she stay in her room, or should she go down and talk to James?

Yes, she would go down and talk to him about Etienne's lessons, and the enlargement of her classes to include the other children.

No, it was late, and he was probably still upset with her over the aerobics session he'd witnessed.

Yeah, but she still wanted to put James in his place, showing him just what he'd be missing when he sent her away.

On the other hand, teasing James might very well turn on her, sort of like offering candy to a lion and being devoured in the process.

She could wear that gauzy wrapper Iris had brought that evening from Mrs. Baptiste, an odd gift for James's mother to have sent, now that she thought about it.

On and on, Selene waged a silent war with herself. Logic versus pure, obstinate, feminine brainlessness.

Brainlessness won out.

There was no winner in this battle, but the war was far from over ...

James sat in the library nursing a tumbler of aged whiskey. He inhaled the intoxicating aroma of the liquor and the pungent odors of the cleaning materials Selene and her household demons had used that day.

He gave up on making sense of the plantation accounts. Instead, he leaned back precariously in his chair and propped his long legs, crossed at the ankles, on the edge of the desk. Picking up Selene's magazine, *We*, he shook his head in weary disbelief. *Bon Dieu!* Who ever heard of naming a magazine *We?* That would be like choosing some foolishly simplistic title, like *People*, or *Life*. Men and women of Selene's time must be incredibly unimaginative.

Selene. There she was again, insinuating herself into his every thought. He rubbed his fingertips back and forth across his upper lip, deep in thought, as he studied the magazine once again, trying futilely to understand her presence in his time . . . his life.

"Oh, how could you? I don't believe this!" The witch in question stormed into the room, glaring down at him from her great height, hands on hips. The whole effect was lost, however, because the wispy garment she wore barely concealed her tall body with its lean curves. Hell, when had her skinny bones translated in his benumbed brain to "lean curves?"

"Get your filthy boots off that clean desk," she demanded. "Do you have any idea how much work it took to polish that monstrosity?"

"Monstrosity?" he asked, amazed by her tirade. "I like this desk." He took a long drink from his glass.

"And drinking again!"

"Shut up, Selene. And go back to bed," he said tiredly. "I'm exhausted. I've been drinking. And I'm in a dangerous mood. Escape while you have a chance."

"No."

He slanted her a look of disbelief. "No? Did you tell me 'no'?"

She raised her hand distractedly to brush a strand of hair off her face, and he saw the long scratch running down her forearm. He gulped with sudden concern. "Did you have the cut tended by Blossom?"

"Yes. It was nothing." She waved a hand airily.

"Cuts get infected easily in the bayou."

"I'm all right, James," she insisted. "I need to talk to you," she added, shifting uncomfortably from bare foot to bare foot.

Oh, merde. If her feet are bare, does that mean she is wearing nothing beneath that flimsy wrapper? "You need to talk to me, naked?"

Her face turned a charming shade of pink, which he could tell annoyed her. "I am not naked."

He studied her boldly, telling her without words just how naked he saw her.

Her eyes shifted guiltily.

He narrowed his own eyes suspiciously. "Selene, have you come here to seduce me into your bed?"

"Absolutely not!"

Before he had a chance to analyze her motives, she dropped down into a chair on the other side of the desk. Light from the oil lamp on his desk and the candelabra near the window flickered in the slight breeze. Seductive shadows danced about the dark room, creating an aura of privacy, an isolation from the rest of the world. A dangerous, tantalizing atmosphere, he decided immediately.

"So do you really believe that Justin Bieber earned ten million dollars last year?" he asked, seeking some neutral subject that would not catapult him onto a course that could only lead to his destruction.

"Huh?" She glanced down at the publication in his lap. "Oh, you've been reading my magazine again. Can I have it back now?"

"No."

She curled her lips with disgust, and he could just hear the gears of her brain grinding out that word she liked to call him. She didn't disappoint him.

"Jerk!"

He smiled smoothly. Then he noticed her eyes riveted to a point just to the right of his mouth and remembered a comment she'd once made about his having a dimple. What had she said? Oh, *oui*, now he recalled. It was something about how he could have anything in the world from a woman if he just showed that dimple once in a while.

Deliberately he smiled wider, pleased to see her lips part with appreciation and her hazelnut eyes grow a misty green with passion. *Passion!* Was he demented, standing here waiting for the kill?

With a grunt of disgust, he threw the magazine to the desk and stood. Walking to a side table, he poured himself another half tumbler of bourbon.

"Thank you. I would like a glass, too."

He glared at her for reminding him of his lack of hospitality, then complied ungraciously. He was rewarded for his efforts when she choked on the first swallow of the potent brew.

"Go to bed, Selene, and stop playing games with me."

Selene felt as if she'd poured liquid fire into her mouth. Heat seared her tongue and throat, then landed like a bolt of lightning in her stomach. But a tingling warmth . . . delicious and almost sensual . . . followed in its wake, and she decided she liked James's bourbon. She took another sip, unamused by his silent laughter at her reaction to the booze. She licked her lips and saw, to her pleasure, that he was no longer laughing, inside or out.

"So what else have you read in my magazine that puzzles you besides Justin Bieber?" Selene asked conversationally.

"Well, I'm not sure I understand these automobile things, or the airplanes that you mentioned to me before," he said. He put his drink down, sitting on the edge of the desk, and flicked through the pages until he came to ads for Chrysler and American Airlines.

"Horseless carriages that travel on roads and in the skies," was the only explanation she could come up with.

"I thought as much."

"I don't think I would like living in your time, though, despite those marvels."

"Really? Why?" She tilted her head in question and sipped her drink, feeling a slight buzz.

"Everyone seems to be in such a rush to get somewhere. Another city. Another job. Another woman, or man. The pressure to move on seems endless. There is no sense of contentment."

"You may be right," she said softly, pondering his words.

"Although I do think I like those teddies," he added, with that blasted dimple of his flashing at her like a neon sign that said, "Sexy. Sexy. Sexy."

"Teddies?" she asked, pulling her gaze away from his enticing mouth with considerable effort. Was that a smile tugging at his lips? Did he know what effect he was having on her, and was he enjoying it? The brute! She was supposed to be teaching him a lesson in what he would be missing, not the other way around.

"*Oui*, isn't that what you call that revealing garment you are wearing on page sixteen?"

Selene had forgotten about that layout for Victoria's Secret. She felt her face grow hot with embarrassment, though why she, a model, should be embarrassed by an advertisement she couldn't really say.

"I must say, Selene, that I am shocked that you would expose your body for one and all to see. Are you sure you're not a fancy lady in your time?"

"A fancy lady? What's that? I always thought of myself as having class. Is that what you mean?"

He shook his head slowly from side to side.

"Oh, you jerk!" she exclaimed, suddenly remembering the New Orleans auction where he had referred to brothels as fancy houses. "I am not a whore. There's nothing wrong with modeling underwear. Standards are different in 2012."

He nodded hesitantly, seeming to accept her explanation. Then he flipped to another page, and winked at her. She leaned forward to see what headline had caught his attention now. *Oh, Lord.*

"So do you know 'Ten Ways to Light Your Lover's Fire'?"

Selene reached for the magazine but he held it out of reach, laughing.

"Sweetheart, I could light your fire ten ways to Tuesday and not even be started," she boasted foolishly, refusing to let him goad her into scurrying off like a frightened mouse.

Selene needed to change the subject, and fast, before the bourbon and James's even more intoxicating closeness turned her brain to putty. She was supposed to be the one in control of this seduction.

"I came down here to talk to you about Etienne," she said huffily, setting down her empty glass. Her lips felt numb as she spoke, and she wondered if that small smile on James's wonderful lips was an indication that she'd slurred her words.

"What about Etienne? Has he been tormenting you in

some way? He hasn't been playing his snake pranks again, has he?"

Snakes! Selene shuddered at that horrid possibility. "No, I've got his tricks under control."

"And what tricks did you use to manage that great feat?"

She ignored his question. "He's gifted, James. You need to know that Etienne is a gifted child, and you must do everything you can to nurture his talents."

"Gifted? What the hell is gifted?"

"He's exceptionally intelligent. He reads at a level twice his age. He grasps complex concepts with ease. I'm not an expert at these things, but I believe his I.Q. is extremely high. You have to plan for his future."

"I won't even ask what an eye-cue is. But, *oui*, I have noticed his brightness." He shrugged. "What would you have me do? There isn't much call for a scholar sugar farmer."

Selene raised her chin indignantly. "There isn't much call for a dumb sugar farmer, either."

"Touché," he said, flashing that damn dimple at her again. "So what are you suggesting? That I keep you here to steer Etienne's education in the right direction?"

Selene brightened. "I hadn't thought of that, actually, but now that you mention it—"

He laughed. "Selene, *ma chérie*, you are as transparent as that outrageous garment you are flaunting. What is it anyway? The mosquito *barre* from your bed?"

"No, you brute. And this is not transparent," she said, looking down to check just in case she'd missed something. "And I'll have you know it was a gift from your mother."

His chin almost dropped to the floor with that news. "My mother? My mother?" he sputtered. "Now you drag my mother into your schemes."

"I did no such thing," she retorted indignantly.

"You are leaving here on Sunday, and that is final."

Don't be too sure about what's final or not final, my good friend. I haven't begun to fight, Rhett, baby.

"What else is on your mind?" he asked, and at first Selene worried that he might have read her thoughts. "You look as if you're ready to engage me in a bout of fisticuffs."

"Someone ought to knock you silly." She counted to ten silently to get her temper under control. "I wanted to know if I could include some of the other children in Etienne's classes. Cain, Abel, whoever might be interested. It wouldn't be any harder to teach ten children than one, in my opinion. And it seems a shame to . . . What? Why are you looking at me so funny?"

"You would be willing to teach the children from the quarters? That wouldn't bother you?"

"Why should it?" she asked in confusion.

"Because they're colored."

"Oh, good Lord!"

He stared at her strangely, swallowing hard several times as if struggling with some internal turmoil. "I just don't understand you," he said finally in a low voice.

"That's okay," she said with a smile, the buzz in her head turning into a roar. Somehow she'd forgotten her original plan—to make the jackass suffer for sending her away. She slanted him a saucy, under-the-lashes look, intended to be seductive. "Do you like what you don't understand?"

He grinned. "*Oui*. I think I like it a whole hell of a lot."

"Well, that's encouraging."

"Why?"

She fluttered her eyelashes at him in an exaggerated demonstration of her supposed coyness. She only hoped she wasn't looking at him cross-eyed with drunkenness. "A girl's got to have a few secrets. Let's pretend I'm just like any other person in the world who likes to be liked."

"Well, I'll tell you a secret," he said, standing. Abruptly he whisked all of the papers and his empty glass off his desk with one wide sweep of his hand. "Let's pretend, instead, that I lie on my back on this desk and you straddle my hips with those *very* long legs of yours. And then let's pretend that you teach me how to do . . . what do you call them? . . . pelvic thrusts."

Touché, James, she thought, repeating his earlier remark to her. Her blood raced, heating her face, swelling her breasts, pooling at the apex of her thighs. She tried, but could not erase the vivid image his husky words evoked. He was teasing her, she knew. He didn't really mean what he suggested.

Did he?

But then suddenly Selene realized his game. Somehow he'd discovered her plan to make him grovel for her affections, to make him want her so badly that he would be sorry when he sent her away. He was turning the tables on her, good and well.

Hah! Two could play that game.

Leaning against the back of a chair to steady her wobbly legs, she pondered aloud, "Hmmm. That sounds interesting. But I know an even more interesting exercise we could practice. Your penis would have to be inside my body, of course—"

"But of course," James choked out, his eyes almost bug-eyed with shock.

"—and then I could employ the Kegel Muscle drill," Selene said conversationally, trying to remember the details of that particular exercise. "That's the one where the woman practices tightening and relaxing her internal muscles so that eventually she can do a sort of milking action. It's hard for the man to remain passive, but his immobility is critical if—"

"You lie. I don't believe any of this."

But Selene could see that he was clearly intrigued.

"Well, you'll never know, sweetheart," Selene said, drifting toward the doorway with what she hoped was a dramatic flourish and not a stagger. She fought desperately against her own heightened passions not to turn and rush into his arms. "Because I'll be long gone from Bayou Noir. At your stupid command."

His ragged breathing was the only sound in the silent room.

"And you can think about it for the rest of your stupid, stubborn life. What you might have had and threw away."

"Touché again, Selene," he called after her with a laugh. "But be careful, *chérie*, I am not checkmated yet. And I never lose a battle once I set my course."

Selene stood in the hall, shivering with foreboding. And anticipation.

Chapter Fourteen

W/*hat a biology lesson!* ...

"Shhhhh! You're makin' too much noise," Etienne hissed.

Hah! There was no way she was going to tiptoe through this snake wonderland with Indiana *E.T.* Even with the clunky leather brogues Blossom had given her Selene knew there must be a million of those slimy suckers just waiting to pounce on her.

Oh, Lord, do snakes even pounce? she wondered, her nerves overwrought with tension. Then she thought of something else. Probably that monster snake that had "attacked" her on the flatboat had followed her to Bayou Noir. Yep, that Jurassic reptile was a marathon swimmer if she ever saw one.

"Let's go back, E.T. This is way too far from the house."

"Why? Are you afraid?" he sneered, looking back at her over his shoulder.

He was carrying a big stick to clear their way through the thick bayou undergrowth. A stick, for heaven's sake! She shook her head at the insanity of her blithely following a three-foot gremlin whose only ammunition against the snake from hell was a measly stick.

"Besides, we're almost there," he added, letting the thin branch of a sapling . . . probably poison something-or-other . . . swing back and catch her pony tail.

With a grunt of disgust, she held her biology book tucked under her chin and combed her fingers through her hair, retying the ribbon at the nape of her neck.

They had almost reached the edge of a bayou stream when Etienne turned and put a finger to his lips, signaling silence. Then he began to climb the split trunk of an ancient cypress tree, motioning for her to follow him onto a wide, almost horizontal branch that spread out about eight feet above the water. It was a good thing she'd worn her exercise outfit—men's pants and a buttoned shirt.

When she sat next to Etienne, he gestured again for quiet. Actually, it was quite nice sitting beside Etienne, listening to the myriad sounds of the bayou's never-ceasing orchestra—croaks and chirps, hisses and grunts, snaps and thumps, splashes and drips.

Etienne pointed, and at first Selene thought he wanted her to look at the muddy bank where a mole burrowed busily through the spongy ground in his species' endless search for worms and grubs.

But, no, he jerked his head toward the edge of the stream, where an odd combination of mud, soggy vegetation, and chunks of fresh reeds formed a platform about six feet in diameter and three feet high. In its center lay about thirty elongated eggs, covered with a layer of mud and more plant material, no doubt intended for camouflage. The eggs were no wider than chicken eggs, but at least three inches long. This must be the nest for some bayou waterfowl. Selene held her biology book at the ready.

But then the proud mama came ambling along the muddy bank, carrying more mud and reeds in its mouth for the large nest. And it was definitely not a bird.

Without thinking, Selene shrieked and almost slipped

off her tree branch. Etienne caught her and pulled her back up to her precarious perch, but her book fell with a clunk to the ground.

Mama Vuitton, with a loud grunt, proceeded to chomp on the book with razor teeth the size of piano keys, combining its learned pages with the goop in its mouth. Then the ten-foot pocketbook walked . . . kerplunk, kerplunk, kerplunk . . . over to the nest on comically short legs, with her impressive tail dragging on the ground behind. There the huge animal deposited the masticated mess in her mouth onto the eggs, and with an agility unbelievable for its size clambered on top of her unhatched babies and smoothed the muddy mess by crawling over and around them.

That job done, the beast-that-could-have-been-a-Buick raised its mammoth snout, peered up at Selene and Etienne in the tree, and let out a loud roar, apparently calling to her mate, who was taking a leisurely afternoon swim about twenty feet away. Mama alligator was probably telling papa alligator, "Hey, Harry, can you believe these two nincompoops up in this tree?"

The alligator's roar also caused a million birds of a million species to squeak and shriek, flying to the sky and scurrying through the trees. And every animal with a breath of good sense left the vicinity pronto. In fact, Selene could have sworn that some of the flowers folded in their stamens and scooted off, as well.

That left her and Etienne.

"You got a spaceship handy, E.T.? What do we do now?"

He looked at her through wide, frightened eyes, his bottom lip trembling. "I dunno. The alligators were never here when I came before."

"You don't know!" she cried out, then raised her feet higher as Mama Vuitton and Harry stood at the foot of the tree, raising their leathery heads, trying to bite their legs off. "Oh, hell," Selene said and did the only thing she could think of. Scream.

"Help! James! Help!" she screeched at the top of her lungs.

Soon Etienne joined in, "Help! Papa! Help!"

Please, God, now would be a good time to send me back to nice, safe New York City.

Over and over, Selene and Etienne screamed for help, taking turns until their voices grew hoarse. It seemed like hours, but probably only ten minutes passed before James and Fergus came storming through the trees with rifles raised. Field workers followed close behind carrying rakes and hoes.

"Sacre bleu!" James cursed, holding out his arms for Etienne. The workers pushed the two alligators back toward the nest with their long-handled tools, and Fergus held his rifle in a firing position. Once, the papa alligator bit off the end of Rufus's hoe and swallowed the metal claw tip with one smooth gulp.

Within seconds of depositing Etienne out of danger, James reached for Selene.

"Jump," he ordered in an icy voice.

"I . . . I . . . ca . . . can't," she stuttered, unable to loosen her grip on the tree branch.

"Merde!" He handed his gun to Fergus and climbed up after her, prying her fingers loose and pulling her roughly after him down the tree. Selene kept her eyes on the two alligators, who were hissing and snapping at Fergus and the slaves, until James picked her up and carried her through the trees to a clearing.

Setting her down near his horse, which was staked along with Fergus's, he grabbed Etienne and lifted the small boy by both upper arms to eye level. Fergus and the workers looked at them with curiosity as they passed on their way back to the sugar fields.

"This is the worst thing you have ever done. How could you, Etienne? How could you?" His voice reeked with disappointment in his child.

"My name is E.T.," Etienne said foolishly.

His father shook him. "Listen! You foolish boy, you could have been killed, along with Selene." James's voice shook with emotion. Exhaling sharply, he pulled Etienne into his arms for a quick hug, closing his eyes with relief, then he set him back down on the ground and swatted his behind. "Go back to the house and stay in your room until I return. You will be punished, of that you may have no doubt."

"But—"

"Go! Now!"

"Don't you hurt him," Selene intervened, coming up to them on shaky legs. "Don't you even think of striking that child again. He never intended to hurt me."

"Good intentions mean nothing if a person dies or is maimed in the process. And I most certainly did not strike the boy. I merely patted his bottom," he retorted indignantly. "Do not think of interfering in how I discipline my child."

"If you want to hit someone, hit me," Selene said defiantly, stepping between him and his son.

James stared at Selene with incredulity. How could she think he would harm Etienne? Exhaling with disgust, he glared at Etienne, who had the good sense to turn and run for the plantation house. Then he told Selene in an icy voice, "Get on my horse."

"No."

"No? *No?* Have a care, lady. I've had more than enough of willful children and even more willful women. Get on the damned horse."

"I can't," she admitted, shuffling her feet in the dirt. "I don't know how to get on a horse."

"Huh?"

"I'm from New York City, you dimwit. We don't ride horses in the city; we ride subways."

"What? Never mind." James wiped a hand across his brow and set his rifle in its leather scabbard on the right side of the saddle. His patience wearing thin, he grabbed Selene by the waist. Since she was wearing men's trousers, he set her astride the horse and, in one smooth leap, mounted behind her. Putting his arms around her, he took the reins and guided the horse in a slow canter.

The light scent of Blossom's lavender soap wafted up from Selene's hair, which was pulled back off her face with a green ribbon. He barely restrained himself from putting his lips to her sharp cheekbones to see if her skin smelled the same.

"Where are we going? The house is the other way."

"You need to calm down before you go back."

"Thank goodness I didn't bring all the kids here for this field trip." The thread of hysteria in her voice belied her calm words, and suddenly her body began to shake with violent tremors of delayed shock.

"Field trip?" he croaked out, wrapping his arms tightly about her slim frame, pulling her closer. A huge lump formed in his throat. The woman was a magnet to danger—first Victor, the sheriff, the snake, now alligators. He couldn't imagine what disaster would befall her next.

All he knew was that he wanted to protect her from all her hurts—those from her past, present, and future. And that was an impossibility. All he had was the moment. "Shhh. It's all right now. You're safe."

"I was so scared. For Etienne. And me," she said tremulously. Her fingertips caressed his bare forearms distractedly, from wrist to elbow and back again, as she spoke.

He closed his eyelids briefly with a silent groan. Did she suspect how that mere touch turned his blood hot, his heart racing? No, she was innocent of her effect on men . . . on him. All those years with that jackass lover of hers . . . Devon . . . had blinded her to her sensual allure.

"You should be proud of Etienne, James. He's a brave little boy, and I don't think he would ever deliberately hurt someone. At least, not seriously," she amended on further thought.

He grunted with amusement. "You're like a lioness protecting her cub." Then he thought about something alarming and spoke the words without thinking. "I don't think

Etienne's ever had anyone stand up for him before, except me. Oh, my mother cares, as well as Blossom, but no one has ever defended him quite so fiercely as you just did. Why would you care?"

"He's your son," she murmured.

His heart slammed against his chest walls at that simply stated explanation. He had to stop this growing fascination for a woman who could not be a part of his life.

She snuggled back against his chest, her tremors finally subsiding, and in the process her bottom rubbed against his thighs and the hardening evidence of his "fascination."

He groaned.

"Did I hurt you?" She shifted forward slightly.

He laughed, a low sound, more resembling a growl, and thought, To hell with it. Putting the reins in his left hand, he placed his right arm firmly around her waist and pulled her flush against his body.

She inhaled sharply, now aware of his desire for her. He thought she might pull away, but after a moment of indecision she relaxed and settled into his embrace.

"Tell me about yourself, Selene," he said, letting the horse follow the pathway that paralleled the course of the bayou. "Tell me about your childhood, your family, your work . . . your lovers."

"Then, will you reciprocate? Will you tell me about your childhood, about Santo Domingo, about the early days on the plantation here . . . about Giselle?"

For several long seconds he said nothing. Finally he spoke. "Perhaps."

That seemed to satisfy her.

"I never knew my father," she started, and went on to tell of a cold, highly structured childhood, a controlling, ambitious mother who spent her entire life telling Selene that her only worth was in her physical appearance. He tucked his chin over her head and ran one callused palm over her bare arm in comfort, never speaking.

When she told him of the death of her friend Tessa from

an odd illness resulting from starvation . . . something called anorexia . . . he shared her dismay with soft words. She turned her head slightly to look back at him with surprise. "When Tessa died, Devon said she always was a dumb broad."

"Devon was a . . . what do you call it? . . . jerk."

She nodded with a faltering smile. "Yeah, Devon was a jerk. And a three-year mistake in my life." An easy silence prevailed between them as the horse ambled along before she added, "Have there been any mistakes in your life, James?"

He couldn't help but chuckle at that. "Ah, Selene, *chérie,* my life has been one long mistake. If I had been able to accept my situation as a bastard child, my early life with my mother in New Orleans would have been tolerable. My father didn't treat us badly. Most times, he just ignored us."

He shrugged at the memories, surprised that they no longer pained him so much. "But I was young and stubborn—"

"And still are."

He squeezed her with mock chastisement and went on, "—and decided when I was thirteen that I was a man. With foolhardy abandon, I signed a three-year indenture that took me to Santo Domingo, then stayed on for an additional seven years until I earned enough to return to my mother. Those years were intolerable beyond belief. But no worse than Negro slaves face every day in the South."

"But not on your plantation, James," she offered. "I can see that you're trying to make it better for them. Can I tell you something about slavery and the future?"

He hesitated, not sure he wanted to know of events to come.

"Slavery will be abolished after the Civil War, which, I think, will start in 1861 with the firing on Fort Sumter. The war between the North and the South will be a horrible, bloody travesty of brother fighting against brother."

James felt the blood drain from his face in horror. "How long . . . how long will it last?"

"Until 1865."

"My God!"

"And, James, you have to know that the South will be brought to its knees. Devastated. Burned to the ground in some places."

James could barely comprehend all she was telling him. Could it be possible? "But the Negroes will then be free?"

"Yes, but the Emancipation Proclamation didn't bring an immediate solution. Heck, a hundred and sixty-some years later, in 2012, blacks will still be fighting for equality, although we have had a black president."

James ignored the black president reference and horned in on something else. "You say the Civil War will start sixteen years from now. I'll be fifty years old then, and Etienne twenty-one. I hope I will be long gone from the South by then."

"You wouldn't want to fight for the North in the Civil War?"

"I don't know. The cause sounds noble, but the idea of fighting my neighbors . . . I just don't know. I wouldn't be very young then, either."

"But Etienne would. Oh, James, I hadn't thought of that when I began to tell you about the future. I don't like this knowing what's coming in the years ahead."

"Neither do I, but now that I do know, I will be forced to make a decision as regards Etienne, won't I?"

She nodded. "And we can't tell anyone else about this, James. I don't know why I've been sent to the past, but somehow I know it's wrong for me to be trying to change history . . . impossible, actually."

"You're right." James would have much to think about later, but not now. It was too much to digest at once. Besides, he was supposed to be taking Selene's mind off her harrowing experience with the alligators. He smiled to himself, remembering something. "Hmmm. The Civil War . . . that's the time of that story you keep dwelling on, isn't it? You know . . . Crimson and Rat."

She pinched his arm playfully. "Oh, you! It's Scarlett O'Hara and Rhett Butler, and you know it. And *Gone With the Wind* is the most famous, romantic love story ever told."

"Well, I think it would have been a better book with the names Crimson and Rat."

"I think you're just changing the subject. It's your turn now. Tell me about your early days at Bayou Noir and . . . and Giselle."

He froze for a moment, then sighed with resignation. "I was almost twenty-four years old when I returned from Santo Domingo with twenty thousand dollars in my pocket."

"That's a lot of money for these times, isn't it?"

"A considerable amount," he agreed, "but not enough to buy a prosperous plantation, or even a flourishing business in New Orleans. So, like many of the Americans coming into the South, and the Creoles down on their luck, I took a chance on a run-down shambles of a bayou sugar plantation."

"The Last Chance Plantation," she remarked with a laugh, reminding him of her earlier nickname for his home.

"The rest of my story is not so unusual. It's lonely here in the swamps. I was able to make even fewer trips into the city then. And when I did, I met Giselle. Ironically, Victor introduced us. I thought she was the answer to my dreams." He made a low sound of disgust before adding, "She wasn't."

"Oh, James." She clasped his hands in both of hers, and the gesture touched him as deeply. Then she asked softly, "And what are your dreams now?"

He didn't hesitate to answer. "I have none. Or, at least, they are more simple dreams. Make a home for my son and my mother away from the ignominy of slavery, perhaps in a less harsh environment, one less susceptible to the moods of nature."

"So you want to move away from Louisiana?"

"Yes, most definitely, but I'm not sure where. Maybe the West, maybe even another country."

They stopped and James slid off the horse, tying its reins to a birch sapling. Then he held out his arms for Selene to slip into his embrace.

They had traveled about a mile from the plantation house, but the sugar fields were only a short distance away. This spot at the curve of the bayou stream was a favorite of his. For some reason, he wanted to share it with Selene . . . before she left.

Selene put her hands on his shoulders as he put his hands on her waist to lift her from the saddle. When she stood before him, still within his arms, she raised the sweeping lashes of her hazelnut eyes—deep pools of liquid brown flecked with shards of green.

"Why did you say we stopped?" she asked huskily.

Disconcerted at first by the awareness of her soft breasts pressed against his chest, both hearts thumping wildly in sweet counterpoint, he stood speechless with gut-wrenching need. Finally, when he could speak above a croak, he jiggled his eyebrows mischievously, much as his son was wont to do, and said enigmatically, "I'm taking you on a . . . what did you call it? . . . field trip."

Selene's head shot up with alertness.

Pushing away slightly, she studied James through half-lidded, suddenly suspicious eyes. Was that a flicker of amusement she detected in his brilliantly blue eyes, so like the warm skies that hovered above them? And that slight twitch at the corners of his lips . . . hadn't he looked at her in the same way last night when he'd thrown out a challenge to her? "I have never lost a battle once I set my course," he'd told her when she'd taunted him with sexual fantasies he would never realize because he foolishly chose to send her away.

"A field trip, huh?" she said, stepping agilely out of his embrace. "So you expect to teach the teacher a lesson, do you?"

"Oui," he admitted unabashedly, taking her hand in his and leading her into a thickly wooded area near a wide curve of the bayou stream.

"Be careful, James, that you don't get hoisted on your own . . . petard."

His only response was a low chuckle and a squeeze of her hand.

When they had almost reached the edge of a bushy screen near the water's edge, he motioned with a fingertip to his mouth for her to remain silent. Then he sank quietly to the ground, taking her with him. With a few efficient adjustments of their bodies, he had her sitting on the ground between his widespread knees, both facing forward.

"It's really mean of you if you intend to scare me with more snakes or alligators," she whispered.

He shook his head vehemently, as if wounded that she would think so ill of him, then indicated once again that she should remain quiet. Tucking her body more closely into the curve of his, he put his mouth near her right ear and whispered, "This is a special place for me. I want to share an extraordinary spectacle with you, *chérie.*"

Selene felt his warm breath near the shell of her ear, then the heady sensation of his lips grazing the curve of her neck. She looked back at him over her shoulder, almost brushing her lips with his.

His compelling eyes held hers for a long moment. "Just watch, *chérie,* and learn about my world."

When Selene turned forward again, she peered through the space he'd made in the brush with their bodies, just large enough for them both to see to the water's edge. She tried to ignore the dreamy intimacy of their private cocoon, sheltered from the rest of the world, and the tingling path of his callused fingertips as they skimmed the sensitive inner skin of her arms from elbow to wrist, over and over.

Relaxing, Selene drank in the spectrum of vivid colors assaulting her vision, then melding into a portrait of such incredible beauty that she wished she had the artistic talent to capture the image for all time. Even the pungent odors of fecund earth, animal musk, and plant life, living and dead, did not offend her senses, merely contrasted beautifully with the heady perfume of wildflowers.

A cuddly, cinnamon-colored muskrat perched on its hind feet only a few yards away, watching them curiously as it nibbled daintily on a long white root resembling a parsnip. As the creature eventually moved on, James pressed her arm and Selene became aware of the animal at center stage, which was obviously the object of James's field trip.

A large female heron, more than two feet long, with streamlined body and elongated neck, perched above the water on the projecting end of a dead tree. Rich grayish purple feathers covered the bird from crown to tail, ending in aigrette plumes on the back that resembled silky strands of hair. Her dagger-sharp beak stuck out a good five inches, and circles of lavender skin surrounded her scarlet eyes.

The female bird tilted its skinny neck this way and that, studying the skies expectantly. She bobbed her head several times, as if in approval, as the male heron she'd obviously been expecting dipped and soared several times before swooping down smoothly to perch beside her on the branch. Identical in appearance to the female, though slightly larger, he sidled inch by inch toward the female, who ignored his presence with universal female haughtiness for the randy male.

"Smart lady . . . ignoring that horny studmuffin," Selene quipped, and James squeezed her arm softly for silence. At the same time, he laid a palm flat against her stomach and pulled her back flush against the vee of his thighs.

The heron wasn't the only horny studmuffin in that clearing.

For a long, long time the birds did nothing, just perched next to each other, though Selene sensed their acute awareness of each other. Just as she was aware of every ragged breath James drew, every flutter of his fingertips as they took increasingly bold liberties in exploring her body—her collarbone, her ribs, her abdomen and belly, always avoiding her breasts which swelled and ached beneath the thin fabric of her cotton shirt.

Finally the female shook herself and dropped down to a lower branch and leaned her long neck against the male's flanks. The gesture was simple and yet so poignant.

"She's signaling that she accepts him for her mate," James murmured near her ear. Selene had to fight the compulsion to lean against James in much the same way, and, in fact, did arch her neck so her head rested back against his shoulder, her breasts lifted slightly.

With just the lightest touch, James placed his fingertips on her hardening nipples, and pleasure, pure and explosive, shot through Selene's body like liquid fire, pooling between her legs in a molten mass of quivering need.

"Mon Dieu!" James muttered under his breath and dropped his hands from her breasts. But Selene felt the involuntary tremors of his arousal in his thighs, which hugged her tightly, and in the hardness which pressed against her backside. With deliberate restraint, he forced her to look back toward the herons.

Once again, the two birds remained almost motionless for an exceedingly long time until suddenly they both raised their heads at the same time. Loud croaking sounds came from their beaks, shattering the stillness of the bayou around them, sounding very much like the groans of lovers driven beyond their control.

And, yes, Selene could sympathize. She, too, was aroused to the point of groaning aloud.

The female stretched and flapped her wings, shuffling from foot to foot as if marking time. Every few minutes, one or both of them would point its beak high, thrust its chest out, and croak hoarsely. Like lovers arching with desire.

And Selene pictured James entering her body, his back arched just so, his neck tense with suppressed passion.

Now the male bird became more aggressive, hopping from one branch to another, shaking himself, raising and lowering his crest feathers. Over and over he performed these motions in a graceful dance of seduction. When he finally stopped the rhythmic movements and perched himself next to his chosen mate once again, he leaned over and twined his neck with hers. She did likewise, and they were soon locked in an incredible love knot.

"Oh, James, it's beautiful."

"*Oui*, I knew you would think so," he commented in a raw voice.

The birds stood, necks entwined, for a long time, periodically unwinding and winding their necks in sensuous embrace.

Selene had seen enough and moved as if to stand.

"The mating ritual of the Louisiana heron," James commented softly, lifting her bodily by the forearms and turning her so that she knelt before him. "What do you think?"

"I think you are a more powerful opponent than I had thought."

"Oh?"

"Did you bring me here deliberately to prove that you will win any battle of seduction? Or did you truly want to share a special experience?" Her eyes clung to his, fearing his answer.

"Both," he admitted. "I cannot deny that, at first, I intended to use this sensuous spectacle to my own advantage. But I think I also wanted you to take this memory back with you to your time." He shrugged miserably. "There is a memory I would have you give me, too, if you would."

"Oh, James." Her heart skipped a beat at the thought that he might finally make love to her. Her senses spun and she blinked with lightheadedness.

"Not *that*, Selene. I just want to look at you one time. Will you remove your shirt and show me your breasts? Please, *chérie?*"

Hypnotized, Selene could no more deny the smoldering

appeal in his burning eyes than the driving need to please him, and to be pleased. With slow clumsiness, Selene undid one button after another, holding his eyes the entire time. His white-knuckled palms pressed to his knees and his ragged breaths betrayed his soul-drenching arousal.

With blood pounding in her veins and a sweet humming in her ears, Selene removed her shirt and brushed the straps of her camisole down, exposing herself to his hot perusal from neck to waist.

She should have been embarrassed. Instead, she raised her shoulders proudly and stared at him in challenge.

"Lift yourself . . . for me," he coaxed with savage persuasion.

Without question, she put her hands under her breasts and raised their heavy weight. Selene looked down, fascinated, as the sun filtering through the trees sparkled on her smooth flesh, and her breasts surged at her own intimate touch.

It was an erotic surrender. But at the same time empowering, Selene realized, as she watched James's jaw clench with agonizing constraint.

Then, one breathtaking inch at a time, James lowered his head, his hands still anchored on his thighs. Gentle as a summer breeze, he kissed one throbbing nipple, then the other, then drew back.

That was all.

But it was enough.

Selene keened low in her throat and gave herself up to a climax so powerful her lethargic limbs trembled and jerked with increasingly larger spasms until all she was, or had ever been, shattered, replaced with the new Selene. She would never, ever be the same again.

Struck with sudden insight, Selene knew that she could throw herself into James's arms now and he would be powerless against the raging fire that connected them. But she also saw how he sucked in huge drafts of air, fighting against the completion of the act that would bind them forever, with blinding consequences.

He was leaving it up to her to decide their fate.

Would she surrender to the passion hurtling them past the point of no return, knowing full well that she might have to leave James at any time? Or would she take the higher road and spare him the pain that would undoubtedly beset him when their inevitable parting came?

With tears running down her face, Selene turned away and donned her shirt again. It was the hardest decision she'd ever made in her life.

Chapter Fifteen

She was a doll . . .

The time for sexual games between them was over.

After they emerged from the woods onto the pathway, Selene was as quiet and grim-faced as James. What had passed between them was too special, and there was absolutely no question that it marked an ending, not a beginning.

Just before he helped her mount his horse, James leaned down and murmured against her lips, in a voice so low she might have imagined it, "Thank you."

Then he kissed her. A light, fleeting brush of firm lips against soft, like fiery butterfly wings. The bittersweet poignancy of the gesture reached into her very soul and made her yearn, beyond her grasp, for things only this man could give her.

"James, I lo—"

He put his fingertips over her lips and shook his head, halting words he refused to hear.

In silence, they rode back to the plantation house, trying their best not to touch. Each inadvertent brush of flesh against flesh, even so innocent as forearm grazing forearm, caused floodtides of emotion to soar through Selene. And she knew by James's ragged breathing that he was experiencing the same soul-wrenching difficulties.

When he dismounted near the back of the house and tied the horse to a hitching rail, he helped Selene down brusquely, avoiding eye contact.

"Now what you done to Mam'zelle Selene?" Blossom demanded of James. Hands on hips, she stood on the back gallery off the kitchen, supervising two young girls in the snapping of green beans. Bob was pecking at some of the discarded ends on the ground, eying James with hostility as he wobbled along on his three legs.

"Me?" James said with a mirthless chuckle. All the time he watched the rooster warily, since he was often the victim of the bird's sharp attacks. "What makes you think I've done anything? Why aren't you worried about me?"

"'Cause her hair looks like you drug her upside down in a bayou hurricane."

With a gasp, Selene put her hands to her wild hair, which had, not surprisingly, lost its ribbon. And, yes, it felt like she'd had her hair styled with a cement mixer.

"She always looks like that," James commented idly, picking up a raw bean and munching on it.

"And her buttons are done up wrong."

Selene's face heated as she adjusted her shirt. Even James blushed. He actually blushed under Blossom's sharp eyes.

"And her mouth looks like bees done stung it."

His eyes shot to Selene's lips, then shifted away guiltily. "It does not," he protested.

"Collagen injections," Selene proffered.

"Hah!" Blossom said, having gained the information she wanted.

"Where's Etienne? I need to talk to him," James said stonily.

"In his room. Don't you be too hard on the boy, now. He's scared somethin' awful."

"He ought to be. Do you know what he did this time?"

"Yessirree, I do. This is the worstest ever. And he gots to have a whuppin', I knows, but remember, he's only a little boy."

"No!" Selene ordered.

James and Blossom both turned on her with surprise.

Selene gulped. "It's my responsibility to discipline Etienne about this incident. I was the one involved, and I should be the one to determine his punishment."

James's eyes narrowed and he was about to argue with her.

"This is something Etienne and I have to work out between us. Talk to him later, if you must, James, but let me go to him first."

He hesitated, then nodded.

"The *caboteur* boat came by this mornin' and left some mail," Blossom informed James, then turned to Selene. "And there's a package for you, too, missie."

"For me?"

Blossom eyed her condemningly before adding, "From Marie Laveau."

Selene's heart skipped a beat, then thundered loudly in her ears. *Oh, no! Not now! Ms. Laveau said she would send the doll, with instructions, when the time was right. Could the time be right, now?*

She looked up at James, who was glaring at her with equal parts anger that she'd deliberately brought voodoo magic into his home, and pain that she'd spun a web of seduction around him this morning, knowing full well she was about to abandon him. He followed after her into the upper entryway of the house where letters had been deposited on a hall table, along with several newspapers and sugar periodicals.

Ignoring the servants who still worked on polishing the brass fireplace andirons and screens with lemon and salt, James grabbed the mail and pulled Selene roughly into the library. With a grunt of disgust, he noted the empty bookshelves and Rose Petal sitting on the floor dusting each tome, one at a time, with a damp cloth.

In a glance, the slave took in James's livid countenance and departed as fast as her big feet could carry her.

James tossed his mail on the desk unread and shoved Selene's packet at her. "Open it," he demanded, a furious tic working at the side of his mouth.

Selene took the silver letter opener James handed her and proceeded slowly, with trepidation. After all, there might be dead toads or something equally repulsive inside.

James swore when he saw the voodoo doll that Selene pulled out—a miniature dark-haired model of herself in a replica of Phillipe's ballgown. He reached for it angrily, but Selene held it behind her back, then proceeded to read Ms. Laveau's letter.

> *St. John's Day.*
> *The doll and the seeds.*
> *Stand by the bayou.*
> *Lightning will strike.*
> *One person only into the door.*
> *Beware the evil ghost.*

Without speaking, Selene handed the letter to James. He read it quickly, then snapped, "What seeds?"

"Ms. Laveau gave me some seeds the day I visited her. They presumably help in the travel through time."

"And you kept this information from me?" he asked icily. "When I specifically forbade you to bring any voodoo into my home?"

Selene shifted uncomfortably. "I couldn't tell you because then I might not ever—"

"—go home," he finished for her with a whoosh of disgust. Then he threw the letter down on his desk. "*Mon Dieu!* Right from the beginning, you were plotting to leave. Dabbling in voodoo. Just like Giselle. Do you conspire with Victor, as well?"

"Victor? James, that's not fair," she started to say, but her attention was diverted momentarily by a flash of lavender skirts outside the library door. At first she thought someone might have been listening, but then decided it must have been a servant passing. When she looked back at James and saw the closed expression on his face, she knew any further explanations would go unheard. "When is St. John's Day?" she asked over a lump in her throat.

"June twenty-third."

She made a quick mental calculation, then brightened slightly. "That means I have six more weeks here."

"Not *here*," he reminded, brushing past her. "You will be long gone from Bayou Noir by then. The note didn't say you had to stand by this bayou." He slammed the library door loudly after himself.

The cumulative effect of the morning's events caught up with her then, and tears streamed down Selene's face as she clutched the macabre doll to her chest.

Almost as soon as the door had closed, it opened again.

It was James.

He stomped forward, pulled her to him roughly, then bent her over one arm and kissed her. A hard, hungry, mind-shattering kiss. His lips coaxed and commanded. His tongue plundered and seared. Rhett could have taken lessons from this guy.

Time and place swirled in Selene's befuddled senses, and she didn't know, or care, that this man in this misplaced time and dangerous place was wrong for her. He felt so right.

When she moaned softly and melted into the kiss with willing fervor, James pulled back slightly. His beautifully firm lips parted, wet from her kiss. His pale eyes grew misty with smoldering passion . . . for her.

Selene's blood sang with the beauty of the moment.

Then he looked down at her, still bent back over his arm. The erotic glitter in his eyes slowly turned to anger.

"Think about that when you're riding your broom through time, Scarlett."

She would.

Dr. Phil would love her group . . .

"You put your right foot in . . . you put your right foot out . . . you put your right foot in and you shake it all about . . ."

Selene and her six pupils—Etienne, Cain, Abel, and three other black children, Daisy, Moses, and Goliath— were doing the hokey pokey three hours later in the school-room.

Etienne and all the young children, none older than seven, had touched Selene beyond measure by scrubbing their young bodies scrupulously and combing their hair before coming for lessons. And their enthusiasm for learning was a joy to behold.

Of course, the other children lagged far behind Etienne, never having learned to read or write, but Selene soon found that Etienne enjoyed the role of teacher's helper. And he exhibited far more patience with his friends than he did with her.

Because their young minds had short attention spans, Selene interspersed the more boring parts of their lessons with games and stories. E.T. and Casper the Friendly Ghost joined Selene's repertoire. She'd discovered she had a spe-cial talent for adapting what she could remember of modern children's stories to the nineteenth-century bayou. For ex-ample, "Kermit, The Bayou Bullfrog," "Red Riding Hood and the Big Bad Snake," "Goldilocks and the Three Alliga-tors," and the ever-popular "Green Eggs and Grits."

Selene had talked to Etienne privately before the lessons started for the day and he'd convinced her of his genuine regret for placing her in danger. He hadn't even balked too much when she said his punishment would be an early bed-time for the next week, with no desserts.

"Can we have lessons this afternoon, too?" Etienne asked when Selene said it was time to break for the midday meal. The other children chimed in their approval with squeals of delight.

Selene raised an eyebrow with disbelief, but nodded, knowing their fascination for schoolwork would probably soon diminish. She wanted to get in all her licks while she could before her forced departure.

After lunch, Selene's aerobics class awaited her in a grassy area behind the house. Two more had joined the class, expanding it to ten women, all wearing work shirts and trousers. Like raw Army recruits, they stood at attention next to their rag rugs, awaiting her orders. Mrs. Baptiste sat knitting in a rocking chair that had been pulled over, while Blossom watched from the porch where she was shelling crawfish.

After an invigorating workout, the women sat in a circle and began their first "group therapy" session. At Selene's urging, each woman introduced herself and was urged to share something private that was bothering her.

Selene started them off. "All my life I've been taught that my only asset is my appearance, and I lived with a man for three years who made me feel as if I didn't have much worth. I need to change my self-image so I can find something else to like about the real me."

The women nodded, surprising her with their understanding.

Reba spoke next. Blushing hotly with embarrassment, she confided shyly, "I'm the opposite. I need to change my appearance so I can look better. If I were better-looking, I know my life would be better. It already is."

The women nodded in agreement with her, also.

Iris told how her husband had died before her twins were born, and he had been the only man to see beyond her big behind. "Once I gets rid of this bustle of muscle, I'm lookin' to take on that Rufus," she warned the other ladies. "So, remember, he's mine."

"I kind of wish I had a bigger bottom," Reba said.

"Oh, yeah, well, I'll give you half of mine, and I'd still have enough lard left over to bake fifty pies," Iris said, shaking her head from side to side at what she considered Reba's foolishness.

Everyone laughed.

"I'm too black," Delphinium, one of the new members of the group, complained.

"Oh, Delphy, don't say that," Selene said. "Where I come from, black is beautiful."

"Really?" a number of the women asked in disbelief.

Selene nodded, knowing she had to step warily on this subject, which might reveal her time-travel background. "Black people came to realize . . . where I'm from . . . that instead of trying to look like white people in appearance . . . you know, straightening hair, mimicking clothing . . . they should take pride in their own heritage. There's beauty in all cultures, all colors." Selene shrugged, not wanting to say more.

All of the black women sat a little taller then, pondering her words. Mrs. Baptiste studied her with fascination, then got up to leave, apparently deciding not to participate in the group. She indicated with a motion of her head that Selene should join her later for tea.

After that the conversation seemed to go downhill, in the direction all women's talk eventually headed: sex.

"Did you know that Jeremiah can keep his . . . you know . . . hard for a whole hour?" one giggling woman revealed about one of the new male slaves. It was Lily of the flat chest.

"No-o-o," the other black women said with a collective sigh of awe.

"How you be knowin', Lily?" Iris asked saucily.

"He timed it with a clock in my cabin," Lily said with boastful mirth.

"And what were you doin' whilst he was doin' all that timin' bizness?" Iris teased.

"I was measurin' with a piece of string." She pulled an outlandishly long string from her trouser pocket, and they all hooted with laughter.

"I think you and Jeremiah were doin' a whole lot of wishin', 'stead of timin' and measurin'," Iris remarked skeptically, looking at the twelve-inch length of twine.

"You know what I likes?" Hyacinth interjected suddenly, her big breasts wobbling as she stood enthusiastically. "I likes a man what talks sweet durin' the lovemaking. Yep, I likes a talker."

"Sweet talkin' is all right, I s'pose, but give me a man what can talk dirty at the right time. Whoo-ee!" Verbena added, rolling her eyes heavenward.

"All I hears from your cabin is moanin'," Hyacinth commented dryly.

"Moanin' is good, too," Verbena agreed, undaunted by the laughter.

Reba was soaking up all this good information like a sponge. No doubt, Fergus would be a happy fella again that night. Then the overseer's wife made the mistake of offering her contribution. "Well, Selene knows about a book called *The Perfect Fit* that tells how a . . . a climax can go on for hours," Reba volunteered, then blushed at being the center of attention.

All the women turned to Selene, mouths hanging open with amazement and, unfortunately, curiosity. Selene shot Reba a look of reproach, but Reba just ducked her head sheepishly.

Selene had no choice then but to try and describe, as best she could remember, what the world's most wonderful sexual position was supposed to be.

"Lordy, how the couple able to walk the next mornin'?" Iris wanted to know when Selene completed her explanation.

"I don't know, and, geez, I never said it worked. I just said I read about this somewhere."

But no one was listening to Selene's disclaimers. They were all making plans for their evening entertainments, and Selene feared she was going to be remembered at Bayou Noir for something other than her schoolroom lessons with E.T. or her aerobics exercises.

The plot thickens ...

Selene entered the *garçonnière* apartment an hour later. Mrs. Baptiste was kneeling on her prie-dieu before a miniature shrine to the Blessed Virgin. Seeing her guest, the slim woman made a quick sign of the cross and stood. She motioned Selene toward a small settee before which a tea service had been laid.

While Selene added a pigload of sugar and cream to her tea, Mrs. Baptiste discreetly snuck a huge dollop of liquor into her cup from a nearby decanter. Her eyes caught Selene's as she was putting the stopper back in the decanter.

"I did not always . . . indulge," Mrs. Baptiste confessed, picking nervously at the weave in her violet patterned cambric morning gown.

"Oh, please, Mrs. Baptiste, don't think I'm judging you. I'm the last person to throw stones about addictions, or any other weaknesses."

Mrs. Baptiste smiled kindly. "I would like to talk to you about my need for . . . liquor. Your group therapy session today touched me so, but I could not bear to speak in front of the servants."

Selene nodded, understanding her reticence completely.

Mrs. Baptiste fidgeted. Then, with a disgusted sigh of exasperation, she folded her fluttering hands in her lap. "James thinks I am a weak woman, but I am much, much stronger than he would ever guess. It's just that there are things he does not know. That's why I invited you here today."

"No!" Selene stood abruptly. "It's not right that you should tell me your secrets, and not James."

"Why should it matter if you are going away?" Mrs. Baptiste asked with a sly, knowing expression on her face.

"You mean because of the Collinses coming on Sunday?"

"*Non*, that is not what I mean, *chérie*."

It took only a moment for Selene to remember the lavender-gowned figure pausing outside the library that morning. With foreboding, she dropped back down to the settee. "You know?" she breathed, fear rippling over her skin.

"*Oui*, but I suspected for days. Your magazine is very . . . interesting."

"You've seen my magazine, too? Oh, James is going to be furious."

"James is not going to know," Mrs. Baptiste said firmly. "This is our secret. I do not understand how you came to be here. I suspect you are the answer to my prayers to the Blessed Virgin." Her eyes shifted pointedly to the shrine in the corner.

Selene felt like giggling hysterically. *Geez! Now I'm the answer to a Southern lady's prayers. Not a Southern gentleman's, mind you, but a Southern lady's. Oh, Lord.*

"I believe God sent you here for James," Mrs. Baptiste added, as if reading her mind.

Selene's eyes widened with amazement.

"Have a beignet, my dear. I had Blossom make them especially for you," she offered with a soft smile. And when Selene's mouth was full of the delicious confection and she was unable to voice a protest, Mrs. Baptiste added, "I need your help to kill the ghost."

Oh, boy.

"Of course, it's Giselle . . ."

Oh, boy.

". . . aided by that diabolical Victor."

Oh, boy.

"Have another beignet. Oh, did I fail to mention . . .

Giselle was having an affair with Victor before she married James?"

Oh, boy.

Selene started to choke, and Mrs. Baptiste poured her another cup of tea.

"I discovered that Giselle was conspiring with Victor from the beginning of her marriage to my son, and that's why I killed her, of course."

Oh, boy. A huge chunk of beignet lodged in Selene's throat, and for a moment she couldn't breathe. *This is not happening to me. I have not landed in Bedlam. This is not Joan Crawford in* Whatever Happened to Baby Jane? *I just imagined that this demure lady sitting before me, sipping tea, said that she killed someone. But if I see anyone remotely resembling Bette Davis come down those stairs, I am definitely going to pee my pants.*

"I enjoyed killing her, you know. I shouldn't admit that, but I did. She was an evil, evil woman who deserved to die."

"Mrs. Baptiste, you really need to talk to James about this." *And a priest or two. Not to mention a psychiatrist.*

Mrs. Baptiste ignored her advice with a dismissive wave of her fingers. "I've been saying a rosary a day in penance since the day I killed Giselle, but God must not have forgiven me yet. That's why the ghost comes back to haunt me, and Bayou Noir. That's why I . . . drink."

Selene put her cup on the table and rubbed her furrowed brow, trying to understand Mrs. Baptiste's jumbled words. "Let me get this straight . . . you killed Giselle? How?"

"I had seen her making love with Victor. I had to stop the wickedness, especially when their devious plots spread to my son and grandson, endangering their lives."

"You didn't answer my question. How did you kill Giselle?"

"Poison," she said matter-of-factly. "Then I dragged her body down to the bayou, near the quicksand pit, and watched as it started to sink—"

"Oh, my God!"

"—but her spirit was picked up by a dark figure in a long black cloak. I think it was Satan." She said the last on a hushed whisper and made the sign of the cross.

"Mrs. Baptiste, confide in James. You must."

"Non, non! I could never do that. James would feel even more guilty than he already does."

Selene frowned, unable to understand the relationship between James's guilt and his mother's actions.

"They argued fiercely that night, as was their pattern so often. I don't think they had even shared a bed for many months," she told her with a knowing nod. "If he suspected what I'd seen and done, he would be consumed with guilt. And he would kill Victor, perhaps be imprisoned and executed for the crime. There are too many risks."

Selene's brain reeled with all that Mrs. Baptiste had told her. "And you want me to help you kill a ghost?"

Mrs. Baptiste giggled, putting her fingertips to her lips in a girlish fashion. "Oh, there's not really a ghost, my dear. Surely you knew that."

"Of course." *Yep, this is Bedlam, and I'm beginning to feel like the star attraction.*

"It's Victor who's trying to kill James, and maybe even me. The ghost is, no doubt, his *placée*, Giselle's half sister, Fleur."

"Giselle's half sister?" Selene asked on a groan. A headache the size of Vermont throbbed behind her eyes. And Selene began to see that this tap dance through time posed even more problems than she'd originally thought.

"Oui. She is a quadroon, of course, but she looks remarkably like a darker version of Giselle, except for the blonde hair, of course. I believe that Victor, in his evil, took great pleasure in bringing both sisters to his bed."

Selene put the heels of both hands against her eyes, hoping to stem the pounding pain. Finally she looked at Mrs. Baptiste, who waited patiently, sipping her tea. "Okay, I think I understand. Now what do you want me to do?"

Mrs. Baptiste reached down to a tapestry reticule lying at her feet and removed a crisp parchment, brown with age. She handed it to Selene significantly, saying, "I give this into your care. I no longer feel it is safe with me. This is what Victor and Giselle sought all those years . . . what Victor continues to search for. Only this paper, or James's death, will satisfy his greed."

"What is it?" Selene asked as she unfolded the aged legal document. It was a will, dated 1810, signed by Marie Verdon Edmunds and Jean-Paul Baptiste and witnessed by Judge Rene Laporte. Eighteen-ten, Selene mused. That would have been before James's birth.

While Selene read the brief document, Mrs. Baptiste explained, "I told you before that Jean-Paul loved me. When I discovered I was *enceinte*, and Jean-Paul was unable to marry me, I decided to go to England to stay with my father's family. Jean-Paul begged me to stay. He promised to provide for me and our child . . . to give us a home and monthly maintenance. But, most important, in the event of his death, half of his estate would go to our child." She pointed to the document in her lap. "And notice the codicil at the bottom . . . his will cannot ever be revised to delete this provision for James."

"Now Victor wants it back," Selene said with sudden understanding.

"*Oui*. Desperately."

"And Jean-Paul?"

Mrs. Baptiste shrugged miserably. "I think he changed his mind, as well . . . if he ever had any intention of providing thus for James. In fact, he once asked me to give it back to him for safekeeping. Safekeeping! Why does everyone think women have syllabub for brains?"

"Why can't you just give this will to James?"

"Hah! He would just tear it up. He wants nothing from his father."

"Well, then?"

"*Non*. I have suffered too much . . . James has suffered

too much. He deserves at least this," she said, her hands shaking with emotion as she tapped her fingertips on the stiff paper.

"Okay, let's suppose I hide this will. That won't help you at all, because you already know that James is sending me away, and—"

"We cannot let James send you away," Mrs. Baptiste said blithely.

"—and that still doesn't solve the problem of the ghost."

"Ah, 'tis simple, my dear," Mrs. Baptiste said, patting her hand. "You and I are going to set a trap for the ghost—"

Oh, boy.

"—using voodoo."

Oh, boy, oh, boy, oh, boy.

You don't scare me, Rhett . . .

No sooner did Selene step out of Mrs. Baptiste's door a short time later than James grabbed her by the upper arms, lifting her off her feet, and slammed her against the wall of the *garçonnière.* The force of his shove caused tiny buds from the wisteria vines that covered the wall to flutter around them in an aromatic shower.

"What did my mother want with you?"

"James, let me go. You're hurting me."

He dropped his hands from her upper arms, but pressed his body up against hers with both arms braced on the wall above.

"James, is that you?" Mrs. Baptiste called, leaning out from the window above them. "Oh, I see you've found Selene," she said in a sweet, pleased voice, deliberately misinterpreting his aggressive stance as an embrace. "Make sure you join me and your fiancée for dinner this evening, darling. I haven't had a chance to talk to you much, *mon cher.*"

James sputtered, about to protest, but his mother had already closed the window. "You told my mother that we are engaged to marry?" he accused.

"I did not," she said huffily, slipping out from his arms and walking toward the house. "I never told anyone that we were engaged. You did, you big . . . galoot."

"What's a galoot?"

"I have no idea, but you fit the description perfectly, I'm sure."

He literally growled with frustration and took her hand, pulling her up the wide staircase in front of the house and then down the hallway toward the library. Selene looked down at their twined fingers and felt an inordinate thrill at the pressure of his palm against hers.

"What?"

"I like holding hands with you," she said in a soft voice.

He immediately dropped her hand.

She smiled.

He frowned.

Selene was having fun.

James was not.

"Do you know what I would like even more?" she said.

"No! I don't want to know." He pushed her in front of him into the library and closed the door after him.

"Are we going to make love on the desk now? Like you mentioned the other night?"

His eyes went wide and his chin dropped like a lead weight. Then he caught himself, and shook his head to clear it of whatever erotic images must have been floating about.

Hey, this teasing business is sort of neat. I think I could develop a real knack for this.

"Selene, what are you doing with my mother?" he asked with exasperation, drawing her attention back to his anger. "She's frail, and I cannot allow you to involve her in your schemes."

"My schemes! Listen here, James. Your mother is a strong woman, don't you ever doubt it. And I don't need to involve her in any schemes, believe me. She's got intrigues coming out the wazoo."

"What intrigues? Oh, Good Lord, don't tell me that she told you about my father's will."

Selene folded her arms over her chest, remaining stubbornly silent.

"If she'd just give me the damn papers, I'd hand them over to Victor gladly, and perhaps all the ghosts and treachery about this plantation would finally end."

"Treachery?"

He nodded grimly. "Someone bashed in the new sugar boiler last night. The day before, there was an attempt to burn some of the northern fields."

"Oh, James! But do you really think returning the document will stop Victor's evil?" Selene asked, feeling in her deep pocket for the paper in question.

"*Non.* Victor will not stop till I'm dead, but I won't give him that satisfaction. I've had men posted about the house at night for the past year, and I've increased their vigilance now, so I'm not too worried about you and Etienne and my mother," he pointed out, as if thinking aloud.

But what about you, James? Who's going to protect you?

"Now I'll have to take much-needed manpower from my day labor to guard the fields and equipment at night," he continued. "Well, there's nothing to be done about . . . What? Why are you looking at me like that?"

Tears welled in Selene's eyes as she gazed at James. He had so many problems weighing him down. She wished he would let her help him. Well, perhaps she could . . . indirectly . . . by working with his mother in her plot.

"I don't want your pity," he snarled, misreading her tears.

"You don't have it."

He blinked with confusion.

She took one step toward him, and he backed up one step.

"I don't want you, Selene."

She laughed, a low, sultry sound, just the kind Eve must have made before she handed Adam the apple.

"Well, I want you, babe."

"This is ridiculous. I brought you in here to tell you to stay away from my mother, to prepare for your departure, and, instead, you're looking at me like a—"

"—beignet?" Selene raised her brows with exaggerated interest. "Do you know what my favorite way is to eat a beignet? First I like to lick all the sugar off, with lo-ong, sloow strokes of my tongue, before I—"

He shot her a look of disbelief.

"—chomp down on it with my teeth."

He winced, then wagged a finger in her face. "I give you fair warning, Selene. Your games are no longer amusing, and I cannot have you meddling with my mother's already muddled mind. I will have my problems, or not have my problems, with Victor long after you are gone. They are none of your concern."

Opening the library door, he hesitated, then threw out one last caution. "And beware of biting too hard on the beignet. Some of them are harder than others."

Chapter Sixteen

T he song from Ghostbusters *could have been the soundtrack to this latest insanity . . .*

"This is the craziest thing I've ever done in all my life," Selene grumbled as she tripped and almost ran into the back of Iris, who was leading them through a path in the woods behind the plantation house.

"Shhh," Mrs. Baptiste said behind her. "We don't want James's guards to hear us."

Carrying candles to light the way in the pitch-black night, they'd already slipped by two of the many men patrolling the periphery of the plantation house and grounds. Fortunately, James had gone into Iberville that afternoon to meet with a sugar broker and didn't intend to return until morning. But he had made good on his promise to provide additional protection to his home and family, and his extra vigilance had made their escape all the harder.

The usual night sounds of crickets and an occasional hoot owl, not to mention the distant rumble of thunder, served as backdrop to their amplified breathing. Actually, it was the brewing storm that had prompted their escapade this night, along with James's absence. Knowing that the ghost usually appeared in the midst of a thunderstorm, Mrs. Baptiste had declared this the perfect opportunity to put their plan into effect.

"Stop shivering, *chérie*. It's only a voodoo ceremony."

Oh, Lord. "What makes you think we can do any better job than James in catching this 'ghost'?" Selene whispered over her shoulder, not that she hadn't been making this argument with Mrs. Baptiste all day. "Heck, we look like ghosts ourselves." All three of them had donned loose gowns, known in modern times as Mother Hubbards, the traditional dress for voodoo participants, but, in addition, they wore long, black veils to hide their identities.

"Because, my dear, James doesn't know how to get to the site of the voodoo ceremonies," Mrs. Baptiste explained patiently, barely above a whisper. "It's the one secret the slaves keep from their masters, even on threat of death."

"Then why is Iris showing us?"

"Because she thinks you have the magic powers, as well."

"Me?" *Oh, Lord.*

"Perhaps you are a priestess in your time, *chérie?*"

"Hardly." *And if one person asks me to chop off a chicken's head, or drink blood, I'm going to barf.* Then she thought of something else. "I'm a Christian. I shouldn't be going to one of these . . . pagan ceremonies."

"But why not?" James's mother asked with surprise. "Many voodoo rituals also include homage to St. John the Baptist. He is the counterpart to the African *loa* for thunder and lightning." The skies provided another clap of thunder at that opportune moment to emphasize her words before she added, "In fact, many ceremonies end with baptism."

Great! St. John the Bayou Baptist. And I'm St. Joan of the Time-Travel Arc.

By now they had traveled about a mile from the plantation house, following a circuitous, sometimes nonexistent path inland. The farther they went, the louder the drums beat, almost in cadence with the continuing thunder and occasional lightning.

Iris had explained earlier that voodoo practitioners came from the surrounding plantations, as well, and drummers were stationed in many locations to mislead any outsiders who sought to discover the hidden ceremonial site.

Turning on them both now, Iris gestured with a raised hand for their silence, pointing to a clearing just ahead. "You must not speak," she said in a hushed voice, "no matter what you see."

Selene and Mrs. Baptiste nodded.

Mrs. Baptiste seemed strangely exhilarated by the whole eerie venture. Selene was scared stiff.

"I swear, if I see one human sacrifice, I'm going home," Selene muttered.

Then she was stunned speechless.

Many candles glowed in a wide circle, throwing frightening shadows on the more than fifty people who jammed the small clearing, swaying to the beat of the mesmerizing drums. Rocking from side to side, the attendees appeared intoxicated, or under the influence of the hypnotizing ritual. A few of them were clearly white and some wore veils like theirs.

Iris drew them to the back of the circle where it was darker, and Selene shuddered with foreboding.

"Hear and come, oh grand *zombi*. Hear and come to work your magic," a compelling male voice called out. Lightning struck suddenly, seeming to hit almost directly behind the makeshift altar. Through the vaporous bayou mists, Selene saw a black man and woman, presumably the voodoo priest, Papaloi, and the queen, Mamaloi.

The tall, majestic man with frizzy gray hair continued to chant, in some other language now, finally turning with significance toward his partner. The woman's coal-black skin gleamed with perspiration as she reached into a wooden box on the ground and picked up a long, black snake.

A snake! Selene's heart just about popped out of her chest.

Then the woman stepped atop the box and began to writhe, like the creature she coiled around her neck. The reptile slithered about her body—over her pointed breasts, around her waist, even up her parted legs under her gown, emerging at the neck.

The whole time, the woman undulated in a sexual parody. And the attendees watching her erotic dance partook of a large cup of drug-laced tafia that was passed around. Under its influence, they worked themselves into a mad dance, speaking in tongues, jerking their bodies, touching themselves intimately.

The voodoo king, who wore a robe covered with strange signs and a necklace of snake rattles, traced a large circle with a black substance, urging candidates to come forward for initiation. The priest tapped each of the kneeling initiates with a wooden paddle. Meanwhile, he intoned a rhythmic African chant, immediately taken up by the crowd, which seemed to be falling into a trance—some fainting, others in a frenzy, spinning around and tearing off their clothes, even biting their flesh in an orgasmic fever.

At the height of the ceremony, a squawking chicken was laid over a low table. The priest severed its head with one smooth stroke of a sharp blade and let the bird's blood drip into a copper bowl.

The young Mamoloi put the snake back in the box and lifted her robe off her still undulating body. The priestess then dipped her fingertips into the blood, smearing the crimson fluid over her now nude body. Other celebrants, one by one, did the same, then paired off, male and female, and began to engage in sex, on the spot.

Revolted, Selene had seen enough.

Turning to Iris and Mrs. Baptiste, she noticed that their

attention centered on a couple on the other side of the circle who were slipping surreptitiously into the edge of the wood. The white man, wearing a mask and a long black cape, was speaking forcefully to a short, veiled woman before him, pointing a finger in her face when she seemed to disagree with his orders. Finally he shoved her in the direction of the plantation house, and he turned back to the orgy surrounding them. No doubt, he intended to participate in the perverted sexual games.

Selene exchanged knowing looks with her two cohorts as a flash of bayou lightning illuminated the clearing for a brief second.

It was Victor and the "ghost."

Iris motioned her head in the direction of the path they had followed from the house, and the three of them fell back into the darkness. When they were beyond hearing range of the voodoo revelers, Iris whispered hurriedly, "I will return to the big house . . . the short way along the bayou. You two follow after the ghost, but keep your distance. And make sure Victor does not come after you on the path."

Selene and Mrs. Baptiste nodded.

"Follow our plan once you get to the house. Rufus is waiting in the appointed spot." Then Iris disappeared into the murky forest.

The storm broke with a fury, soon drenching Selene and James's mother, making them unable to see more than two feet in front of them. Selene kept darting fearful glances over her shoulder in case the voodoo orgy broke up early and Victor followed them. She was more afraid of Victor than any "spirit."

By the time they got to the plantation, there was no sign of the ghost; so Selene and Mrs. Baptiste parted company, going to their previously designated spots for trapping the ghost. If it was Fleur, as Mrs. Baptiste suspected, Selene didn't want her killed, and she'd made all her accomplices promise to use only minimal force in the capture. They wanted information from Fleur, not her death.

Mrs. Baptiste, looking like a wet, bedraggled cat, waited until one of James's guards walked by on his rounds, then slunk through the kitchen door where Blossom awaited her with formidable weapons—brass soup ladles and a wooden apple-butter paddle. Selene heard the lock click into place behind Mrs. Baptiste, as planned.

Then she slipped around to the front. Rufus was stationed on the third floor near the sleeping quarters, with a rifle in case Victor showed up, and a huge swath of fish netting to throw over the "ghost." Iris had gone to the fourth floor to guard Etienne.

It was Selene's job to double check all the doors and windows, except for the central door on the second floor, so that the "ghost" wouldn't be able to escape once surrounded. Selene's sodden slippers squished noisily in the eerie silence. Satisfied that the second floor was secure, Selene was about to climb the stairs when she heard a faint rustling noise in the library, then saw a dim light under the closed door.

She peeled off her noisy shoes and tiptoed down the hallway, grabbing a closed parasol from the hall stand. With fringed umbrella raised, she rushed into the room, then stopped suddenly. By the light of a single candle, she could see the "ghost" pouring a white powder into James's bottle of bourbon on a sideboard.

Poison?

With a gasp of surprise, the "ghost" dropped the packet of powder and pulled a dagger from its skirts, lifting the sharp blade overhead. But instead of storming toward Selene in assault, the veiled specter backed up warily. The hand holding the knife shook, and the fearsome "ghost" whimpered pitifully.

"Fleur, is that you?" Selene asked, lowering her parasol.

The hand shook even more and the "ghost" began to sob.

"Don't be afraid, Fleur. I won't hurt you. Just lower the knife, and we can talk."

Selene stepped forward and took the knife out of Fleur's trembling hand. Then she lifted the veil off her frightened face, steering her toward a chair. Meanwhile, Victor's *placée* wept loudly into a dainty lace handkerchief, wailing, "Oh, Mam'zelle, I didn't want to do it. Victor made me. Forgive me, forgive me. Oh, he will kill me now for failing."

Just then Selene heard a loud crash below in the kitchen, followed by a male voice cursing. "*Sacre bleu!* What the hell is going on here? Why did you strike me with that soup ladle?"

Uh oh!

At first Selene thought, even hoped, it might be Victor. No such luck!

James had returned.

And by the sounds of his colorful epithets resounding throughout the house, someone was going to have a lot of explaining to do.

"Are you all insane? Ah, I know who is responsible. Where is Selene? I'll kill the witch," she heard him yell. Then, he pounded up the back steps, looking for her.

An old sixties' tune kept flicking through her head—"James is back and there's gonna be trouble . . ."

Yep, my brain is definitely splintering off into rock 'n roll cyberspace.

She lit his fire, no matter how he denied it . . .

An hour later, James had gotten all the information he could out of the sobbing Fleur. She'd admitted being sent by Victor to put poison in James's liquor in the library and in his bedchamber, although she claimed, unbelievably, that this was the first trip she'd made to Bayou Noir. Someone else must have played the part of the ghost. Fleur did say that his cowardly brother had given up on physical assault by the "ghost," for the time being, and had decided to try a new tactic—poison.

James couldn't blame the pitiful *placée*, however. Fleur was in no position to disobey her master, no matter her objections to his evil plots.

Still, Fleur obviously hid some secret that she feared to divulge. Her terrified, doe-like eyes had darted about the room evasively, avoiding his scrutiny, but she'd refused to say more.

In the end, James sent for Fergus, ordering him to take Fleur to a hiding place they'd used in the past, both for her safekeeping from Victor who would surely seek her out and to interrogate her further in the morning.

Now, James lined the rest of the guilty parties up in the kitchen like recalcitrant children—Selene, his mother, Iris, and Rufus. Blossom declined to obey his orders, grumbling about the puddles of water they were all making on her clean kitchen floor. Instead, she set a huge pot of coffee to boil and laid some food on the table, her answer to any problem being a full stomach.

Blood roared furiously in James's head, and he feared he might do bodily harm to any one of them for their foolishness. Selene, more than any, should know better than to place his mother, Blossom, and two slaves in such danger. Instead, she kept licking her delicious lips, her eyes darting involuntarily to the table where Blossom had placed a plate of beignets. He would have laughed if he weren't so angry.

His mother remained oddly quiet, shivering in her sodden clothes. Her eyes had flashed defiantly when he'd questioned her about her participation in this outlandish scheme, but she'd clamped her lips shut stubbornly.

"Iris, I want you to dry my mother off and put her to bed in one of the guest rooms. I don't want her sleeping in the *garçonnière* tonight with Victor possibly lurking about. Rufus, you go out and help the guards. I will talk to both of you tomorrow about your part in this scheme. Surely you know that I cannot abide slaves who work against me."

They both hung their heads contritely, but Selene's chin whipped up with outrage. "Against you! Why, you lout, they were trying to help you."

Everyone's mouths dropped open in amazement at her temerity in rebuking him, except for his mother, whose blue eyes twinkled with appreciation. James gritted his teeth. How could Selene presume to question his orders?

He grabbed Selene by the upper arm and pulled her from the room, not wanting to chastise her in front of the others. Or kiss her silly, in relief over her safety. *Mon Dieu,* she could have been killed tonight, he thought as delayed shock set in.

"Don't you dare punish Rufus and Iris for helping your mother . . . I mean, me," Selene snapped at him the moment the library door was closed.

His voice rose in surprise. "My mother is at the bottom of this brainless plot?"

Her face flushed guiltily at having inadvertently revealed the truth. "No," she lied, "it was all my idea. And it wasn't a brainless plot. The plan would have worked if you hadn't come home before you were supposed to. Actually, it did work since the 'ghost' is now in custody. So there! Why did you come home early anyhow?"

"Not that it's any of your business, but I had my own plan for capturing the 'ghost' . . . which you hampered with your actions tonight, by the way."

He started to pour himself a drink, then decided that would be a fatal mistake in light of the powder Fleur had put in it. Opening the gallery door to the cool night air—the storm had abated to a slow drizzle—he walked out onto the gallery and poured the decanter's contents over the railing.

When he returned to the library, he saw Selene wiping up the excess powder with the edge of her damp gown. "I wouldn't want Etienne, or even Dreadful, to go near this poison," she explained, shivering with cold.

Lord, she looked like a drowned rat. Her wet hair clung to her face in thick clumps, rivulets still running down her cheeks to her neck and a puddle forming on the wood floor at her feet. Her loose gown hugged her slim body, delineating her magnificent breasts and the smooth curve of her hips, even her excessively long legs.

His eyes feasted on her, and then he gulped, especially when her hazelnut eyes welled with tears and she gazed back at him needfully. He knew she'd been through an ordeal that night and that she wanted him to take her into his arms for comfort.

Instead, he took a key from his desk and opened a cabinet that held several unopened bottles of liquor. He poured two tumblers of bourbon and handed one to her. "Drink," he ordered, "before you shiver your skin off."

Her eyes glittered with resistance at his harsh tone, but then she sank down into a chair before the desk, holding the glass in both hands as she sipped. "Where did you take Fleur?"

He refused to tell her.

She made a tsk-ing sound of rebuke. "Will she be safe?"

He nodded.

"Do you think Victor will come after her?"

"Undoubtedly. In his own twisted way, he will view this as my taking something that belongs to him."

She nodded sadly in agreement. "And when he comes, will you be able to trap him?"

"Only if he makes an assault himself, which he rarely does, coward that he is."

"Will it ever end?" she asked wearily.

"One way or another, *oui,* it will." He intended to bring matters to a head with his brother, and soon, but Selene didn't need to know that.

"James, it was awful tonight . . . that voodoo ceremony. I've never witnessed anything so bizarre, and evil. Have you ever attended one yourself?"

"*Oui,* many times in Santo Domingo. Voodoo is not

always evil in character, though. In fact, sometimes the rites resemble a Christian church service."

"Your mother said that."

He was momentarily speechless with surprise. Apparently his mother was not quite the ill-informed, weak woman he had thought her of late. He would have to watch her more carefully. "Tell me what you saw tonight."

As she sipped her drink, tracing the lip of the glass with a fingertip as she talked, Selene told him about all they had done and seen that night.

"Are you sure the chicken wasn't Bob?" he asked hopefully at one point, and she laughed spontaneously . . . a moment of shared mirth as their eyes connected. And his heart slammed against his chest walls in longing.

He took another huge swallow of his drink for strength, draining the glass, and poured a refill.

"If you went to your father and gave him back the will, do you think he could put a stop to Victor's schemes?" Selene asked.

"I don't think so. I believe Victor is out of control, mad with greed and envy . . . though why he should envy me, I cannot fathom."

"Perhaps it has something to do with Giselle," Selene said tentatively.

"Why should you think that?" he asked with curiosity, surprised at his own lack of anger at her personal question.

"Well, your mother seems to believe that Victor and Giselle had been . . . involved . . . before your marriage . . . and you said yourself that you had met Giselle through Victor."

"My mother said that? Truly, I need to have a long talk with her. But you are right. I suspect Victor did have feelings for Giselle, but my father would never have agreed to their marriage. I wish, in retrospect, though, that Victor had claimed her for himself."

He saw Selene's open face brighten at his words, and he chuckled at their impossible situation. He wanted her. She wanted him. And neither could have the other.

"Tomorrow is Thursday. On Sunday you will be going off with the Collinses, *chérie,*" he said softly. "After tonight, I am even more convinced you will be better off away from Bayou Noir. Your safety is important to me, no matter what you may think."

She held his eyes for a moment in question before her long lashes fluttered downward. "Yes, I think you do care."

"I didn't say I cared," he immediately amended.

Slanting him a knowing look, she remarked with certainty, "You care."

He was trying to keep some balance in this tightrope he walked between self-control and mind-boggling lust. "Don't push me, Selene."

"You can't even bear to touch me, James, for fear of the spark that would ignite between us."

"Oh, and you think you could 'light my fire' so easily. Think again, my dear," he scoffed.

"James, James, James," she said with mock despair, "your fire has been lit for weeks. Hell, it's a raging wildfire, as far as I can see. You just can't admit that you care." She stood then, her shoulders slumped with weariness, and left for her bedchamber to sleep off her exhaustion.

"I admit it," he murmured aloud after she left, taking another long swallow of bourbon. "I admit it, *chérie.*"

Now she knew what slavery was really like . . .

The next afternoon, Selene and her ten students were sitting in the grassy plot Rufus had cleared in the front of the plantation house. She stacked their math papers in front of her, satisfied with all they'd accomplished that day, both in their morning session and again after lunch. Selene's heart

swelled with pride at the children's enthusiasm for learning
and her recognition that she had a talent for teaching.

"Can we sing the name song again?" Etienne asked.

Selene ruffled his hair and was inordinately surprised
when he didn't immediately pull away. "Sure. Who wants
to start?"

"Me! Me!" Hollyhock lisped through her two missing
front teeth.

"Okay, Holly, you start, and we'll all repeat the refrain.
Then we'll continue around the circle, like we did before."

The little, wiry-haired girl stood and sang out merrily,
"Holly, Holly, fo folly, fee fie, fo folly. Holly."

Cain stood as Holly sank to the ground with a giggle and
began, "Cain fain, fo fain . . ." His words trailed off in mid-
sentence as his eyes widened with fright, staring over Selene's shoulder. The other children gasped and whimpered,
pulling closer to her skirts.

Confused, Selene stood and turned around to see Jake
Colbert, the overseer to James's father, Jean-Paul. He was
docking a flatboat on the bayou landing. James had pointed
him out to Selene at the slave auction in New Orleans.

Colbert and two other brutish looking men jumped off
the boat, leading a half-dozen vicious, barking bloodhounds in front of them on long leashes. Dreadful, who had
been sleeping at her feet, raised his huge head, saw the
loudly snarling canines approaching, blinked several times
in disbelief, then had the good sense to take off with a flying leap for the safety of Blossom's kitchen.

"It's a slave patrol," Etienne informed her, moving to her
side with touching protectiveness.

Colbert and his men moved up the incline toward them,
barely able to keep the frothing dogs under control. When
they got closer to Selene and her students, who cowered
behind her skirts, Selene could see the cruelty in the overseer's thin lips beneath a huge drooping mustache and in
the white-knuckled fingers of his right hand, which flexed
on the handle of a knotted whip, almost with anticipation.

"Where's that bitch, Fleur?" he asked Selene without any introduction.

"Who?" Selene answered evasively.

"You know damned well who, missie, and don't you be lyin' to me."

Selene raised her chin haughtily. "You're trespassing here, Mr. Colbert. Besides, Fleur is a free black . . . a *placée.* You have no right to seek her out."

His evil eyes narrowed craftily and he spit tobacco juice on the ground with deliberate disdain. "So the bitch *is* hidin' here. Well, let me tell you somethin', missie," he said, poking her in the chest with the handle of his whip, "I hear you got a bit of the blood in you, too. You're nothin' but a high yaller yourself. You kin be put on the auction block same as Fleur. Papers don't mean nothin'. Victor owns Fleur, and he kin own you, too. Best you accept that."

Then his eyes lit on the children surrounding her. "What're you doin' with these pickaninnies?"

Selene clenched her fists, and her lips curled contemptuously. "These are my students, Mr. Colbert."

"She's teachin' niggers," one of the men exclaimed with outrage. "Wait till they hear 'bout this back in Nawleans. Not only is Baptiste freein' his niggers, now he's givin' 'em an ej-e-ca-tion, too."

Selene ignored the man's words and directed her attention to the overseer. "I would suggest that you wait here in the yard, Mr. Colbert, while I send someone for Mr. Baptiste." Her eyes raked each of the men in turn, settling on their muddy boots. "I don't think Mr. Baptiste would want you to come indoors."

"You're right about that," James said in an icy voice.

Selene turned to see him approaching from the fields, along with Fergus and several of the black workers. They all carried raised rifles.

James's eyes connected with hers for an instant. When assured that she was safe, he indicated with a wave that Selene and the children should go inside. She heard angry words being exchanged behind her, but she wasn't really worried about James's safety in this instance. Colbert and his buddies were outmanned.

The viciousness of the times stunned Selene, though. To read about slave patrols in a history book was one thing; to actually witness the sadistic practice was quite another. Her heart wept for the poor slaves subjected to this demeaning travesty of justice—to be hunted down like animals.

Selene's head swam with conflicting emotions. She wanted to race back and stand at James's side, to fight off whatever adversities came his way. And she wanted nothing more than to slip back into the future and her nice, uncomplicated life.

It wasn't really much of a mental fight. Selene knew she would never be happy without James, whether away from Bayou Noir at another plantation or in 2012 New York City.

Two people who cared about each other . . . and there was no question in her mind that James cared . . . should be working together to solve their problems. Not running away from them.

Selene had three days to convince James not to foist her off on the Collins family. Tears of frustration welled in her eyes. She had no idea what to do.

Well, maybe she needed reinforcements . . . back-up forces, so to speak . . . if she was going to launch a full-blown attack. Hmmm. She tapped her chin thoughtfully as she and the children entered the kitchen where Blossom and several slaves sat whispering nervously, jerking involuntarily anytime one of the bloodhounds barked in the distance.

"Children, I have something to tell you. We will only be able to have classes for three more days. Mr. Baptiste is sending me away on Sunday," she announced firmly for all to hear.

They all protested loudly, and Etienne exclaimed, "*Non*, my papa would not do that. You lie. You lie." His eyes shot daggers of accusation at her before he fled the room, running up the back stairs to his room.

Selene felt only a momentary twinge of guilt at her underhanded tactics. *Well, fiddle-dee-dee! A girl's gotta do what a girl's gotta do.*

"And, Iris, we've got to make sure that all the cleaning is done by then and the schedule is down pat," Selene added, turning to the black woman who eyed her suspiciously from her great height. "And tell Mrs. Baptiste I need to talk to her this afternoon about my departure."

She glanced around the room. "Blossom, you and I will have to go over my list again to make sure we've covered all the workers and their jobs. I want everything to run smoothly . . . even when I'm gone."

Blossom just chuckled and shook her head as she stirred a pot of gumbo over the *potager*. "The master don't stand a chance. He's a dead duck, he is."

She fought dirty . . .

Over the next three days, James began to feel like a leper in his own home.

He stood leaning against a tree in the woods behind the house, watching Selene give her women one last arrow-backs class before the Collinses' arrival this afternoon. He felt like a real . . . what did Selene call him? . . . ah, yes, a jerk. But he would not, could not, change his mind about sending her away.

She was from another time. She might fly away at any moment. She disrupted his life and his carefully laid plans. And she was in danger here at Bayou Noir until Victor's perfidy was stopped.

But Selene had somehow . . . deliberately, no doubt . . . drawn his family and workers to her bosom, and they had all rallied against him. Knowing of his plans to send Selene away, they assaulted him with vocal and silent protests in her defense.

Etienne berated him continually. "Why? Why do you

hafta send her away? She's a good teacher, the best I ever had. I hate you. I hate you."

Blossom scoffed at him. "Those aliens Etienne's always talkin' 'bout musta stole your brains, boy. She's the best thing that ever happened to Bayou Noir or you, and you know it. Yessirree, you do. Jist look around you. The house sparkles. Your people love 'er. Etienne ain't behaved so good since the day he was borned."

And Reba! Oh, Lord, she wept every time he came within her sight. He had to admit that Fergus's wife looked mighty good since Selene had arrived and instructed her on improving her appearance. But couldn't Reba continue without Selene's constant tutelage?

Even Fergus, who'd benefited indirectly from Selene's sexual advice, was barely civil to him in their everyday dealings. No doubt Fergus thought his newly enhanced bedroom activities would take on a boring tone once Selene left.

In fact, a number of his workers had turned sullen. These same blacks had been arriving in the fields each morning of late with satisfied smiles, leaving James with the nagging suspicion that the black women were learning more than tush crunches from Selene.

Worst of all, his mother wouldn't speak to him *at all*, and he feared she was drinking more.

Miserable, he looked straight ahead, watching as Selene raised her hips in the air, calling out, "Thrust, up, hold, release . . . thrust, up, hold, release."

James felt a thickening in his loins and his hardening erection as he watched Selene, but he couldn't blame her seductive exercises. In truth, he'd been in a continual state of arousal for weeks, ever since he'd first met her at the Quadroon Ball.

To his dismay, he realized that he wanted her not only when she thrust her open thighs upward in invitation, as she did now, but he wanted her almost every time he saw her. When she was gobbling up beignets. When she was covered with mud, or when she wore her ridiculous makeup, even the spider lashes. When she defended his son, then berated him shrilly. When she cried out in fear, then tried to save his life.

Turning away, James groaned at the difficult choice he was being forced to make. Selene continually told him that he couldn't even be her Rhett. He finally admitted to himself, though, that, more than anything, he'd like to be.

But unfortunately, in this fairy tale, he was going to be the frog, not the prince. And that was a fact.

Chapter Seventeen

𝒯he women was driving him to drink . . .

When James finally made his way toward his guests on the front gallery early Sunday afternoon, he realized that he'd failed to take into account three important factors regarding Selene's removal to the Collins plantation:

—Andrew Collins's brother Pierce was home from the West, where he was a wagon scout.

—Pierce Collins was unmarried.

—Women lapped up Pierce Collins's good looks and wild reputation like cats did a bowl of milk.

And, to James's scowling chagrin, Selene was practically purring, along with his mother and Ellen Collins. They leaned forward in their chairs, enthralled with the fascinating story Pierce was telling them.

Oh, merde!

". . . and after that, the Indians took us back to their village where Chief Black Scar . . ."

Indians! Wonderful! I get to hear all of Pierce's heroic exploits again.

". . . James, my friend, I didn't see you standing there."

Rising politely as James walked onto the galley, Andrew and Pierce towered over him at six-foot-five at the least. *Lord, what do women see in gangly giants like these two?*

About thirty years old, both men had sandy brown hair and muddy brown eyes, but that was where the resemblance ended. Andrew was thicker in the waist and more bull-like in stature, his muscles honed by hard labor in his sugar fields. Pierce, on the other hand, was lean and wiry with excessively long hair for a man, a rakish mustache, and an equally rakish smile. *He probably practices that damned smile in front of a mirror every day. And that wink! Did he just wink at Selene? I'll kill him.*

Pierce clapped a hand on his shoulder. "James, how are you? I don't think I've seen you since I was back here three years ago. So sorry to hear about Giselle."

James accepted his condolences and nodded toward Andrew in greeting. Then he bent down and took Ellen Collins's limp hand in his, kissing it in the Creole manner. Dressed in various shades of pink and white, she looked like a sweet confection. "Ellen, *chérie*, you look lovely, as usual."

Selene stiffened.

Hah, he thought, seeing her eyes fixed on Ellen's pale blonde hair, which was parted in the middle and hung in ringlets at the side of her face. With an oozing drawl, he complimented Ellen: "Is that a new hairstyle, dahlin'? I swear you have the most beautiful hair in all the South. Everyone always says it looks like spun gold."

Ellen simpered coyly, peeking at him over a pink fan.

Selene made a small gagging sound behind him.

He grinned.

"*Mère*," he said, leaning down to kiss his mother's cheek, "how good of you to honor us with your presence . . . finally." His mother had refused to leave her room for days in protest over his sending Selene away, and her eyes flashed defiantly at his mild rebuke now.

"James, sit and join us, *s'il te plaît*," his mother said,

motioning toward the empty seat next to Selene. "You are making an unpleasant shadow in front of me."

He frowned at his mother's testy tone. Sensing that it was going to be a long day, he dropped down to a low porch chair, crossing his ankles casually.

Indifferently he took his first good look at Selene. Then immediately looked again. His eyes almost bugged out.

Selene had taken infinite care with her appearance, employing all the makeup at her disposal. Her skin glowed flawless as warm peaches on a summer day, right down to the expert blush on her cheeks and the hint of color on her full lips. The green in her hazelnut eyes was accentuated by a subtle blending of kohl on the lids and, of course, those blasted spider lashes.

The smooth column of her neck and the pearly shells of her ears appeared almost naked under the graceful arrangement of her hair. She had swept the glossy, dark brown swath up and off her face into a loose knot at the back of her head, with teasing strands dangling about her face.

But the worst part was the dress—no doubt one of his mother's, altered to fit her like a second skin. The jade silk bodice, edged with cream lace, was cut low in a vee, almost to the exposed cleavage between her magnificent breasts. Its shimmery fabric hugged her from shoulders to waist, then swirled out into a full skirt, which only called attention to her long legs every time she moved in her chair. Unlike Ellen, who wore at least five crinolines, Selene wore only one . . . if that.

"James, you're staring," she admonished him under her breath.

"Damn right I'm staring. What are you wearing under that gown?"

Her eyes held his in challenge. Then she fluttered those ridiculous spiders at him and whispered, "Nothing."

Nothing? She wouldn't. Yes, she would. The witch!

He grinned and shook his head incredulously.

"Do I get one point?" she asked sweetly and didn't need to explain that they were engaged in a contest of wills.

"For that, you get two," he conceded with a laugh. Looking over at Ellen Collins, he winced at her giggling voice, which grated on his already frazzled nerves as she relayed to his mother the latest exploits of her five- and six-year-old daughters, Celestine and Eglantine. Etienne had taken the little darlings to the schoolroom to show off his E.T. drawings. James half expected to hear the girls shriek anytime now as Etienne also showed them a snake, or an alligator eyeball, or one of his own forbidden body parts.

Misinterpreting his continued stare at Ellen, Selene inclined her head toward him, asking in an undertone, "How do you put a gleam in a blonde's eye?"

"Selene, this is not the time," he hissed in warning.

"You shine a candle in her ear."

The others were still engaged in conversation, so she continued, "Why do blondes wear underwear?"

"Do they? Wear undergarments?" he asked.

She made a tsk-ing sound of disgust at his interruption. "To keep their ankles warm."

Unfortunately, she took his grim smile as encouragement. "What does a blonde have when she has two green balls in her hand?"

To his amazement, he realized that he was beginning to understand her foolish riddles and answered, "A frog's undivided attention?"

Her pink glossed lips parted with surprise. "That's not the right answer."

He smiled with satisfaction. "Ah, but a better one, don't you think? I believe that's my point, Selene. What's the score?"

He turned to ask Andrew how his crops did in this hot summer weather, but his neighbor had been pulled into a discussion with his wife and James's mother about the landscaping work Rufus had started. Pierce, on the other hand, had been following his conversation with Selene, as evidenced by his appreciative eyes raking Selene's body, no doubt imagining all that bare skin beneath. A grin twitched beneath his mustache.

God, I hate mustaches. James barely stifled a growl.

"I've always liked a good joke, Miss Selene. In fact, the Indians are great ones for telling riddles, you know. Perhaps you would like to hear a few I learned whilst a Sioux captive a few years back."

"No!"

Selene and Pierce both raised their eyebrows at James's vehement response. He counted to ten to calm himself, then asked bluntly, "So when will you be returning West?"

"Oh, I don't know," Pierce drawled. "I had thought to stay only a few weeks, but now . . ." He shrugged, his eyes still locked on Selene's body.

She twisted in her seat slightly to get a better view of the hyacinth blossom his mother held up for Ellen, and James could have sworn he saw the seams pull in the tucks just beneath her upraised breasts.

Pierce noticed, too. His eyes connected with James's as if to say, *And you're getting rid of this woman? Are you mad?*

Selene stood abruptly. "I think I'll go to the kitchen and see if Blossom has some drinks prepared for us. We won't be eating dinner for another hour."

"I'll go with you," Pierce volunteered, standing. He winked suggestively at Selene as he spoke.

"Over my dead body."

Selene and Pierce looked at James questioningly once again.

"I'll help Selene. I have to go to the library anyhow to get some bourbon," James explained weakly, hating the heated blush that crept up his neck to his face.

Selene blinked at him in confusion. Pierce nodded in sudden understanding.

Shoving Pierce rudely back into his chair as he passed, James said in a low voice, "If you wink at Selene one more time, I'm going to cut off your balls."

He heard Pierce chortling with amusement behind him as he entered the house.

"What did you say to Pierce?"

"I told him his trousers were unbuttoned."

She gasped. "You did not."

"How do you know, Selene? Were you looking . . . *there?*"

With quick thinking, she countered saucily, "You betcha I was, James, and I liked what I saw. A lot."

She had the good sense to duck out of his reach, heading down the back stairs to the kitchen. "Gotcha, James. That's another point for me," she called gaily over her shoulder. Then she peeked back around the corner, her wonderfully expressive eyes twinkling with devilment. "How do you know when a blonde is really conceited?"

He shook his head in mock despair.

"She calls out her own name when she comes." With those blunt words, she was gone, leaving him to marvel at her warped sense of humor. Ladies of his acquaintance would never tell such a risqué joke. But then, he admitted, ladies of his acquaintance bored him. Selene did not.

While he was pulling several bottles from the cabinet, Andrew and Pierce entered the library, closing the door after them.

"We've been hearing some alarming stories about activities here at Bayou Noir," Andrew said with concern. "Is it true someone's been trying to kill you?"

James nodded and updated them on Victor's activities. Both men offered their help in trapping his nefarious brother and bringing him to justice. He might need them.

She tasted sweeter than wine . . . uh, syllabub . . .

A short time later, Selene looked up to see James enter the kitchen where Blossom was showing her how to make syllabub. He carried two bottles of bourbon, one of which he handed to the cook for the mint juleps, along with several crystal goblets.

"James, I've just discovered the most fabulous drink. It's like liquid beignets."

He raised an eyebrow skeptically.

Selene was whipping together fresh cream, sugar, and apple cider in a pottery bowl until it frothed. Dipping a finger in, she tasted the sweet drink and closed her eyes in ecstasy. "Ummmm. That's delicious." She couldn't resist and stuck her forefinger in again.

"Here, let me see," James said, laying the bottles on the table and taking her wrist in his.

"What?"

He raised the dripping finger to his mouth, holding her eyes the entire time, then lapped up the frothy mixture from the base of her finger to the tip, over and over. With each long stroke, Selene felt the caress over her peaked breasts, between her thighs, even on the sensitive balls of her feet. She could swear her toes curled.

"Oh."

He chuckled and took the end of her finger in his mouth, sucking hard, and Selene felt an answering pull deep in her woman's center. She leaned back against the kitchen table for support.

"Touché, James. Your point."

"Lordy, you two are like cats in heat."

"What?" they both said at the same time, having forgotten that Blossom was in the room.

"You want I should send everyone home so you two can lick each other's . . . fur?" Blossom suggested.

Embarrassed, Selene turned back to mixing the drink, but James just grinned. *The tomcat!*

"Here, syllabub tastes better with a little kick." He poured a generous dollop of bourbon into her bowl.

"Uh oh," Blossom said.

"I don't know, James. It's only afternoon. We'll be crocked before dinner."

"The way I'm feeling right now, crocked sounds pretty damn good."

Selene carried the tray of glasses out to the gallery, some with mint juleps, some with the spiked syllabub, and some with plain lemonade. James brought the bourbon and glasses, taking a swig right out of the bottle twice before they joined his guests. Once he put a palm to her backside and squeezed. "*Mon Dieu!* You really aren't wearing any undergarments."

Selene would have slapped the silly grin off his face if she had a free hand.

"Behave yourself, Selene," he advised just before they rejoined the smiling company. But Selene soon realized that he didn't intend to take his own advice.

"Has Selene told you about her arrow-backs classes and group therapy?" James asked Ellen, who accepted only lemonade as she blushingly admitted she was in a "delicate condition," fanning herself girlishly.

"Why, no, she hasn't," Ellen said, looking toward Selene as she passed out mint juleps to Andrew and Pierce and James' mother, taking a glass of syllabub for herself.

Ignoring her frown, James poured himself enough bourbon to stun a horse and settled into his chair for the entertainment.

For a fleeting moment, as Selene looked around the gallery, a picture from *Gone With the Wind* swept through her mind. This is just how Tara would have been before the war, she thought.

"I do declare, you must tell me all about yourself, Miss Selene," Ellen simpered.

Well, fiddle-dee-dee, Selene thought, forcefully reminding herself that she was not Scarlett and that the roguish, half-drunk oaf ogling the neckline of her dress was definitely not Rhett.

"I'm so looking forward to your company. Why, I'm sure you and I will have so many interests in common. Do you embroider?"

Selene shook her head.

"Only stories," James contributed.

She shot him a look of disgust.

"Play the piano?" Ellen asked.

Once again, Selene shook her head.

"Dance?"

"Not much."

"Only the boogie," James offered, studying his finger-nails innocently.

The jerk! He must have heard of her latest exercise class.

"Sing?"

Selene almost gurgled with dismay. "No."

"Well, now, Selene, that's not quite true," James said, eying her over his raised goblet, which was already half empty. "Remember that achy breaky heart song."

"Achy breaky . . . ?" Ellen choked out almost as if they were vulgar lyrics.

"Of course, I have a decided preference for 'Who Put the Bop in the Bop She Bop,'" James noted.

Selene snarled.

"Now, now, my dear," Mrs. Baptiste cautioned, no doubt noticing her clawed hands.

At first Ellen looked upset, probably questioning just what kind of governess she was getting for her young daughters. But then she beamed with the graciousness of a pure Southern belle. "Never fear, my dear, I'm sure we'll find some hidden talent of yours." She stretched out her hand and patted Selene's arm patronizingly, and in the process dropped her fan.

All three men jumped up to recover it.

Gawd! Maybe there was something to the simpering, helpless, batting-the-eyelashes style of coquettishness practiced by these antebellum women. She took a swig of her syllabub and decided to experiment, fluttering her false eyelashes at Pierce. She knew better than to try such obvious tactics on James.

Pierce's eyes widened, registering her flirtation. Then he winked.

She heard James mutter something about cutting off more body parts.

"What are arrow-backs?" Pierce asked.

"And group therapy?" Andrew added.

Mrs. Baptiste sipped daintily at her mint julep, her blue eyes dancing with delight at the unusual turn the conversation was taking.

Before Selene could respond, James launched with relish into a full-blown explanation of her exercise classes.

"What's a tush?" Ellen asked in a squeaky voice, already having expressed her concern over the inappropriateness of Selene's engaging the slaves in her aerobics. *Wait till she finds out about my integrated classroom.*

Selene rolled her eyes and chugged down the rest of her glass of syllabub, then reached for another on the tray.

James's knowing eyes followed her actions, and he smiled approvingly. "How shall I say this, Ellen, without offending your sensibilities? A tush is a . . . derriere."

"Oh . . . oh . . . oh," Ellen gasped out, waving her fan furiously in front of her flushed face.

James addressed Andrew and Pierce then, explaining, with fake consideration. "Actually, tush crunches are pelvic thrusts." He turned to Selene. "Perhaps it would be better if you demonstrated for everyone, Selene. I could do the counting for you. 'Thrust, up, hold, release . . . thrust, up, hold, release.' "

Mrs. Baptiste giggled behind her fingertips, and Ellen looked as if she were about to have a seizure.

"Oh, that's right, Selene," James continued, hitting the side of his head as if he'd just thought of something, "you have to be wearing trousers."

Ellen's face turned green, a ghastly contrast to all that pink she wore. She gulped for breath.

"Darling, perhaps I should take you inside to rest before dinner," Andrew suggested soothingly to his wife. He shot a look of condemnation at James for causing his wife such distress.

"*Oui*," Mrs. Baptiste agreed, standing to lead the way into the parlor. "A woman in your condition should not sit in the hot sun too long." Before she left, Mrs. Baptiste also cast a disapproving glare at her son.

"She's probably just got her corset laced too tight," Selene said meanly as everyone showed such concern for the blonde woman who clung to her husband as they left the gallery into the main hallway.

Pierce glanced back and forth between her and James, obviously confused.

"You know," Selene said, her lips beginning to feel numb from the second glass of syllabub, "I think you Southern men are all full of yourselves."

"I'm from Pennsylvania originally," Pierce said.

"Big deal!" James snapped, echoing one of the phrases Selene used.

"Yep, you Southern men are all male chauvinist pigs."

James snorted with disgust. "Would you care to explain that remark and its relevance to anything in the world?"

Pierce smiled from ear to ear.

"Take Ellen, for example—"

"All right," James said.

Selene gave James a black look.

"Oh, by the way, Pierce, you must ask Selene to 'strut her stuff.' She's a model, you know."

"Really?" Pierce asked, his eyes telling her just how much he'd like a demonstration. "I like models."

"You like anything in a gown."

"As I was saying before you so rudely interrupted me, James . . . Ellen is the quintessential Southern belle. Just what all you men want. Weak, simple, clinging, swooning, deferring to your more superior judgment. God, I think I'm going to puke."

"Perhaps you've had too many syllabubs."

"Perhaps I've had too much of arrogant, domineering, self-centered Southern gentlemen." She looked at Pierce speculatively. "James has a real thing for blonde women, Pierce. Tell me, do you like blondes?"

"Oh, I much prefer brunettes," he answered with charming good sense.

James took another bolt of booze.

"Did you hear about the blonde who walked into a tavern with a duck under her arm?" she asked Pierce, ignoring James's warning frown. "No? Well the bartender said, 'You can't come in here with a pig.' And the blonde said, 'This isn't a pig. It's a duck.' Then the bartender said, 'I wasn't talking to you. I was talking to the duck.'"

Pierce laughed.

James warned him dryly, "Don't encourage her. She has a whole repertoire of these stupid blonde jokes."

"Amazing," Pierce said.

"How did the blonde happen to have a wooden baby?"

James rolled his eyes when Pierce asked, "How?"

"She got nailed by a carpenter."

"*Sacre bleu!* Pierce will think you're a loose woman, Selene."

"I like loose women."

"I'm not loose."

"I think you're driving me mad," James said on a groan.

"You were already mad before I got here."

"Do you two always behave like this?" a confused Pierce asked.

"Only when we're crocked," Selene observed.

They all laughed then.

"You have a mustache," James remarked after a few moments, looking at her upper lip.

"Huh?" She raised her fingertips to touch her wet upper lip, and hit her nose, instead. Batting her eyes at him, she asked with drunken candor, "Would you like to lick it off?"

To her supreme delight, James choked on the bourbon he continued to imbibe in startling quantities.

Pierce hooted with amusement, clapping a hand on his

knee. "Lord, I haven't had so much fun since Effie Morgan dropped her drawers at the Magnolia Cotillion."

"Will you excuse us, Pierce?" James said, dragging Selene to her feet with an iron grip on her wrist. "I have to discuss . . . the dinner menu with Selene."

Before she knew it, Selene was standing in the back parlor with James. Through the closed sliding door, she could hear the murmur of Mrs. Baptiste's voice addressing Andrew and Ellen.

Selene leaned back against the wall and closed her eyes for a second, hearing a low buzzing in her ears, feeling as light as the frothy beverage she'd been drinking. When she opened her eyes, she saw James standing a few feet away, hands on hips, scowling at her, as usual.

"So are you going to lick off my mustache?"

That practically shocked the pants off him.

He inhaled sharply. "No." Then, just as quickly, he changed his mind. "*Oui*, perhaps I will." His pale eyes turned stormy with passion and his lips parted with anticipation as he moved closer and closer. "And perhaps I'll lick the honey from your hair, as well."

"What honey?" She raised a hand to her head, then blushed when she realized what he'd meant. "I was just kidding . . . about licking off the mustache."

"I'm not."

"Do you know there's a whole ad campaign in my time where the models all have milk mustaches?"

"Shut up, Selene," he said, his lips lowering toward hers, his breath a whispery caress.

"Is this going to be a good-bye kiss?" she asked huskily.

"*Merde*, how do I know! Hello . . . good-bye . . . I'd-like-to-lay-you-on-the-carpet-and-practice-tush-crunches-on-top-of-you . . . Would-you-stick-your-tongue-in-my-mouth . . . whatever. Take your pick."

"All of the above . . . and then some," she sighed, putting one hand behind his neck and the other at the side of his face, pulling him closer. The scent of his skin and the heat of his body pulled at Selene's senses like the most powerful aphrodisiac.

He braced both arms on the wall above her and lapped her upper lip with his tongue, like a cat, with long wet strokes. Then he did the same to the seam and the lower lip. "You taste so sweet, *chérie*."

She purred, "Let me see," and drew his tongue into her mouth, suckling softly. "You're right."

With a low growl, James dug one hand into her hair and with the other behind her buttocks jerked her forcefully against his hardness. Parted and hungry, his lips ravaged hers, alternately coaxing and devouring, firm and pliant. She answered his kisses with a matching intensity, trying to show him with her lips, and soft moans, and caressing hands over his neck and back just how much she wanted him.

This was their moment out of time, all that they would probably have, and both seemed to want to squeeze a lifetime of feelings into the little time they had left together.

"I love to kiss you, *chérie*," he whispered against her neck, kissing and biting along the curve from shoulder to earlobes.

"I wish it could go on forever."

His body stiffened at her mention of "forever," then relaxed. They both knew there was no forever for them.

When James began to grind himself against her in a tantalizing rhythm, Selene arched her neck, inadvertently offering her ear to his ministrations. He pulled the lobe into his mouth and tugged on it gently with his teeth. She told him with a reluctant whimper how sensitive her ears were, and he gave a low, sexy laugh. Tracing the delicate whorls with the tip of his wet tongue, he asked in a raspy voice, "Do you like that?"

"Yes."

He pressed the tip as deep in the ear as he could, then pulled it out. "And that?"

"Oh . . . maybe you'd better do it again so I can decide."

He chuckled and began a seductive, wildly erotic, in-and-out stroking dance to match the rhythmic pressing of his erection against her pulsing center. He smothered her keening wail by pressing his lips against hers once again.

Meanwhile, his impatient hands shoved the neckline of her gown off her shoulders and down to her elbows. He pulled back slightly and gazed with passion-glazed eyes and parted lips at her exposed breasts. "You are so beautiful, Selene."

"I told you I was beautiful."

He smiled, a pulse-stopping smile that tore at her heartstrings and turned her blood warm and churning with a lifetime of pent-up emotions. Almost instantly, his expression turned bleak. "What do you want from me, Selene?"

"Now or forever?" she asked, her fingertips caressing his rigid jawline.

He swallowed several times before answering. "Now . . . just now."

She wanted so much from James, and she wanted to do so much for him. But there was so little time. She would have to settle for now. "Kiss me . . . there," she pleaded, looking downward.

His breath grew ragged with understanding, and he lowered his head, taking one hardened nipple into his mouth, laving it with his wet, abrasive tongue, then flicking and gently biting it to an aching point. "Like that?" he asked, raising his eyes to hers.

"O-o-o-oh."

"Is that a yes?"

"That's yes, yes, yes, yes . . ."

He moved to the other breast, and Selene's knees buckled. He caught her by putting both of his hands under her buttocks, making a low, masculine sound of satisfaction deep in his throat.

"James, Selene . . . it's almost time for dinner," Mrs. Baptiste called out, tapping on the hallway door. "Fergus and Reba have arrived. Come, dears, and no more arguments."

"Arguments?" they both said, groaning, as her footsteps moved down the hall toward the gallery.

"Your mother's timing is perfect," Selene grumbled as she drew up the bodice of her dress.

James pulled away with a soft curse. "Perhaps it's for the best," he said, tucking his loosened shirt into the waistband of his trousers and straightening his suspenders.

She shot him a look of disbelief.

He shrugged sheepishly. "I didn't say I liked the interruption." He pointed toward a pier mirror on the wall across the room. "And you'd better fix your hair before you go back out or everyone will know what you've been doing."

"Yeah, and you'd better check out your pants, Mr. Baptiste, or everyone will definitely know what you've been doing."

He looked down at his crotch and grinned.

Her heart did a cartwheel. He was so handsome. *God, how I love him!*

He tried to adjust his pants to hide his erection, to no avail.

"Do you want me to help?"

"Are you totally mad?"

She could barely walk across the room on her wobbly legs. When she got to the mirror, she shrieked, "Oh, my God! My hair! My makeup! And what happened to my eyelashes?"

He bent to the floor, lifting the two objects in his hands, grinning. His dimple emerged slowly as the grin bloomed into a full-blown, dazzling smile, heart-wrenching in its open splendor.

I love you, James. She had to bite her bottom lip to keep from saying the words aloud.

Turning back to the mirror, she squeaked out, "Why, you jerk! You gave me a hickey."

"What's a hickey?" he said, coming up behind her.

"A passion mark," she replied, laying her fingertips on the dark bruise at the side of her neck.

"So I did," he noted without apology.

"How could you have said I look beautiful, James? I look absolutely horrid," she moaned, wondering how she was ever going to repair the damage before dinner.

He stood behind her, looking at her image in the mirror. His lips were just as kiss-swollen as hers, his face flushed with unfulfilled passion, his black hair rumpled from her caresses.

"You look beautiful to me," he said simply.

All those years with Devon when she had tried so hard to please, he'd always made her feel inadequate. Now here she was with James, looking her worst, and he made her feel so special. "Oh, James, I'm afraid that you're better than any old Rhett Butler. Much, much better."

"That's what I've been telling you all along, *chérie*," he said with a wink and began to help her fix her hair. "Rhett was just a fairy tale. I'm . . . I'm—"

"—the answer to my dreams."

"Well, I wouldn't go that far," he said dryly, and winked at her in the mirror.

Chapter Eighteen

T̶alk about mixed signals! . . .

Selene felt a bit like Alice in Wonderland at the tea party by the time dinner rolled around. And that rogue sitting at the other end of the table, inhaling bourbon and staring at her with blatant eroticism, was unquestionably the Mad Hatter.

A dark cloud hung thickly in the atmosphere, portending an ominous storm. And James was going to be the lightning rod or die trying.

She'd had the good sense to stop her intake of spiked syllabub, and James definitely needed to cut off his supply of bourbon or he'd soon have his face in the crab gumbo before him.

"James, would you like a glass of lemonade?" she offered politely.

"No."

"What?"

"No, I don't want any lemonade, Selene. No, I'm not drunk. No, I don't need you to tell me what to do."

"But—"

Standing abruptly, he pulled the monstrous epergne centerpiece toward him and, one by one, dumped the roses and
water from each of the ten miniature crystal vases onto the
floor. Then he proceeded to fill each of them with bourbon.
Taking one of the vases in hand, he sank back to his seat,
shot a "so there!" look at Selene, and quaffed the liquor
down in one swallow.

Everyone at the table stared at him as if he were a luna-
tic. Then, with pure Southern graciousness, they just pretended he hadn't done such an outrageous thing in polite
company.

Fergus and Reba had joined them at the dinner table,
along with Mrs. Baptiste, Andrew, Pierce, and Ellen, who
seemed to have recovered nicely from her fit of the vapors.

Ellen kept looking at the new and improved Reba, no
doubt seeing Selene and her talents in a new light. Andrew
kept looking at his wife to make sure she didn't swoon or
need help with some brain-straining activity, like buttering
her bread.

Fergus kept looking at the passion mark on Selene's
neck and grinning at James.

Pierce kept looking at Selene and winking.

James kept looking at his vases of bourbon . . . when he
wasn't glaring at Pierce, or sending Selene sexual signals
that would scorch a girl's body at ten paces.

And Mrs. Baptiste kept looking from one to the other
with supreme satisfaction, as if everything were just hunky-
dory.

When the conversation lulled, between the shrimp *étouf-
fée* and the chicken and fresh vegetables, Ellen addressed
Mrs. Baptiste, "I got a letter from my mother last week. She
tells me that Mr. Audubon is now living in New York City
and is quite the rave there in artistic circles."

"Did you hear that, James?" Mrs. Baptiste said, then informed Selene, "When James was only twelve years old, he
earned extra money guiding M'sieur Audubon through the
bayou wilds to paint his bird pictures."

"Are you talking about John James Audubon?" Selene asked in awe.

"*Oui.* In fact, he sent James a folio of his bird sketches." She turned to her son. "You still have that folio, don't you, *cher?*"

He nodded, tracing the rim of his vase with a forefinger, seemingly bored.

"I can't believe you actually knew John James Audubon. Do you know that those sketches you have are priceless?"

James smiled grimly, his eyes full of dull remoteness. "No, they're not, Selene. They're barely worth the paper Audubon scribbled on incessantly." And Selene saw in his bleak eyes the reminder that she was not of his time, and never would be.

Her throat aching with defeat, Selene fought back a rising panic as the grandfather clock chimed four o'clock. How much longer would it be before the Collins party departed? How much longer before James was no longer a part of her life?

Her meager supply of clothing and worldly goods were packed and waiting near the front door, including the ballgown. She'd already said her good-byes to a tearful Etienne, Blossom, Iris, her aerobics class, and her other young pupils.

Blinking back tears, Selene tried to maintain some semblance of dignity. "Tell us about Mr. Audubon, James," she encouraged, her eyes pleading for his help.

"He was a crazy old coot who could spend hours and hours just sitting and staring at a bird. Sometimes he even killed them in order to study them up close." He shrugged. Then his eyes lit up with remembrance, and his gaze locked with hers. "But I have one thing to thank him for," he said softly. "He introduced me to the mating ritual of the herons."

Selene inhaled sharply. Oh, how could he remind her of that intimate interlude now? "You are cruel, James."

"*Moi?*" he asked with wide-eyed innocence and drank

another vase of bourbon. "Now that I've told you about Audubon, why don't you tell us some blonde jokes?" He'd been barely picking at his food, but now he was tossing fresh peas in the air and catching them in his mouth one at a time, like peanuts.

Everyone ignored his rude behavior. But, for sure, Ellen Collins would have enough gossip to relate up and down the bayou for a lifetime.

"Blonde jokes? Are you crazy?"

"*Oui*, I am feeling a bit mad." He offered her a stark, tight-lipped smile. "You don't want to regale us with your blonde riddles, Selene? Ah, how unfortunate. Perhaps, I can remember some of the hundreds you've told me."

"I never told you hundreds of jokes," she said indignantly.

"No? Well, dozens, at least," he said, winking at her. Lord, between Pierce and James, she was being winked to death.

First he explained to everyone at the table the point of a blonde joke, as if there were one. *The dolt!* Ellen didn't look too happy about jokes based on the dumbness and loose morals of blonde women, but Reba giggled behind her fan. Mrs. Baptiste sipped at what must be her sixth mint julep of the day.

Oh, Lord.

"Why is a blonde like a bottle of wine?"

"Why?" Pierce asked enthusiastically.

"They're both empty from the neck up." James looked at Selene to see if he had told the joke right, and winked again.

She crossed her eyes at him.

He gave her a cross-eyed look back. Criminey! How could the man look so handsome even when cross-eyed?

"What's the quickest way to drown a blonde?"

"James!" Selene exclaimed, knowing the insult to come.

"You put a mirror on the bottom of a lake."

Ellen started hyperventilating, and her husband glared angrily at James.

"That's enough!" Selene stood. "James, could I please talk to you in the hall?"

"Why? Do you have another mustache?"

Selene felt her face flame crimson as everyone turned to see if she did indeed have a mustache. They didn't understand what he meant by the suggestive question, except Pierce, of course, who winked at her. *Argh!*

When they got to the hall, James reached for her with a devilish grin, but she ducked under his arm. "Stop it! Stop it right now, James!"

"What, *chérie?* What do you want me to stop?" He managed to pull her into his embrace with a deft hook of an arm. Bracing his shoulders against the wall with both arms looped around her waist, he nuzzled her neck. "This? Do you want me to stop this?"

Selene bit her bottom lip to stifle a moan. His hot breath teased her skin as his lips pressed against the pulse beat in her throat. "Yes . . . no . . . I mean, stop this ridiculous behavior of yours. O-o-oh!"

He raised his head and peered at her with the blatant artlessness of an experienced lech. "You don't like my kisses?" he asked with wounded pride, grazing his knuckles over the edge of her jaw.

Delicious shivers of electricity ran over every inch of her skin, from scalp to toes. She would like nothing better than to lean into his caress, to surrender to the overpowering pull on her senses. But she could not. Guests awaited them in the dining room . . . guests with whom Selene would soon be leaving Bayou Noir.

Confused, Selene tried to understand James's behavior. He was sending her away and yet, at the same time, seemed to be doing everything in his power to prevent her departure.

She slapped his rascally hand away from her neckline and shoved hard against his chest. Hands on hips, she demanded, "Why are you doing this, James?"

"Why are you crying, *chérie?*" he said, genuinely contrite. "I didn't mean to make you weep. Truly I didn't."

Selene wiped at the tears and sniffed. "James, you've got to stop these wild antics. Andrew and Ellen will never take me with them if you continue to make me look so bad in their eyes. Is that what you want?"

His long lashes fluttered in confusion before he pressed the fingertips of both hands to his eyes. When he looked up at her again, his eyes were forlorn. "I don't know what I want anymore." Regret—sharp and painful—turned his voice raw. "I do know what's best for you, though, and for me. Go back into the dining room, Selene. I'll join you shortly."

She hesitated, then moved away from him. Just before she entered the dining room, she asked, "Are you going to behave now?"

He grinned mirthlessly. "I doubt it."

Oh, the promises he made! . . .

A subdued James rejoined them during the dessert course. He didn't comment on the fact that the epergne and the bourbon had been removed from the table. Instead, he listened attentively to Pierce recounting one of his experiences in a wild Western cow town where the women were loose and the men lawless.

Although James no longer seemed on the verge of drunkenness, a dangerous light glittered in his clear blue eyes. Like a tightly wound spring, he grew tenser and tenser.

Selene felt like a time bomb herself. Any minute now, the Collinses would announce that it was time to leave, and everything Selene had come to love and cherish at Bayou Noir, especially James, would be lost to her. She struggled to keep tears from welling in her eyes.

So at first she didn't hear James ask Pierce, "Have you ever met Dr. Ruth in your travels?"

"Who?"

"Dr. Ruth," James repeated.

Selene started to choke.

Pierce clapped a hand on her back with gentlemanly consideration, then asked James, "Does she live out West?"

"She might." James raised questioning eyes to Selene.

Selene shrugged as she reached for a glass of water. How the hell did she know where Dr. Ruth Westheimer lived? The only place she'd ever seen her was on a TV talk show.

"Dr. Ruth is an expert who writes books," James informed Pierce in a deceptively conversational manner, "among other things."

"Like Mr. Poe?" Pierce asked.

"Not quite," James replied dryly. "Did you know that, according to an article I just read, the majority of women enjoy . . ." He paused dramatically.

Uh oh! Selene shot a warning glare at James, which he blithely ignored. She took another gulp of water.

"—oralsex," he slurred out.

Selene sprayed everyone within three feet of her with water when she coughed.

"I know what that is," Ellen said brightly.

"You do?" James and Selene asked at the same time, gaping at the dimwitted lady.

"Yes. *Orulsis.* It's a kind of needlework pattern. I read about it in an embroidery book." Ellen looked at her husband for approval, and he beamed as if she were a rocket scientist. Then she turned back to James. "What type of stitch did this article recommend?"

"Tongue and groove," James answered without even blinking.

Selene literally gaped at him.

"And what kind of needle?" Ellen asked eagerly.

"Oh, pointed." He waved a hand airily.

"Huh?" Ellen looked confused.

"And the article also suggested a sort of fluttery motion of the . . . needle." James flicked his fingertips back and forth in the air to demonstrate.

I'm going to kill him, Selene thought.

He grinned at her and winked.

She shook her head in amazement and couldn't help but smile at the comedic turn this dinner party was taking.

James tamed down for the remainder of the meal. But he looked so sad and miserable, sitting there tracing the rim of his coffee cup, that Selene almost forgot how sad and miserable she was herself.

When Andrew shifted in his chair, Selene stiffened with foreboding. "I suppose we should be going soon," he told Ellen. "Shall I gather the girls and get the boat ready?"

A wild panic thrummed through Selene and she had to press her knuckles to her trembling mouth to keep from crying out.

Ellen nodded and stood.

"I suppose you think I love you," James blurted out, his eyes locking with Selene's.

Everyone gasped with surprise.

Selene's heart stopped beating for a second, then jump-started into a wild, erratic thumping against her chest wall.

"I never thought that," she said weakly, clutching the lacy edges of the tablecloth.

"Liar," James accused her gently.

"I think we'd better leave before it gets dark," Andrew blustered. His florid face flushed with discomfort and confusion as he led his equally confused wife from the room. He added over his shoulder, "It's obvious you won't be sending Selene with us now."

"You won't?" Selene asked James, tilting her head questioningly. "Be sending me away?" Suddenly, ripples of hope turned Selene's deadened spirits alive.

James declined to answer, just continued to stare at her enigmatically.

"Well, it's been nice seeing you again," Pierce said mockingly as he stood. "I don't suppose I'll be passing this way again for a few years."

"My pleasure, Pierce. I have you to thank for . . . a number of things today." James inclined his head meaningfully at Selene.

Pierce chuckled, bending down to kiss Selene's cheek.

James made a low, snarling sound but said nothing more.

Reba and Fergus departed, as well, leaving only Mrs. Baptiste. James's mother looked from him to Selene and then back to her son, nodding with satisfaction. James stood when his mother did, and she hugged him warmly.

"I'm taking Etienne to sleep in the *garçonnière* with me tonight. You need privacy to resolve your issues, my son."

James seemed overcome with emotion, unable to respond to his mother's kind words.

Mrs. Baptiste patted his arm as he sat back down. "Be happy, James. Grab the moment in your fist and hold on tight. You may never have another." She walked gracefully from the room then, humming a song. Selene could have sworn it was "Achy Breaky Heart."

In fact, Selene felt a humming in her own head as the implications of the afternoon's events began to become clear. She was staying at Bayou Noir . . . with James . . . and, oh, had he really hinted that he might be in love with her?

"You never answered my question, Selene," James reminded her when they were alone, seated still at opposite ends of the table. "You think I've fallen in love with you, don't you?"

Selene couldn't answer his question. Instead, she started to weep—huge, silent tears that testified to her deep emotion.

"Why are you crying, *chérie?* You have won. You will be staying at Bayou Noir. I thought that would make you happy."

"I am happy," she sobbed.

"And so you weep?" He lifted an eyebrow dubiously.

"I'm crying because I'm happy—"

"Hah!"

"—and because you're *not* happy."

"What makes you think I'm not happy?"

"Because you're still frowning." She held her breath, trying to stop crying, and hiccupped loudly.

James's lips turned up ever so slightly, as if he were fighting a smile. "Ah, perhaps I'm just stunned that I could have ever thought to send you away."

James continued to scrutinize her for a long time, leaning back in his chair lazily, tapping his fingertips thoughtfully on the tabletop.

Finally Selene could stand the throbbing silence no longer. "What now, James?"

There was no mistaking the smile that pulled at his lips . . . his beautifully firm lips. "Well, *chérie*, I'm not quite certain. First off, I think I'd like to 'light your fire' and then . . ."

Light my fire? The humming in Selene's head grew louder and she felt all the fine hairs on her body stand at attention. "And then what?" she asked huskily.

His smile grew wider, seductively teasing. "Perhaps I'll stoke it into a roaring bonfire."

She snuffled back the last of her tears. "A bonfire sounds good," she agreed, returning his smile.

She was rewarded with the first sign of his emerging dimple, and her heart did three quick cartwheels . . . flip, flip, flip. "Then what?"

"You are a greedy little witch, aren't you, darlin'?" he said, chuckling, as he braced both elbows on the table and put his chin in his hands.

"Well?"

"Then, Selene, I intend to put out your fire, good and proper."

"Is that a promise, James?"

"Written in my heart's blood."

"Oh, James."

"Don't you 'Oh, James' me."

Selene suddenly remembered something significant. "James," she said, biting her bottom lip nervously, "don't

expect too much of me. I know I talk outrageously some-times, but I've never really had much luck with . . . sex."
Boy! That's the understatement of the year.

James flashed a devastating smile at her, dimple and all. "Ah, Selene, your luck is about to change."

Her heart did three more cartwheels *and* a backspring this time—*flip, flip, flip, oomph!* She stood and was about to come to him with open arms.

He put up a halting hand. "Not yet, Selene. I'm coiled tighter than a bayou snake. If you touch me now, *my* fire will be doused in the midst of the *crème Brûlée*," he said with a laugh, pointing to the remaining desserts on the table.

She plopped back down to her chair in a rustle of shim-mering silk, waiting.

"I have to find Rufus and assign additional guards to the *garçonnière* for my mother and Etienne. And there are other precautions that must be taken for security against Victor if I am going to be indisposed for the next twelve hours."

"Twelve hours?" Selene squeaked out.

The air resonated with the intense physical awareness that held them in its thrall. Some tangible bond grew palpa-bly between them—a slender thread spun by the silkworms of time, reinforced by a growing love.

He stood and walked slowly toward her. Putting both hands on her shoulders to prevent her rising, he pressed his warm lips to hers briefly in a tantalizing promise. A spark flashed between them, and delicious flames of erotic antici-pation rippled over Selene's already heightened senses. In truth, the man did know how to light a fire. He really did.

"At least twelve hours," he said in a thick voice, brushing a forefinger over her parted lips.

Then he left her staring after him, heart beating a wild tomtom accompaniment to the humming in her brain. At the doorway he paused, turned back, and winked.

Rhett couldn't have done it any better.

As bonfires go, theirs was amazing . . .

An hour later, Selene stood staring out the front parlor windows, watching the approaching dusk settle over the bayou like a sigh. The very chirping of the crickets—large enough to intimidate a New York cockroach—rang musically in her ears.

When had she come to appreciate the serenity of the wild swamplands?

Even the raucous croaking of mating frogs drew a smile to her face. *I'll bet there's some Rhett-bullfrog sitting on a lily pad right now, winking at some unsuspecting Scarlett-frog.*

Lifting a hand to brush a strand of hair behind her ear, she inhaled deeply as the smell of Blossom's lavender soap rose to her nostrils. Selene had bathed in James's absence, although she'd donned the same dress again, leaving her shoes and stockings upstairs.

A door slammed below and soft voices wafted up through the silent house. James's deep, masculine voice mingled with Blossom's rumbling laughter in the kitchen. Selene heard Blossom shuffling noisily to her room on the lower floor, then James locking doors and windows. He then went up the back stairs to the third and fourth floors and did the same.

At last she heard his step. Hesitating, he looked through the dusky light into the parlor. His hair had been slicked back wetly, and his white shirt lay open almost to the waist. He must have bathed somewhere outdoors, probably in the stream behind the mansion.

His eyes, smoky blue with passion, held hers for a moment, then swept over her body in appreciation. "Don't move," he ordered in a low, husky voice as he secured the doors and windows on this floor, too.

Selene turned back to the tall window, trembling with anticipation. Truly, this marked the first day of her life. Nothing that had happened before mattered. The fact that she came from another time melted into oblivion. She and this man were meant to be. The how and the why were irrelevant.

James came up behind her, wrapping his arms around her waist. She lolled her head back on his shoulder, exposing the curve of her neck for his soft kiss.

"Ah, *chérie*, I have been waiting for this moment for so long."

"A lifetime," she agreed, turning in his arms.

He put his hands on her hips and pulled her closer, letting her know just how hard the waiting had been on him.

"Why are you smiling, James?"

"You make me smile, darlin'." And he smiled even wider.

If her heart did any more cartwheels, Selene thought she might just go into cardiac arrest. "Is that good? Making you smile?"

"Very, very good," he assured her as he lowered his mouth toward hers, one tempting inch at a time. At first his misty eyes held hers captive. Then the sinfully long lashes fluttered shut in surrender to the overpowering sensuality enveloping them.

Selene moaned.

James smiled against her lips. "Have I lit your fire yet?" he teased, his breath a whispery caress against her parted lips.

"Well, I definitely feel the heat of your flame."

He chuckled, then turned serious. "I want to make this last forever."

"Forever? Hmmm. You are confident of your abilities."

"Supremely." He gripped her face in both hands, angling her to fit his kiss. At first, he just brushed the firm flesh of his lips against hers—pleading, coaxing, murmuring soft sounds of pleasure.

When her lips turned pliant, he changed the kiss from gentle and persuasive to hard and demanding. He claimed her then with savage intensity. Open-mouthed and clinging, sucking and nipping, he turned her into a mewling creature, dying for the sustenance only he could give.

"I never knew a kiss could be so erotic, James," she confessed, breathing raggedly. She pulled back and traced the lines of his mouth with utmost tenderness. "I love your kisses."

"I love the way you respond to my kisses," he rasped out. Putting a hand to her throat, he lowered his face again, but this time the kiss was dramatically different. "Open for me, Selene," he murmured against her mouth.

When she complied, his tongue glided into her mouth, searing her, filling her with incredible completeness. And every erogenous zone on her body—including some she hadn't known existed—turned into a pulsating quiver.

Drawing on his tongue, she encouraged him without words to begin the slow, sensual strokes that were a prelude to that culmination their bodies were already seeking.

"You're killing me, Selene," he groaned out finally, panting against her neck.

"I don't think I can wait, James," she said, taking one of his hands in hers and pressing it against her aching breast. She gasped. The sheer pleasure of that slight touch against her sensitized nipple almost brought her to climax.

James saw her reaction. And he knew.

Laughing softly, he pulled his hand away from her breast. "It's too soon, Selene . . . far too soon. I think you are a mere ember now. You are a long way from the bonfire I promised you."

"Ember!"

"Well, I could be mistaken. Perhaps I should check," he said cryptically and stepped back, holding her at arm's length. "Will you let me, *chérie*. Hmmm?"

"What?" Lord, every hormone in her body was humming for satisfaction. At this point, she'd probably jump off a cliff if he asked her.

Instead of answering, he took her hand and led her to a nearby fainting couch—one of those decadent pieces of furniture indolent ladies used to loll during lazy afternoons, reading a book, eating bonbons.

James had neither literature nor food in mind.

Laying her down on the upholstered couch, he began to lift the hem of her gown.

"James, I don't know about this," she protested.

"Shhh. Indulge me, *chérie*. I want to examine your . . . embers." Before she had a chance to think, he drew up the edge of her gown to bunch at her waist, exposing her nude body.

"Embers," she choked out as he dropped to one knee near her bare feet. Her hands reached out for him to pull her upright. "I'm not sure I like this, James."

"Trust me, darling," he said in a thickened voice.

She hesitated, then let her hands fall back. He ran his fingertips along the outside of her legs. "Why are your legs so smooth?"

"I shaved."

He laughed.

"With your razor."

"Now that would be a sight." He moved between her legs, parting them. "But nothing compared to this."

Selene felt vulnerable and incredibly excited.

"I see your fire, Selene," he informed her, "but it is a wet heat." Embarrassed, she tried to close her legs, to no avail. "Ah, finally I see the source of your heat."

Lightly he placed a fingertip against her wetness and the swelling bud. Selene began to keen with the rising waves of her coming orgasm.

But he didn't want her satisfied yet. Abruptly he flicked her gown back to her ankles and pulled her to her feet, kissing her gently on the lips.

"You're going to stop now?" she asked incredulously.

"*Oui*," he said, hugging her to his side and drawing her toward the stairs.

"I'm in agony."

"Savor the agony . . . of anticipation."

"Are you in agony, too?"

"Most definitely."

When they stood at the bottom of the wide staircase, he regarded her with a slight, knowing smile.

Then she understood.

With the skill of a pure Southern gentleman, he scooped her into his arms and proceeded to carry her up the stairs, fulfilling her fantasy. Halfway up, he warned her with a sexy growl, "I swear, Selene, if you call me Rhett, I'm going to drop you."

Chapter Nineteen

Rhett couldn't have done it better . . .

Dusk had turned quickly to nightfall by the time James carried Selene into her bedchamber. He set her on her feet, then held her at arm's length, gazing at her with wonderment. His heart thundered wildly with the knowledge that they had finally come to this point in their relationship—the beginning.

Selene had pulled her dark hair off her face with a green ribbon. He reached behind her neck and undid the bow, watching appreciatively as the curly tresses ballooned out around her, down to her shoulder bones in the back and the upper curve of her breasts in front.

A primitive, elemental need exploded in his vitals.

"Would you like to take off your gown, or shall I?" he asked with husky bluntness.

Through the shadowy light, he saw her jaw drop into a gape.

He struck a match, moving toward the many-pronged candelabrum on the dresser. A full moon cast sufficient light in the room through the French doors, but he didn't want to miss one single detail of the night to come.

"Why didn't we go to your room?" she asked, shifting self-consciously from bare foot to bare foot, her slender toes digging into the carpet.

Hah! You'd better not turn shy on me now, Selene. Not with the plans I have in mind for you. "Because my room doesn't have that mirror." He pointed to the freestanding, pedestal mirror in the center of the room.

She tilted her head questioningly.

"I have plans for the mirror, *chérie*. And you."

"You do?"

"Oh, yes, I definitely do," he said, patting her bottom suggestively as he passed behind her. Reaching for two oil lamps, he lit and placed them on either side of the mirror.

Her face colored becomingly as she began to comprehend his plans. "I don't know, James. This looks a little perverted."

"It does, doesn't it?" he agreed unabashedly, then winked at her. "It's all your fault, Selene. You gave me the idea."

"I never did."

"Selene, Selene, Selene," he chided her. "You talk incessantly about your *Gone With the Wind* fantasies. Did it never occur to you that I have a few fantasies of my own?"

"Fantasies?" she gulped.

"And, believe me, *chérie*, none of my fantasies involve gallant Southern gentlemen or sweet, simpering belles."

"More like wicked men and wickeder women, I bet," she said with a slight smile.

"Exactly."

"I've never been very wicked before," she confessed, her mouth turning down forlornly.

"I'll teach you."

"Oh, my!"

" 'Oh, my!' I plan on making you say that a lot tonight."

"Oh, m . . . ," she started to say, but stopped herself, eying him suspiciously.

He pulled his galluses off his shoulders to hang from his waist and removed his half boots with the toe of first one foot, then the other. He wriggled his toes sensuously once they were free of their leathery confines.

Her gaze fixed oddly on his toes.

"What? Why are you staring at my feet?"

She jerked to attention. "I was just remembering . . ." She dropped her lashes modestly.

"Remembering what, Selene? Don't stop now."

She waved a hand dismissively. "It was nothing. . . ."

Lord, he loved the way she blushed.

"Just . . . well, that first morning when I woke up in your hotel room in New Orleans, I saw you sleeping on the bed. And I remember thinking that you had beautiful feet—"

"Beautiful feet?" he choked out incredulously. He was so aroused he felt disoriented, and she talked about feet.

"—and I couldn't believe that I was actually getting turned on by a man's feet."

He brightened. "My feet 'turn you on'?"

"Among other things," she added impishly.

"Perhaps I'll let you touch them later if you are very good," he said offhandedly, trying hard not to laugh.

"And perhaps I'll suck on one or two . . . if you are *very* good." Her eyes glittered with challenge.

It was his turn to gulp. *Sacre bleu! What an erotic image! Involving feet, of all things! Apparently, perversion can be a learned taste.* He chuckled as he started to unbutton his shirt.

Intently she watched his every move. Once she even licked her dry lips. Hell, he might need to take another cold bath in the stream before they even started.

He moved in front of the mirror and crooked his finger at her.

Her eyes widened.

He saw the points of her breasts ruching beneath the thin silk of her gown and could barely restrain his hands from tearing away the offensive fabric. Suddenly his mouth turned parched, and he followed Selene's suit in licking suddenly dry lips.

It was time to take back control of this loveplay. "Are you dewing with need for me, Selene?" he asked in a thick, unsteady voice.

Her quick intake of breath told him without words that he had guessed correctly.

"Do your nether lips swell and part, yearning for my invasion?"

She moaned and nodded, a willing slave to his graphic questions.

"Does your woman's center pearl for me?"

A low, mewling sound of assent escaped her parted lips.

Slowly, slowly, his brain whispered.

Hurry, hurry, his raging lust shouted.

Mon Dieu! Her open ardor and his careening passions would unman him before he even began. And he wanted this first time with Selene to last all night.

"Come here, *chérie*," he coaxed, turning serious. "I have something important to tell you before my ravenous lust turns me into a wild beast of perversions."

She moved toward him with downcast eyes, shuffling her feet nervously. When she stood so close that he could smell the lavender soap on her skin, he lifted her chin upward with a finger. Her womanly allure enveloped him with heat.

"*Je t'aime, chérie,*" he whispered fervently. Then he repeated, "I love you, darling."

At first she just blinked at him in confusion. He saw the moment comprehension dawned.

"Oh, James, I love you, too. I really do." She threw herself into his arms, almost knocking him backward, and bestowed little kisses all over his face and neck. "I love you . . . I love you . . . I love you . . . ," she declared between her nibbling kisses.

Tunneling his fingers into her hair to hold her still, he leaned down and kissed her softly on the lips, hoping to convey with just the tenderest brush of his mouth how strong his feelings were for her. "I love you," he said against her mouth, and then pulled back a hairbreadth. "I don't know what tomorrow will bring, Selene, or how many to-morrows we will have together—"

"I hope forever," she interrupted, her eyes filling with tears.

He nodded, fearing there might be tears in his own eyes, as well. "We can talk about the future later, but for now I just wanted you to know . . . I just wanted you to know . . ." His voice broke with emotion, and he shrugged, unable to find the words to tell her what was in his heart.

But she knew.

Selene looked up at James and smiled with the sheer joy of the moment. *He loves me! He really loves me! Thank you, God!* "Rhett couldn't have said it any better," she told him.

"I thought I told you not to mention that rascal's name," he growled.

"I forgot."

"Well, *Crimson*," he teased, "don't you think it's about time you showed me what scandalous things a *scarlet* Southern belle can do?"

"You are a *rat*, Rhett," she countered with a saucy laugh.

"I try to be." Holding her eyes, he finished unbuttoning his shirt, pulled it from his waistband, and threw it care-lessly to the floor. Then he proceeded to remove the rest of his clothing while she watched.

Already deeply excited by James's loveplay in the parlor and his seductive words of a few moments ago, Selene felt a hot wetness pool between her legs at this first sight of his bare skin. Her breasts swelled and ached against the con-fines of her tight bodice, especially when James's eyes lin-gered there knowingly.

James was a handsome, sexy man. His wide shoulders swept down in muscled planes and perfect symmetry to a chest of tight black curls, a tapering waist, and narrow hips.

She intended to examine every suntanned inch as soon as possible.

One by one, with deliberate, sensual slowness, he undid the buttons of his trousers, finally freeing the evidence of how very much he wanted her. Then he dropped the pants to the floor and kicked them aside.

"You are beautiful, James."

His eyes shot up with surprise. "Do you think so? What part of me do you find most beautiful?"

"You're outrageous."

"*Oui*." He smiled, an open, dazzling expression of his joy.

"Your turn, Selene," he announced, posing her in front of him before the long mirror. His eyes held hers captive as he began to undo the many buttons down the back of her gown. "How are the embers doing, my dear?" he asked when he finished, having seared a path of erogenous flames down her spine to the small of her back.

"Hot as blazes."

He laughed, a low barbaric sound of satisfaction.

She leaned her head back on his right shoulder, closing her eyes, as he smoothed the shimmering gown off her arms, down over her hips and legs to the floor.

Selene heard his sharp inhale of breath and felt his body stiffen behind her. Especially his steely erection, which pressed against the cleft of her bare buttocks.

"Look," he demanded in a raspy voice.

Her eyelashes lifted slowly.

"You are the beautiful one, Selene."

And she was. Selene had posed for thousands of photographs because of her renowned beauty, but she had never looked this good. Never.

James was half a head taller than she, and she was very tall. She had gained some weight the past few weeks, to her advantage, she had to admit. Jutting bones and harsh angles had been replaced with soft curves and tempting, secret shadows. Through James's eyes she saw her full breasts and narrow waist, the dark curls of her femininity and long, tapered legs.

She hardly recognized the wanton creature with the wild hair and passion-bruised lips. The green-eyed seductress that stared back at her with flaming desire was not the "sexless mannequin" Devon had once described. Yes, she was beautiful, and for once she was happy that beauty defined her, if only because it brought pleasure to this man she loved.

"Put your hands behind my neck," he urged, placing one palm possessively against her taut belly, pulling her back against his body, and using the other hand to guide her hands up and behind his neck.

The motion brought her full breasts even higher and arched her back, as if she were offering her engorged nipples for a lover's sustenance. She was.

Selene felt James's erection jerk against her.

"Oh."

With his left hand still pressing against her stomach, James used his right hand to pull her hair off her face. "Oh?"

"Oh, if you don't touch me soon, I think I'm going to die."

He looked as if he wanted to laugh but was in too much pain.

"I love your breasts," he whispered against her ear, the hot breath teasing the inner whorls erotically. He used both hands to lift her breasts even higher, then swept his palms upward over the aching centers.

"A-a-ah."

"Does that feel good?" He used his palms to draw light circles on them.

"It feels wonderful . . . and terrible. It's too much . . . and not nearly enough."

His palms left her breasts, leaving the swollen mounds unfulfilled and yearning with a throbbing intensity for more. His luminous eyes trapped hers in the mirror as his exploring hands moved lower, skimming over the wetness that coated even her outer curls. She lowered her eyes, but he immediately forced her chin upward.

"No, *chérie*, I want to see your pleasure, as you see mine."

"I want you inside me when I come, James," she admitted in a small voice.

She felt his breath suspend momentarily. Then he exhaled with a loud whoosh. "I will be, darling. I will be. Just let me . . ." He pressed his fingertips between her legs, then shuddered. *"Mon Dieu!* You are like warm honey melting over me. I wanted to make this last. I really did, Selene. But I don't think I can wait."

She turned in his arms and gripped his face. "No more torture, James. Later . . . you can torture me later if you want, but for now I just want you to . . . I just want *you*. That's all."

With a deep, masculine sigh of compliance, he hooked his arm under her knees and carried her to the bed. Dropping her down to her back on the feather mattress, he followed immediately after, covering her with the welcome weight of his body.

"Now," she demanded, parting her legs and bending her knees to cradle him. She reached for him, hoping to draw his hardness into her body, but he slapped her hand away with a low laugh.

"Not yet. Your embers have not yet become a bonfire."

"Hah! If you're not careful, I'm going to sizzle your pizzle," she warned, quoting Etienne's favorite vulgar word.

James laughed. "I'll hold you to that promise, Selene. Later."

"Now, James."

With sublime Southern charm, he grinned at her and refused, doing just as he damned well pleased. Not that it didn't please her, too.

Bracing himself on one elbow, James slid off her to his side and traced a forefinger over her mouth, along her chin, down the thin column of her neck, to her breasts. He took a nipple between his thumb and forefinger, squeezing gently. "Have I told you that I love your breasts?"

"Yes." She stretched her upper body with a cat-like purr at the delicious, agonizing pleasure.

Lowering his mouth, he laved the aching pebble with his tongue, bringing it to even more heightened sensitivity, rolling it between his lips, flicking it back and forth. When he began to suckle rhythmically, Selene reached overhead to grasp the spindles of the headboard. He moved to the other breast, giving it equal attention, murmuring naughty words of appreciation.

"Sweet . . . sweet . . . your moans are so damned sweet, *chérie.*"

With each suckle, Selene felt a tantalizing pull deep in her woman's center, and the wetness between her legs grew thick and molten.

Suddenly Selene began to ride upward on the waves of an overpowering climax, keening aloud.

James stopped. *He stopped.*

Dropping to his back, he threw an arm over his face, gasping for breath.

Selene stared at him in shock. "You drive me to the point of madness, and then you stop. Are you really that cruel?"

He peeked at her through the splayed fingers of one hand. "This hurts me more than it hurts you, darlin'."

"Hah!" The she looked downward and saw his huge erection, so engorged the veins stood out in waiting for the tight embrace of her sheath. "Why?" she asked, placing a hand on his chest, playing with his flat nipples, just as he had hers. His sharp inhale pleased her immensely. She trailed her fingertips lower, over his ridged abdomen and flat stomach. When she reached for that male part of him, he grabbed her wrist.

"No."

"No?" she asked and swung her leg over his hips, straddling him. "Do you mean no, you don't want me to do this?" she asked and slipped her tongue between his parted lips, kissing him hungrily.

He groaned.

"Or do you mean this?" she teased, nipping at his nipples.

He sucked in his stomach muscles, fighting the raging arousal that consumed them both.

"Or this?" she said, sighing, and took his male organ between both hands guiding it into her slickness.

"Yes," he said in a voice that seemed to come from far off, and he bucked upward, filling her, impaling her almost to the womb. Placing both hands on her hips, he held her in place, gritting his teeth to hold back his climax.

But Selene was not so strong. Like a tightly wound ball of fiery threads, she began to unravel. And her hot inner folds convulsed around him in fierce waves of flowing lava.

"*Mon Dieu!*" he ground out. "You feel like velvet fire."

Her chin dropped to her chest as she fought for breath.

Only then did he begin to rock her gently. Reaching up, his slender fingers with their work-callused pads touched only the tips of her throbbing breasts, then moved lower to the wet pearl that seemed more like a marble between her legs.

Her womanly sheath clasped him spasmodically. And she climaxed again, to her amazement and his delight.

She whimpered incoherently.

He murmured tender words of encouragement. "You look so . . . so beautiful when you peak."

"I never . . . I never . . ." In the throes of her continuing passion, she could barely speak.

"You are trembling."

"Your heart is beating madly," she answered.

"Your skin tastes like smooth satin."

"Your skin tastes better than beignets."

He laughed joyfully as he began to explore her body more leisurely.

She sighed.

"Ah, Selene, tell me what you like."

"Everything."

"I should have known when you ate so many beignets that you would be a greedy wench."

"Hah!" Then her voice turned sultry. "Tell me what you like, James. Tell me what you are going to do."

And he did. Oh, Lord, he did.

Soon neither of them could stand any more of the verbal foreplay. James flipped her to her back, still embedded in her depths, and began a slow, stroking rhythm. The only sounds in the room were the soft murmurs of their voices and the wet sounds of their lovemaking.

"I love you, Selene," he said, panting, as his strokes grew harder and shorter.

"I love you, too. Oh, how I lo—" She gripped the head-board for support, unable to speak coherently, and wrapped her legs around his waist. Unbelievably, his huge organ grew larger inside her and went in even deeper.

"O-o-oh," he rasped out, giving up the fight. He slammed into her body one last time, climaxing with hot spurts.

They lay still for endless minutes, breathing raggedly. James's face was buried in her neck, and his weight pressed her to the bed.

For the first time in her life, Selene felt womanly and desirable and sated. Definitely sated. She smiled, running a caressing hand over the supple muscles of his back. "I love you, James," she whispered, not sure if he could hear.

But he did.

James rolled over onto his back, taking her with him, and tucked her warm body under his arm at his side. "You're just saying that because I put out your bonfire," he teased, kissing the top of her head.

She peeked up at him mischievously. "Hey! What makes you think the fire's out yet, Rhett baby?"

His eyes shot wide with surprise. Then she felt a low rumble of laughter begin in his chest.

"What?" she asked.

"I think I know how Rhett died."

This time their lovemaking was a slow, gentle celebration as each began to know the other's body. Soft words expressed their awe over this rare gift they'd been given.

"I have no desire to return to my time," Selene told James when they lay limp once again in each other's arms.

"Shhh," he cautioned, pulling her tightly into the cradle of his arms. "Don't make promises you might not be able to keep."

She lifted her head and looked at him, then traced the line of his jaw lovingly with a forefinger. "James, I love you. I want to be with you. If I choose not to don that gown on St. John's Eve, the choice is mine."

He seemed to swallow with difficulty. "I'm almost afraid to believe it's possible. I've had so many problems that I'm afraid to be happy now, to hope."

"I know exactly what you mean, honey. It's like you're afraid if you're too happy, you'll jinx yourself. Like some jealous god will look down and nix the whole deal."

He smiled. Lord, he had the most beautiful smile in the world. "Well, I wouldn't have said it in quite that way, *chérie*, with those jinx-es and nix-es." He shifted to his side and looked down at her, his expression suddenly serious. "What now, Selene?"

She raised her eyes mockingly. "Again, James?"

"No, not again, Selene," he said with exaggerated horror. "I meant tomorrow and day after that. There are people in my home—Etienne, my mother, Blossom, slaves, servants—people who see and hear everything. I wouldn't want to compromise you by making you my mistress. Even if I leave your bed at dawn, they will know I slept here. Believe me, they will know."

She smiled at his consideration. "What are you suggesting?"

"That we get married . . . as soon as possible."

Selene's heart slammed against her ribcage, and her blood rushed joyously through her veins. Still, she hesitated. "I love you, James. Nothing would make me happier than to be your wife. Nothing. But do you really think it's wise to rush into marriage? I mean . . . well, I know I said the choice is mine about staying here. But what if you should have second thoughts later?"

"I won't."

"And what if—"

"Selene, let's take one day at a time. That's all anyone can do. There are no guarantees in life. Love's a gamble, don't you think?"

"And you think the odds are in our favor?"

"Absolutely."

They drifted off to sleep together.

Just before dawn he awakened her again. "Hurry, Selene, it's almost light."

"No more," she groaned and rolled over onto her stomach, burying her head under a pillow.

He swatted her on a bare buttock. "Get up, Selene. You have to dress."

She lifted one side of the pillow and peered up at him. "Dress? For what?" He had already pulled on a pair of black trousers and was tucking a white shirt, unbuttoned, into his waistband.

"I want to show you something."

"Again? In the middle of the night?"

"Tsk-tsk, Selene. You have a dirty mind. Besides, it's not the middle of the night. It's four o'clock, and it will be dawn soon. Come on."

He dragged her out of bed then and pulled her toward the armoire, where he grabbed a long skirt and shirtwaist blouse.

"Let me wash first." She looked down with embarrassment at the slickness that covered her inner thighs.

"No." His pale eyes gazed at the vee of her legs with carnal appreciation. "I like knowing . . . seeing . . . that some part of me is still in you . . . and on you."

She started to balk, but he drew her over to the mirror

and sat on a chair in front of it with her on his lap, facing forward. He spread his knees wide apart, taking hers with them. "Look, Selene. See what I see when I look at you. It's beautiful. You're beautiful."

A blush crept up Selene's neck to her face, but she looked. And through James's eyes she saw her femininity exposed, like the petals of a dew-covered flower, not hidden away like some dirty, forbidden secret.

"Oh, James." She felt a savage lurch of arousal unfurl between her legs.

He laughed softly and set her on her feet. "Not now, you greedy witch." He gave her a light butterfly kiss on the lips, then stepped away. "Put this gown on before I forget where I wanted to take you."

A short time later, sitting before James on his horse, she realized where they were headed. The special place at the curve of the bayou stream where the herons performed their mating ritual.

"I dreamed about making love to you here," he whispered against her ear as he helped her alight, then staked the horse. He pulled a coarse blanket off the saddle and twined her hand with his, directing her toward the secluded spot. The same two herons sat patiently on the limb, as if awaiting their arrival.

"You're right, James. This is the perfect place to seal our love."

Surrounded by primitive nature and timeless creatures, James laid her on the blanket. And Selene soon came to believe that two lovers really could cross the thresholds of different worlds . . . worlds which were not so different after all.

"Your people and mine are not unlike, Selene. I see that now. Love is the common bond," James murmured as he knelt and entered her body, reverently, as if he, too, sensed the symbolism of their act.

Selene rose upward in one fluid motion, following

James's receding stroke. Sitting back on his haunches, still embedded in her depths, James pulled her with him until she straddled his thighs. Sighing, she pressed her breasts against the wiry hairs of his chest. "Two heartbeats . . . I can actually feel our two heartbeats," she cried out in awe.

"*Oui,* two heartbeats, but one rhythm."

Her spirit soared and twined with James's, like the necks of the two herons who sat before them. "You're right, James. Love knows no boundaries. Neither time nor place."

In that moment, when their cries of passion rose to the skies, mingling with the eternal forest sounds, Selene understood why she had been sent back in time.

Tears of happiness streamed down her face as she arched her back and climbed a crescendo of ever-increasing waves, then crashed, splintering into a whirlpool of the most intense, shattering pleasure she had ever experienced in her life. Followed by an immense sense of completeness.

James's strangled cry of satisfaction echoed after hers. She looked up to see his eyes filled with tears, as well. And her heart welled almost to overflowing.

In that one split second in the spectrum of eternity . . . that frozen limbo of the gods . . . time stood still. And they knew they were blessed.

Chapter Twenty

Whoever said true love runs smooth was a fool . . .

It was seven o'clock before Selene and James got back to the house. They'd returned the back way, circumventing the sugar fields to avoid any embarrassing questions from Fergus or the workers who were already hard at work.

Sitting astride the horse in front of James, Selene yawned and arched her back against his hard chest in a sensuous stretch. Her body felt bruised and sore and abraded. And absolutely wonderful.

James dismounted in one lithe movement, tying his horse to the back rail. Then he placed his hands on Selene's waist, lifting her to the ground. He did not immediately release her, however. Leaning down, he kissed her lightly on the lips.

"I love you, Selene," he said solemnly.

"I love you, too, James." Overwhelmed with emotion, she had difficulty speaking. "I've never been happier in my life."

"We have much to talk about later today, *chérie*. Our future."

"I look forward to it."

"Perhaps I'll disclose some more of my fantasies to you then," he added, jiggling his eyebrows with mock lasciviousness.

"Be still, my heart," she replied, laughing, as she basked in the glow of this wonderful, frivolous bantering. Then she wagged a finger at him. "But don't be too sure that I don't have a few more of my own fantasies tucked up my sleeve."

"I'm counting on it, *chérie*."

Smiling, they walked into the kitchen with arms looped around each other's waists.

"Lordy, Lordy, where you two been? We been lookin' for you everywhere," Blossom said anxiously. She stood over the *potager*, turning strips of bacon.

Iris's wide eyes swept over their crumpled attire, and her mouth dropped practically to the tray she was preparing for Mrs. Baptiste.

Etienne's hand, holding a slice of buttered bread and jam, stopped midway to his mouth. The scamp also had a cup of coffee in front of him. As if the outrageous kid needed more energy! Next he'd be having a shot of bourbon and a cigar after dinner.

Grinning, Etienne remarked, "I know what you been doin'." Then he resumed eating, the subject apparently not of that much importance to him. Dreadful lolled, open-mouthed, under the table, catching the many crumbs the boy dropped.

"Etienne!" James warned.

Selene pulled away from James. With chin averted to hide her red face, she announced, "I'm going to go take a bath."

Selene was about to escape the room when she heard Blossom exclaim, "Will everyone just shut up!"

Stunned, they all turned to look at the cook. Blossom pointed her ladle at James. "If you would stop babblin' long enough, I would tell you why everyone's been lookin' for you, you fool."

"Why?" James asked, suddenly alert to the concern in Blossom's voice.

" 'Cause Victor and the po-lice are here. I put 'em on the front gallery with some breakfast to hold 'em off. But they wants to begin a search for that Fleur girl, startin' inside the house. And they gots legal papers."

Selene exchanged an apprehensive glance with James. He'd refused the past few days to tell her where Fleur was hidden, only assuring her that Victor's quadroon mistress was safe. Now he didn't look so sure.

Selene started to come back, intending to go with James to confront Victor.

"No!" James put up a halting hand.

"No?"

"Change your clothes and go to my mother. Take Etienne with you. I'll handle this. I mean it, Selene. No interference." Then he told Iris, "Send for Fergus, and tell him to bring men with him. Armed men."

"But—" Etienne started to say.

"One more word out of you today and you won't be able to sit for a week."

"But—" Selene protested.

"Or you either."

"I can't sit anyway," she muttered under her breath.

James heard her. And despite the danger surrounding them, he grinned with masculine satisfaction.

God, she loved the brute. "Okay," she agreed finally, wanting to help him in any way she could.

Their solution was doggone good . . .

Hours later, Victor and the guardsmen had searched the house, sugar fields, outbuildings, and quarters, to no avail. They finally left, without Fleur, swearing to come back with tracking dogs.

With a loud exhale, James sat down next to Selene on the

settee in the *garçonnière* parlor. His mother handed him a cup of strong Creole coffee.

"But I don't understand, James. How can Victor track a free black woman?" Mrs. Baptiste asked.

"Atwood forged documents detailing Victor's purchase of a slave named Fleur two years ago."

"Then there is nothing to be done," Mrs. Baptiste said with a shrug. "You must return the girl to Victor."

"No!" Selene cried out, speaking up for the first time. "Fleur is pregnant, and Victor is going to kill her."

Mrs. Baptiste raised an eyebrow in question at her vehemence. "And how do you know this, *chérie?*"

"I just do," Selene said weakly, casting her eyes downward at James's warning glare.

"I must tell you, *mere,* that I would return the will to Victor if I thought his perfidy would stop." He turned to Selene. "I know you have the will. I demand you give it to me."

"Fine, I'll run upstairs and get it," Selene replied.

"The will is not yours to relinquish, James," Mrs. Baptiste snapped when Selene had left the room. "I have no objection to Selene handing the document over to you. But until I am dead, I do not want to hear of your giving up rights to what *I* earned."

James lifted his hands in a begrudging gesture of acceptance. Then he turned to Selene, who had returned, taking the will from her hand. "I have no intention of returning Fleur. But I must get her off the plantation before Victor brings the dogs."

"I was thinking, James . . . do you suppose Pierce would be willing to take Fleur with him?" Selene asked tentatively. "Maybe some family traveling on one of his wagon trains would need a girl to help them."

James's troubled face brightened. "Hmmm. That might work."

Suddenly Selene thought of something else. "Victor sent dogs here once before with his overseer," she reminded him, "and they didn't do him any good then."

"Ah, but he had no legal right to search then. The dogs were not let loose."

Selene nodded with understanding.

But Mrs. Baptiste no longer listened. Instead, her attention honed in on her son's hand now laced intimately with Selene's on the couch.

"Do you plan to wed?" she blurted out to James.

He made a low, hooting sound of laughter at her bluntness. "*Oui,* I hope to."

"And you, Selene? Are you sure you want this stubborn son of mine?"

"I'm sure," Selene said, locking eyes with James. Her heart thrummed wildly at the love she saw reflected in the blue depths.

"I will send notice to Father Sebastian in St. Martinsville to begin announcing the banns this Sunday. Perhaps he can perform the ceremony here at Bayou Noir in, say, one month?" Mrs. Baptiste said, her fertile mind already making detailed plans.

"Now, *mere,* there's no rush," James said.

Mrs. Baptiste's clear eyes swept over both of them with knowing appraisal, missing nothing. "I would say there is most definitely a *big rush.*"

Mrs. Baptiste looked from one to the other, preening like a Cheshire cat. You'd think she had maneuvered their whole romance. She glanced toward the miniature shrine to the Blessed Virgin in the corner, commenting to herself, "I must remember to say a novena of thanks."

She knew the perfect way to thank him . . .

James was unable to see Selene again until late that evening. Reeling with exhaustion, he ate a hasty cold supper in the quiet kitchen. Everyone had already gone to bed. Then he bathed and went to Selene's bedchamber.

"Good heavens, James! I've been so worried. Where have you been?" Selene said, rushing into his arms.

"Ah, the woman has turned into a shrew already," he teased.

She kissed his face and neck, hugging him warmly.

Suddenly he wasn't quite so tired. He sank down into a low slipper chair, taking her with him onto his lap.

"I followed up on your suggestion concerning Pierce," he informed her when he felt welcomed enough by her nibbling kisses. "I visited the Collins plantation this afternoon. Luckily, Pierce agreed immediately to our plan. In fact, he already has a family in mind." He was examining the ribbons that tied her gown together as he spoke.

"Oh, James, that's wonderful."

"Victor might be back tomorrow with the dogs. So I took Fleur tonight to her new hiding place at the Collins'. Pierce and Fleur will be leaving within days for Missouri."

"This is such a relief. I've been so concerned about Fleur."

"And you had every reason to be," he admitted in a grim voice. "I didn't want to tell you before, but Fleur's body is covered with bruises and scars—old and new—from the many beatings my brother has administered."

"What a beast!"

"*Oui,* he really is. I wonder . . . do you think he is mad?"

Selene shrugged, unknowing. "The most important thing is that you saved Fleur."

She looked at him with tear-filled eyes of adoration, then blinked with surprise when his hand caressed a naked thigh. Looking down, she seemed to realize for the first time that her gown lay open, exposing miles of bare, delicious skin.

"James, I love you so much. Thank you for helping Fleur."

"Hah!" he said, pushing her off his lap and standing. "Don't think I went to all this trouble for a few paltry words of thanks."

"What did you have in mind?" she asked, slanting him a sultry look.

"Arrow-backs."

"Aerobics? Now?"

"That's right, darlin'. Pelvic thrusts. Kegel muscle drills. Everything. I'm at your mercy."

She laughed. "Is that all?"

"Well, in some ways, I'm a lot like Etienne . . ." He grinned at her, intentionally showing her the dimple she liked so well. He was rewarded by seeing her nipples peak under her thin dressing gown.

"Meaning?" She ducked away from his reaching fingers. "Are you gifted?"

"Some say so. And I definitely have a 'gift' for you, *chérie*."

"And just what kind of instruction would an experienced bayou lover like you want from an old city girl like me?" she asked, surrendering to his exploring hands, twining her arms around his neck.

"The Perfect Fit."

"Oh, Lord," she gasped. His fingers had just discovered a spot where they fit quite nicely.

"Now is not the time for prayer, Selene," he whispered, nuzzling the smooth slope of her neck, "because I am definitely having impure thoughts."

"Maybe you should kneel down and let me hear your confession," she said on a sigh as his lips roved lower.

"I'll kneel down all right," he growled huskily, "but you're not going to be giving me any blessings, *chérie*. You're going to be counting your blessings."

"O-o-oh," Selene moaned a short time later. "That's the first one. Blessing, I mean."

He showed her a new way to make sugar . . .

The next morning, Victor, his father's overseer Jake Colbert, Corporal Atwood, two guards, and six vicious, snarling dogs arrived at Bayou Noir. After several hours of intensive searching, and much swearing at the terrified slaves and servants, they were only able to find a slave cottage where the dogs howled repeatedly. But Fleur, of course, had long since vacated the hidden closet on the premises.

"This is not the end of this, you bastard," Victor railed at James in fury. But for now there was nothing more he could do, and he left in a huff.

Early that afternoon, it was Selene's turn to be livid. She stormed out to the sugar fields where James and Fergus were helping the workers inspect the cane for the hated worms that often appeared at this time of the year. The blistering sun beat down unrelentingly. They had all removed their shirts, but kept hats on to shade their eyes.

"What's the matter, *chérie?*" he asked, walking up to her, using his discarded shirt to wipe the perspiration from his chest.

"I want you to see what Etienne has done now!" she said in a shaky voice. He could tell that she'd been crying because the black substance she always put on her lashes was smudged. There were also rivulets in the liquid powder she applied in a ritual she called "putting on her face."

"What? What's he done now?"

Selene raised her chin indignantly and sniffed. "You'll see. Iris is bringing him and the other children now. I didn't want you to have to come back to the house just for this, but . . . but, oh, I am so mad at that brat."

James looked up to see Iris marching toward them with a half dozen frightened children in tow, like a troop of midget soldiers—Etienne, Cain, Abel, Samson, the gaptoothed Hollyhock, and a wiry-haired Primrose. Chins dragging for whatever shameful transgressions they'd committed, they looked a bit like that Our Gang group that Selene had described one time when her hair had turned to buckwheat.

Fergus walked over to James's side as the children came

closer, then lifted their faces. The men both gasped at the same time, then burst out laughing.

Apparently, the children had confiscated Selene's cosmetic case. Lip rouge circled their mouths in grotesque caricatures. Etienne had drawn wide black rings around his eyes like a raccoon. Hollyhock wore Selene's false eyelashes—upside down. Cain had used her black wand . . . mascara, Selene called it . . . to draw a mustache above his now trembling upper lip.

James shook his head with laughing amazement.

"It's not funny," Selene exclaimed and started to sob. "They took my private property and destroyed it. And now . . . and now, oh, God, I have no makeup at all."

"Etienne," James said, trying to sound stern, "explain yourself."

His son lowered his eyes and shuffled his feet in the dirt. "We didn't mean to make Mam'zelle cry. We were jist playin', and . . ." Despite his explanation, Etienne didn't sound very sorry.

"Iris, take the children to the house and scrub their faces. Then send Etienne back to the fields. Apparently he has too much time on his hands. Perhaps a day of hoeing under this hot sun will occupy his mind to better advantage."

"Papa! You wouldn't make me work in the fields! I'm too little."

"Be back here in one hour, Etienne," he ordered. "And know that this will not be the end of your punishment. I blame you for this debacle."

"It wasn't my fault."

"Oh, let there be no doubt, my son. You were the leader of this mischief, and you will be the one to pay. But first, *all of you*, I think you know what you must do." And one by one they dragged their feet up to Selene and offered their apologies.

After they departed, James sent the men back to work and drew Selene along the path and into the sugar house.

Pulling a handkerchief from his pocket, he wiped the smeared makeup from her face.

"Selene, *chérie*, I'm sorry for what Etienne did. Is it really so disastrous, though?"

"Of course it's disastrous. What am I going to do without makeup?"

He stared at her, puzzled. "This makeup . . . it is a necessity to you?"

"Of course it is," she said, slanting him a look of exasperation. "I need it to look beautiful. God, I don't think I've gone without makeup a single day since I was twelve years old."

"You have been wearing makeup every day here?" he asked, tilting his head with confusion.

She made a clucking sound of disgust and blew her nose loudly in his handkerchief, then tucked it into her skirt pocket.

"But your skin always looks so . . . natural."

"Oh, Lord, spare me from the blindness of men. Of course my skin looked natural. That's the point of makeup."

"It is?"

Selene exhaled loudly with impatience. "The bottom line here, James, is that I no longer have any makeup, and I'm probably going to be"—she gulped—"homely."

His lips twitched with a smile.

"And you probably won't love me anymore when I'm homely." Her voice cracked with what was undoubtedly going to be the onslaught of another bout of tears.

"Selene, sweetheart, I think you're beautiful, even without artifice." He reached out, about to take her into his arms.

"How do you know?" she asked cautiously. "You've never seen me without makeup."

"We could go to the bayou stream and wash your face. Then I could give you an honest appraisal," he offered.

She lifted her eyebrows mockingly. "The bayou stream, huh? You wouldn't be thinking of that spot with the herons,

344 Sandra Hill

now would you, James? Really! You've got a one-track mind."

"You liked that track last night," he reminded her, moving closer.

"And I'm not blonde, either," she commented irrelevantly, slipping out of his grasp.

"What the hell does that have to do with anything?"

"If I were blonde, that would make up for not having makeup," she said.

"That's ridiculous."

"Did you hear about the seventy-five-year-old blonde woman who walked into a tavern with a pigeon on her head?"

"Now? You are going to tell blonde jokes now?"

"Don't interrupt. Where was I? Oh, and then the seventy-five-year-old blonde with the pigeon on her head shouted, 'Whoever can guess the weight of this bird gets to make love to me.'" Selene paused dramatically. "Way in the back of the tavern, a drunk shouted, 'One thousand pounds.'"

"Oh, good Lord!"

"And the blonde said cheerfully, 'Close enough!'"

Selene's voice sounded thready and almost hysterical. Over makeup, for God's sake!

James grinned and shook his head. "What's the point, Selene? I don't see a pigeon on your head."

She laughed and backed up with a loud clang into the scales behind her.

"What are these?" she asked.

"The scales that we use to weigh the hogsheads of sugar."

"Scales?" she said, eying them oddly. "Could a person weigh herself on one of these?"

"I suppose."

Selene stepped up onto the scale, almost as if approaching a guillotine. "I guess I might as well get all the bad news in one day."

He adjusted the weights and moved her so that she stood in the center of the scale. "One hundred and twenty-five pounds," he announced.

"That's impossible! Check again."

He did, then shrugged. "It's the same."

She stepped down and began to wail. Again. "Oh . . . oh," she gasped out. "I've gained fifteen pounds. Fifteen pounds! I must look like a tub of lard. I must look like a . . . a hogshead, whatever that is."

"Enough! I've had enough of this nonsense about your beauty, or lack of it." He pulled her over to the far side, away from the door and windows. Bracing his hands on the wall on either side of her head, he told her, "I've told you I love you. Repeatedly. Some of those times were in the dark. I think you're beautiful, but I think I would love you even if you were homely as a . . . a . . ."

"Warthog," she offered, apparently remembering that he had called her that at one time. *Mon Dieu*, her memory was entirely too sharp.

"Precisely. Now, there is something I must teach you about sugarmaking." He dipped his head and whispered against her lips, "Do you know what the two sweetest occupations are in the world, *chérie?*"

"Is this a riddle?" she asked, then moaned as his lips brushed back and forth across hers in delicious temptation.

"No, it is not a riddle." He put his left hand on the smooth column of her neck, holding her in place for his kiss, and swept his right hand lower, cupping her full breast.

She sighed and parted her lips under his, inviting his plundering tongue.

He pulled away, teasing. "The two sweetest occupations in the world are making sugar and . . ."

". . . and?" she purred, arching her chest as he rolled her nipple between his thumb and forefinger through the fabric of her blouse.

". . . and making love."

"And you're an expert at both, I suppose," she choked out, allowing him to ease the hem of her gown up to her waist and pull down her drawers. Belatedly she added, when his fingers were already parting her moist folds, "Do you think it's wise to make love here? Someone might walk in."

"No one will walk in," he gritted out, unbuttoning his trousers and adjusting himself between her legs. "Just try to restrain your moans so the workers don't think I'm beating you."

"Hah! I know a saying, too, about making sugar."

"Tell me later," he grunted out, unable to restrain his roiling need.

She laughed. "I've heard that the longer the cane stands, the sweeter the sugar. Maybe you should think about holding onto that *cane* a bit longer."

"No!" he asserted, wrapping her legs around his waist and plunging himself into her hot depths. "This cane is about to be cut. Now!"

A very short time later, Selene commented with a gasp, "I think the cane was pretty damn sweet anyhow."

He made a low rumbling sound of male approval as he adjusted his clothing.

"You think you're hot stuff, don't you, James, darlin'?"

He eyed her suspiciously.

"Did you hear about the blonde whose lover rolled off her and asked, 'Do you smoke after sex?'?"

"Not another joke!" he groaned.

"And the blonde said, 'I dunno.' Then the blonde looked down her body and added, 'I never looked.'"

"You are impossible, Selene," he said, pulling her to his side as they walked toward the doorway. "But, *oui*, it is true."

"Huh? What's true."

"You do smoke."

Back from the dead, part two . . .

Two weeks later, Selene still floated on a cloud of bliss. She had never been happier in her life and had absolutely no regrets about staying in the past.

She leaned her head on James's shoulder under the keel-boat shelter, and sighed with contentment. Etienne slept on his father's lap, exhausted from the day's mind-boggling events.

To celebrate the boy's sixth birthday the day before, Selene, with Blossom's help, had given Etienne a party he would never forget, complete with improvised tomato and cheese pizzas and a homemade book of illustrated E.T. and Casper stories. James's gift had been today's trip to the visiting circus in St. Martinsville.

"Why are you sighing, my love?" James asked, kissing the top of her head.

She turned her face upward, offering her lips. He kissed her sweetly, tenderly. "I was sighing because I still can't believe you love me. It's as if this love we've been given is a gift."

He chuckled her playfully under the chin. "From whom?"

"I don't know. God, maybe. Or the fates. Yeah, maybe fate ordained that I come to this time to be with you."

He laughed.

"What? You don't believe that?"

He shrugged. "A fanciful notion, don't you think?"

"I suppose, but how else can you explain my time-travel? Look, it's obvious, really. You needed me. I definitely needed you. Together . . . it's as if we are two parts of one whole that was mistakenly divided by the quagmires of time."

"So you think I needed you? What a conceited wench you are!"

Selene swept a teasing hand down his back to his buttocks,

and he inhaled sharply, almost jolting Etienne off his lap. The boy whined in protest, squirmed a bit, then went back to sleep.

"That's not fair, Selene," he said, grinning. "Tantalizing me when you know I'm in no position to rise to the occasion."

"Oh, and are you . . . rising?"

"Always, Selene. Always, for you." He chuckled and slapped her straying fingers away with a free hand.

"That's a promise I'm going to make sure you keep after we're married," she said, snuggling once again into the curve of his shoulder. "Only two more weeks until the wedding, James. No second thoughts?"

"None, *chérie*."

"Have you thought any more about what I told you about the gold rush in California which is to come? About how we might go there?"

"No. It all seems too incredible."

"Everything about us is incredible."

He couldn't argue with that.

It was already dark by the time their flatboat docked and two of the slaves tied it up for the night. James and Selene walked up the incline to the house. An overtired, half-asleep Etienne stumbled along between them.

"Why are there candles lit all over the house?" Selene asked suddenly.

"I don't know," James said warily. "Perhaps there are guests."

They had almost reached the front steps when James stopped suddenly and gasped out, "No, it's impossible. God would not be so cruel."

A riffle of foreboding swept the back of Selene's neck, like a ghostly vapor.

A woman stood at the top of the steps, wearing an exquisite off-the-shoulder gown of pale blue silk over wide petticoats. She raised a dainty hand in greeting.

"Fleur? Why is Fleur here?" Selene asked with alarm. "She should be all the way to Missouri by now."

James looked at Selene oddly, then turned back to the figure on the gallery. The color drained from his face, and he shook his head in disbelief.

"What? What's wrong?"

Just then a slight breeze came up from the bayou, causing a strand of the woman's blonde curls to come loose from her chignon.

Blonde hair! But . . . but Fleur has black hair.

The fine hairs stood out on Selene's body in alarm. She raised frightened eyes to James in question.

"Giselle. It's my wife, Giselle," he informed her in an icy voice.

And with those words, Selene felt her wonderful, loving world with James come crumbling down around her.

Chapter Twenty-one

I *t was hard to bow out gracefully when wearing a hoop skirt . . .*

"James! *Chéri!*" the exquisite creature cried out and threw herself into James's arms. "Oh, it has been so long, my husband. I didn't think I would ever get back to you."

While she talked, the fragile, china-doll figure kissed James's face and neck in welcome. And Selene realized to her horror that the woman had every right to do so. She was his wife.

His wife! Selene's brain spun with bewilderment and she choked back the urge to scream. *No! This can't be. Giselle is dead. James is a free man. We're going to be married in two weeks.*

Raw grief clawed at Selene. She understood none of what was happening. She only knew that her perfect world—her perfect love—was about to end.

James remained stiff in Giselle's fluttery embrace, but his shock soon yielded to fury. "Where the hell have you been, Giselle? What kind of game are you playing?"

"Game? How can you accuse me of such when I have

suffered so this past year?" Giselle said in a wounded voice, pulling back and dabbing at her eyes with a frilly lace handkerchief. "That night . . . that horrible night when we quarreled, I ran into the swamp. I almost drowned."

She peeked up at him to see if he was feeling appropriately guilty.

He just glowered at her.

Raising the back of her hand to her forehead, she continued soulfully, "Fortunately, a Cajun fisherman rescued me, but a fever of the mind has held me captive these many months. I remembered nothing, not even my name. Till recently." She sniffled dramatically.

"And where is this fisherman? Give me his name!" James scoffed.

Just then Etienne started to whimper, pulling on Selene's gown. And they all remembered that the child was still in their presence.

"*Mon fils!* My son!" Giselle gushed, reaching out for the cowering boy.

"*Non, non,*" Etienne protested, burrowing even deeper into Selene's skirts. "Don't want no ghost."

Blossom stepped out of the shadows and onto the gallery, flashing a look of contempt at Giselle. "Hush, child. Come with me. Blossom'll put you to bed. Yessirree, everythin' gonna be all right. Ol' Blossom will stay with Etienne."

"You overstep yourself, you nigger wench. He's *my* son. I will care for him," Giselle snarled.

"'Bout time you remembered that," Blossom snapped back.

Giselle raised a hand, about to strike the old woman.

Selene grabbed Giselle's wrist in midair. It was not her place to intervene, but she just couldn't allow the spiteful woman to hit Blossom, or anyone else.

Recovering himself, James motioned with a jerk of his head for Blossom and Etienne to leave, then for Selene to release Giselle's hand. She did so gladly. There was a feel of evil in the mere touch of Giselle's clammy flesh.

"Don't think you can take my place with my son," Giselle hissed, shooting a look of pure hatred at Selene as she rubbed her bruised wrist. Then Giselle seemed to remember where she was, and the expression on her Barbie Doll face changed from fury to hurt. "James, darling, aren't you happy to see me? I have dreamed of this day ever since I regained my memory. It will be a new beginning for us."

With lethal calmness, James told his wife, "Let us go inside. You have much to explain."

"I think I'll go to my room," Selene said weakly. Bereft and desolate, she felt as if she were floating on a cloud of despair. What would she do now that Giselle had returned? How could she live in the same house with James and his wife?

"No!" James said firmly. Then he softened his voice with entreaty, his eyes pleading for understanding in a situation that defied logic. "You will stay. Whatever Giselle has to say affects us all."

"Oh?" Giselle said. "I hardly think this . . . this mere housekeeper . . . or governess . . . should be present for our joyous reunion."

Joyous reunion! Selene's heart felt like the most delicate crystal, and it was shattering bit by bit as each moment passed.

"I can't stay, James," she said in a shaky voice. "I just can't." Selene desperately needed to be by herself, to sort out all the devastating implications of Giselle's return. She needed privacy to cry.

She fled, starting for the center stairway leading to her third-floor bedchamber. At the bottom of the steps, James stopped her with a hand on her shoulder.

She turned.

"Trust me, *chérie*. Please, just trust me," he said bleakly.

Selene nodded, unable to speak over the lump in her throat, and walked stiffly up the stairs. She soon discovered the first of the changes to come. Iris informed her that

Giselle had ordered all of her clothing and personal belongings moved to one of the cramped fourth-floor bedchambers normally reserved for servants.

"Now all the evil deeds gonna start again," Iris predicted. "The beatings, the voodoo . . ." She looked at Selene expectantly. "What you gonna do about it?"

"Me?" Selene squeaked out.

"You're the only one what can stop her."

Oh, yeah. Me and a platoon of Marines.

Throughout the evening, sitting alone in her tiny room, Selene repeated James's words over and over as she wept silent tears of pain. Yes, she would try to trust in James, but she didn't see any way he could find a solution to this horrible predicament.

The man she loved was married.

And he did not come to her that night.

For whom the bleepin' bell tolls . . .

Selene awakened early the next morning, before seven, but already a heavy miasma of gloom hung over the house. The kitchen, which normally bustled with chattering voices at this hour, resounded with quick, efficient movements carried out in quiet fear.

"What you gonna do 'bout that one?" Blossom asked, pointing upward to what Selene presumed was Giselle's bedchamber. *James's bedchamber*, she realized with hopelessness. Blossom, Iris, Hyacinth, and Verbena all stared at her, as if she had magic answers. Poor Etienne sat at the table, staring into his bowl of porridge with unaccustomed dolefulness.

"Me? What can I do?" Selene felt the weight of their dependency, when all she wanted was just to run away and hide. James must feel this same way at times, overburdened with responsibility. But these were not her people. Not now. "Where is James?"

"He went off somewheres," Blossom informed her, "prob'ly to hunt down that Cajun family the mistress claims she stayed with. Hah! More likely she bin sleepin' in Victor's bed all this time."

Selene was amazed at Blossom's perceptiveness. She'd already come to the same conclusion herself. She even wondered if Giselle was the "ghost." She was about to voice that possibility to Blossom when she saw Etienne listening to their every word. She darted a look of warning at Blossom and the others.

"Come on, E.T., let's start our lessons early today. Perhaps we can experiment with some of those paints we bought yesterday in St. Martinsville."

He stood and shuffled to his feet. "Bet *she* won't let me have the name E.T. anymore. Bet *she* won't let me study bye-olive-gee outdoors. Bet *she* won't let me do anything fun."

Selene watched despondently as the boy made for the corridor leading to the back stairs. She would have to be careful. After all, Giselle was Etienne's mother.

And Selene's heart wept at the thought.

The jingling of a bell jolted them all to attention.

"What is *that?*" Selene exclaimed.

"Now it begins," Iris stated grimly. "It's the mistress ringin' the bell for a servant."

"I didn't even know there was a bell."

"You're gonna be hearin' it a lot," Blossom predicted.

"I ain't goin'," Verbena said, rolling her eyes. "Not me. Las' time she hit me with a flat iron for not pressin' her crinoline jist right."

"An' before she went away, she threatened to put a voodoo curse on me when I wouldn't get her one of them powders for makin' the monthly flow come," Hyacinth added. "As if I know where to find one anyways!"

"An abortifacient?" Selene asked, and realized when everyone stared at her dumbly that they wouldn't understand the word. "Never mind."

"I'll go," Iris said with a sigh of resignation, "but if she tries to hit me with that little whip of hers, I swear I'm gonna whack her back this time." The fearful look in her eyes belied her brave words.

Blossom was right when she'd said they would be hearing the bell a lot. It seemed as if every fifteen minutes that morning the bell resounded throughout the house reminding one and all that the real mistress had come home.

The end was galloping fast forward . . .

Selene stood in the schoolroom early that afternoon with Etienne and the half dozen black children who'd had the courage to show up for class.

After failing miserably to get their participation in a spelling bee or even their favorite Hokey Pokey, she arranged the unnaturally silent children on the floor. Dropping down with them into a cross-legged position, Selene made up a new story for them, "Beauty and the Bayou Beast," and then taught them "Old MacBaptiste Had a Farm."

It took a long time, but finally she got the children to relax and sing along with her. ". . . and on his farm, he had a three-legged chicken. Ee-aye, ee-aye, oh. With a squawk, squawk here, and a squawk, squawk—"

"What is the meaning of this outrage?"

The room went deathly silent, and everyone looked up to see a livid Giselle standing in the doorway. A midnight-blue riding habit adorned her petite frame, and her golden blonde hair was arranged neatly under a pert black hat with swaths of blue netting. She tapped a small riding crop against her leg, waiting impatiently for an answer.

The children were struck mute with fright.

"I'm giving the children their lessons," Selene said, standing. She towered over the diminutive Creole lady by at least a head.

"By singing some foolish song about chickens?" Her cupid's-bow mouth made a moue of derision.

"Yes, by singing." Selene clenched her fists at her sides and forced herself to be polite. "Would you like to join us?"

"Me?" Giselle laughed. "*Non*, I have come for my son. We will go riding together."

Etienne shuddered at her side. Selene saw the absolute terror in his eyes.

"A ride would be pleasant, E.T.," she tried to convince him. After all, he needed to get reaccustomed to his mother sometime.

"I don't feel good," he lied.

Selene patted him on the head and addressed Giselle, "Perhaps tomorrow would be better."

Giselle raised her whip slightly, almost as if she considered striking Selene. Then, slowly, she lowered it.

"What is this E.T.?"

"My nickname," Etienne answered in a small voice.

"*Non*, it is not. Etienne is the name I gave you at birth, and the only one you will answer to. Is that clear?"

The boy nodded.

"And what are all these pickaninnies doing here in the house? Out, out!" She waved her hand toward the doorway, and the children scampered out, except Etienne, who slipped a hand in Selene's.

Giselle's eyes narrowed with hatred as she noticed Etienne's gesture.

"Come to my room, Mademoiselle Selente. It would seem you and I have much to discuss." Without waiting for an answer, she swept from the schoolroom, never questioning that her orders would be obeyed.

It took Selene a half hour to calm Etienne down and straighten out the schoolroom before she made her way to James's bedchamber. By then, Giselle was pacing with increasing furor at Selene's failing to follow immediately.

Selene's eyes darted around James's room. She inhaled

sharply with pain on seeing the shirt and trousers he had worn the night before thrown carelessly over a chair back.

Giselle smiled maliciously.

"Sit," she ordered, pointing to a wingback chair. She dropped gracefully into the one opposite. Staring thoughtfully at Selene, she tapped her riding whip on her knee.

"Has James returned yet?" Selene asked finally, breaking the awkward silence.

Giselle forced her lips into a rueful pout. "*Oui*. Unfortunately, the Cajun family that provided safe harbor for me all these months has mysteriously disappeared. Their home abandoned. Nothing left but an old gown of mine to prove that I was there."

"How unfortunate!" Selene commented, not really surprised by the news.

"So tell me, mademoiselle, when do you intend to leave?"

Selene blinked with surprise. "Leave?"

"*Oui*, of course. Now that I am back, reunited with my husband, did you really think I would countenance his lover in my home?"

Selene swallowed hard. It was too soon to make such an important decision.

"Do not make things awkward for us all, *my dear*. Do not force James to ask you to leave. Surely your pride is greater than that."

Selene tried to draw on James's words of last night, begging for her trust. She did trust him, but this was a situation beyond trust.

"He will not divorce me, you know. We were married in the church, and there is no divorce in our religion."

Selene had suspected as much.

"Would you be satisfied with the role of mistress? Away from Bayou Noir? Perhaps in some house in the swamps?"

Selene recoiled with horror. *No! Never!*

"James loved me once," Giselle reminded Selene with

relish. "There is no doubt he will love me again. Men are so easy to . . . manipulate."

And all Selene's insecurities about her sexual allure slammed back with a vengeance. Giselle was probably right. If she left, James would forget about her eventually. Perhaps he and Giselle could reconcile their differences, make a true family with Etienne. It was for the best, really.

"I could leave on St. John's Eve," she offered in a shaky voice. "I had made arrangements once before to leave on that date."

Giselle pondered her words. "Hmmm. Twelve days from now. Well, that will have to do, I suppose. In the meantime, I expect you to know your place in this household. You are a governess and housekeeper. No more than that."

Whoa! I don't like the tone of this woman. Just who does she think she is? No way is she going to get the last word here. "Tell me, Giselle . . . did you know that doctors have finally discovered the cause of pockmarks on a blonde's face?"

Reflexively, Giselle gasped and put her fingertips to her face.

"They're not pimple scars, according to the doctors. The pockmarks are caused by dumb blondes trying to learn how to use a fork."

"Wha . . . what did you say?" Giselle fumed. "Are you saying . . . oh, how dare you speak to me so! You'll be sorry."

"Fiddle-dee-dee!" Selene said with a smile, and the phrase felt *really* good on her lips. Then, employing her years of modeling experience, Selene swept out of the room in her best Scarlett imitation, head held high.

Once she closed the door, however, Selene struggled to hold back her tears. She had just made a decision to leave everything she held most dear in the world, the only man she had ever loved. And she felt as if she had just signed her own death warrant.

Yeah, but is love enough? . . .

That evening the drums started soon after dusk, along with another storm. The rolling thunder to which Selene had become accustomed portended one of those quick bayou showers—violent in its onslaught, over within minutes. An hour later, the ground was often bone dry again.

Selene sat with Etienne until he fell asleep, having told him one bedtime story after another to soothe his troubled spirits. The audacious, mischievous boy had turned overnight into a trembling, overserious child, and Selene didn't know how to help him. More important, she didn't know how to prepare him for the time when she would be gone, no longer the buffer between Giselle and himself.

She would have to talk to James about that. Along with so many other things. But she hadn't seen him since the night before.

Selene fell asleep to the steady beat of raindrops on the roof and awakened hours later from her deep slumber, with a jolt. She wasn't sure what had disturbed her sleep, but now she sensed a presence in her small room, quiet except for the swish of a cool breeze through the open window. No, there was another sound—breathing.

Is it Giselle? Oh, Lord! And I have no weapon with me.

Peering through the shadowy room, Selene exhaled with a sigh of relief. James sat in a low rocking chair, his hands shoved in his trouser pockets, his long legs braced against the edge of her cot, using it as a lever to push himself back and forth. That motion must be what had awakened her.

He watched her with an unreadable expression on his face. He was keeping a silent vigil. Like a good-bye, Selene thought, gulping back tears.

She sat up and pulled the sheet up near her shoulders to hide the bare skin exposed by her thin camisole.

James's eyes flashed with hurt at her gesture of embarrassment. It bespoke the sudden distance between them.

"Why are you sleeping up here, *chérie?*"

Selene looked at him with surprise. "Giselle's orders."

His lips curled with disgust. "I should have known. I'll help you move everything back to your chamber."

"No! This is fine. I'd rather be next to Etienne anyhow."

He was about to object, then nodded with understanding.

"James, where have you been?"

"Searching for evidence."

"And?"

"Bits and pieces. Nothing definitive yet."

"And what do you suspect?"

"Victor and Giselle . . . working together."

"To what end?"

"Mine."

Selene pressed a palm over her heart in distress. "You don't believe Giselle's story."

"Do you?" he scoffed.

She shook her head.

"My room was ransacked this morning when I came in from the barn, where I slept. Apparently, she was searching for the will. Luckily, I'd hidden it elsewhere."

So he hadn't slept with his wife last night. Selene was comforted by that thought, at least. "I just don't understand any of this. I know there have been threats on your life, but why would Giselle pretend to be dead? And where has she been all this time? Why not just get a divorce if she wants to be with Victor?"

"There is no divorce in our church," he informed her in a flat voice.

Selene's heart sank. "Yes, that's what Giselle told me," she whispered brokenly.

James's eyes shot up at that and his feet landed loudly on the floor. "What else did she tell you?"

"That she's back here for good. That she's your wife. That the most I could ever hope for now is to be your mistress somewhere away from Bayou Noir. That in the end she will win you back."

He stood abruptly. "And did you tell her that I promised to love you forever, to never let you go?"

She slid her legs over the edge of the bed. Her toes curled in the soft rag rug at her feet. Unable to meet his questioning eyes, Selene hung her head. "No. I told her I would go away on St. John's Eve."

James sucked in his breath loudly, as if she had punched him in the stomach. When he recovered, he sank down on the cot next to her. Tilting her chin up with a forefinger, he asked, "How could you, Selene? I asked you to trust me."

Hot tears rolled down her cheeks as she fought for words. "This isn't about trust, James. It's about morality. You're married, and apparently you're going to continue to be married. What other solution is there?"

"I don't know, but I'll find one. I promise."

"Even if you uncover evidence of Victor and Giselle collaborating together, you will still be married."

"Shhhh. Trust in me, *chérie*," James said, brushing her hair off her face and behind her ear. His warm breath caressed the shell of her ear, and Selene felt an electric current of pleasure shoot through her blood.

"No, this isn't right," she protested, even as she leaned into his shoulder.

"*Au contraire*, it is the only thing that is right in this nightmare. Our love"—he sought for the right words—"is powerful enough to withstand this threat."

Selene wanted to believe him, but it was so hard. She had told him at one time that their love was a gift from God. Did God give with one hand and take with the other? She just didn't know.

"I am not myself tonight." His voice carried an odd composure, but his eyes glittered with feral turmoil. Gently he touched his fingertips to the pulse beat in her neck, his eyes holding hers imploringly. "I need you, Selene."

And that was all Selene had to hear. She fell back on her small bed in surrender, taking James with her.

Roughly he tore the camisole from her body and dispatched his own clothing with haste. His fingers dug into her forearms as he returned to the bed, breathing raggedly. Selene tried to soothe the tense muscles of his neck and back with sweeping caresses and soft words, but James seemed beyond hearing.

Pressing his lips on hers with barely controlled aggression, he marked her as his possession. Gentle bites, firm pressure, and then the plundering claim of his tongue . . . all bespoke a man out of control, pushed beyond his limits. He stabbed her nipple with his tongue, then took the bud and aureole into his mouth, sucking hard. His hands and lips roamed everywhere at once, frantic, rapacious.

"You are mine," he kept repeating over and over in a raw voice.

Selene forced herself to relax, to trust in James that he would not truly harm her. Love flowed through her, and she tried to transmit those feelings to James through the haze of his frenzied handling.

Almost immediately, he settled, shaking his head as if to clear the raging madness that had overcome him. "I'm sorry," he murmured.

"Hush," she whispered, placing her bruised lips to the wildly beating pulse at the base of his straining neck. She thought she felt a wetness on his face.

Now James's hands turned gentle, persuasive. Methodically he searched for all the pleasure points on her body and made sexy sounds of male approval when her soft sighs affirmed his discoveries.

Taking her hand, James guided it to the steely evidence of his need for her. Whispering, he told her how he wanted her to touch him, what pleased him most.

He gripped her ankles in both hands, pushing her knees upward and out, and entered her body. Selene writhed and rolled from side to side, fighting the waves of a rising crescendo of pleasure . . . too intense, too overwhelming, far beyond her control.

Over and over, James drove her to the point of release. Then he would stop with a triumphant cry . . . and start her on her journey again. With each long stroke, Selene felt herself splintering bit by bit, but she yielded herself to James, giving herself into his care, trusting that he would help her put the pieces back together.

Finally James braced himself on corded arms, his head reared back, and teeth bared savagely. With a primitive moan, he buried himself in her, and her body welcomed his jerking manhood with loving clasps.

Sated, at last . . . panting with sublime exhaustion . . . he lay heavily atop her as he grew soft inside her body, but still he did not pull himself out. "You are mine," he said once again, this time in a gentle voice of entreaty.

"I am yours," she agreed.

Then, holding James in place with her hands on his buttocks and her knees locked around his hips, she kissed him softly, murmured sweetly, even chuckled, until he was ready again. And then it was Selene who cried out in the end, "You are mine."

Chapter Twenty-two

*W*ho says trouble comes in twos? Try threes . . . or fours? . . .

Starting the next morning, disasters began exploding throughout Bayou Noir, one after another, like popcorn over an open fire.

"Bob is dead," Blossom informed Selene the minute she entered the kitchen.

Bob? The three-legged chicken?

"And someone dug a hole in the south levee, floodin' the fields," Hyacinth added dolefully. "All the cane there is buried in mud."

"Mam'zelle Baptiste is drinkin' tafia like it be water," Iris contributed, clicking her tongue against her teeth with disapproval. "An' she claims someone been messin' in her personal belongings."

Selene looked about the busy kitchen where the slaves worked briskly as they talked. They glanced repeatedly up at the bell on the wall, waiting for its first dreaded tinkling.

James had long since gone to the fields, leaving Selene's

bed before dawn with a sweet kiss and the whispered plea, "Trust me." That left her to handle these household problems, when she'd rather think about the wonderful night that had just passed in James's arms and how they were going to resolve their own monumental problems.

"Is that all?" she asked, putting a hand to her suddenly throbbing head.

"No, that ain't all." Blossom slammed her copper spoon down on the table. "Reba locked herself in her bedchamber 'cause she's got a pimple and ain't got no more makeup. And Verbena's been cryin' and cryin' over in the laundry house. Says she gots PMZ. What's PMZ?"

"PMS," Selene corrected her with a groan. She sank down on a chair and took the cup of steaming coffee Blossom set before her.

"There be voodoo signs all over the place from las' night," Iris told her in a hushed whisper.

Selene remembered then that she, too, had heard the drums last night before the onslaught of the bayou storm.

"Amen says he saw Mam'zelle Giselle in the woods, and she was the Mamoloi at the voodoo ceremony. Says she was the one what slit Bob's neck," Blossom noted. "I swear, I'm gonna whack some sense into that Amen with my soup ladle for bein' there hisself. The fool!"

First things first, Selene told herself. "Where's Etienne? Has anyone told him about Bob?"

Blossom nodded her head. "The master tol' him. Lordy, Etienne was sobbin' somethin' awful. He went to the fields with his papa today."

"Good. Now I'll go talk to Mrs. Baptiste. Let me take her tray, Iris."

Just then the bell rang and they all winced. Another day at the Last Chance Plantation, Selene thought, wondering if her last chance for happiness was dwindling away with each tinkle of the bell.

Selene didn't talk to James the rest of that day as he and every able-bodied man on the plantation fought to save the south field. From afar, she watched as they dug drainage trenches, rebuilt the levee, fought against time and the rot that could soon destroy a good portion of the sugar crop overnight.

But Selene did talk to Giselle . . . a lot more than she would have liked.

"James will be ruined," Giselle said with malicious satisfaction. Silent as a slithering snake, Giselle had come up behind Selene, catching her unawares where she stood at the edge of the field. Her blonde hair was perfectly coifed with ringlets framing her delicate face, and she wore a day dress of rose cambric over at least six crinolines. Her only deference to the heat was a pert straw bonnet and a feathered fan.

"Why would James's ruin please you?" Selene asked in puzzlement. "He's your husband. If the plantation fails, your well-being will suffer, too."

"Perhaps," Giselle said, studying her fingernails with lack of concern. "Perhaps not."

"Did Victor do this?"

Giselle quickly drew a blank expression over her face. "Why would you ask me? I have nothing to do with Victor."

"I think you do. I think you and Victor have concocted some evil plan to destroy James and Bayou Noir."

"You think too much, my dear," Giselle said patronizingly. "No doubt it comes from being so . . . tall . . . and thin. *Oui,* I have found that women who have no beauty think too much."

Selene dug her nails into her palms, fearing she might scratch the witch's eyes out. When she was more calm, she said, "And I've found that dumb blondes like you don't know their tongues from their toenails. In fact, Giselle, do you know what you get when you cross a blonde with a pig?"

Giselle just gaped at her.

"Nothing. There's some things even a pig won't do."

At first the dense woman didn't understand. When she

did, her face turned scarlet with rage. "Are you saying that I am . . . oh, you *salope* . . . you bitch . . . oh, I could kill you. I could kill you right now," Giselle sputtered.

"Yeah, I'll bet you could . . . *try*, that is," Selene snapped back. "Just like you and Victor have tried to kill James and anyone else who gets in your way."

Mrs. Baptiste was waiting for her when she returned to the house. Pulling Selene into the *garçonnière*, the trembling woman handed her a ball of black wax, which Selene immediately dropped onto a low table.

"Holy cow! Where did you get this?" Selene asked, wiping her hands on her skirt with distaste. The object looked very much like the gris-gris that Selene had found in her hotel room in New Orleans, the one presumably left by Lilith.

"It was on my bed this morning," Mrs. Baptiste said. "Giselle has put a curse on me, I know she has."

Selene could smell alcohol on Mrs. Baptiste's breath, and the frightened woman swayed as she paced.

"Sit down," Selene ordered. *Before you fall down.*

Mrs. Baptiste obeyed, wringing her hands in her skirts. "All of my belongings were scattered about. Giselle and Victor are looking for the will. And . . . and I think they put laudanum in my tafia last night. Why else would I have slept so soundly?"

Maybe because you were drunk.

Mrs. Baptiste looked up at her hopefully through bleary eyes.

Lord, why did everyone think she could solve their problems?

"First of all, you're going to move into the big house. You can share a bedroom with me until the danger has passed." Though when that would be, Selene had no idea.

"*Oui.* I think that would be best."

Selene realized with sudden dismay that her invitation meant James could not come to her at night again. Well, that was just as well. Maybe she had unconsciously made the offer for that very reason. Despite Giselle's viciousness, she was James's wife, and Selene had trouble reconciling her morals and making love with a married man. She could trust in James to try to find a solution, but that didn't mean she would continue to participate in adultery in the meantime.

The pieces of the puzzle came together . . .

For the next five days, Selene avoided James, who had enough problems without a confrontation over their personal relationship. The only words they exchanged were in the company of others, usually involving the plantation work.

Part of the south field had been saved, but three cows and one of the mules had died from poisoned oats. Reba reported that many of the slaves ate only fresh fruit and vegetables from their own gardens for fear of being poisoned themselves.

Dreadful had chased an intruder near the house one night and been sliced with a knife. As a result, he hobbled about with a big bandage on his hind leg proclaiming his bravery. James muttered something about never being able to get rid of the mangy mutt now. And Etienne beamed, proud of his "guard dog."

James had decreed that Selene's lessons continue with Etienne *and* the Negro children, much to Giselle's fury. But since then, Giselle had had many more reasons to hate James. He had posted a guard at the hall and gallery doors of his wife's bedchamber, giving strict orders that the man was to follow her everywhere.

As days went by under this close surveillance, Giselle grew wild-eyed and impossible to control. And everyone realized that she was addicted to some drug, probably laudanum—a diluted form of opium. Being prevented from going out at night to the summons of the voodoo drums apparently translated into a cutoff of her drug supply, and she suffered deep withdrawal pains.

After sustaining slaps, slashes from her riding crop, broken pottery, tongue lashings, threats, and curses, none of the servants would go to Giselle's room, and they scurried away whenever she came downstairs. Selene was the only one willing to approach her, and even she was a bit frightened.

She carried a breakfast tray up to Giselle now, no longer able to put off the task. The guard—a black man of about twenty—rolled his eyes at the smashing noises inside Giselle's room when Selene knocked on the door. "She be wilder than usual today, mam'zelle. Best you be careful."

"I will," Selene said, inhaling deeply to brace herself. Opening the door, she stepped inside and almost staggered back at the chaotic scene. Selene closed the door behind her and laid the tray on a side table.

Practically nude, Giselle wore only a thin camisole-style garment. In her frantic search for drugs, she had strewn every item of clothing she owned about the room—on the bed, the floor, over chairs.

Giselle's glazed eyes turned on Selene, unfocused. "I need my medicine," she said in a thready, childlike voice. "Can you find my medicine?"

Suddenly Selene noticed the old bruises and scars that covered Giselle's too-thin body. "Did Victor do this to you?" Selene asked, touching a yellow spot on her shoulder with sympathy. Selene understood codependency too well to remain unmoved. Although Devon had never struck her physically, he had wielded emotional blows right and left.

Giselle waved her hand dismissively. "They're nothing. Victor and I have always liked a rough edge to our lovemaking. He carries as many bruises as I do." She flashed a look of disdain at Selene, as if she were incapable of understanding "real" lovemaking.

Selene's mouth dropped open in astonishment.

Giselle laughed with a trill of hysteria. "Victor is a wonderful lover, not a milksop like James."

James a milksop? Never! "Do you love Victor?"

"*Oui.*" She frowned. "I think I do . . . I used to . . . oh, I don't know." Tunneling her fingers in her hair, which hadn't been washed in days, Giselle pulled at the lank strands in frustration.

"Why didn't you marry Victor? Why did you marry his brother?"

"Victor's father forbade our marriage. He threatened to cut Victor off without a penny." She narrowed her eyes craftily. "So we came up with a plan. I would marry James, and when he was gone, I would have not only Bayou Noir to sell, along with its slaves, but I would have the will to half of Jean-Paul's estate."

Selene tilted her head in puzzlement. "But wouldn't James's estate go to Etienne?"

Giselle's lips twisted with disgust. "I had not planned to have a baby. Actually, I rid myself of two of James's other unborn children without his knowledge."

Selene cringed inwardly in horror, but she wanted to get as much information from Giselle as she could. "I still don't understand. Why did you go away for a year?"

"Oh, you are so stupid. All of you are. That stubborn woman . . . James's mother . . . tried to kill me. She refused to give me the will. . . ."

Giselle was pacing the room, her body movements jerky in the throes of her withdrawal. She seemed to have lost her train of thought.

"And?" Selene prodded.

"I was ill for a long time, I think. I don't remember. I stayed in a room in New Orleans, and Victor gave me my medicine . . . do you know where my medicine is? . . . and Fleur was there . . . where's Fleur? . . . oh, my head hurts so, and my heart is beating so fast . . . please, please, can't you get me some medicine?" Giselle rambled on, almost delirious with the craving for her addictive drug.

She needed help desperately, but first Selene sought

more answers. "Why did you come back now? Why didn't you stay with Victor?"

"You . . . you are the reason I came back."

"Me?"

Giselle blinked at her with confusion. "I told you. We need the plantation *and* the will. James was going to marry you. We could not allow that to happen. One more person obstructing our dream."

What a dream! Selene thought, but found it hard not to pity this wretched woman. "Oh, Giselle. Do you really think killing James and gaining this plantation would satisfy Victor? Can't you see that you're just a means to his evil ends?"

A flicker of doubt swept Giselle's flushed face, but she quickly shook it off. "I believe Victor. And soon we will attain our goals. Then we will move away . . . somewhere gay . . . perhaps Paris . . . and I will have my medicine, and Victor, and . . ." Her voice grew faint as she tried to remember all the details of their dream.

Selene wondered where Etienne fit into those plans, and decided not to ask. Because she knew, even if Giselle did not, that Victor would never harbor James's child.

After that, Giselle made little sense. Selene changed the sheets and tied Giselle's flailing body to the bed with strips of linen, aided by Iris, Hyacinth, and the guard. She knew nothing about treatment for drug addicts, but it seemed to her that Giselle posed a danger to herself unless restrained.

For days after that, she and the servants took turns wiping Giselle's convulsing body with cool cloths when she was feverish, and covering her with blankets when the chills came. They tried to force some broth down her parched throat.

After three days they removed the restraints because Giselle just lay listlessly, whimpering occasionally for her medicine and Victor. James came once to see her and left almost immediately, shaking his head with revulsion.

Exhausted, Selene plodded to the bath chamber late that afternoon with clean clothing and linen towels. A tear slipped down her cheek as she made a mental note of the date—Saturday, the day she and James had planned to marry.

Selene bathed in a zombie-like fashion, unable to gain her usual pleasure from the luxurious bathtub. After her bath, she dressed and tidied up the room, then leaned against the wall.

With hot tears streaming down her cheeks, she finally accepted the facts that she had resisted for days. Witnessing firsthand Giselle's sickness and her need for love and a helping husband had driven home to Selene that she could not stay at Bayou Noir.

Selene couldn't help but liken this situation to the death of her friend Tessa. What if Tessa had had a husband who failed to understand her anorexia and addiction to diet pills? What if that husband had fallen out of love with Tessa and had been involved with another woman? Selene would have expected Tessa's husband to stay with her, to help her survive, to rebuild their marriage.

Selene couldn't justify her own position in this triangle.

It was two days until St. John's Eve, and Selene decided that she would go home then, back to 2012. She had no choice.

With that decision made, she dragged herself up to her fourth-floor bedroom. It was past time to make preparations for her departure. Minutes later, she came storming out.

Her precious ballgown, her key to the future, was gone.

I'll kill him, she raged to herself. *I can't believe James would take my ballgown. I can't believe he would force me to stay here against my will.*

Should she go out to the fields and confront him, or should she wait until dinner? She decided to wait for him in the kitchen. She was passing through the lower-floor corridor when she saw him approaching.

James saw Selene before she saw him. Looking right

and left to see that no one else was about, he smiled to himself. At last, an opportunity to catch Selene alone.

Before she had a chance to protest, he pulled her into the cold cellar, maneuvering around the hanging hams and barrels of leftover winter vegetables and fruits.

"I've been looking for you," Selene said when he backed her up against the cool stone wall. "Oh . . . stop that," she added, swatting at his right palm that circled her breast, drawing the nipple into a hard point. He loved the way her body responded so readily to his touch.

"Stop what?" he murmured against her lips. He nibbled at her lower lip until she parted for him, then devoured her with his lips and tongue. "So long . . . it has been too long, *chérie*," he whispered. "I am so hungry for you."

She moaned and tried to push against his chest. "I need to ask you something . . . I need to . . . a-a-ah . . ."

"I will fill your needs," he promised with an exultant cry as he pressed his hardened manhood against the cleft of her thighs.

"Don't . . . you can't . . . we can't . . ." Her words of protest weakened as he lifted the hem of her skirt and inserted a finger into the slit of her drawers. "O-o-h."

"I love the way you say that, *ma chérie*."

"What?" she gasped.

"The way you say 'oh.' Did you know you have dozens of ways of saying 'oh'? And I'm beginning to recognize each of them."

She flashed him a look of disbelief, still trying to wriggle out of his embrace.

At his first touch of the slick heat of her womanhood, she cried, out, "Oh . . . I mean . . ."

He groaned with pure male satisfaction. "That 'oh' means you like to be touched in just that spot." He repeated the strokes to prove his point, and her eyelids fluttered erotically.

"Stop it, James. We can't do this."

"I love you, Selene. And we can, and will, do *this*."

She exhaled loudly in surrender at his words and parted her legs further for his carnal explorations. When he found the nub of her pleasure and played it to a swollen bud with his callused fingertips, her knees trembled.

"Oh . . . oh, my God!"

"That 'oh' means you are amazed at my dexterity."

She choked out a laugh while her fingers bit into his shoulders for support.

He undid his trouser buttons with one hand, then put both hands under her buttocks, raising her up and canting her hips outward for his entry.

"Tell me," he coaxed hoarsely as he plunged deep into her woman's center.

"I love you," she responded, and her silken folds caressed his manhood as they adjusted to accommodate his burgeoning size.

He pulled out, almost completely, and repeated, "Tell me."

"I love you. I love you. I love . . ."

Over and over, in and out, he glided into her body, each time demanding her avowal of love. He craved the emotion as much as the physical gratification, he realized. The two were one and the same in his mind.

She mewled helplessly against her body's raging fire, and he grew larger with his desire for her. When he imbedded himself in her clasping sheath to the hilt, he inserted a finger between their bodies and flicked the sleek pearl back and forth.

Her heart lurched against his chest, and a tremor rippled down to her womb through her womanhood until he felt her climax around his shaft with violent shivers. Only then did he withdraw one last time and then thrust into her with a guttural shout, releasing his seed into her body, and his soul into her keeping.

They both slid weakly to the dirt floor. James pulled her into the curve of his shoulder, kissing her hair and cheek, realizing belatedly that she was weeping silently.

"Ah, *chérie*, what troubles you? Did I hurt you?"

She shook her head and pulled away from him. "Where's my gown?"

He blinked at her in confusion. "Your gown? You're crying about a ballgown? Now?"

"Yes, you bastard," she said on a sob. "You seduced me before I could tell you why I was looking for you."

"Seduced you? I thought we were making love . . . with each other." He averted his face to hide his hurt.

She tried to slap him, but he gripped her wrist firmly.

Standing abruptly, he adjusted his clothing. "Tell me," he said, a cold foreboding ringing in his voice.

"I decided that . . . I decided that I have to return to my home—"

"This is your home."

She shook her head. "No. No, it's not, James. I have to go back to my own time."

"Why? Why now? You promised," he accused harshly. "You promised to trust me."

"I do trust you, James. But I admitted today what I've known for days. Giselle is sick . . . physically and mentally . . . and she needs you. There's no way you could ever put her aside in this condition. And maybe, if I were out of the picture, you could grow to love her again."

"Not in a million years," he said in a steely voice. "Selene, listen to me. Victor grows desperate. He will act soon. I can feel him drawing closer to my trap."

"And when he does? Then what?"

"What are you saying?"

"I'm saying that even if Victor is convicted of all his crimes . . . even if he were dead, that still doesn't solve the problem of Giselle."

"I'll get an annulment."

She slanted him a scoffing look. "And declare Etienne illegitimate? I wouldn't allow you to do that."

"Don't go," he pleaded. He took her by the upper arms and pulled her closer.

"I can't go. That's the point. You've taken my ballgown, and I want it back. *Now*."

His eyes widened with surprise, and pain stabbed at his heart. "You think I stole your gown? That I would force you to stay against your wishes?"

She glanced at him guiltily. It was exactly what she'd thought.

"Without trust we have nothing," he lashed out angrily. Then he shoved away from her and moved toward the door. "I'm sick of all the turmoil, Selene. I need you at my side, not fighting me." He lifted his hands in a hopeless gesture. "I'll find the damned gown for you. And then you can go to your time, or go to hell. I don't care. Frankly, my dear, I don't give a damn."

But he did care. Desperately.

How would he ever survive without Selene?

The most terrible trouble of all finally arrived . . .

An hour later, Selene was in the sewing room helping Reba cut fabric for the slaves' clothing. She looked up to see Mrs. Baptiste enter, carrying her ballgown.

"I took the gown," James's mother confessed, handing it to her. "I knew you were thinking of going away. I heard you and James talking in the library one day, and I thought . . ." She shrugged and dipped her chin guiltily. "Please forgive me, my dear."

"You're going away?" Reba asked in alarm. "You can't leave us now."

Selene patted her friend's hand.

Reba jerked away from her. "You would desert us . . . abandon us to that madwoman?"

"Reba, she's his wife . . . the mistress of this plantation," Selene tried to explain. "I have no place here now."

"You wormed your way into our lives . . . our hearts . . . and then you just strut away, like one of your modeling shoots," Reba accused, throwing down her scissors and running for the door.

"That's not fair," Selene started to say, but Reba was already gone.

Mrs. Baptiste cast Selene an equally condemning look and left her alone.

By St. John's Eve, no one was speaking to Selene. They all treated her like a rat about to jump ship. It was not the way Selene had wanted to leave.

No one knew how she planned to leave, except James and Mrs. Baptiste. The others didn't ask, probably assuming she would hitch a ride on one of the grocery or mail boats that floated by on a regular basis.

That afternoon the drums began beating early, announcing one of the most important of all voodoo celebrations—St. John's Eve. The festivals held throughout Louisiana on that feast day would worship both the snake god known as the *gran Zombi* and St. John the Baptist, called by the African name Agomme Tonnerree.

The day took on an even more bizarre note when Giselle came strolling down the staircase, laughing gaily, dressed to the nines in a green silk, off-the-shoulder gown with wide hoops. The listless look had left her eyes, and although she was thinner than when she had arrived, her body carried a bounce of unnatural vigor.

Everyone realized immediately that Giselle had somehow obtained more drugs. And they soon learned how when a shout from above alerted them that the slave who guarded her gallery door lay unconscious, having been struck on the head.

Giselle refused to answer any questions, even James's angry interrogation. She just smiled secretively and acted as if it were another normal day at Bayou Noir.

Before he left again for the fields, Selene tried to talk to James, to say her last good-byes. He walked away from her, but not before Selene saw the hurt and despair in his pale blue eyes.

Bracing herself with determination, knowing she did the right thing, Selene tied up all the loose ends of her existence in the bayou house. She set out lesson plans for Etienne, whose idea of a good-bye was to kick her in the shin and run away. She instructed the brooding Iris, Hyacinth, and Verbena on the continued upkeep of the house and laundry. She hugged a stiff Blossom, who refused to return her embrace.

James stayed away all day. As the afternoon progressed, the servants avoided the house and Giselle's hysterical laughter.

By nightfall, Selene had to take one of Blossom's headache powders. Her head throbbed to the beat of the incessant drums and her aching heart, not to mention the claps of thunder.

Just then a loud bang shot through the air. The lightning was striking precariously close now. She would have to check on Etienne.

Selene had already moved her ballgown and the seed packets to her old bedroom on the third floor, not wanting to disturb James's sleeping mother. With a heavy heart, she went there at about eleven o'clock, and with painstaking care she pressed exactly 167 black seeds into the voodoo doll, one for each year she wanted to travel forward. Then she donned the precious garment, which seemed somehow hateful to her now.

Or she *tried* to don the gown.

It was too tight.

Selene laughed and looked at herself in the mirror. Ruefully she noted a one-inch gap in the back of the gown. No way would she be able to close it.

But Selene was not upset. Oh, she would never be able to return to her modeling career in this shape. But she looked and felt better than she ever had in her life.

Selene peered closer. The collagen injections in her lips had worn off, and her suntan had faded. She decided then that she wouldn't abuse her face again in that fashion, no matter what Georgia advised.

And she made other decisions, too. After her success with Etienne and her other students, she realized she had an innate talent for teaching. She would pursue teacher training at Columbia, not a degree in psychology.

A flicker of light through the side window diverted Selene's attention. Perhaps lightning had struck nearby, as she'd thought earlier. Frowning, she moved away from the mirror and then gasped as she saw flames shooting through the sugar fields.

"Oh, my God!" she exclaimed. After barely saving the fields from the recent flooding, how would James be able to survive a fire? Instantly she recognized that he couldn't put out a fire of this proportion.

"*Oui*, best you should pray, Selene. For you will all die now."

Selene turned with a start to see Giselle standing in the doorway, a gun aimed precisely at her heart. Her eyes danced with evil glee, but her hand was steady.

"Giselle, put the gun down. Someone will come."

"*Non*, they are gone to the fields to help put out the fires. Victor has ensured their absence. Now I must do my part." She laughed with macabre humor.

"Where are Mrs. Baptiste and Etienne?"

"Etienne is tied on the boat we have hidden away for our escape. He will attend the boarding school in New Orleans."

"And Mrs. Baptiste?" Selene asked fearfully.

"Dead," she replied with no remorse. "Did you not hear the shot? Finally the meddlesome woman is gone."

"No-o-o," Selene wailed and rushed for Giselle.

Giselle pulled the trigger of her small gun, and the shot hit Selene in the shoulder. She recoiled and put a hand to the bloody wound.

I'm shot, Selene thought, stunned, as she watched the

red fluid seep through her fingers. Then the next shot rang out, hitting lower, knocking her to the floor.

As blood poured from her wounds, pooling beneath her, Selene saw Giselle approach through dimming eyes. She grew weaker. Leaning down, Giselle gazed at Selene to see if she had dealt her a fatal blow.

"I think I would rather you not be quite dead, Selene," she said cheerily. "I think it would be appropriate for you to die by fire, don't you?"

Unable to move or speak, feeling her strength seep out with her life's blood, Selene could only stare up at the insane woman.

Giselle dropped her gun to the floor and began to tug on Selene's skirts. "This gown is too beautiful to be wasted on you. And you are staining it with your nasty blood."

Selene watched Giselle through a hazy veil of approaching delirium as the madwoman pulled the garment completely off her body. Giselle removed her own gown then and put on Phillipe's ballgown, oblivious to its excessive length. Pirouetting before the mirror, she hummed, then broke into a soft French melody, as if she had not just shot a woman . . . no, two women.

In that moment before Selene's eyes closed, she saw Giselle pick up the voodoo doll. "Why, Selene, you surprise me. I would not have thought you a believer."

That was the last coherent thought Selene had before she smelled the acrid odor of billowing smoke.

James! Please, God, save him. Don't let evil prevail. Let my time here have some meaning. Please, God, I pray . . .

Chapter Twenty-three

Happily-ever-afters don't get any better than this . . .

"Selene . . . Selene, can you hear me?" James's voice came to her from far off.

Drifting in a place beyond her understanding, Selene no longer fought against death's mesmerizing pull. *So much blood. I feel ethereal, like an angel.* She smiled in her dream state.

"No!" James cried out. "Don't you dare die on me now. Don't you dare!"

Selene heard the sob of fear in his voice. She tried to reach out for him, but a curtain was growing between her and this mere mortal.

James wouldn't let her go, however. Through excruciating pain, she felt him and Iris probing the wounds in her shoulder and abdomen. Iris put a cup of some liquid to Selene's lips, forcing her to drink. And she felt no more pain until she awakened to the searing pull of a needle passing through her skin, stitching her bullet holes shut.

"I'll never be able to model again," Selene muttered. "No one wants a scarred woman."

"I do," James said simply, and Selene felt a teardrop fall onto her chest from above.

Oh, James, she thought, seeking the respite of death once more.

But death did not come easily to Selene. Days passed and she alternated between racking fever and painful chills.

"Let me go," she whispered on more than one occasion.

"Never!" James said in a hoarse voice. "*As God is my witness*, you will not die."

Selene tried to smile at the odd twist of fate that would have James quoting *Gone With the Wind*, but her lips would not move.

One day she grew more lucid and asked, "How is Etienne?"

"Fine. Worried about you," James responded.

"And your mother?"

A poignant silence followed.

Selene fought her fever and opened her eyes. "Tell me."

"Dead," he said, a hard edge to his voice. "She died instantly from her gunshot wound."

"Oh, James." She wanted to hold this tortured man, but her arms seemed frozen at her sides. Then she remembered something else. "Victor and Giselle?"

"Both dead. Victor died in the fields. He struggled with me and landed accidentally in the fire he started. Giselle died . . . elsewhere."

So many deaths! So much misfortune for James! Selene tried to swallow over her parched throat, and James tipped a cup of cool water to her lips. "How . . . how did Giselle die?"

James seemed to hesitate. "Her body was found down by the bayou. She was wearing your gown and clutching that damned voodoo doll in her hands. I don't know if drugs or lightning killed her." He shrugged, uncaring.

Selene's heart started to beat madly. "James, do you

think she traveled to the future in my place? Do you think her dead body was just a shell? Maybe that's what you would have found if I'd gone back to my time."

"I don't know, Selene. I don't care. It's over now. Just rest."

After that, the fever overtook her again and raged for days.

When she awakened finally, Blossom was fussing about her bed. Selene moved her head tentatively on the pillow and realized that she lay in James's huge canopied bed.

"Why am I here?" she asked in a croaky voice.

"Well, missie, you took your good time comin' back to us," Blossom said tartly, coming closer, but Selene could see the tears welling in her eyes. "And you're in this room 'cause the other bedchamber burned in the fire.

The fire. Selene's murky mind registered the memory of fire but couldn't assimilate all the implications.

"How long . . . how long . . . since that night?"

"Three weeks."

"Three . . . three . . . how is that possible?"

"You been sick, honey chile. We almos' lost you a few times, but the master, he wouldn't let you go. Nosirree. You gots him to thank for your life, you surely do."

Yes, she knew that. Selene fought back a sob. Even in the depths of her pain, she had felt James calling to her, refusing to let her go. "Where's James?"

"Gone to Nawleans on bizness. With Fergus."

"Huh?" Selene said. How could he leave her now? Her brain reeled with confusion. She was so tired.

Through a haze, she heard Blossom explain, "He didn't leave till yesterday when he saw you was gettin' better."

After that, she slept long hours and drank the strong broth Blossom forced on her. Hour by hour, she grew stronger and gradually began to heal.

The next day, Selene sat up in bed and even had a few visitors—Etienne, who fought back tears and told her of a story he was writing for her about a skinny teacher with magical powers, sort of like a bayou superwoman; Reba, who apologized profusely for her sullen silence before the tragic day; and the hovering Blossom, who fretted over her like a mother hen.

The following day, Selene walked about her room on shaky legs and began to really believe she might recover. When Blossom brought her a heaping tray of beignets and a carafe of oversweet café au lait, Selene's stomach growled loudly. She hugged the black woman warmly.

"Now I knows for sure you gonna be all right."

"I've lost so much weight," Selene complained when she got her first horrified look in the mirror.

"Yep, and you ain't got no suntan anymores, either," Blossom informed her bluntly. "And that cold-gin in your lips has gone away."

"Collagen," Selene corrected Blossom with a smile.

"Whatever. Even your hair ain't so kinky now."

"In other words, I'm a mess," Selene concluded.

"Nosirree, honey chile. You is plumb beautiful. You surely is."

Selene wasn't so sure about that, especially with no makeup.

The day after that, Iris assisted her in walking downstairs and she sat in the kitchen for a short while.

"When you gonna start our arrow-backs again?" Iris asked. "And the therapy classes? I been leadin' 'em since you been sick."

"You have?" Selene asked in amazement.

"Now don't you be startin' on the mistress yet," Blossom admonished Iris. "She ain't gonna be up to all that for a long time."

Iris's face fell dramatically.

"Is something wrong?" Selene asked with concern.

"Well, I wanted to tell you all somethin' important. But I guess it'll have to wait till we meets again."

"What?" she and Blossom both asked at once.

"Rufus and me are gonna get married," Iris blurted out, unable to hold back her delightful news.

"Oh, Iris, that's wonderful," Selene said.

"Humph! I knew it all the time," Blossom proclaimed.

"An' we found the Perfect Fit," Iris added with a mischievous gleam in her huge eyes.

Selene giggled, and Blossom asked, "What fit?"

"I have some news, too," Reba announced shyly.

"You're going to have a baby," Selene guessed, reading the warm blush on her face.

Reba nodded excitedly.

"I knew that, too," Blossom said.

More joyous hugs were exchanged.

"But what's a perfect fit?" Blossom still wanted to know.

Yes, things were beginning to feel like the normal lunacy at Bayou Noir.

Three more days passed and Selene grew stronger and stronger. Now she worried over James's absence. Reba claimed she had no idea why her husband and James had hurried off to New Orleans, just that some compelling business with bankers and agents had forced their hasty departure. But Selene saw all the women exchange furtive glances on occasion and knew they kept some secret from her.

The fire had destroyed more than half of the cane, along with a portion of the mansion. Selene sensed that these catastrophes spelled disaster for James. The banks would foreclose. He could lose everything.

And she also feared that in his fierce pride he would refuse to marry her now. He would feel he had nothing to offer her. Oh, she wished he would return so she could tell him that he had the world to give her, if he only would.

Seven days after James had left for New Orleans, Selene sat in the classroom with Etienne. Distracted, she looked out the window and saw a flatboat pulling up at the bayou dock.

"Papa! Papa's home!" Etienne shouted and ran for the door. Selene rushed after him, but had to pause at the third-floor landing, gasping for breath. When she got to the second-floor entryway leading out to the main gallery, James was already striding up the wide outside steps.

He slowed when he saw her.

In a frozen tableau, Selene watched James move closer. A slow smile moved over his lips, then spread wider into a glorious, wondrous display of dazzling white teeth and that delectable dimple. He took off his wide-brimmed hat and tossed it to a chair without looking.

Dark circles smudged his eyes and new wrinkles of worry crinkled the edges of his lips. A dark shadow of beard covered his face, which seemed thinner, and his ebony hair lay unkempt and too long down his neck. He looked disreputable and absolutely gorgeous.

Behind him she saw Etienne, Fergus with his arm wrapped around Reba's shoulder, several slaves carrying bundles, and a strange man wearing a clerical collar . . . a priest. Selene frowned with puzzlement, then concluded that James had brought the priest to perform belatedly the funeral rites over his mother, and maybe even Giselle. Victor's body had been taken back to New Orleans by his father.

Selene's heart still ached for the loss of James's precious mother.

"Selene," James said simply when he stood in front of her. Then he whooped with joy, startling her, and scooped her up in his arms, twirling her around in a circle. Selene heard Etienne giggle behind her. Finally he set her on her feet and she leaned dizzily against his chest.

"You're better," he said, leaning down to kiss her gently on the lips and trace a fingertip along her jaw, as if to make sure she was really alive and well. Then, unable to help himself, he clutched her tightly in his arms and held on tight. Against her neck, he whispered, "Selene . . . my Selene . . . I was so afraid that I would lose you. I prayed . . . oh, *chérie*, how I prayed!"

She pulled back and smiled up at him through her tears. "So you got deathbed religion, huh? You told me once that God had abandoned you."

He grinned at her. "He gave me you. I can't argue with that."

One of the slaves approached carrying several packages and asked, "Where you wants me to put this?"

"Right here." James pointed to the parlor, then looked at Selene and winked. "I have some presents for you."

He winked. Oh, Lord. "You are a rascal, James. In my weakened state, you're going to make me swoon."

He gave her a quick look of mock horror. "Not now. I have too many plans for you."

"Plans? James, you really shouldn't be spending money on me now with all the repairs needed here at the plantation."

"Are you nagging me, Selene? Tsk tsk." He looped an arm around her shoulder and pulled her into the parlor, pushing her gently into a chair.

First he handed her a large package. She opened it carefully to find a moss green velvet dress with a fringe edging. She raised an eyebrow in question.

"Your wedding dress," he said and smiled with immense satisfaction.

"A green wedding dress? And velvet? In Louisiana?"

He waved a hand airily. "Minor details. I remembered you admiring the drapes in the hotel one time. So I purchased them for you and took them to a dressmaker's."

"You didn't!" Selene's mouth dropped open.

James leaned down and kissed it shut. "I did."

"You must be the talk of the city."

"For a certainty," he said dryly.

Next he dropped a heavy leather bag in her lap. Selene untied the leather thong opening and saw an enormous pile of paper money and gold coins. She raised questioning eyes to James. "Where did you get this?"

"It's our grub stake."

"Huh?"

James pulled a low chair close to hers and sat down in front of her, knee to knee. Taking her hands in his, he held her eyes earnestly. "I sold the plantation."

Selene inhaled sharply.

"To Fergus and Reba. Oh, Fergus didn't have enough money right now to buy it outright. But I figured he and Reba could pay us back over the years when they could. Is that all right?"

She nodded dumbly, still not understanding. "Then where did you get all this money?"

"My father," he said with a grimace. "I couldn't let my mother's death be for nothing. I took the will and went to him, demanding he buy out my half of my inheritance."

"And he did?" she asked, truly astonished.

"He did, but it took a while to convince him." James's beautiful eyes clouded over, and Selene knew how painful it must have been to go to his father on humble knee. "Truly, you would have been proud of me. I am a shrewd negotiator."

A fierce, sweet joy blossomed in her heart as Selene began to realize the implications of James's news. Was he finally free of all his burdens, both the past and his current financial woes?

"This really isn't much, Selene. Just enough for us to start over."

"Start over?" she questioned, beginning to feel like a parrot.

James slanted her a seductive, teasing glance. "How do you think I'll look as a prospector?"

Suddenly Selene understood. "We're going to California!" She remembered now how she'd told James of the opportunities to be had in California during the coming gold rush.

James nodded. "Rufus and Iris want to come with us, and some of the free blacks. What do you think, Selene?"

"Well, fiddle-dee-dee, James, why didn't you tell me all

this to begin with?" Selene said with a tinkling laugh and threw herself into his arms, landing in his lap. She kissed his face and neck, over and over.

Etienne walked up to them tentatively, as if unsure of his welcome in this intimate scene. James pulled him onto his other knee and hugged them both.

"Are you sure this is what you want, James?" Selene asked finally. "To leave your land, and everything that's familiar to you?"

Gruffly James answered, "Hell, yes."

Then he stood them both on their feet. "Why is everyone dawdling around here? We have a wedding to conduct. I brought the priest. Blossom promised to make beignets and a punchbowl of syllabubs for the wedding dinner. What are we waiting for?"

Selene in her "Scarlett" wedding gown looked better than she ever had as a cover model. Etienne put a frog in the priest's cassock, but once the cleric survived that shock, the ceremony went on beautifully. Dreadful was a real gentleman with a red ribbon tied in a huge bow around his neck, and he only ate ten of Selene's beignets. Blossom cried profusely, and Iris wore a new, slim gown which she declared showed off her much trimmer tush.

Later that evening, lying next to James in his wide bed, they spoke softly of the day's events. Cuddled close to James now, whispering soft endearments, Selene trailed a hand teasingly down his naked chest, over the flat male nipples and crisp hairs, then lower.

"Did I tell you I've thought of some new embroidery strokes?"

"I didn't know Southern gentlemen knew how to embroider."

"Honey, there's a lot I could have taught that Rhett." She peeked up at him with wide Southern-belle eyes.

"Oh? And what might those embroidery strokes be?" he asked with a chuckle.

"Nip and tuck."

"Ouch."

"Knit and purl."

"Hmmm. That has possibilities."

"Nook and cranny."

"Now that sounds interesting."

"Tongue and groove."

"Definitely interesting." But then he had second thoughts. "Selene . . . ," he said hesitantly, "you're still weak. We should wait. We have a lifetime ahead of us. Remember—"

"I swear if you say. 'Tomorrow is another day,' I'll scream. Scarlett didn't know everything."

And as she taught him a few "embroidery strokes" that Scarlett never dreamed of, James gasped for breath and soon conceded, "Forget that *Gone With the Wind* fantasy. I'll take today's fantasy anytime."

Epilogue

Time travels fast when you're having fun . . .

"And then the man puts his pizzle . . ." Etienne was explaining the facts of life with all the worldliness of a ten-year-old rake to his awestruck friends, Cain and Abel.

"Etienne Baptiste! Wait till your father hears about this," Selene said, waddling onto the front porch under the weight of her behemoth stomach.

She put one hand to the small of her aching back, meanwhile cradling ten-month-old Ashley on her hip. Lord, she hoped the baby came soon. She felt like a walking bus. Scarlett wobbled after her on her chubby toddler legs, holding onto her skirts for balance, cooing, "E.T. . . . E.T. . . . E.T."

"I thought you boys were supposed to be watching the children," Selene reminded Etienne.

"We are," the rascal answered lazily, pointing to the two four-year-olds. His brother Rhett and Rufus and Iris's darling Lily Belle were making mud pies near the pump, covered from head to toe with muck. The only supervision Selene could see came from Dreadful, who kept licking their faces.

Selene made a clucking sound of disgust, then jerked up alertly at the sound of horses. James led a group of riders through the road separating the north and south pastures.

As always, Selene felt a surge of pride when looking at their prosperous cattle ranch. She and James had done well in California, not from panning gold but from selling beef to the prospectors in the blossoming gold rush towns. And her small school had grown from five to twenty students this past year.

Her only regret was that Blossom hadn't been able to make the trip with them. The elderly black woman had become like a mother to her. And she missed Reba, even though they exchanged letters regularly.

Turning back to the riders as they came closer, Selene ordered Etienne, "Take the children back to Iris." She handed Ashley to him and watched as he led the band of youngsters around the house.

"Oh, Lord," Selene muttered as she recognized the men. When James dismounted and tied his horse to the rail, she asked peevishly, "What are you doing with Ignacio and his ragtag gang of desperadoes?"

James rolled his eyes. "They're just stopping for water." His expression turned suddenly serious. "They have two captives."

"I don't know who to pity more, Ignacio or the captives," she remarked, knowing how inept these particular bandits were. "The last time they took a captive for ransom their victim bopped them over their thick heads and robbed them."

James chuckled in remembrance.

Selene made her way carefully down the steps toward her husband and slapped his hand away when he reached reflexively to caress her stomach.

"What's the matter, *chérie?* Are you feeling discomfort?"

"Discomfort? Hah! I know firsthand how a bloated cow feels!"

"You are beautiful to me, Selene."

Selene did feel beautiful, even without her makeup and slim figure. Even though she still took great care with her grooming, she no longer defined herself by her physical appearance. Now she was wife, mother, friend, teacher, and beautiful woman . . . in that order. Thanks to James.

But then the brute ruined her whimsical mood by laughing. "Would you like me to check out your udders?"

She ducked away from his reaching hands. "If you dare, I'll step on your toe and probably break your foot."

Ignacio and his scruffy thieves drew their horses over to the water trough. Two horses trailed behind, carrying a man and a woman who were arguing vehemently. Their hands were bound in front of them.

"Oh, shut up, Rafe. I saw you looking at that blonde in the saloon," the woman snapped shrewishly, tossing a wild mane of red hair over her shoulder.

"Helen, Helen, Helen. I was only admiring Larita's . . . dexterity with cards," the devilishly handsome Hispanic man shot back with a grin.

"Bull! By the way, Lech of the Month, what do you call a zit on a blonde's butt?"

The gorgeous dark-skinned man winced. "Oh, shit! Another blonde joke."

"A brain tumor."

"Blonde jokes?" Selene and James said at the same time, looking at each other in amazement. Then she noticed the fearful, vulnerable look in her husband's eye. "What? What's wrong?"

He jerked his head toward the still-bickering couple, who were dismounting awkwardly to the curses of Ignacio and his pals. A chill of foreboding passed over her as she noticed their clothing for the first time.

U.S. military uniforms.

And blonde jokes.

Then Selene understood. She was not the only person to ever travel back in time. Marie Laveau had hinted as much.

And James, despite their five years of happiness together, worried that one day she would wish to go back to the future. As often as she told him how much she loved him, he still harbored doubts. He must think that this precious gift they'd been given could sift through his fingertips . . . like time.

Her heart expanded with love for him, and the proof of that love leapt in her stomach with a jolt. She decided to give him his answer in the only way she could. Deliberately, she turned her back on the modern couple—a tangible link to her past.

"You meet these people, James. I'm going into the house to feed your baby," she told her husband in a soft voice, patting her big belly. "Iris made a fresh batch of beignets."

And thus she closed the door on her old world forever.

"I love you," James whispered after her.

"I know."

Reader Letter

Dear Readers:

I hope you liked this reissue of one of my favorite books. A time-travel classic, in my opinion.

Look for the upcoming reissue of *Sweeter Savage Love*, its sequel featuring Etienne as its hero. And the Rafe and Helen mentioned in the epilogue? They're the hero and heroine of the coming reissue of *Desperado*.

Some folks wonder why I veered from Vikings to the Old South. The answer is simple. My grandmother Flora was a proud old peacock, and as mean as a coot. "Mum Mum," as she was called, stemmed from *the* Butlers, dontcha know.

The rest of the world knows that Rhett Butler was a figment of Margaret Mitchell's wonderful imagination. But Mum Mum claimed that good ol' Margaret based her fictional rogue on one of our ancestors. And who were we to argue with our cane-wielding grand dame?

Now, I probably carry a few of Mum Mum's genes, especially those generating pride and a tart tongue (yes, tart tongues are hereditary, the Q-chromosome, I think it's called), but more than that, her bent for the fanciful is surely in my blood. From the time I was twelve years old and read *Gone With the Wind,* I just knew there had to be some basis for my grandmother's recollections. And when I visited the South for the first time at age thirty, my internal synchronicity bells clanged louder than the bells of New Orleans's famous St. Louis Cathedral.

Mum Mum passed on to me a few family books tracing our ancestry back to the tenth century, including *The Butler Family in America.* I'm not saying Rhett is mentioned in any of these tomes, but if you read between the lines . . . well, a perceptive person could conclude a few things.

Naturally, I wanted to name my first son Rhett, but my husband balked, unimaginative as he is. So, I settled for Beau, a good Southern name. And Beau's a rogue in the vein of Rhett, no doubt about it.

Through the years, I keep searching for evidence of a Rhett in our family tree. Failing that, I created my own "Rhett" in *Frankly, My Dear* . . . I hope you like him.

As always, I wish you smiles in your reading.

Sincerely,

Sandra Hill
www.sandrahill.net

Can't get enough of *USA Today* and
New York Times bestselling
author Sandra Hill?
Turn the page for glimpses of her amazing
books. From cowboys to Vikings, Navy
SEALs to Southern bad boys, every one
of Sandra's books has her unique blend of
passion, creativity, and unparalleled wit.

Welcome to the World of Sandra Hill!

The Viking Takes a Knight

⊗

For John of Hawks' Lair, the unexpected appearance of a beautiful woman at his door is always welcome. Yet the arrival of this alluring Viking woman, Ingrith Sigrundottir—with her enchanting smile and inviting curves—is different . . . for she comes accompanied by a herd of unruly orphans. And Ingrith needs more than the legendary knight's hospitality; she needs protection. For among her charges is a small boy with a claim to the throne—a dangerous distinction when murderous King Edgar is out hunting for Viking blood.

A man of passion, John will keep them safe— but in exchange, he wants something very dear indeed: Ingrith's heart, to be taken with the very first meeting of their lips . . .

Viking in Love

✣

*C*aedmon of Larkspur *was the most loathsome lout* Breanne had ever encountered. When she arrived at his castle with her sisters, they were greeted by an estate gone wild, while Caedmon laid abed after a night of ale. But Breanne must endure, as they are desperately in need of protection . . . and he is quite handsome.

After nine long months in the king's service, all Caedmon wanted was peace, not five Viking princesses running about his keep. And the fiery redhead who burst into his chamber was the worst of them all. He should kick her out, but he has a far better plan for Breanne of Stoneheim—one that will leave her a Viking in lust.

The Reluctant Viking

❦

*T*he self-motivation tape was supposed to help Ruby Jordan solve her problems, not create new ones. Instead, she was lulled into an era of hard-bodied warriors and fair maidens. But the world ten centuries in the past didn't prove to be all mead and mirth. Even as Ruby tried to update medieval times, she had to deal with a Norseman whose view of women was stuck in the Dark Ages. And what was worse, brawny Thork had her husband's face, habits, and desire to avoid Ruby. Determined not to lose the same man twice, Ruby planned a bold seduction that would conquer the reluctant Viking—and make him an eager captive of her love.

The Outlaw Viking

☙

As tall and striking as the Valkyries of legend, Dr. Rain Jordan was proud of her Norse ancestors despite their warlike ways. But she can't believe it when she finds herself on a nightmarish battle-field, forced to save the barbarian of her dreams.

He was a wild-eyed warrior whose deadly sword could slay a dozen Saxons with a single swing, yet Selik couldn't control the saucy wench from the future. If Selik wasn't careful, the stunning siren was sure to capture his heart and make a warrior of love out of **The Outlaw Viking**.

The Tarnished Lady

❧

Banished from polite society, Lady Eadyth of Hawks' Lair spent her days hidden under a voluminous veil, tending her bees. But when her lands are threatened, Lady Eadyth sought a husband to offer her the protection of his name.

Notorious for loving—and leaving—the most beautiful damsels in the land, Eirik of Ravenshire was England's most virile bachelor. Yet when the mysterious lady offered him a vow of chaste matrimony in exchange for revenge against his most hated enemy, Eirik couldn't refuse. But the lusty knight's plans went awry when he succumbed to the sweet sting of the tarnished lady's love.

The Bewitched Viking

&

Even fierce Norse warriors have bad days. 'Twas enough to drive a sane Viking mad, the things Tykir Thorksson was forced to do—capturing a red-headed virago, putting up with the flock of sheep that follows her everywhere, chasing off her bumbling brothers. But what could a man expect from the sorceress who had put a kink in the King of Norway's most precious body part? If that wasn't bad enough, Tykir was beginning to realize he wasn't at all immune to the enchantment of brash red hair and freckles. Perhaps he could reverse the spell and hold her captive, not with his mighty sword, but with a Viking man's greatest magic: a wink and smile.

The Blue Viking

⧖

For Rurik the Viking, life has not been worth living since he left Maire of the Moors. Oh, it's not that he misses her fiery red tresses or kissable lips. Nay, it's the embarrassing blue zigzag tattoo she put on his face after their one wild night of loving. For a fierce warrior who prides himself on his immense height, his expertise in bedsport, and his well-toned muscles, this blue streak is the last straw. In the end, he'll bring the witch to heel, or die trying. Mayhap he'll even beg her to wed . . . so long as she can promise he'll no longer be . . . **The Blue Viking**.

The Viking's Captive

(originally titled MY FAIR VIKING)

⊗

Tyra, Warrior Princess. She is too tall, too loud, too fierce to be a good catch. But her ailing father has decreed that her four younger sisters—delicate, mild-mannered, and beautiful—cannot be wed 'til Tyra consents to take a husband. And then a journey to save her father's life brings Tyra face to face with Adam the Healer. A god in human form, he's tall, muscled, perfectly proportioned. Too bad Adam refuses to fall in with her plans—so what's a lady to do but truss him up, toss him over her shoulder, and sail off into the sunset to live happily ever after.

A Tale of Two Vikings

❧

*T*oste and Vagn Ivarsson are identical Viking twins, about to face Valhalla together, following a tragic battle, or maybe something even more tragic: being separated for the first time in their thirty and one years. Alas, even the bravest Viking must eventually leave his best buddy behind and do battle with that most fearsome of all opponents—the love of his life. And what if that love was Helga the Homely, or Lady Esme, the world's oldest novice nun?

A Tale of Two Vikings will give you twice the tears, twice the sizzle, and twice the laughter . . . and make you wish for your very own Viking.

The Last Viking

☖

He was six feet, four inches of pure, unadulterated male. He wore nothing but a leather tunic, and he was standing in Professor Meredith Foster's living room. The medieval historian told herself he was part of a practical joke, but with his wide gold belt, ancient language, and callused hands, the brawny stranger seemed so . . . authentic. And as he helped her fulfill her grandfather's dream of re-creating a Viking ship, he awakened her to dreams of her own. Until she wondered if the hand of fate had thrust her into the loving arms of . . . **The Last Viking**.

Truly, Madly Viking

❧

A Viking named Joe? Jorund Ericsson is a tenth-century Viking warrior who lands in a modern mental hospital. Maggie McBride is the lucky psychologist who gets to "treat" the gorgeous Norseman, whom she mistakenly calls Joe.

You've heard of *One Flew Over the Cuckoo's Nest.* But how about *A Viking Flew Over the Cuckoo's Nest?* The question is: Who's the cuckoo in this nest? And why is everyone laughing?

The Very Virile Viking

⊗

*M*agnus Ericsson is a simple man. He loves the smell of fresh-turned dirt after springtime plowing. He loves the feel of a soft woman under him in the bed furs. He loves the heft of a good sword in his fighting arm.

But, Holy Thor, what he does not relish is the bothersome brood of children he's been saddled with. Or the mysterious happenstance that strands him in a strange new land—the kingdom of *Holly Wood*. Here is a place where the folks think he is an *act-whore* (whatever that is), and the woman of his dreams—a winemaker of all things—fails to accept that he is her soul mate . . . a man of exceptional talents, not to mention . . . **A Very Virile Viking.**

Wet & Wild

What do you get when you cross a Viking with a Navy SEAL? A warrior with the fierce instincts of the past and the rigorous training of America's most elite fighting corps? A totally buff hero-in-the-making who hasn't had a woman in roughly a thousand years? A dyed-in-the-wool romantic with a hopeless crush? Whatever you get, women everywhere can't wait to meet him, and his story is guaranteed to be . . . **Wet & Wild**.

Hot & Heavy

In and out, that's the goal as Lt. Ian MacLean prepares for his special ops mission. He leads a team of highly trained Navy SEALs, the toughest, buffest fighting men in the world and he has nothing to lose. Madrene comes from a time a thousand years before he was born, and she has no idea she's landed in the future. After tying him up, the beautiful shrew gives him a tongue-lashing that makes a drill sergeant sound like a kindergarten teacher. Then she lets him know she has her own special way of dealing with over-confident males, and things get . . . **Hot & Heavy**.

Frankly, My Dear . . .

🔅

*L*ost in the Bayou . . . *Selene had three great passions:* men, food, and *Gone With the Wind*. But the glamorous model always found herself starving— for both nourishment and affection. Weary of the petty world of high fashion, she headed to New Orleans for one last job before she began a new life. Little did she know that her new life would include a brand-new time—about 160 years ago! Selene can't get her fill of the food—or an alarmingly handsome man. Dark and brooding, James Baptiste was the only lover she gave a damn about. And with God as her witness, she vowed never to go without the man she loved again.

Sweeter Savage Love

❦

*T*he stroke of surprisingly gentle hands, the flash of fathomless blue eyes, the scorch of white-hot kisses . . . Once again, Dr. Harriet Ginoza was swept away into rapturous fantasy. The modern psychologist knew the object of her desire was all she should despise, yet time after time, she lost herself in visions of a dangerously handsome rogue straight out of a historical romance. Harriet never believed that her dream lover would cause her any trouble, but then a twist of fate cast her back to the Old South and she met him in the flesh. To her disappointment, Etienne Baptiste refused to fulfill any of her secret wishes. If Harriet had any hope of making her amorous dreams become passionate reality, she'd have to seduce this charmer with a sweeter savage love than she'd imagined possible . . . and savor every minute of it.

The Love Potion

☩

*F*ame and fortune are surely only a swallow away when Dr. Sylvie Fontaine discovers a chemical formula guaranteed to attract the opposite sex. Though her own love life is purely hypothetical, the shy chemist's professional future is assured . . . as soon as she can find a human guinea pig. But bad boy Lucien LeDeux—best known as the Swamp Lawyer—is more than she can handle even before he accidentally swallowed a love potion disguised in a jelly bean. When the dust settles, Luc and Sylvie have the answers to some burning questions—can a man die of testosterone overload? Can a straight-laced female lose every single one of her inhibitions?—and they learn that old-fashioned romance is still the best catalyst for love.

Love Me Tender

*O*nce upon a time, in a magic kingdom, there lived a handsome prince. Prince Charming, he was called by one and all. And to this land came a gentle princess. You could say she was Cinderella . . . Wall Street Cinderella. Okay, if you're going to be a stickler for accuracy, in this fairy tale the kingdom is Manhattan. But there's magic in the Big Apple, isn't there? And maybe he can be Prince Not-So-Charming at times, and "gentle" isn't the first word that comes to mind when thinking of this princess. But they're looking for happily ever after just the same—and they're going to get it.

Desperado

&

*M*istaken *for a notorious bandit and his infamously* scandalous mistress, L.A. lawyer Rafe Santiago and Major Helen Prescott found themselves on the wrong side of the law. In a time and place where rules had no meaning, Helen found Rafe's hard, bronzed body strangely comforting, and his piercing blue eyes left her all too willing to share his bedroll. His teasing remarks made her feel all woman, and she was ready to throw caution to the wind if she could spend every night in the arms of her very own . . . **Desperado**.